IRON MAN
AND SPIDER-MAN

Writers: **Paul Tobin, Fred Van Lente, David Michelinie, Bob Layton & Gerry Conway**
Artists: **Chris Samnee, James Cordeiro & Scott Koblish, Jackson Guice & Bob Layton, Ross Andru & Frank Bolle**
Colors: **Sotocolor, Studio F's Martegod Gracia, Bob Sharen & Stan Goldberg**
Letters: **Dave Sharpe, Blambot's Nate Piekos, Janice Chiang & Charlotte Jetter**
Cover Artists: **Skottie Young, Michael Golden, Jackson Guice, Bob Layton, John Romita & Joe Sinnott**
Assistant Editor: **Michael Horwitz**
Editors: **Nathan Cosby, Mark Paniccia, Howard Mackie & Roy Thomas**

Collection Editor: **Cory Levine**
Assistant Editor: **Alex Starbuck**
Associate Editor, Special Projects: **John Denning**
Editors, Special Projects: **Jennifer Grünwald & Mark D. Beazley**
Senior Editor, Special Projects: **Jeff Youngquist**
Senior Vice President of Sales: **David Gabriel**
Color Reconstruction: **ColorTek**

Editor in Chief: **Joe Quesada**
Publisher: **Dan Buckley**
Executive Producer: **Alan Fine**

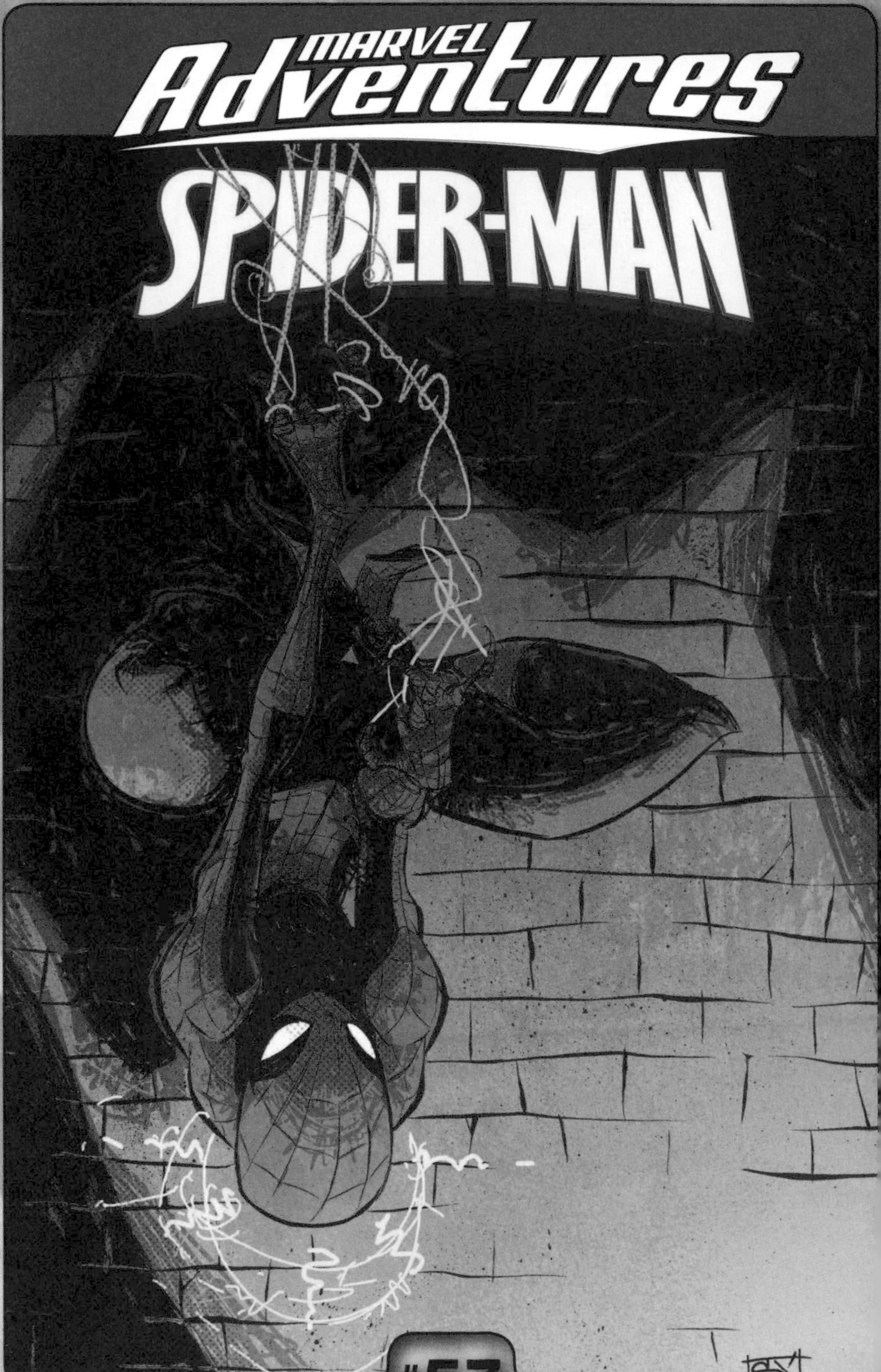
MARVEL
Adventures
SPIDER-MAN
#57

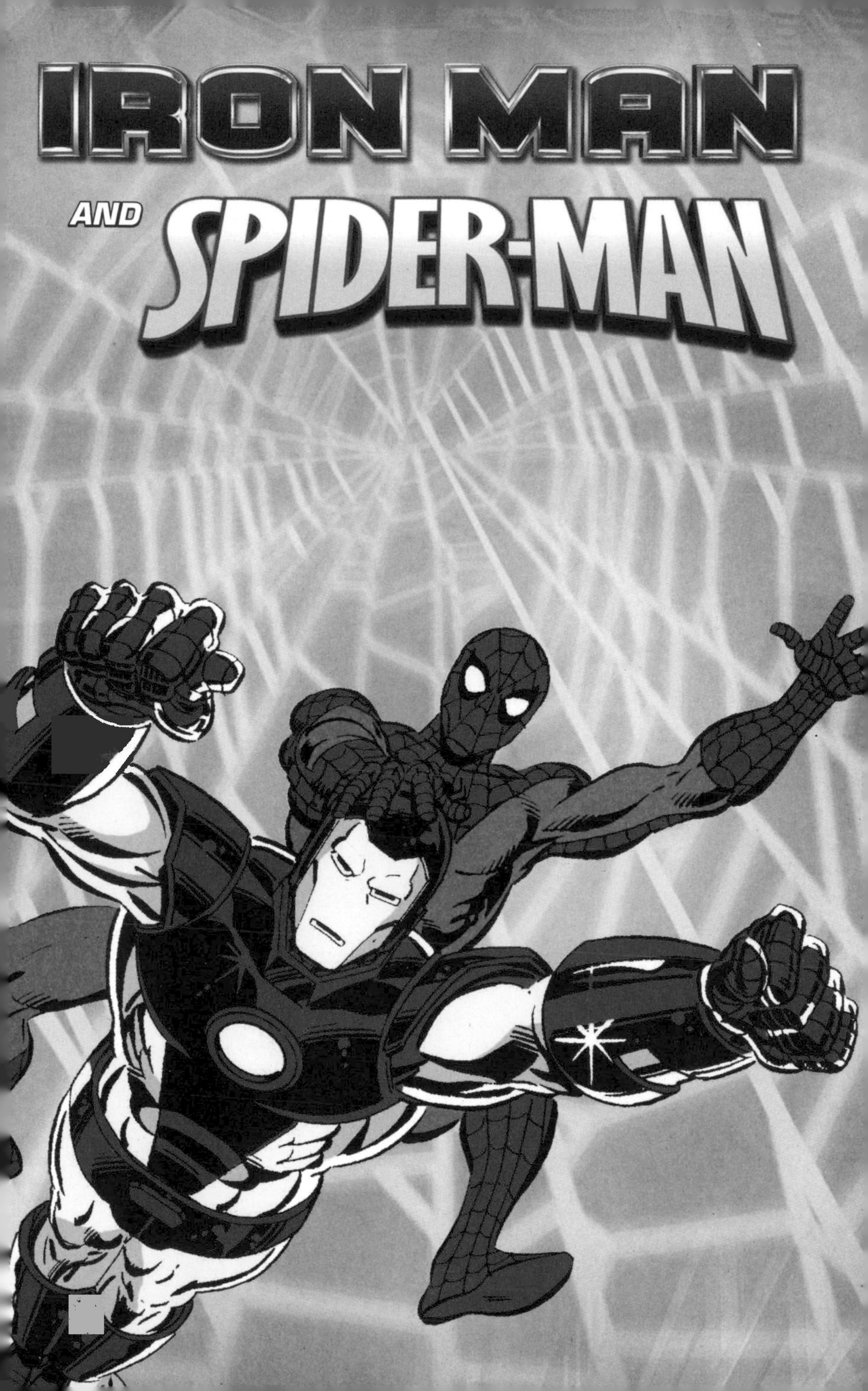
IRON MAN
AND
SPIDER-MAN

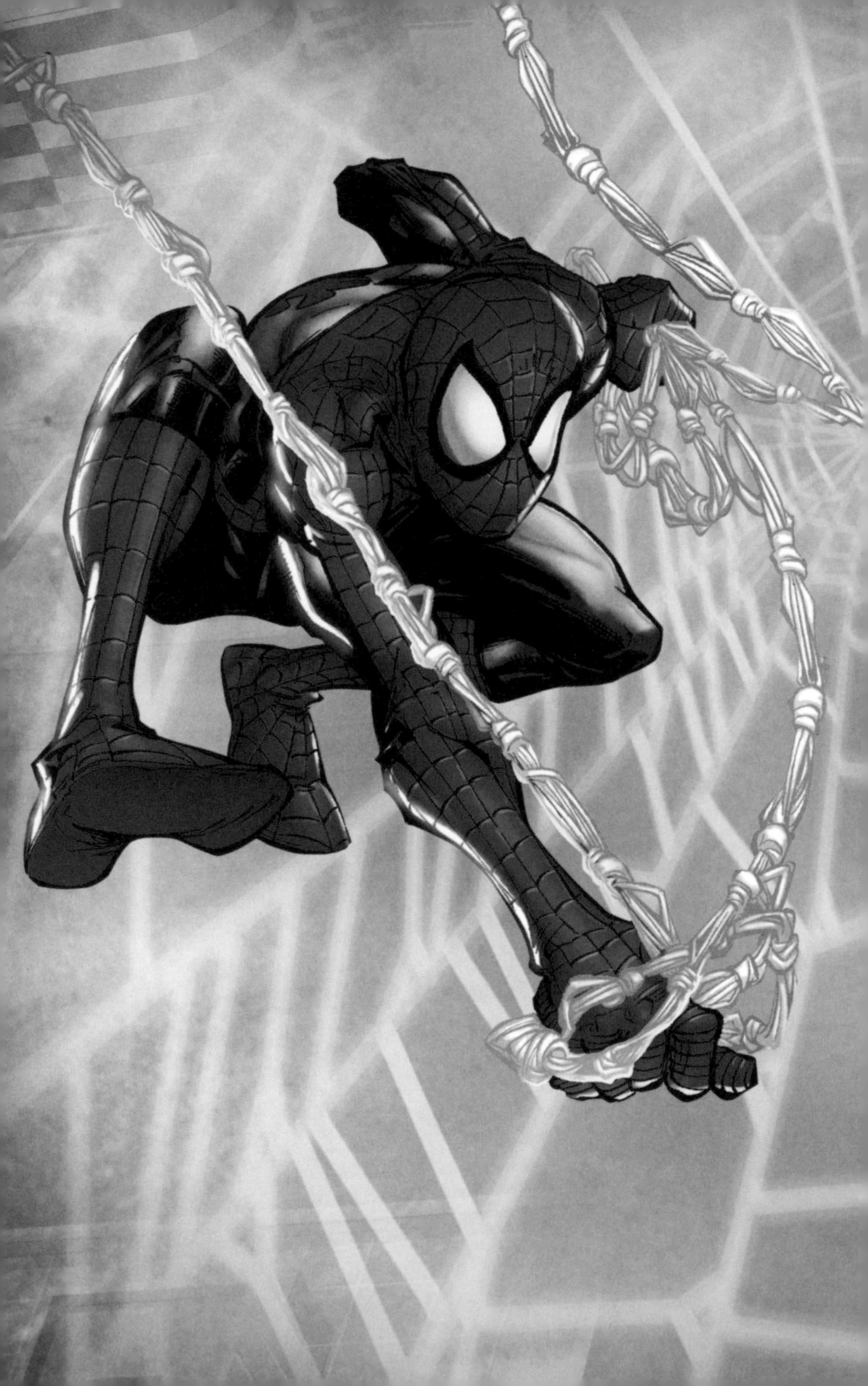

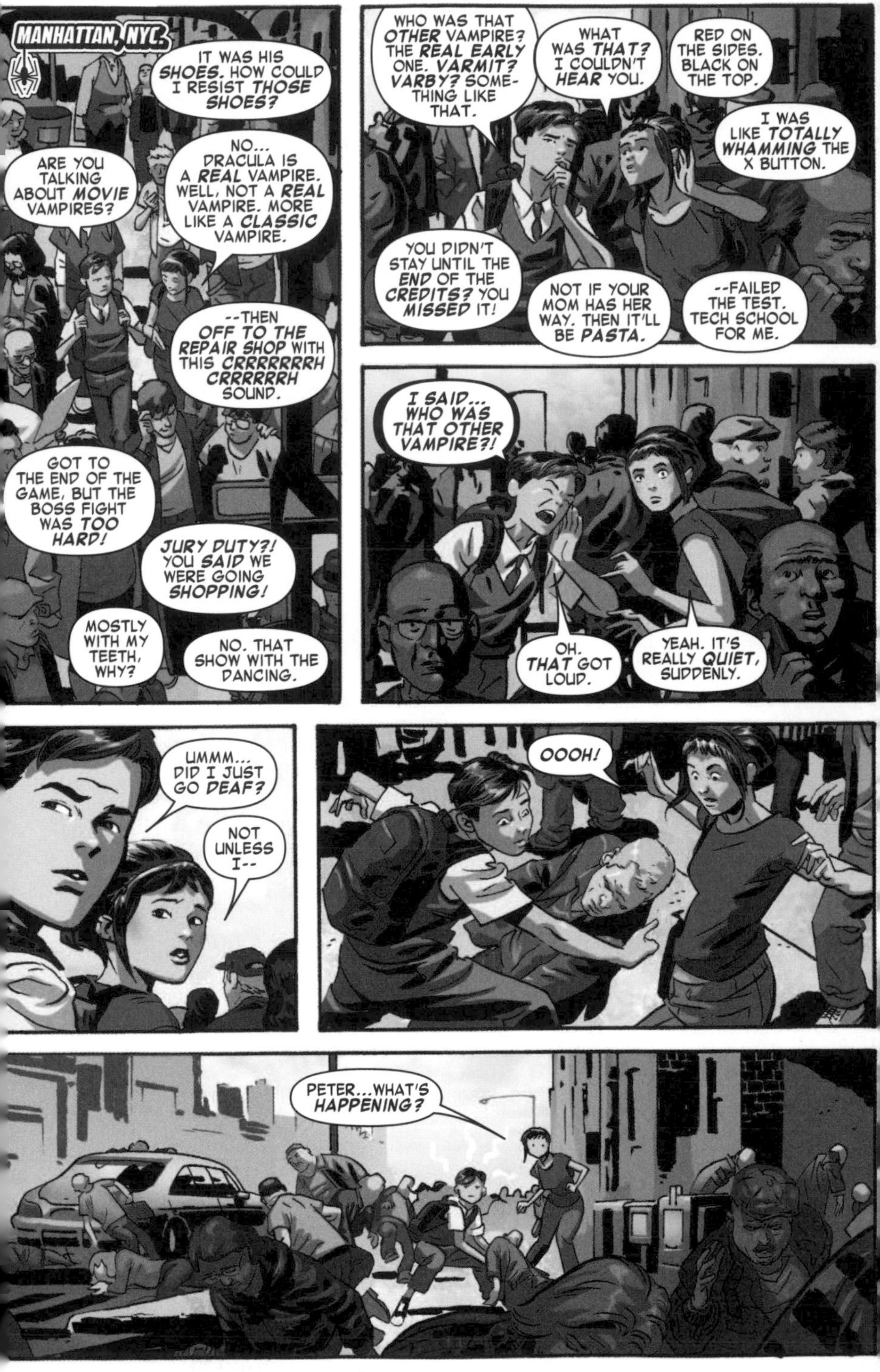
MANHATTAN, NYC.
IT WAS HIS SHOES. HOW COULD I RESIST THOSE SHOES?
ARE YOU TALKING ABOUT MOVIE VAMPIRES?
NO... DRACULA IS A REAL VAMPIRE. WELL, NOT A REAL VAMPIRE. MORE LIKE A CLASSIC VAMPIRE.
--THEN OFF TO THE REPAIR SHOP WITH THIS CRRRRRRRH CRRRRRRH SOUND.
GOT TO THE END OF THE GAME, BUT THE BOSS FIGHT WAS TOO HARD!
JURY DUTY?! YOU SAID WE WERE GOING SHOPPING!
MOSTLY WITH MY TEETH, WHY?
NO. THAT SHOW WITH THE DANCING.
WHO WAS THAT OTHER VAMPIRE? THE REAL EARLY ONE. VARMIT? VARBY? SOMETHING LIKE THAT.
WHAT WAS THAT? I COULDN'T HEAR YOU.
RED ON THE SIDES. BLACK ON THE TOP.
I WAS LIKE TOTALLY WHAMMING THE X BUTTON.
YOU DIDN'T STAY UNTIL THE END OF THE CREDITS? YOU MISSED IT!
NOT IF YOUR MOM HAS HER WAY. THEN IT'LL BE PASTA.
--FAILED THE TEST. TECH SCHOOL FOR ME.
I SAID... WHO WAS THAT OTHER VAMPIRE?!
OH. THAT GOT LOUD.
YEAH. IT'S REALLY QUIET, SUDDENLY.
UMMM... DID I JUST GO DEAF?
NOT UNLESS I--
OOOH!
PETER...WHAT'S HAPPENING?

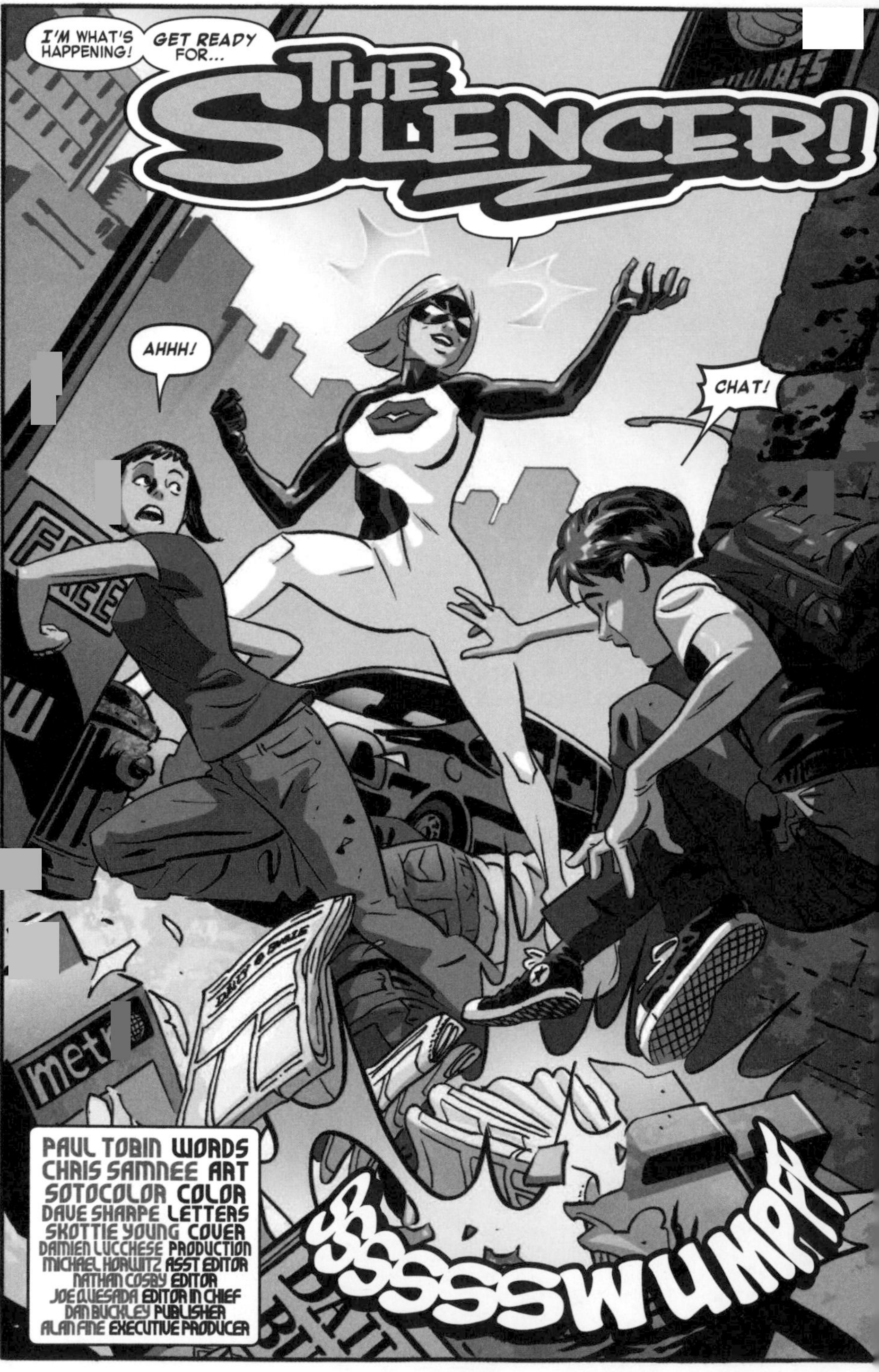
I'M WHAT'S HAPPENING!
GET READY FOR...
THE SILENCER!
AHHH!
CHAT!
SSSSSSWUMP!
PAUL TOBIN WORDS
CHRIS SAMNEE ART
SOTOCOLOR COLOR
DAVE SHARPE LETTERS
SKOTTIE YOUNG COVER
DAMIEN LUCCHESE PRODUCTION
MICHAEL HORWITZ ASST EDITOR
NATHAN COSBY EDITOR
JOE QUESADA EDITOR IN CHIEF
DAN BUCKLEY PUBLISHER
ALAN FINE EXECUTIVE PRODUCER

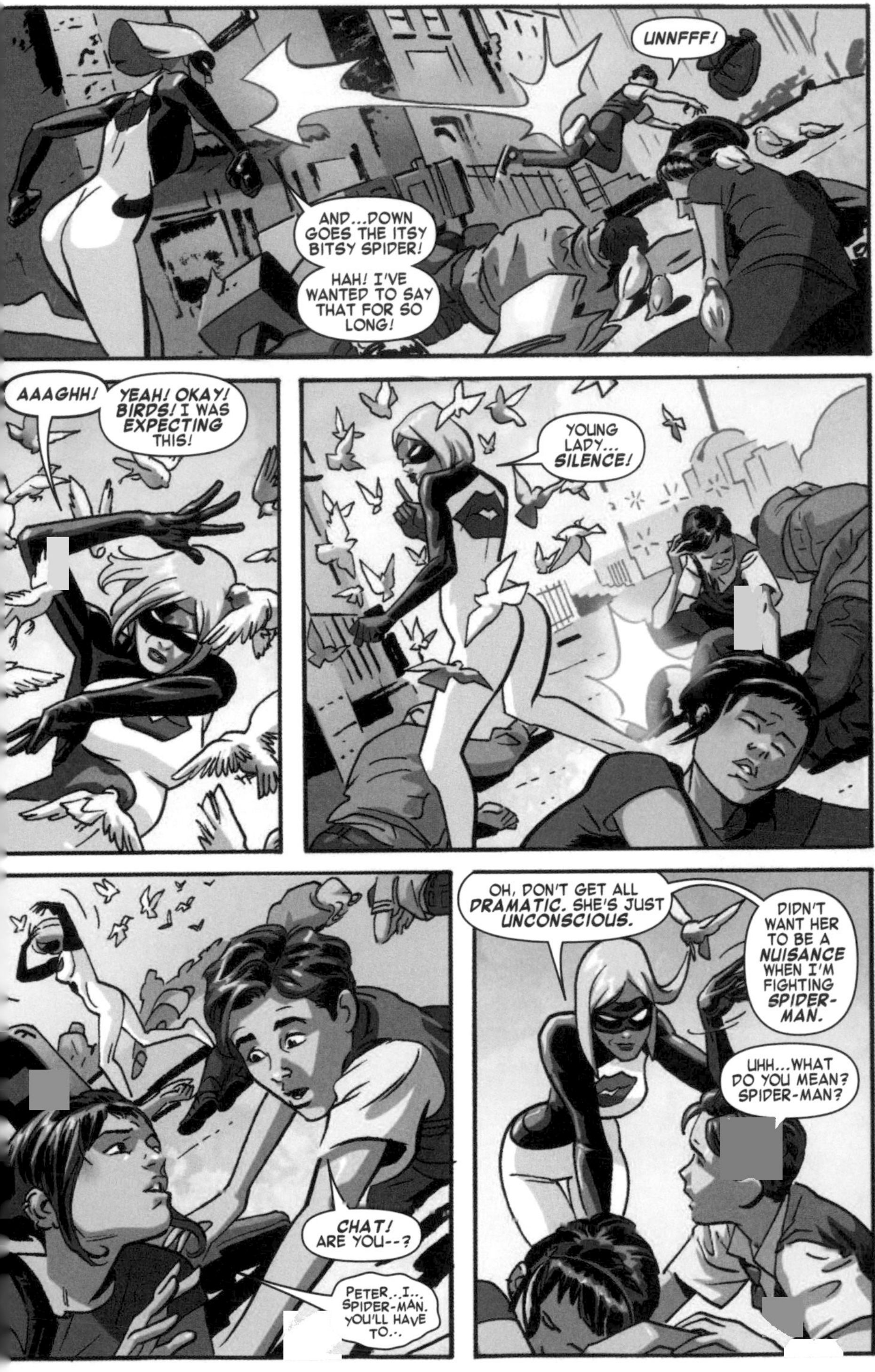
UNNFFF!
AND...DOWN GOES THE ITSY BITSY SPIDER!
HAH! I'VE WANTED TO SAY THAT FOR SO LONG!
AAAGHH!
YEAH! OKAY! BIRDS! I WAS EXPECTING THIS!
YOUNG LADY... SILENCE!
CHAT! ARE YOU--?
PETER...I... SPIDER-MAN. YOU'LL HAVE TO...
OH, DON'T GET ALL DRAMATIC. SHE'S JUST UNCONSCIOUS.
DIDN'T WANT HER TO BE A NUISANCE WHEN I'M FIGHTING SPIDER-MAN.
UHH...WHAT DO YOU MEAN? SPIDER-MAN?

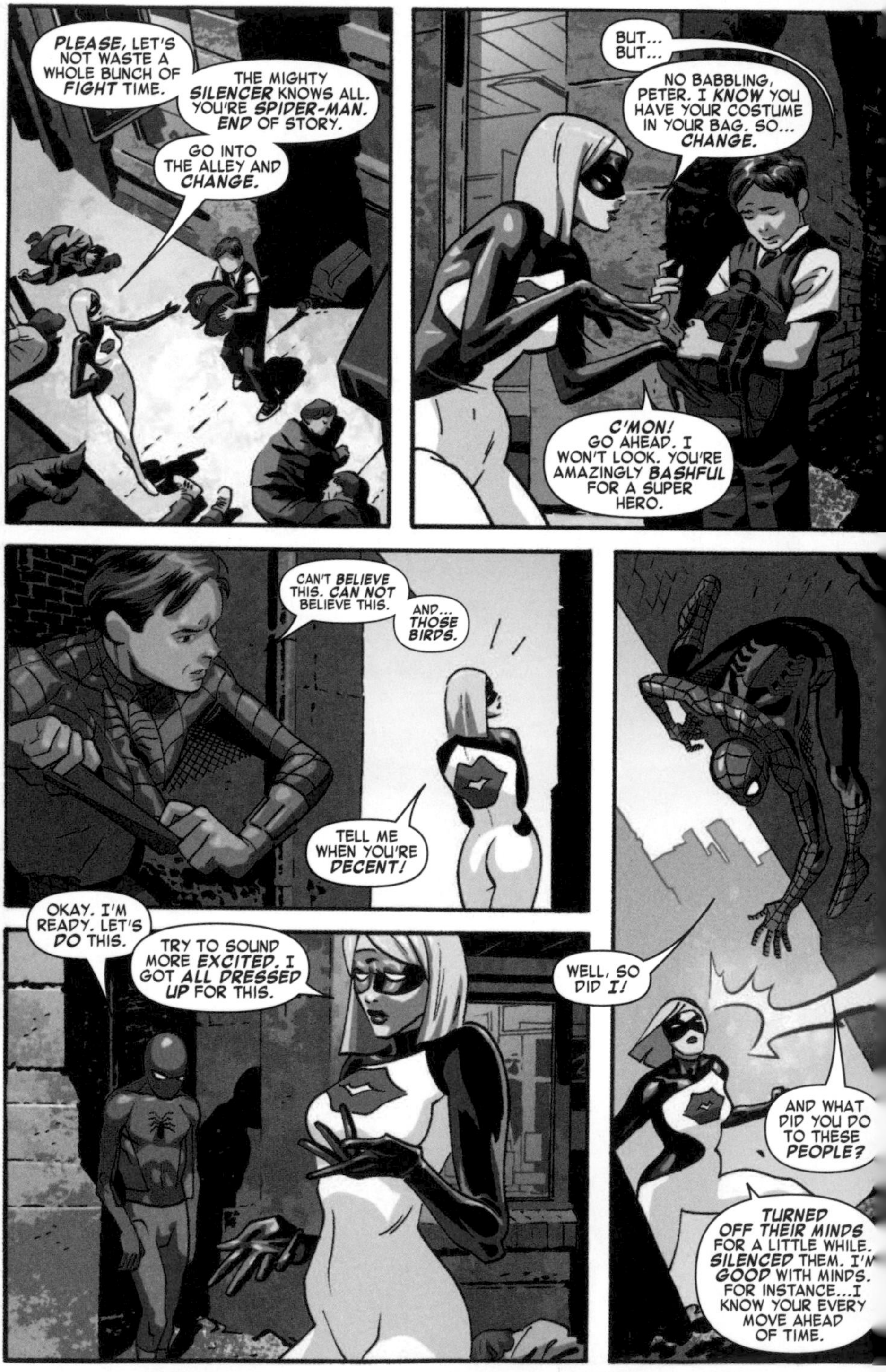
PLEASE, LET'S NOT WASTE A WHOLE BUNCH OF FIGHT TIME.
THE MIGHTY SILENCER KNOWS ALL. YOU'RE SPIDER-MAN. END OF STORY.
GO INTO THE ALLEY AND CHANGE.
BUT... BUT...
NO BABBLING, PETER. I KNOW YOU HAVE YOUR COSTUME IN YOUR BAG. SO... CHANGE.
C'MON! GO AHEAD. I WON'T LOOK. YOU'RE AMAZINGLY BASHFUL FOR A SUPER HERO.
CAN'T BELIEVE THIS. CAN NOT BELIEVE THIS.
AND... THOSE BIRDS.
TELL ME WHEN YOU'RE DECENT!
OKAY. I'M READY. LET'S DO THIS.
TRY TO SOUND MORE EXCITED. I GOT ALL DRESSED UP FOR THIS.
WELL, SO DID I!
AND WHAT DID YOU DO TO THESE PEOPLE?
TURNED OFF THEIR MINDS FOR A LITTLE WHILE. SILENCED THEM. I'M GOOD WITH MINDS. FOR INSTANCE...I KNOW YOUR EVERY MOVE AHEAD OF TIME.

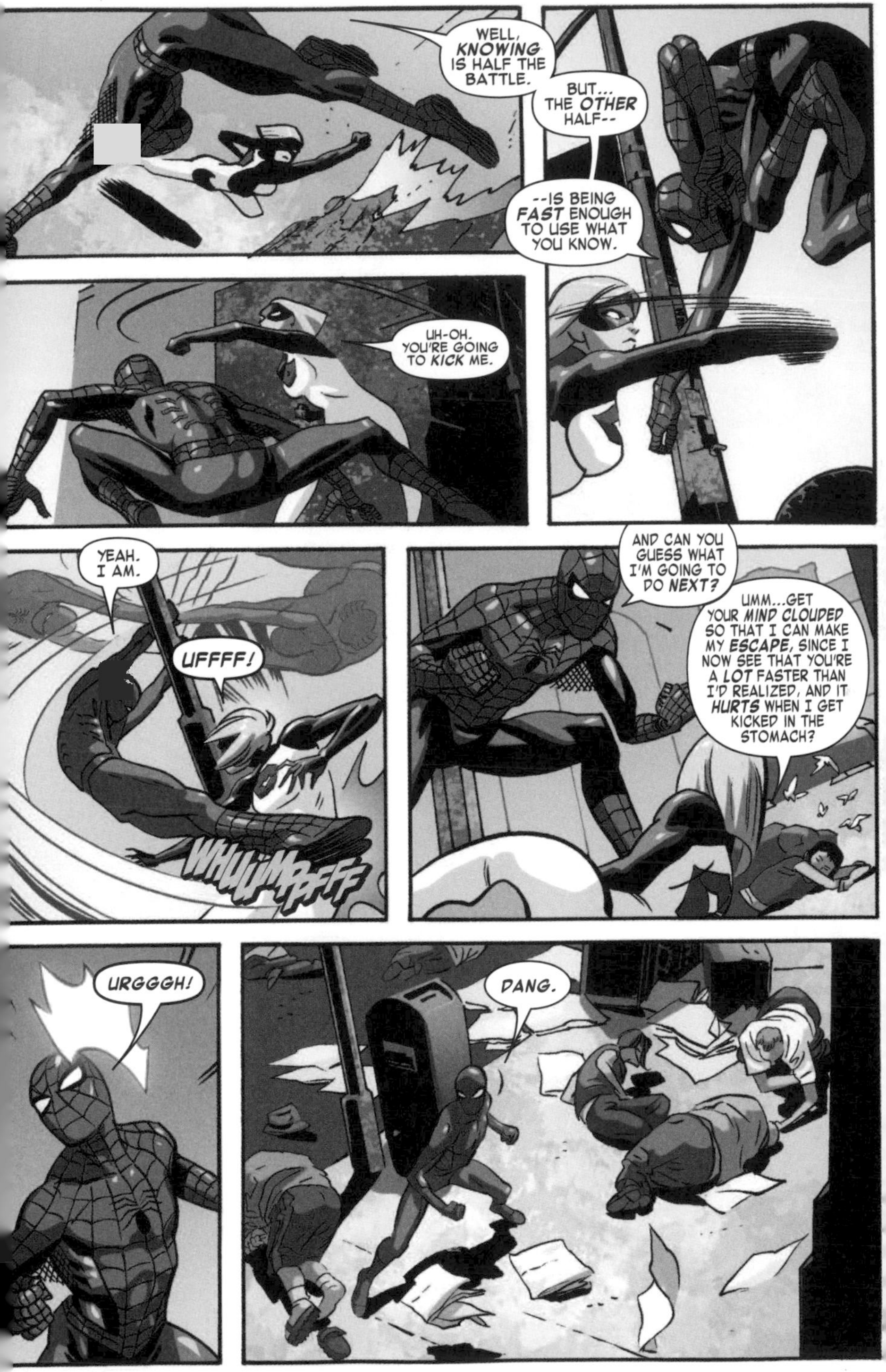
WELL, KNOWING IS HALF THE BATTLE.
BUT... THE OTHER HALF--
--IS BEING FAST ENOUGH TO USE WHAT YOU KNOW.
UH-OH. YOU'RE GOING TO KICK ME.
YEAH. I AM.
UFFFF!
WHUUMPFFF
AND CAN YOU GUESS WHAT I'M GOING TO DO NEXT?
UMM...GET YOUR MIND CLOUDED SO THAT I CAN MAKE MY ESCAPE, SINCE I NOW SEE THAT YOU'RE A LOT FASTER THAN I'D REALIZED, AND IT HURTS WHEN I GET KICKED IN THE STOMACH?
URGGGH!
DANG.

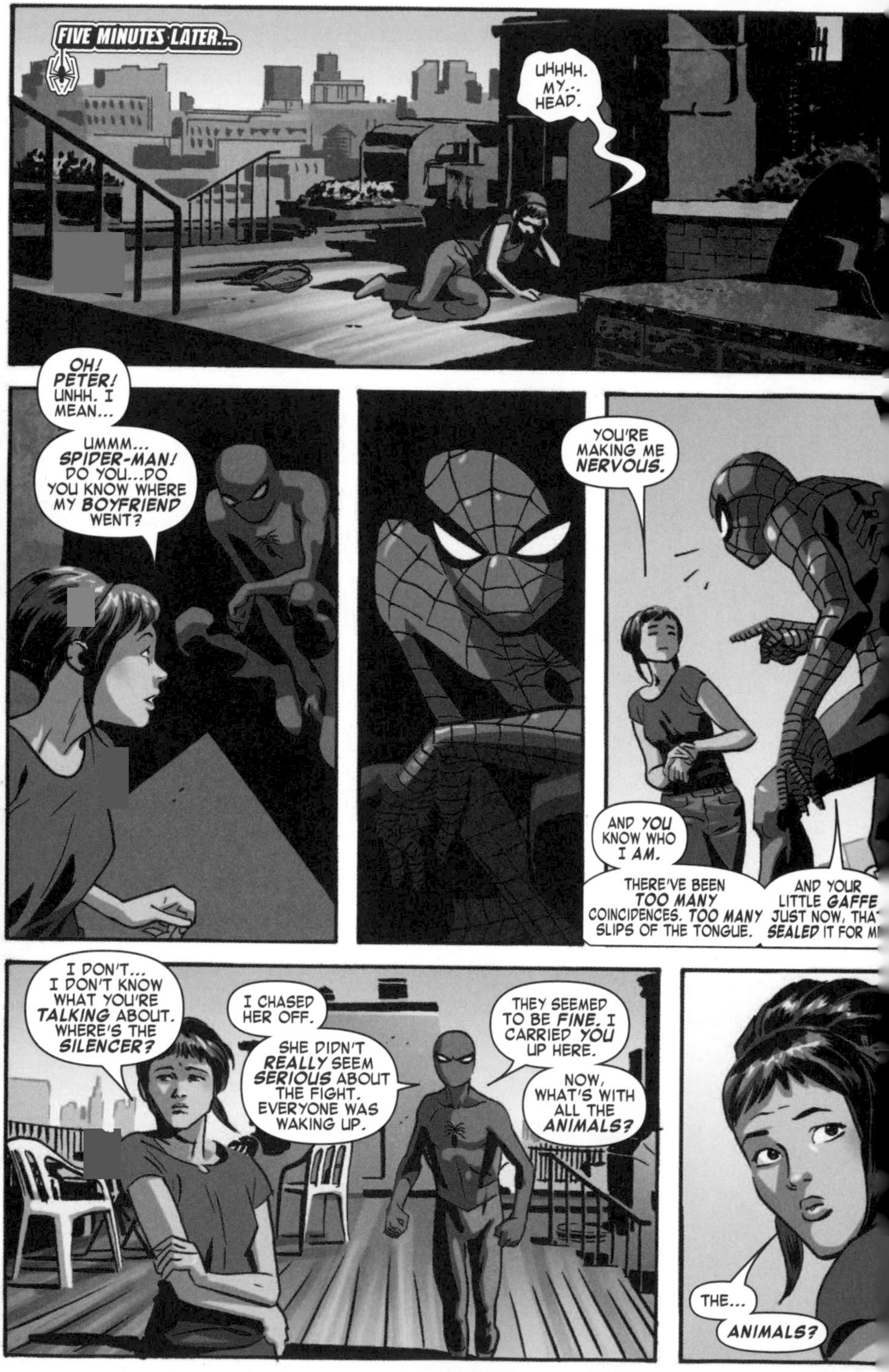
FIVE MINUTES LATER...
UHHHH. MY... HEAD.
OH! PETER! UNHH. I MEAN...
UMMM... SPIDER-MAN! DO YOU...DO YOU KNOW WHERE MY BOYFRIEND WENT?
YOU'RE MAKING ME NERVOUS.
AND YOU KNOW WHO I AM.
THERE'VE BEEN TOO MANY COINCIDENCES. TOO MANY SLIPS OF THE TONGUE.
AND YOUR LITTLE GAFFE JUST NOW, THA SEALED IT FOR M
I DON'T... I DON'T KNOW WHAT YOU'RE TALKING ABOUT. WHERE'S THE SILENCER?
I CHASED HER OFF.
SHE DIDN'T REALLY SEEM SERIOUS ABOUT THE FIGHT. EVERYONE WAS WAKING UP.
THEY SEEMED TO BE FINE. I CARRIED YOU UP HERE.
NOW, WHAT'S WITH ALL THE ANIMALS?
THE...
ANIMALS?

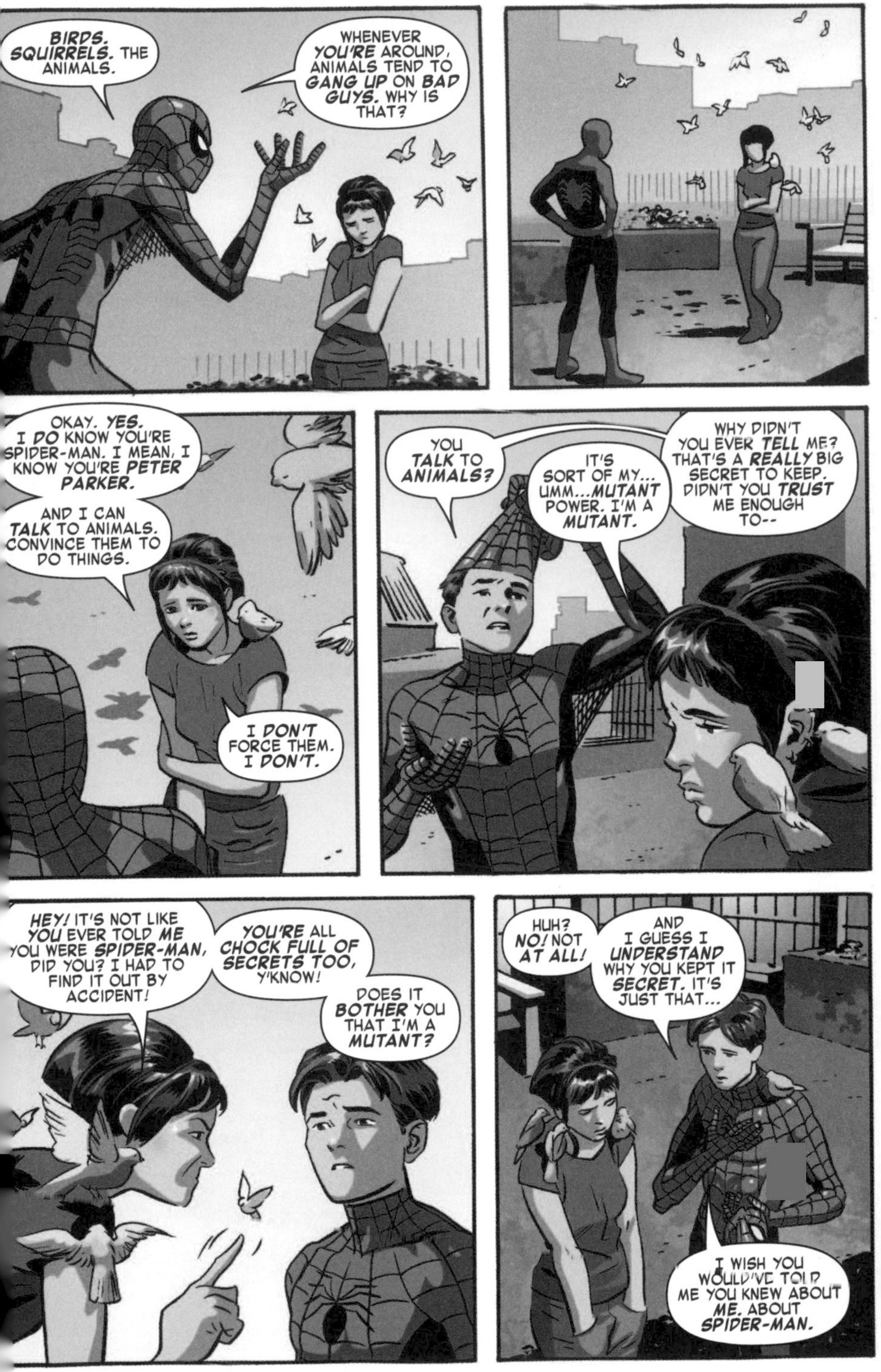
BIRDS. SQUIRRELS. THE ANIMALS.
WHENEVER YOU'RE AROUND, ANIMALS TEND TO GANG UP ON BAD GUYS. WHY IS THAT?
OKAY. YES. I DO KNOW YOU'RE SPIDER-MAN. I MEAN, I KNOW YOU'RE PETER PARKER.
AND I CAN TALK TO ANIMALS. CONVINCE THEM TO DO THINGS.
I DON'T FORCE THEM. I DON'T.
YOU TALK TO ANIMALS?
IT'S SORT OF MY... UMM...MUTANT POWER. I'M A MUTANT.
WHY DIDN'T YOU EVER TELL ME? THAT'S A REALLY BIG SECRET TO KEEP. DIDN'T YOU TRUST ME ENOUGH TO--
HEY! IT'S NOT LIKE YOU EVER TOLD ME YOU WERE SPIDER-MAN, DID YOU? I HAD TO FIND IT OUT BY ACCIDENT!
YOU'RE ALL CHOCK FULL OF SECRETS TOO, Y'KNOW!
DOES IT BOTHER YOU THAT I'M A MUTANT?
HUH? NO! NOT AT ALL!
AND I GUESS I UNDERSTAND WHY YOU KEPT IT SECRET. IT'S JUST THAT...
I WISH YOU WOULD'VE TOLD ME YOU KNEW ABOUT ME. ABOUT SPIDER-MAN.

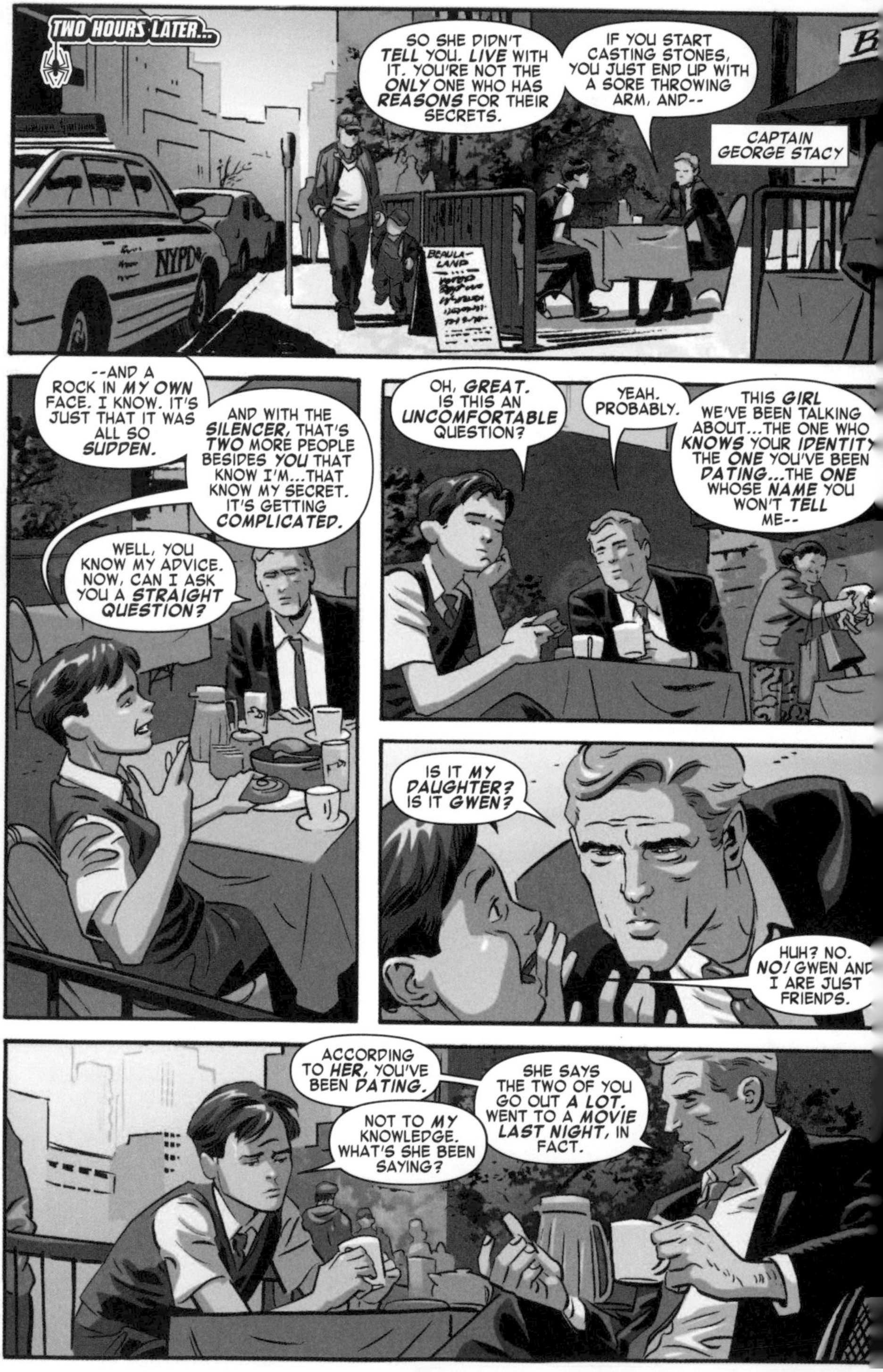
TWO HOURS LATER...
SO SHE DIDN'T TELL YOU. LIVE WITH IT. YOU'RE NOT THE ONLY ONE WHO HAS REASONS FOR THEIR SECRETS.
IF YOU START CASTING STONES, YOU JUST END UP WITH A SORE THROWING ARM, AND--
CAPTAIN GEORGE STACY
NYPD
BEAULA-LAND
--AND A ROCK IN MY OWN FACE. I KNOW. IT'S JUST THAT IT WAS ALL SO SUDDEN.
AND WITH THE SILENCER, THAT'S TWO MORE PEOPLE BESIDES YOU THAT KNOW I'M...THAT KNOW MY SECRET. IT'S GETTING COMPLICATED.
WELL, YOU KNOW MY ADVICE. NOW, CAN I ASK YOU A STRAIGHT QUESTION?
OH, GREAT. IS THIS AN UNCOMFORTABLE QUESTION?
YEAH. PROBABLY.
THIS GIRL WE'VE BEEN TALKING ABOUT...THE ONE WHO KNOWS YOUR IDENTITY THE ONE YOU'VE BEEN DATING...THE ONE WHOSE NAME YOU WON'T TELL ME--
IS IT MY DAUGHTER? IS IT GWEN?
HUH? NO. NO! GWEN AND I ARE JUST FRIENDS.
ACCORDING TO HER, YOU'VE BEEN DATING.
NOT TO MY KNOWLEDGE. WHAT'S SHE BEEN SAYING?
SHE SAYS THE TWO OF YOU GO OUT A LOT. WENT TO A MOVIE LAST NIGHT, IN FACT.

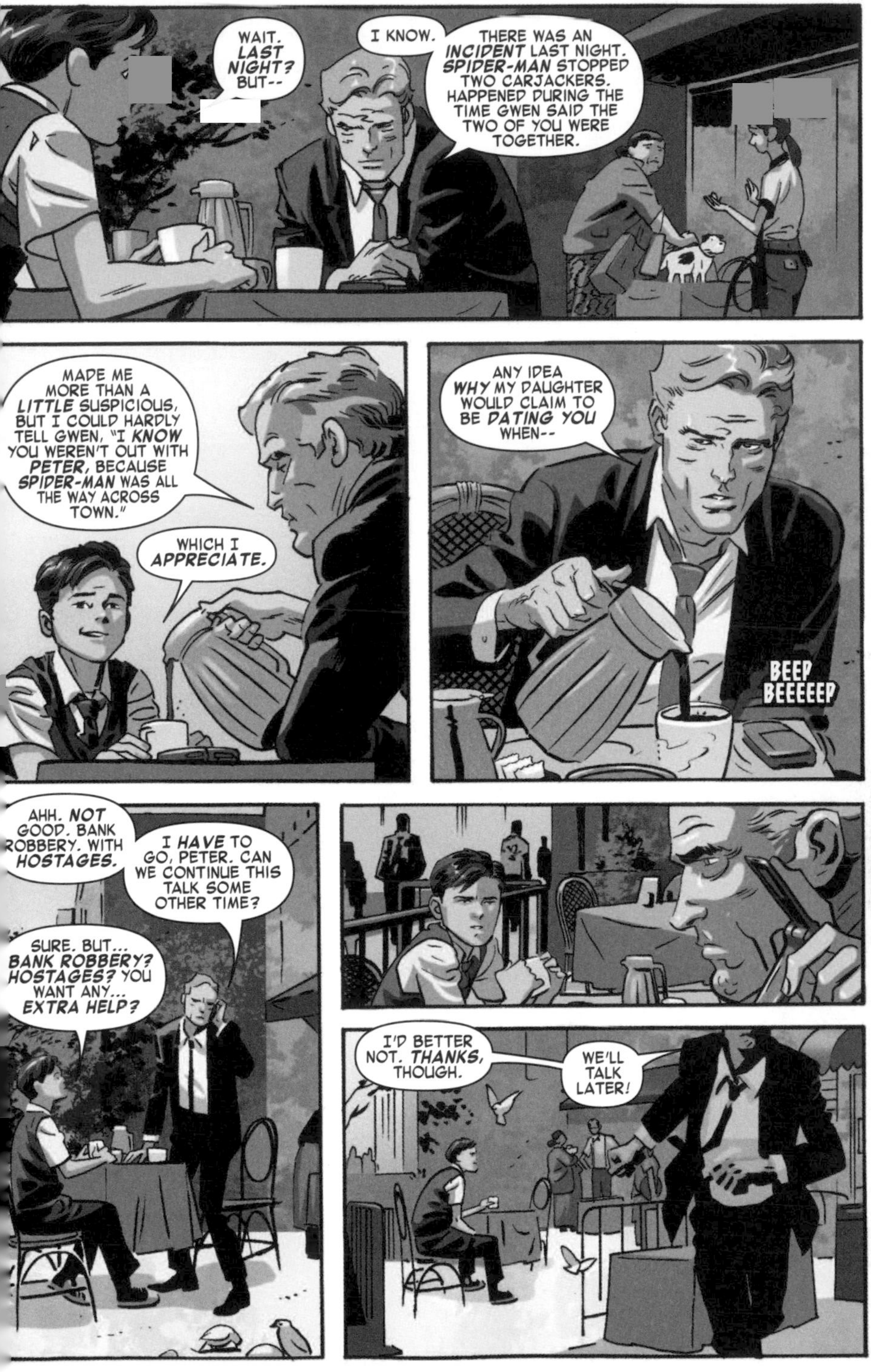
WAIT. LAST NIGHT? BUT--
I KNOW.
THERE WAS AN INCIDENT LAST NIGHT. SPIDER-MAN STOPPED TWO CARJACKERS. HAPPENED DURING THE TIME GWEN SAID THE TWO OF YOU WERE TOGETHER.
MADE ME MORE THAN A LITTLE SUSPICIOUS, BUT I COULD HARDLY TELL GWEN, "I KNOW YOU WEREN'T OUT WITH PETER, BECAUSE SPIDER-MAN WAS ALL THE WAY ACROSS TOWN."
WHICH I APPRECIATE.
ANY IDEA WHY MY DAUGHTER WOULD CLAIM TO BE DATING YOU WHEN--
BEEP BEEEEEP
AHH. NOT GOOD. BANK ROBBERY. WITH HOSTAGES.
I HAVE TO GO, PETER. CAN WE CONTINUE THIS TALK SOME OTHER TIME?
SURE. BUT... BANK ROBBERY? HOSTAGES? YOU WANT ANY... EXTRA HELP?
I'D BETTER NOT. THANKS, THOUGH.
WE'LL TALK LATER!

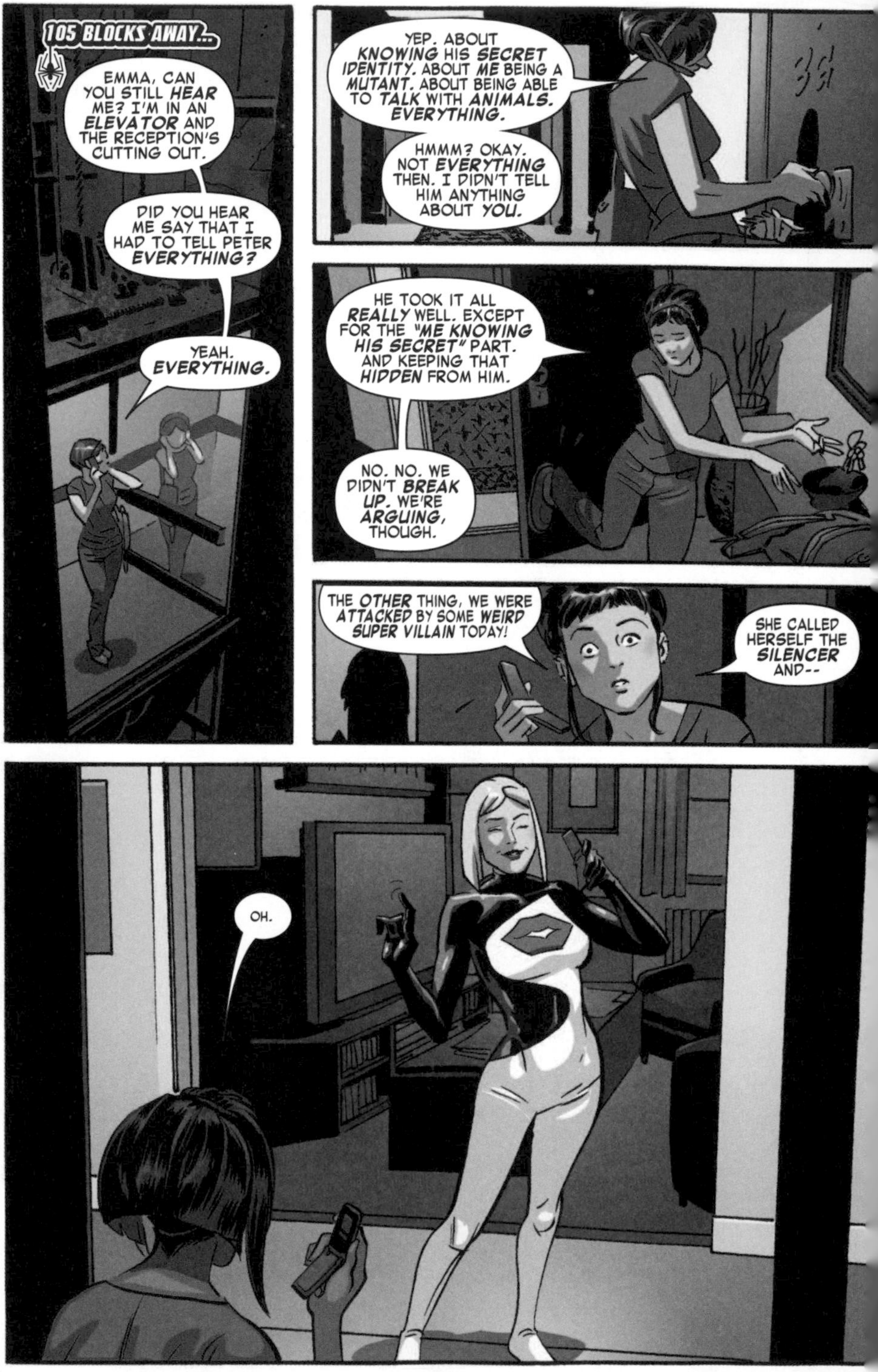
105 BLOCKS AWAY...
EMMA, CAN YOU STILL HEAR ME? I'M IN AN ELEVATOR AND THE RECEPTION'S CUTTING OUT.
DID YOU HEAR ME SAY THAT I HAD TO TELL PETER EVERYTHING?
YEAH. EVERYTHING.
YEP. ABOUT KNOWING HIS SECRET IDENTITY. ABOUT ME BEING A MUTANT. ABOUT BEING ABLE TO TALK WITH ANIMALS. EVERYTHING.
HMMM? OKAY. NOT EVERYTHING THEN. I DIDN'T TELL HIM ANYTHING ABOUT YOU.
HE TOOK IT ALL REALLY WELL. EXCEPT FOR THE "ME KNOWING HIS SECRET" PART. AND KEEPING THAT HIDDEN FROM HIM.
NO. NO. WE DIDN'T BREAK UP. WE'RE ARGUING, THOUGH.
THE OTHER THING, WE WERE ATTACKED BY SOME WEIRD SUPER VILLAIN TODAY!
SHE CALLED HERSELF THE SILENCER AND--
OH.

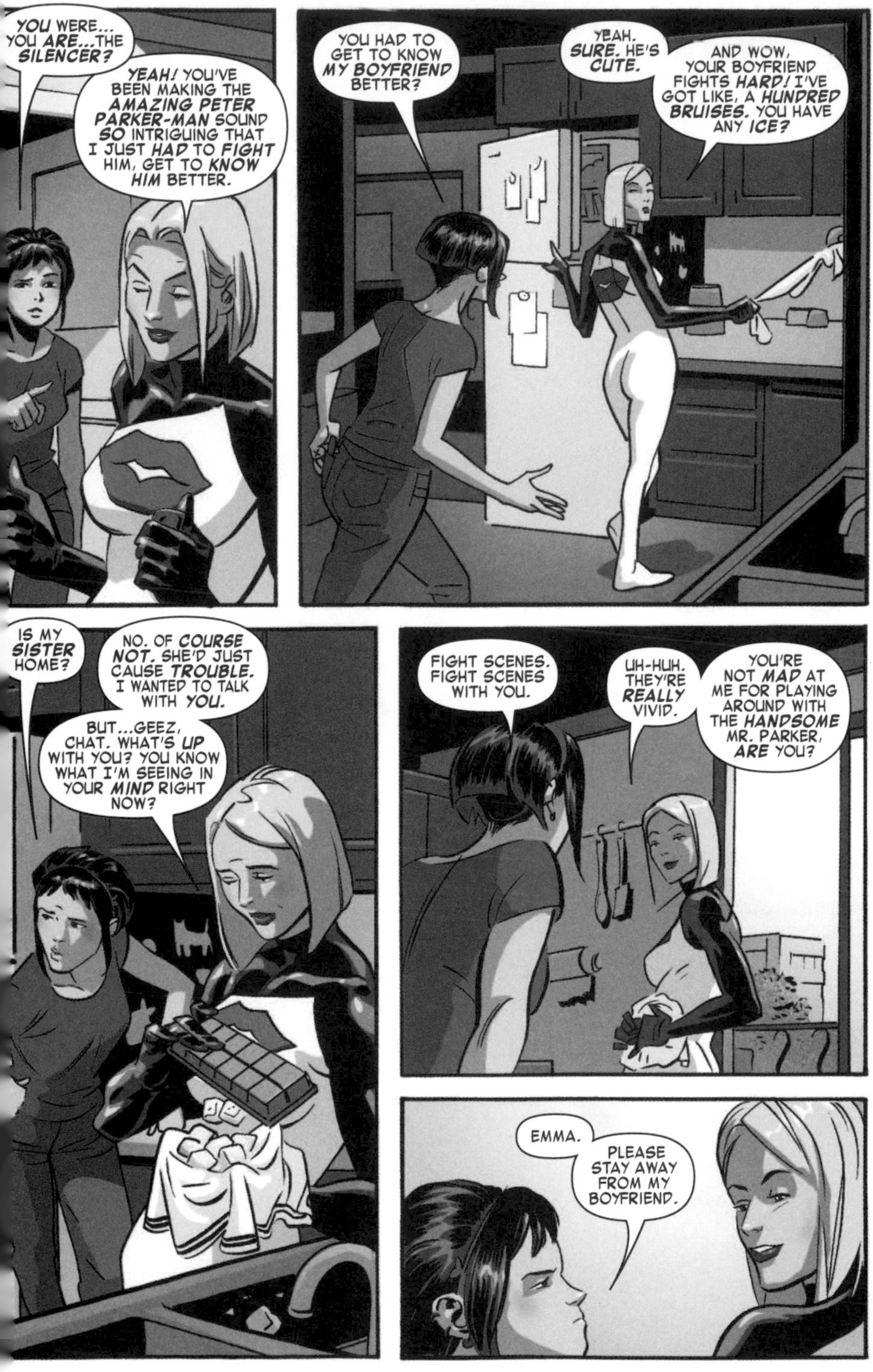

YOU WERE... YOU ARE...THE SILENCER?
YEAH! YOU'VE BEEN MAKING THE AMAZING PETER PARKER-MAN SOUND SO INTRIGUING THAT I JUST HAD TO FIGHT HIM, GET TO KNOW HIM BETTER.
YOU HAD TO GET TO KNOW MY BOYFRIEND BETTER?
YEAH. SURE. HE'S CUTE.
AND WOW, YOUR BOYFRIEND FIGHTS HARD! I'VE GOT LIKE, A HUNDRED BRUISES. YOU HAVE ANY ICE?
IS MY SISTER HOME?
NO. OF COURSE NOT. SHE'D JUST CAUSE TROUBLE. I WANTED TO TALK WITH YOU.
BUT...GEEZ, CHAT. WHAT'S UP WITH YOU? YOU KNOW WHAT I'M SEEING IN YOUR MIND RIGHT NOW?
FIGHT SCENES. FIGHT SCENES WITH YOU.
UH-HUH. THEY'RE REALLY VIVID.
YOU'RE NOT MAD AT ME FOR PLAYING AROUND WITH THE HANDSOME MR. PARKER, ARE YOU?
EMMA.
PLEASE STAY AWAY FROM MY BOYFRIEND.

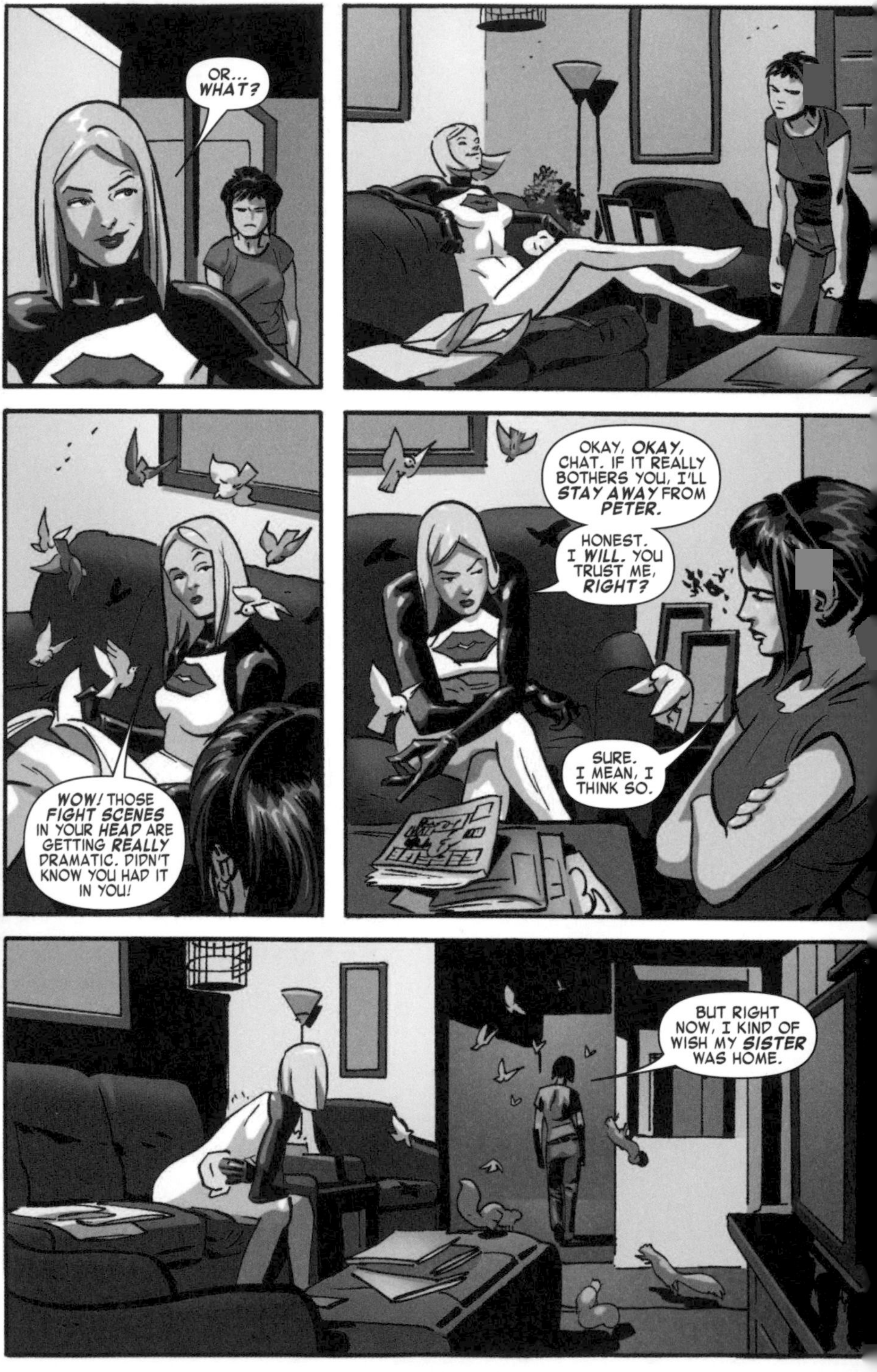
OR... WHAT?
WOW! THOSE FIGHT SCENES IN YOUR HEAD ARE GETTING REALLY DRAMATIC. DIDN'T KNOW YOU HAD IT IN YOU!
OKAY, OKAY, CHAT. IF IT REALLY BOTHERS YOU, I'LL STAY AWAY FROM PETER.
HONEST. I WILL. YOU TRUST ME, RIGHT?
SURE. I MEAN, I THINK SO.
BUT RIGHT NOW, I KIND OF WISH MY SISTER WAS HOME.

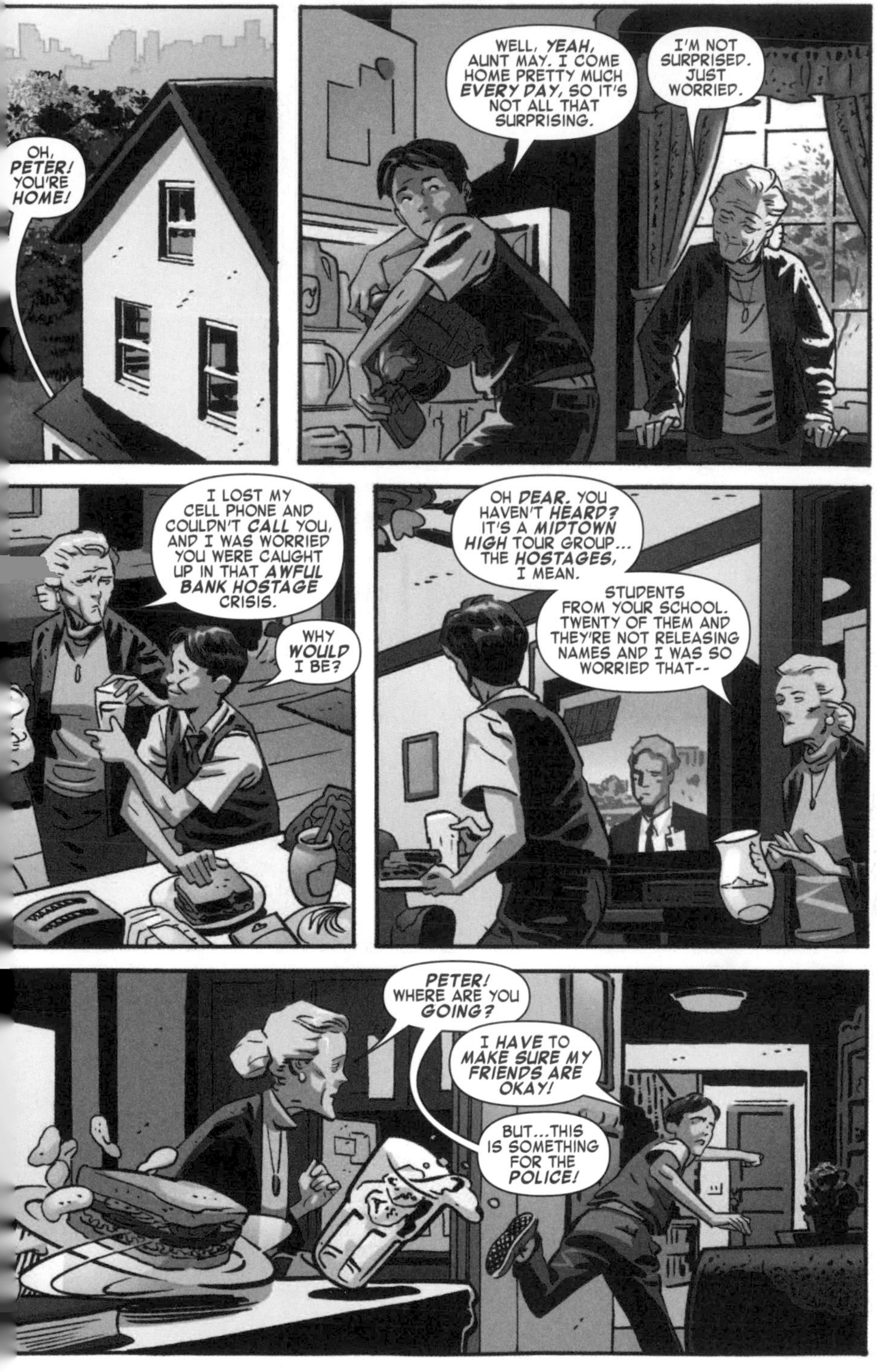
OH, PETER! YOU'RE HOME!
WELL, YEAH, AUNT MAY. I COME HOME PRETTY MUCH EVERY DAY, SO IT'S NOT ALL THAT SURPRISING.
I'M NOT SURPRISED. JUST WORRIED.
I LOST MY CELL PHONE AND COULDN'T CALL YOU, AND I WAS WORRIED YOU WERE CAUGHT UP IN THAT AWFUL BANK HOSTAGE CRISIS.
WHY WOULD I BE?
OH DEAR. YOU HAVEN'T HEARD? IT'S A MIDTOWN HIGH TOUR GROUP... THE HOSTAGES, I MEAN.
STUDENTS FROM YOUR SCHOOL. TWENTY OF THEM AND THEY'RE NOT RELEASING NAMES AND I WAS SO WORRIED THAT--
PETER! WHERE ARE YOU GOING?
I HAVE TO MAKE SURE MY FRIENDS ARE OKAY!
BUT...THIS IS SOMETHING FOR THE POLICE!

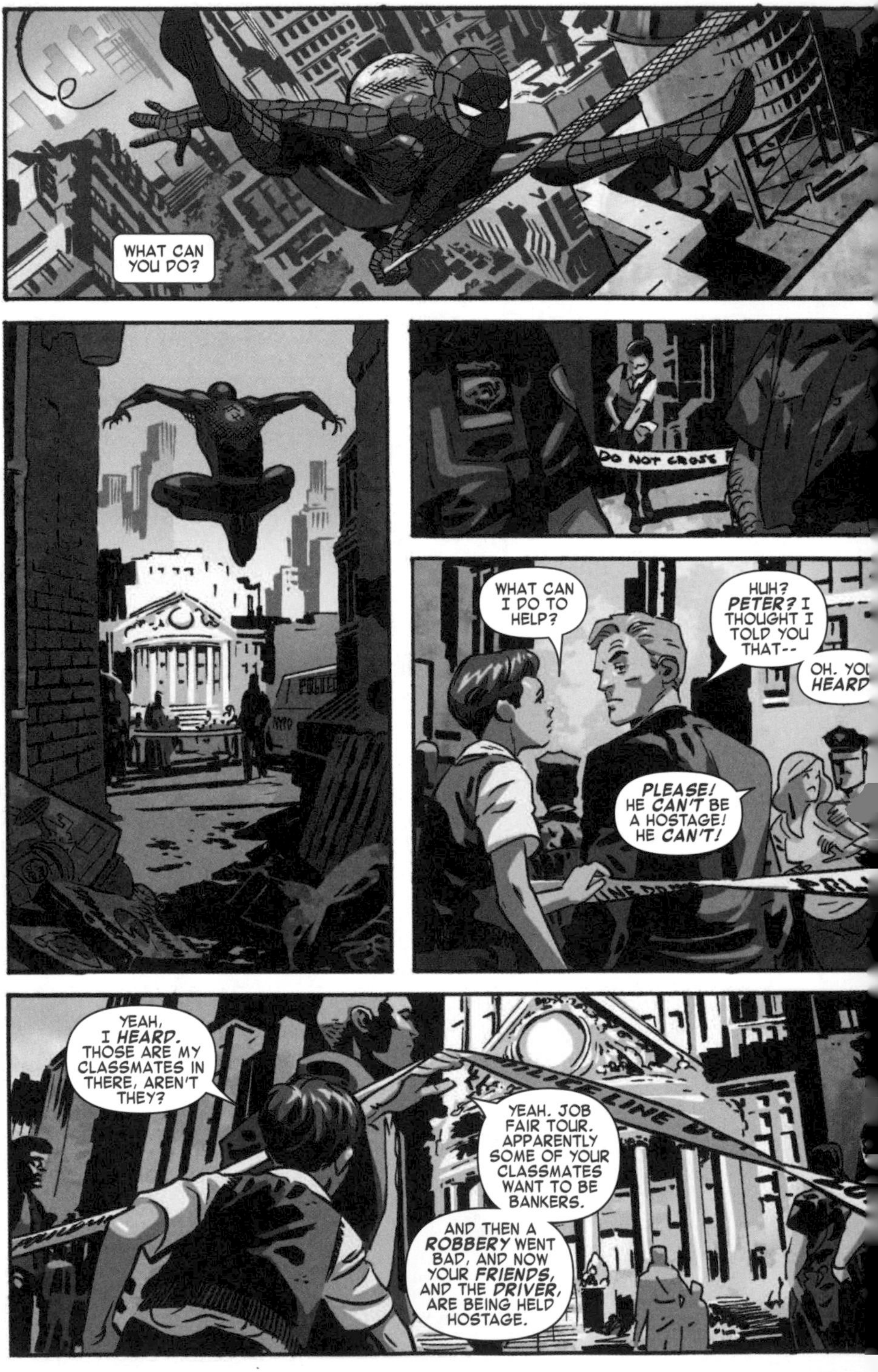
WHAT CAN YOU DO?
DO NOT CROSS
WHAT CAN I DO TO HELP?
HUH? PETER? I THOUGHT I TOLD YOU THAT--
OH. YOU HEARD
PLEASE! HE CAN'T BE A HOSTAGE! HE CAN'T!
YEAH, I HEARD. THOSE ARE MY CLASSMATES IN THERE, AREN'T THEY?
YEAH. JOB FAIR TOUR. APPARENTLY SOME OF YOUR CLASSMATES WANT TO BE BANKERS.
AND THEN A ROBBERY WENT BAD, AND NOW YOUR FRIENDS, AND THE DRIVER, ARE BEING HELD HOSTAGE.

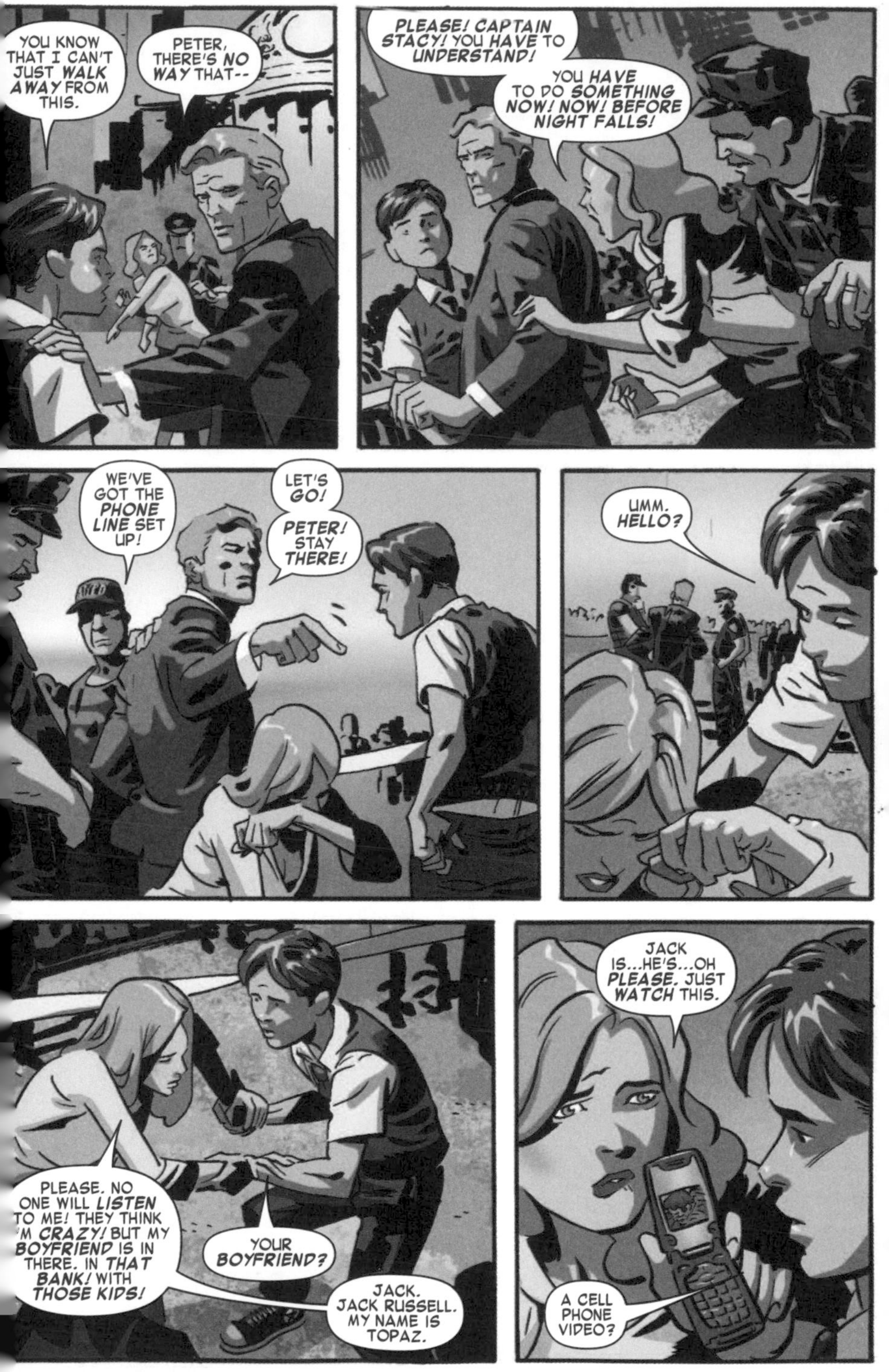
YOU KNOW THAT I CAN'T JUST WALK AWAY FROM THIS.
PETER, THERE'S NO WAY THAT--
PLEASE! CAPTAIN STACY! YOU HAVE TO UNDERSTAND!
YOU HAVE TO DO SOMETHING NOW! NOW! BEFORE NIGHT FALLS!
WE'VE GOT THE PHONE LINE SET UP!
LET'S GO!
PETER! STAY THERE!
UMM. HELLO?
PLEASE. NO ONE WILL LISTEN TO ME! THEY THINK I'M CRAZY! BUT MY BOYFRIEND IS IN THERE. IN THAT BANK! WITH THOSE KIDS!
YOUR BOYFRIEND?
JACK. JACK RUSSELL. MY NAME IS TOPAZ.
JACK IS...HE'S...OH PLEASE. JUST WATCH THIS.
A CELL PHONE VIDEO?

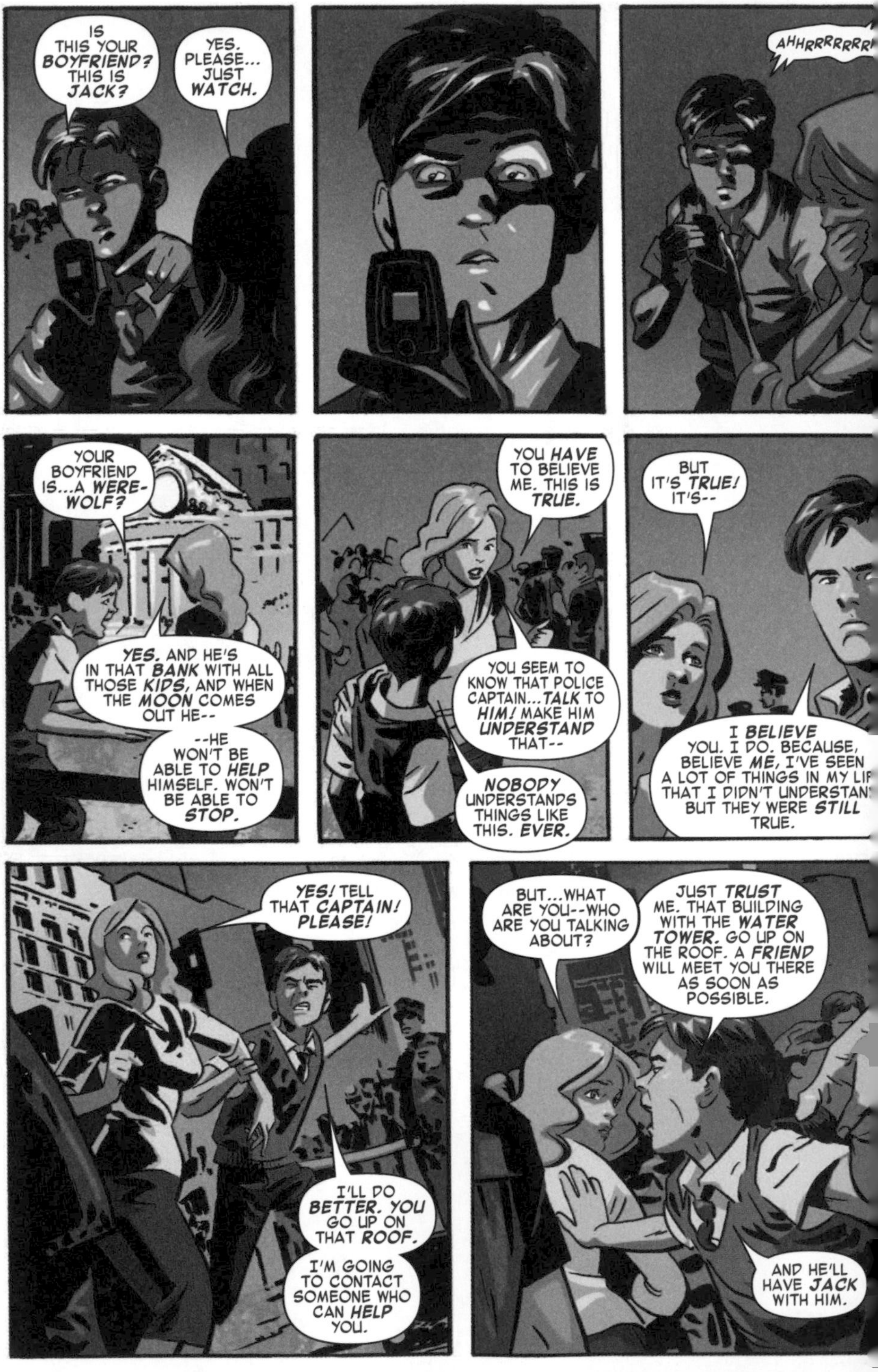

IS THIS YOUR BOYFRIEND? THIS IS JACK?
YES. PLEASE... JUST WATCH.
AHHRRRRRRR
YOUR BOYFRIEND IS...A WERE-WOLF?
YES. AND HE'S IN THAT BANK WITH ALL THOSE KIDS, AND WHEN THE MOON COMES OUT HE--
--HE WON'T BE ABLE TO HELP HIMSELF. WON'T BE ABLE TO STOP.
YOU HAVE TO BELIEVE ME. THIS IS TRUE.
YOU SEEM TO KNOW THAT POLICE CAPTAIN...TALK TO HIM! MAKE HIM UNDERSTAND THAT--
NOBODY UNDERSTANDS THINGS LIKE THIS. EVER.
BUT IT'S TRUE! IT'S--
I BELIEVE YOU. I DO. BECAUSE, BELIEVE ME, I'VE SEEN A LOT OF THINGS IN MY LIF THAT I DIDN'T UNDERSTAN BUT THEY WERE STILL TRUE.
YES! TELL THAT CAPTAIN! PLEASE!
I'LL DO BETTER. YOU GO UP ON THAT ROOF.
I'M GOING TO CONTACT SOMEONE WHO CAN HELP YOU.
BUT...WHAT ARE YOU--WHO ARE YOU TALKING ABOUT?
JUST TRUST ME. THAT BUILDING WITH THE WATER TOWER. GO UP ON THE ROOF. A FRIEND WILL MEET YOU THERE AS SOON AS POSSIBLE.
AND HE'LL HAVE JACK WITH HIM.

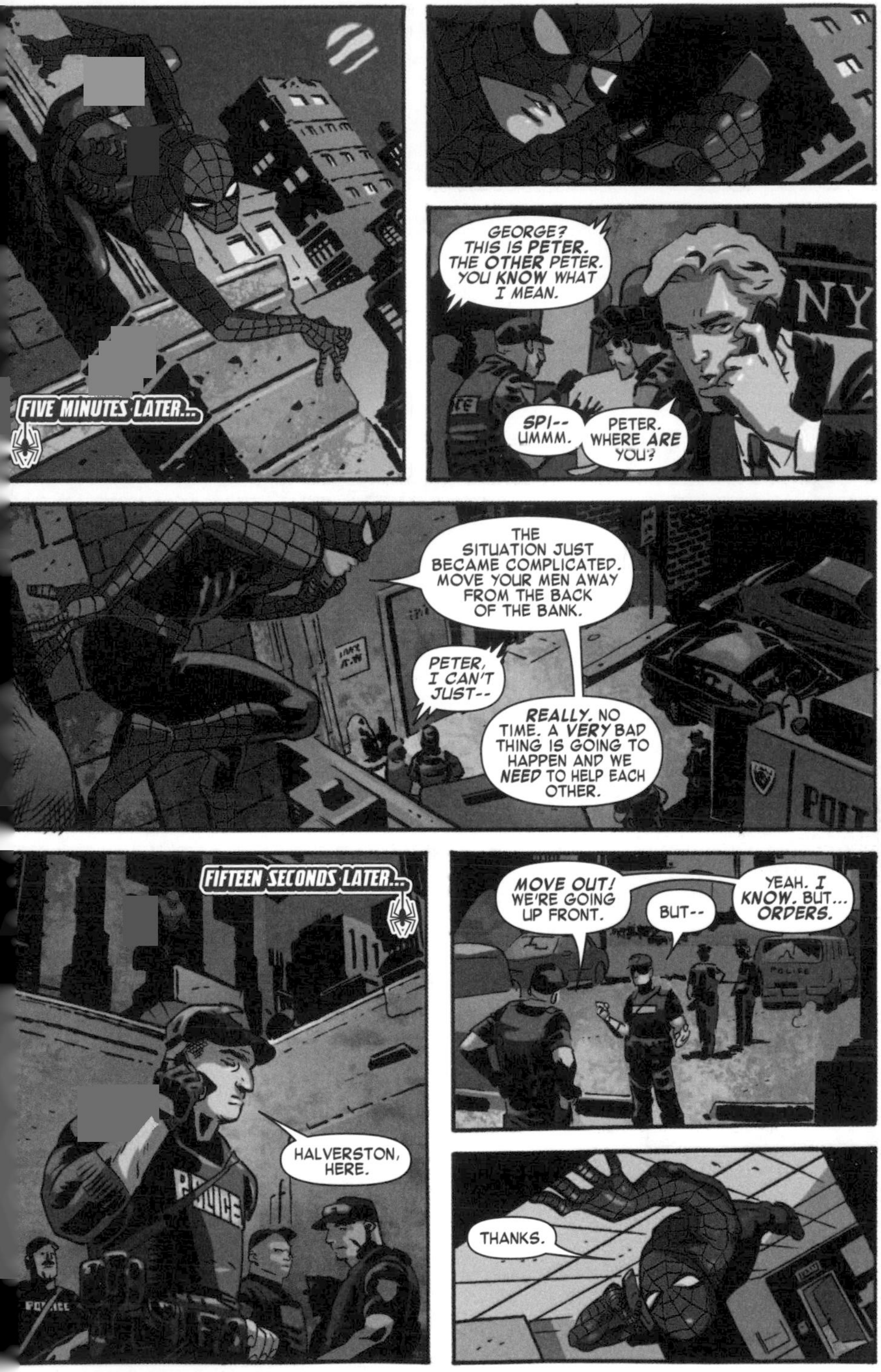
FIVE MINUTES LATER...
GEORGE? THIS IS PETER. THE OTHER PETER. YOU KNOW WHAT I MEAN.
SPI-- UMMM.
PETER. WHERE ARE YOU?
THE SITUATION JUST BECAME COMPLICATED. MOVE YOUR MEN AWAY FROM THE BACK OF THE BANK.
PETER, I CAN'T JUST--
REALLY. NO TIME. A VERY BAD THING IS GOING TO HAPPEN AND WE NEED TO HELP EACH OTHER.
FIFTEEN SECONDS LATER...
HALVERSTON, HERE.
POLICE
MOVE OUT! WE'RE GOING UP FRONT.
BUT--
YEAH. I KNOW. BUT... ORDERS.
THANKS.

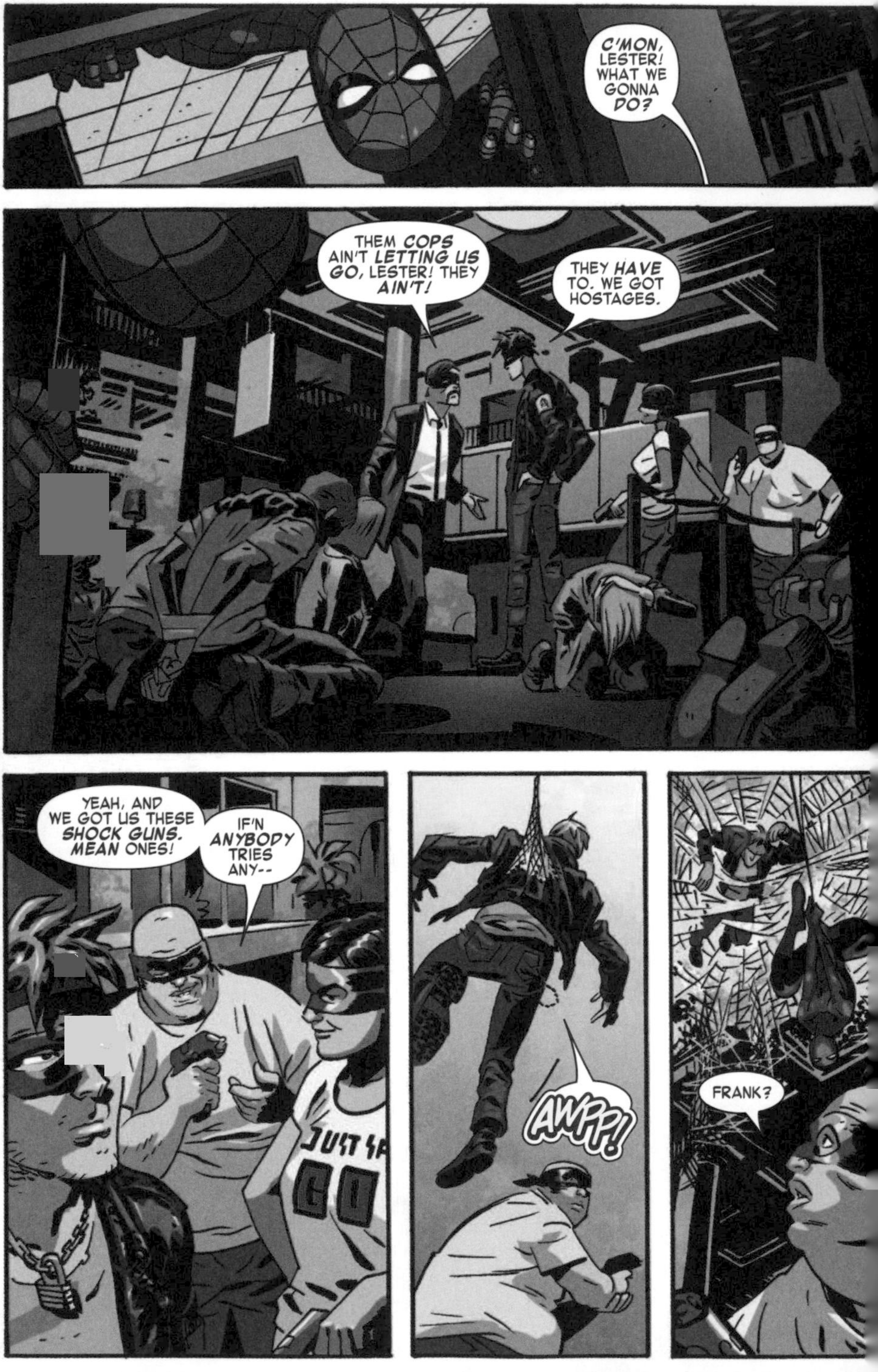
C'MON, LESTER! WHAT WE GONNA DO?
THEM COPS AIN'T LETTING US GO, LESTER! THEY AIN'T!
THEY HAVE TO. WE GOT HOSTAGES.
YEAH, AND WE GOT US THESE SHOCK GUNS. MEAN ONES!
IF'N ANYBODY TRIES ANY--
AWPP!
FRANK?

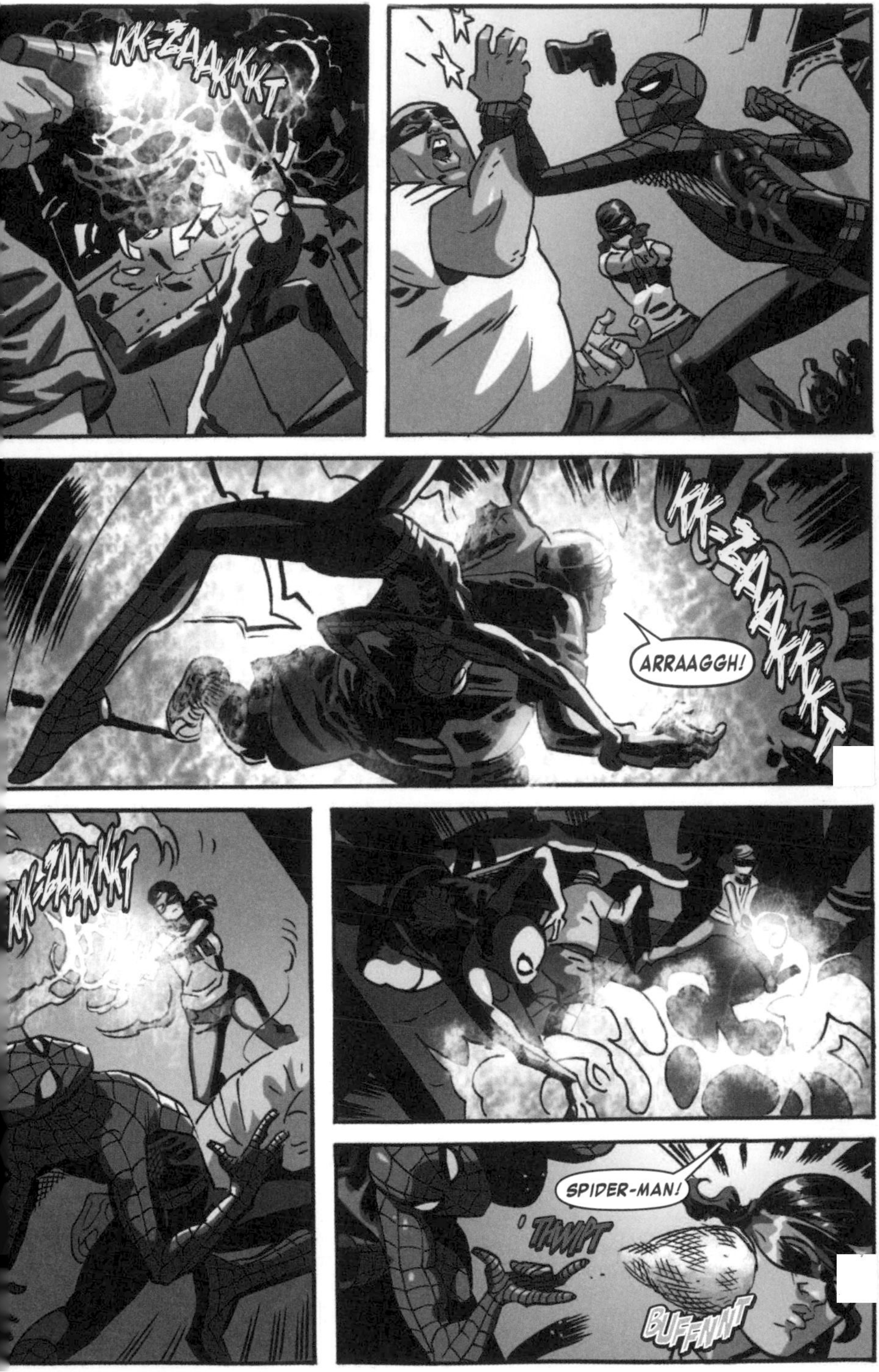
KK-ZAAKKKT
KK-ZAAKKKT
ARRAAGGH!
KK-ZAAKKKT
SPIDER-MAN!
THWIPT
BUFFNNT

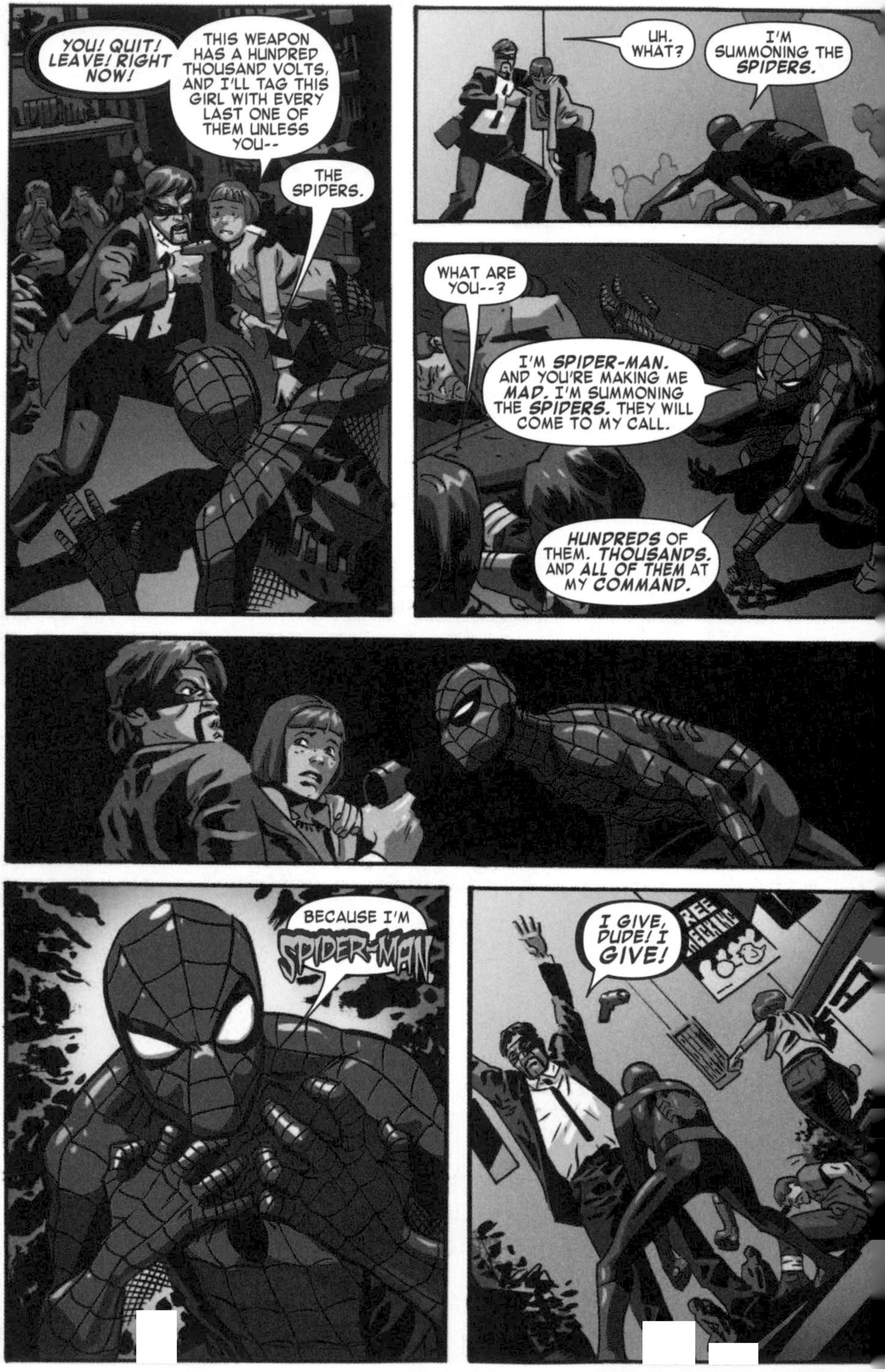
YOU! QUIT! LEAVE! RIGHT NOW!
THIS WEAPON HAS A HUNDRED THOUSAND VOLTS, AND I'LL TAG THIS GIRL WITH EVERY LAST ONE OF THEM UNLESS YOU--
THE SPIDERS.
UH. WHAT?
I'M SUMMONING THE SPIDERS.
WHAT ARE YOU--?
I'M SPIDER-MAN. AND YOU'RE MAKING ME MAD. I'M SUMMONING THE SPIDERS. THEY WILL COME TO MY CALL.
HUNDREDS OF THEM. THOUSANDS. AND ALL OF THEM AT MY COMMAND.
BECAUSE I'M SPIDER-MAN.
I GIVE, DUDE! I GIVE!

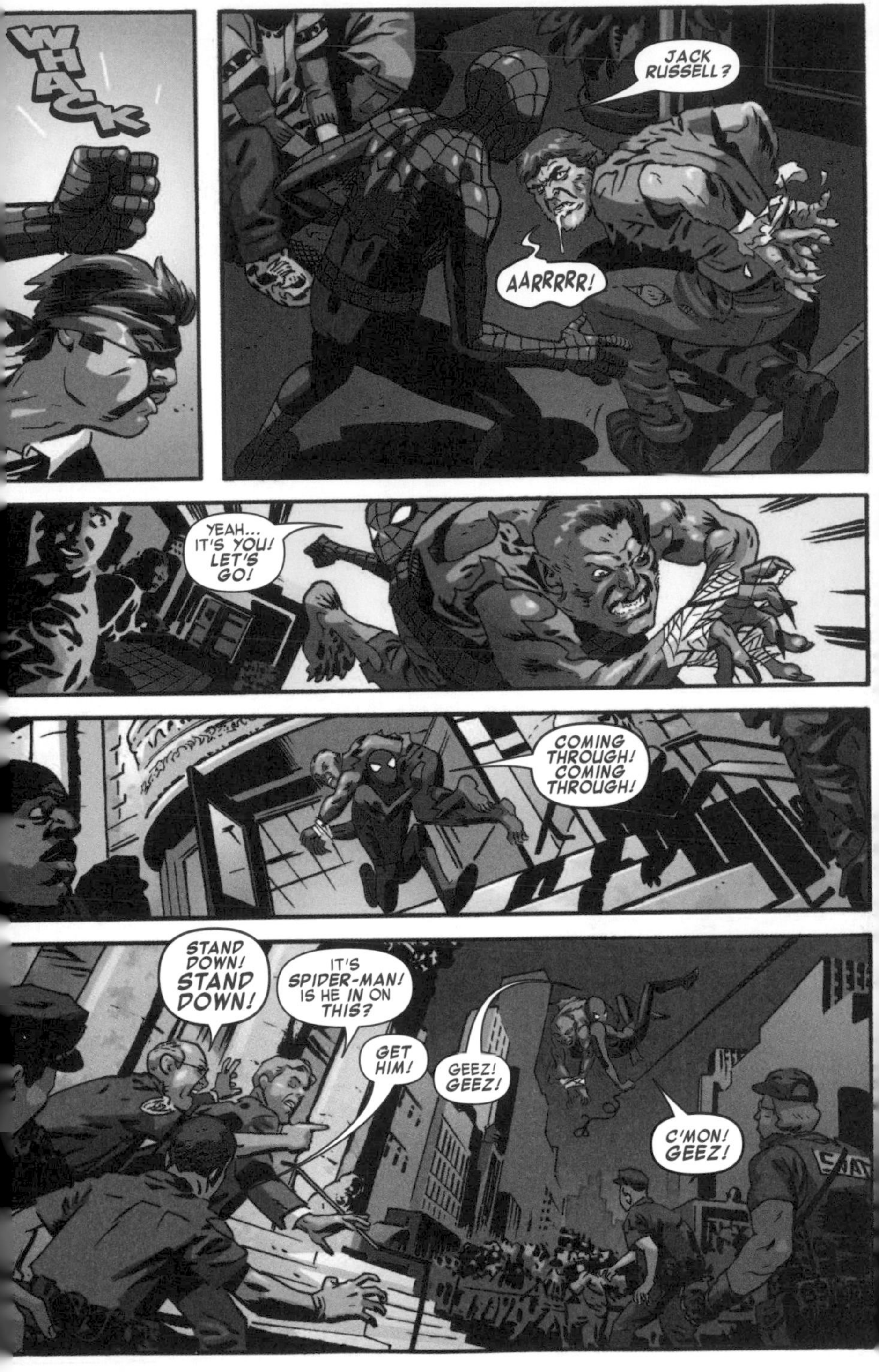
WHACK
JACK RUSSELL?
AARRRRR!
YEAH... IT'S YOU! LET'S GO!
COMING THROUGH! COMING THROUGH!
STAND DOWN! STAND DOWN!
IT'S SPIDER-MAN! IS HE IN ON THIS?
GET HIM!
GEEZ! GEEZ!
C'MON! GEEZ!

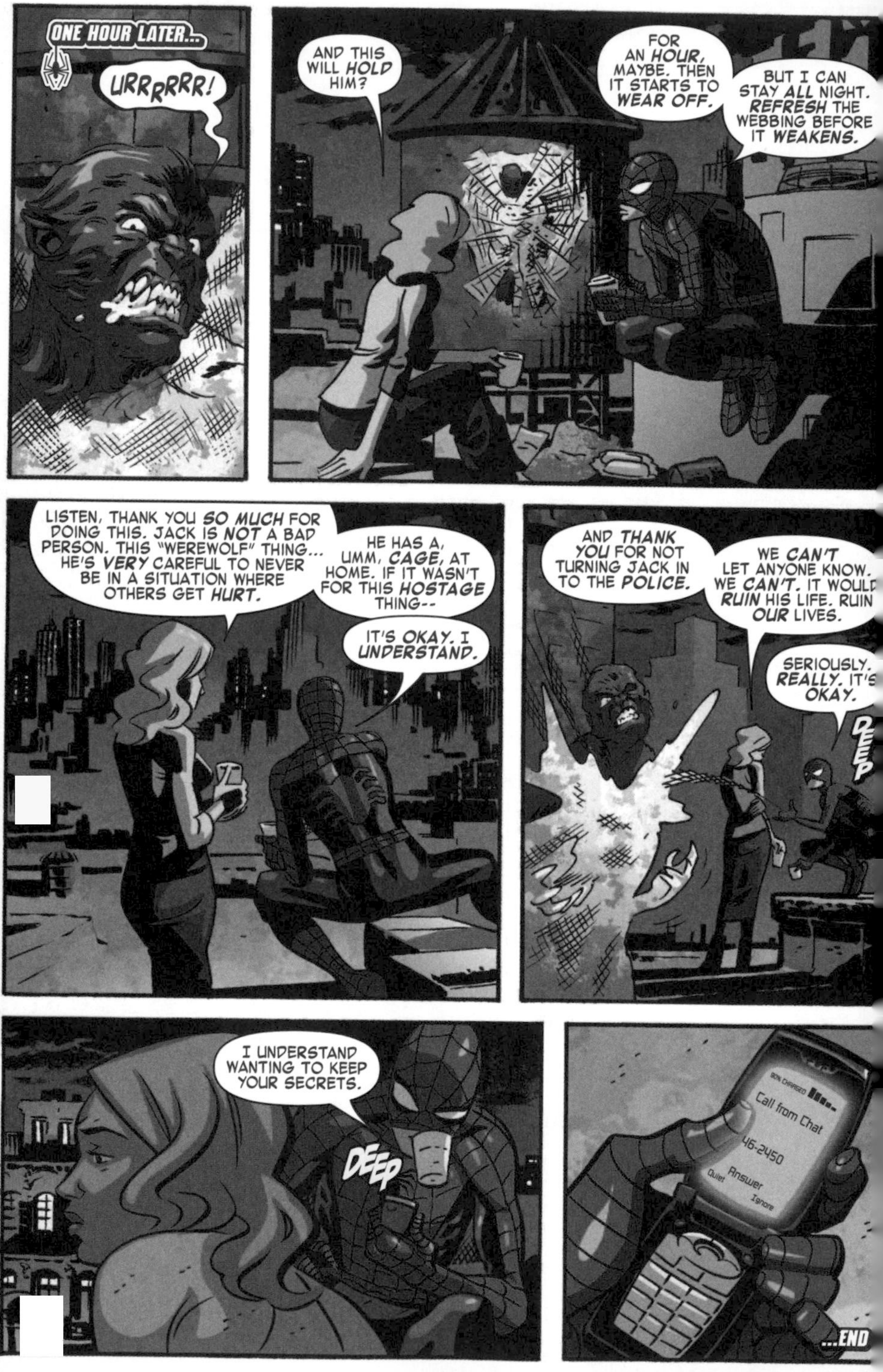
ONE HOUR LATER...
URRRRRR!
AND THIS WILL HOLD HIM?
FOR AN HOUR, MAYBE. THEN IT STARTS TO WEAR OFF.
BUT I CAN STAY ALL NIGHT. REFRESH THE WEBBING BEFORE IT WEAKENS.
LISTEN, THANK YOU SO MUCH FOR DOING THIS. JACK IS NOT A BAD PERSON. THIS "WEREWOLF" THING... HE'S VERY CAREFUL TO NEVER BE IN A SITUATION WHERE OTHERS GET HURT.
HE HAS A, UMM, CAGE, AT HOME. IF IT WASN'T FOR THIS HOSTAGE THING--
IT'S OKAY. I UNDERSTAND.
AND THANK YOU FOR NOT TURNING JACK IN TO THE POLICE.
WE CAN'T LET ANYONE KNOW. WE CAN'T. IT WOULD RUIN HIS LIFE. RUIN OUR LIVES.
SERIOUSLY. REALLY. IT'S OKAY.
DEEP
I UNDERSTAND WANTING TO KEEP YOUR SECRETS.
DEEP
Call from Chat
46-2450
Answer
Quiet
Ignore
...END

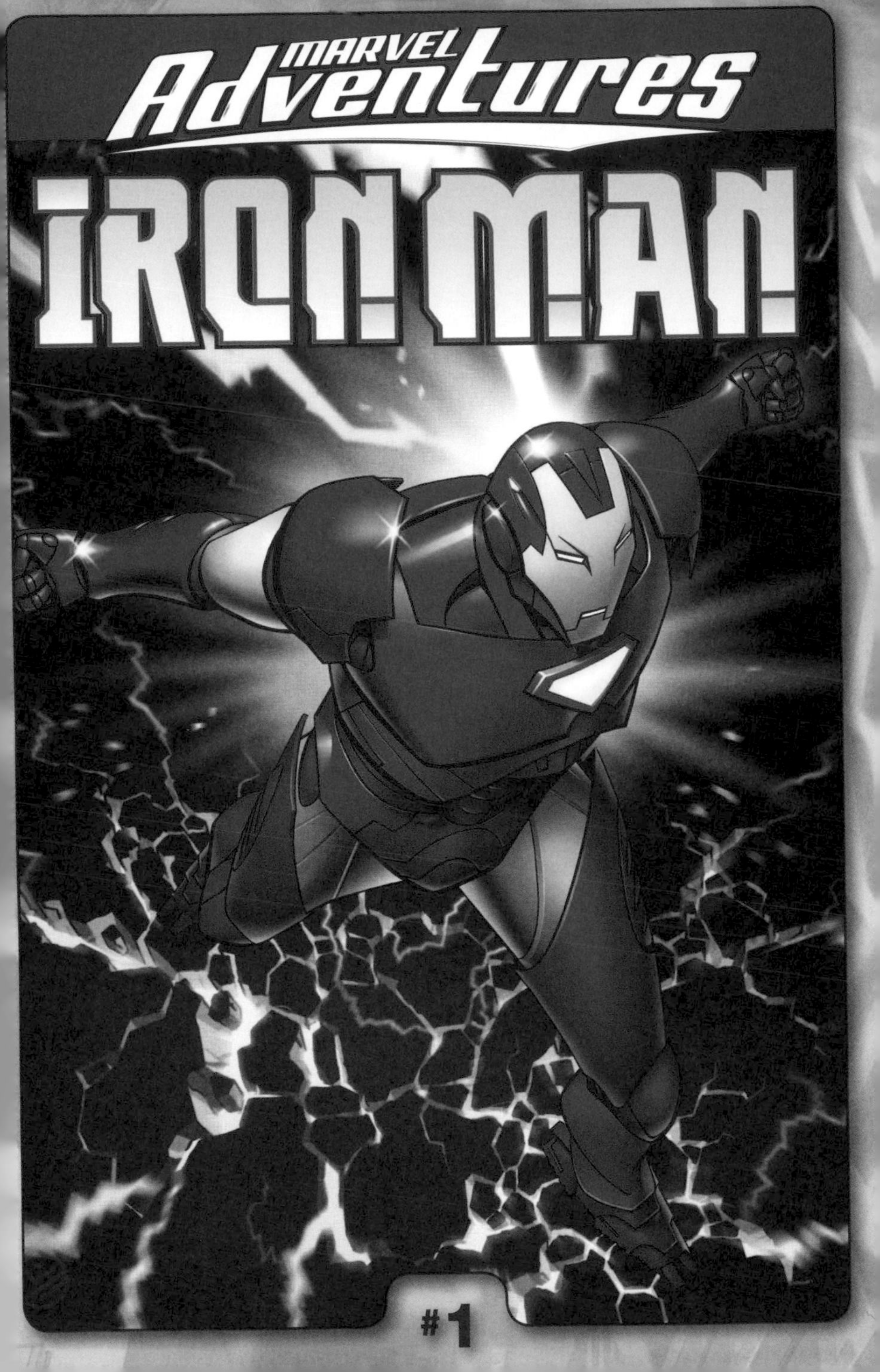
MARVEL
Adventures
IRON MAN
#1

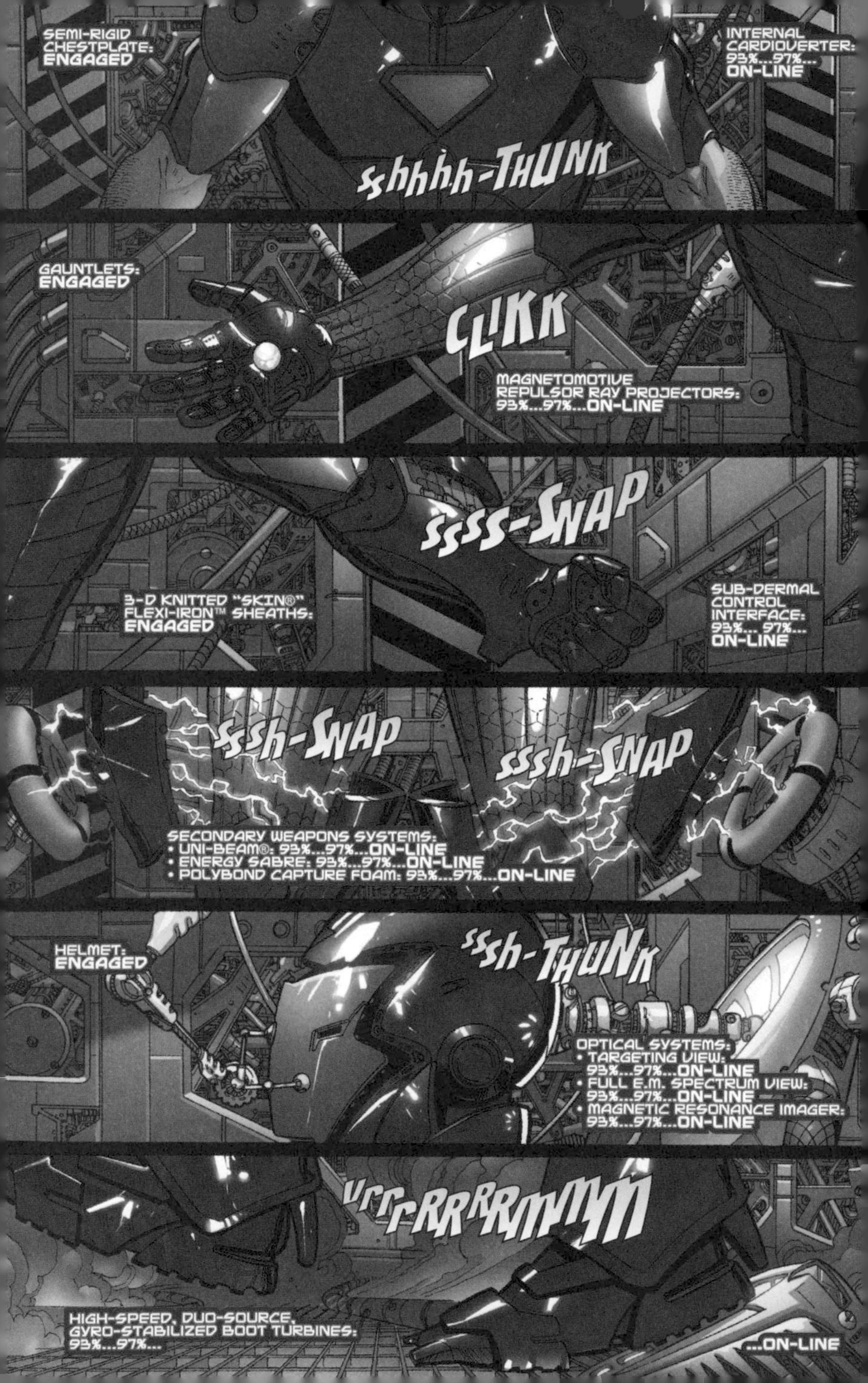

SEMI-RIGID CHESTPLATE: ENGAGED
INTERNAL CARDIOVERTER: 93%...97%... ON-LINE
SSHHHH-THUNK
GAUNTLETS: ENGAGED
CLIKK
MAGNETOMOTIVE REPULSOR RAY PROJECTORS: 93%...97%...ON-LINE
SSSS-SNAP
3-D KNITTED "SKIN®" FLEXI-IRON™ SHEATHS: ENGAGED
SUB-DERMAL CONTROL INTERFACE: 93%... 97%... ON-LINE
SSSH-SNAP
SSSH-SNAP
SECONDARY WEAPONS SYSTEMS:
• UNI-BEAM®: 93%...97%...ON-LINE
• ENERGY SABRE: 93%...97%...ON-LINE
• POLYBOND CAPTURE FOAM: 93%...97%...ON-LINE
HELMET: ENGAGED
SSSH-THUNK
OPTICAL SYSTEMS:
• TARGETING VIEW: 93%...97%...ON-LINE
• FULL E.M. SPECTRUM VIEW: 93%...97%...ON-LINE
• MAGNETIC RESONANCE IMAGER: 93%...97%...ON-LINE
VRRRRRRRRMMM
HIGH-SPEED, DUO-SOURCE, GYRO-STABILIZED BOOT TURBINES: 93%...97%...
...ON-LINE

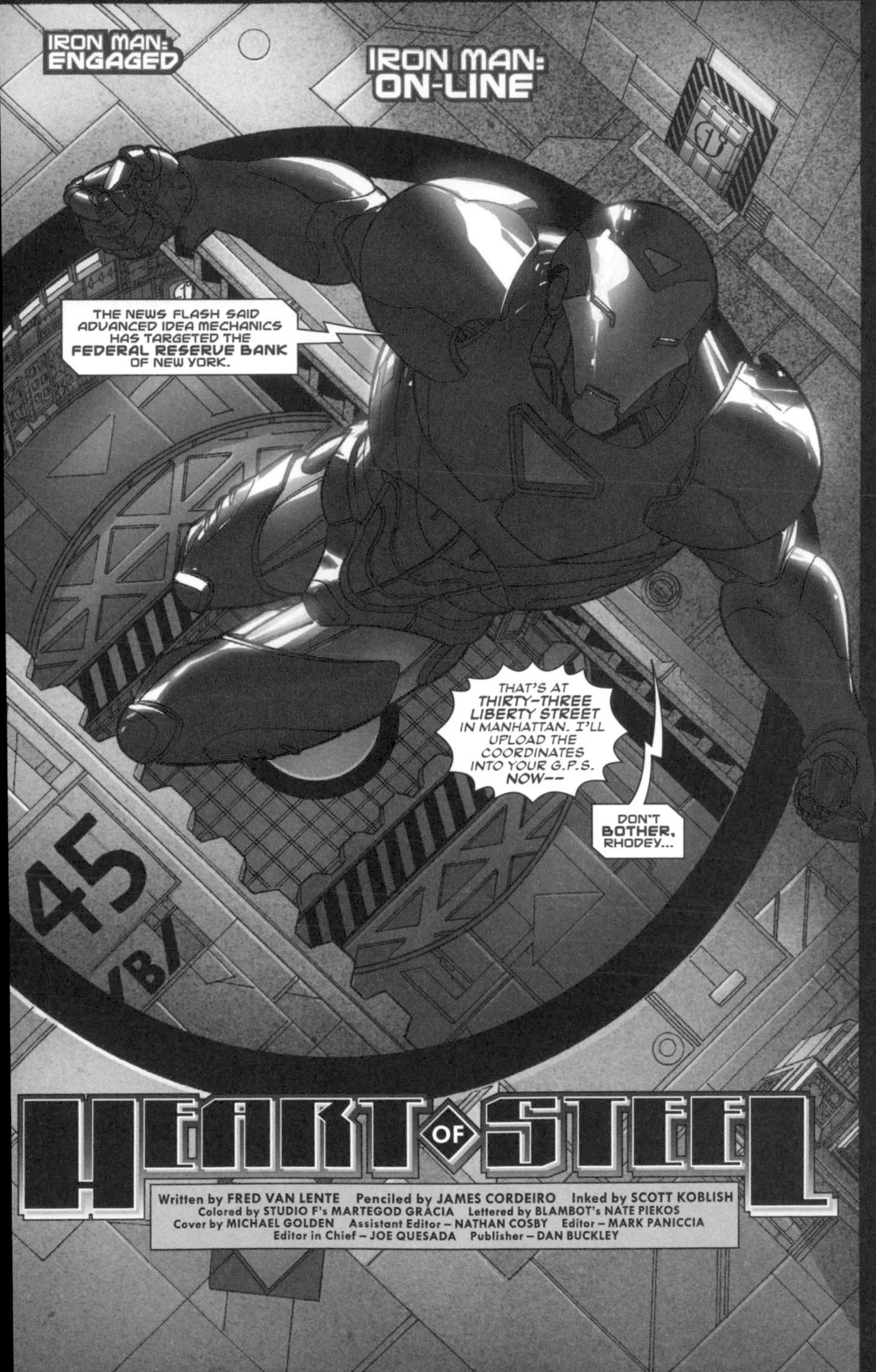
IRON MAN: ENGAGED
IRON MAN: ON-LINE
THE NEWS FLASH SAID ADVANCED IDEA MECHANICS HAS TARGETED THE FEDERAL RESERVE BANK OF NEW YORK.
THAT'S AT THIRTY-THREE LIBERTY STREET IN MANHATTAN. I'LL UPLOAD THE COORDINATES INTO YOUR G.P.S. NOW--
DON'T BOTHER, RHODEY...
45
HEART OF STEEL
Written by FRED VAN LENTE Penciled by JAMES CORDEIRO Inked by SCOTT KOBLISH
Colored by STUDIO F's MARTEGOD GRACIA Lettered by BLAMBOT's NATE PIEKOS
Cover by MICHAEL GOLDEN Assistant Editor – NATHAN COSBY Editor – MARK PANICCIA
Editor in Chief – JOE QUESADA Publisher – DAN BUCKLEY

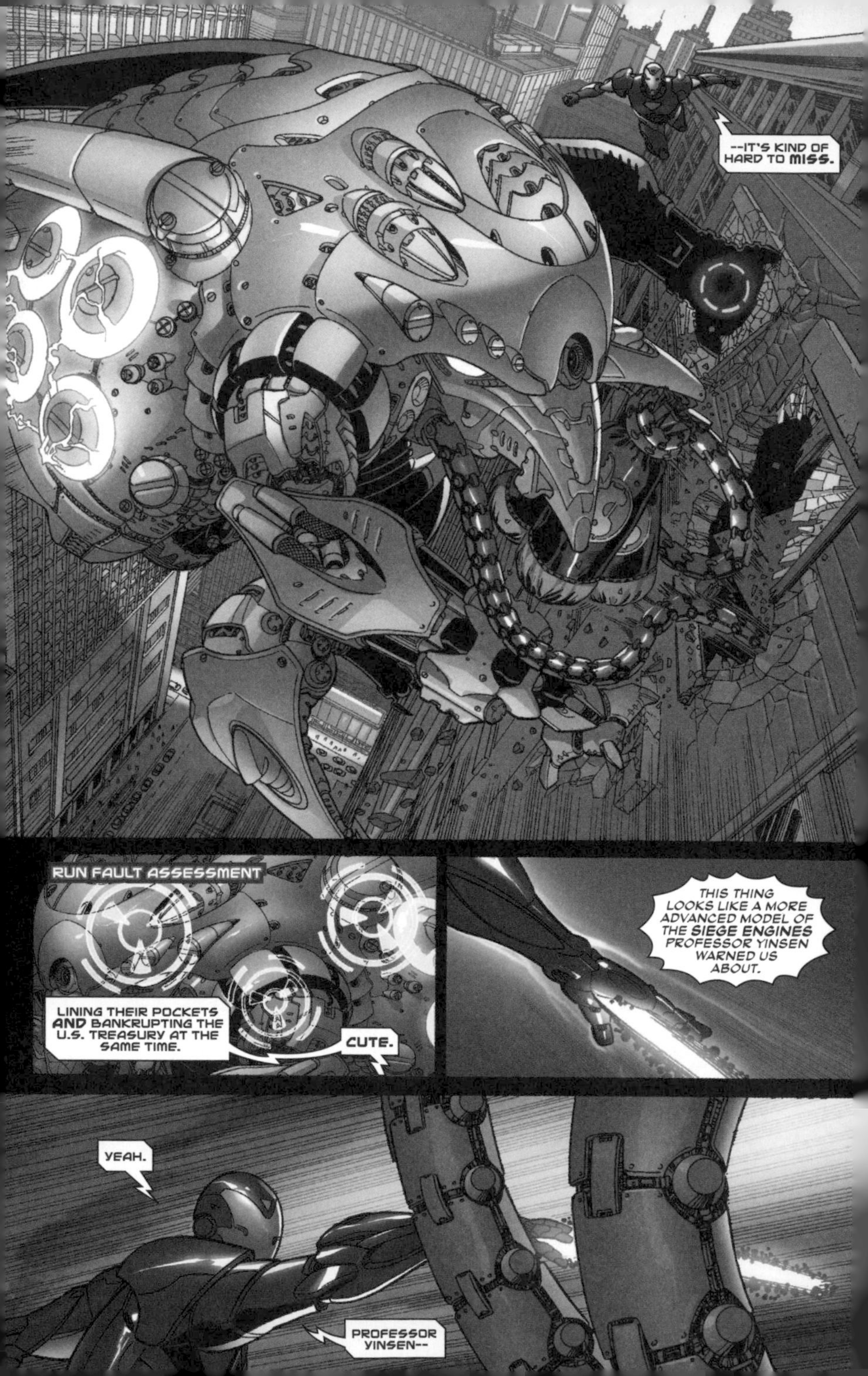
--IT'S KIND OF HARD TO MISS.
RUN FAULT ASSESSMENT
LINING THEIR POCKETS AND BANKRUPTING THE U.S. TREASURY AT THE SAME TIME.
CUTE.
THIS THING LOOKS LIKE A MORE ADVANCED MODEL OF THE SIEGE ENGINES PROFESSOR YINSEN WARNED US ABOUT.
YEAH.
PROFESSOR YINSEN--

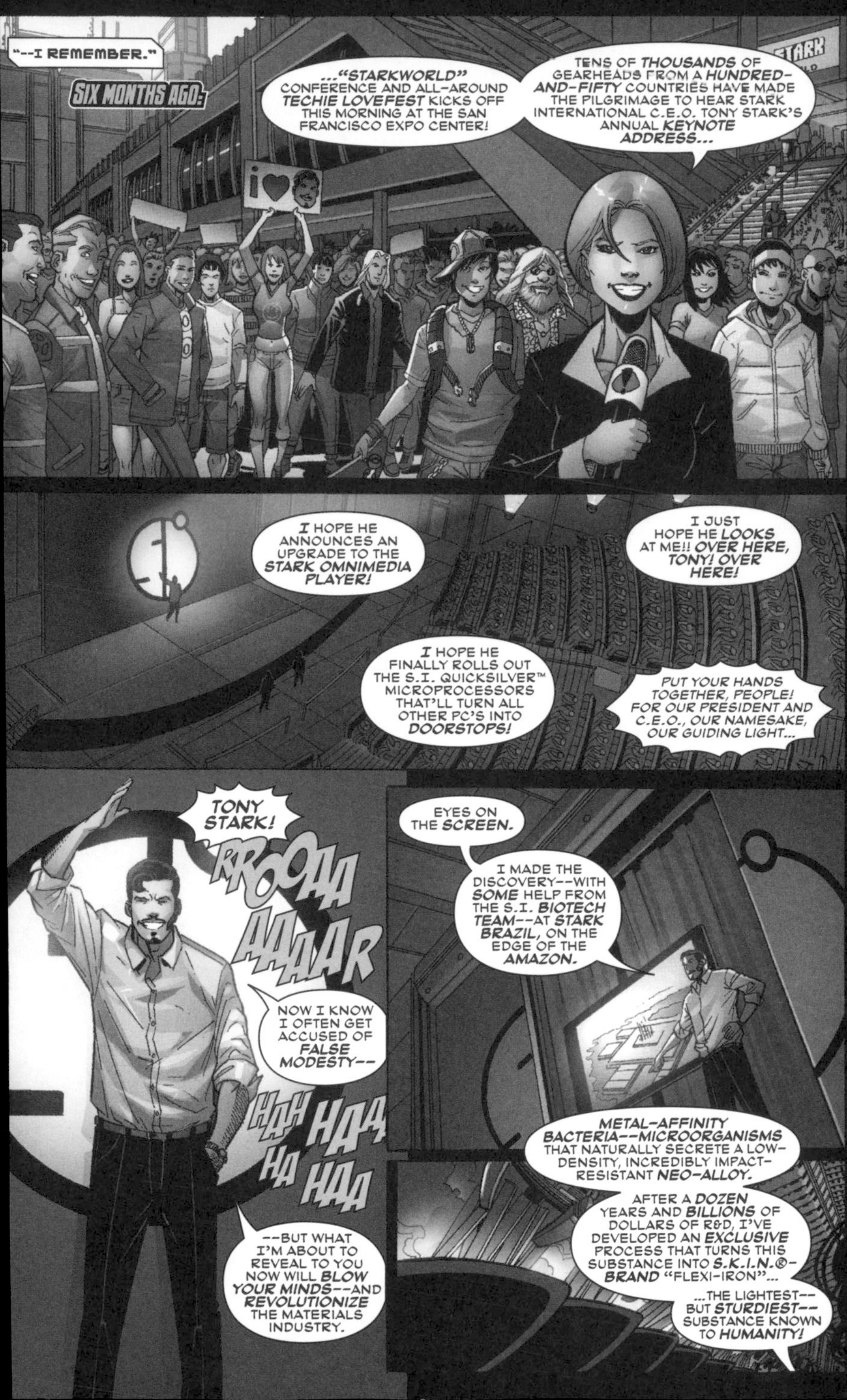
"--I REMEMBER."
SIX MONTHS AGO:
..."STARKWORLD" CONFERENCE AND ALL-AROUND TECHIE LOVEFEST KICKS OFF THIS MORNING AT THE SAN FRANCISCO EXPO CENTER!
TENS OF THOUSANDS OF GEARHEADS FROM A HUNDRED-AND-FIFTY COUNTRIES HAVE MADE THE PILGRIMAGE TO HEAR STARK INTERNATIONAL C.E.O. TONY STARK'S ANNUAL KEYNOTE ADDRESS...
STARK
I HOPE HE ANNOUNCES AN UPGRADE TO THE STARK OMNIMEDIA PLAYER!
I JUST HOPE HE LOOKS AT ME!! OVER HERE, TONY! OVER HERE!
I HOPE HE FINALLY ROLLS OUT THE S.I. QUICKSILVER™ MICROPROCESSORS THAT'LL TURN ALL OTHER PC'S INTO DOORSTOPS!
PUT YOUR HANDS TOGETHER, PEOPLE! FOR OUR PRESIDENT AND C.E.O., OUR NAMESAKE, OUR GUIDING LIGHT...
TONY STARK!
RROOAA AAAAR
NOW I KNOW I OFTEN GET ACCUSED OF FALSE MODESTY--
HAH HAA HA HAA
--BUT WHAT I'M ABOUT TO REVEAL TO YOU NOW WILL BLOW YOUR MINDS--AND REVOLUTIONIZE THE MATERIALS INDUSTRY.
EYES ON THE SCREEN.
I MADE THE DISCOVERY--WITH SOME HELP FROM THE S.I. BIOTECH TEAM--AT STARK BRAZIL, ON THE EDGE OF THE AMAZON.
METAL-AFFINITY BACTERIA--MICROORGANISMS THAT NATURALLY SECRETE A LOW-DENSITY, INCREDIBLY IMPACT-RESISTANT NEO-ALLOY.
AFTER A DOZEN YEARS AND BILLIONS OF DOLLARS OF R&D, I'VE DEVELOPED AN EXCLUSIVE PROCESS THAT TURNS THIS SUBSTANCE INTO S.K.I.N.®-BRAND "FLEXI-IRON"...
...THE LIGHTEST--BUT STURDIEST--SUBSTANCE KNOWN TO HUMANITY!

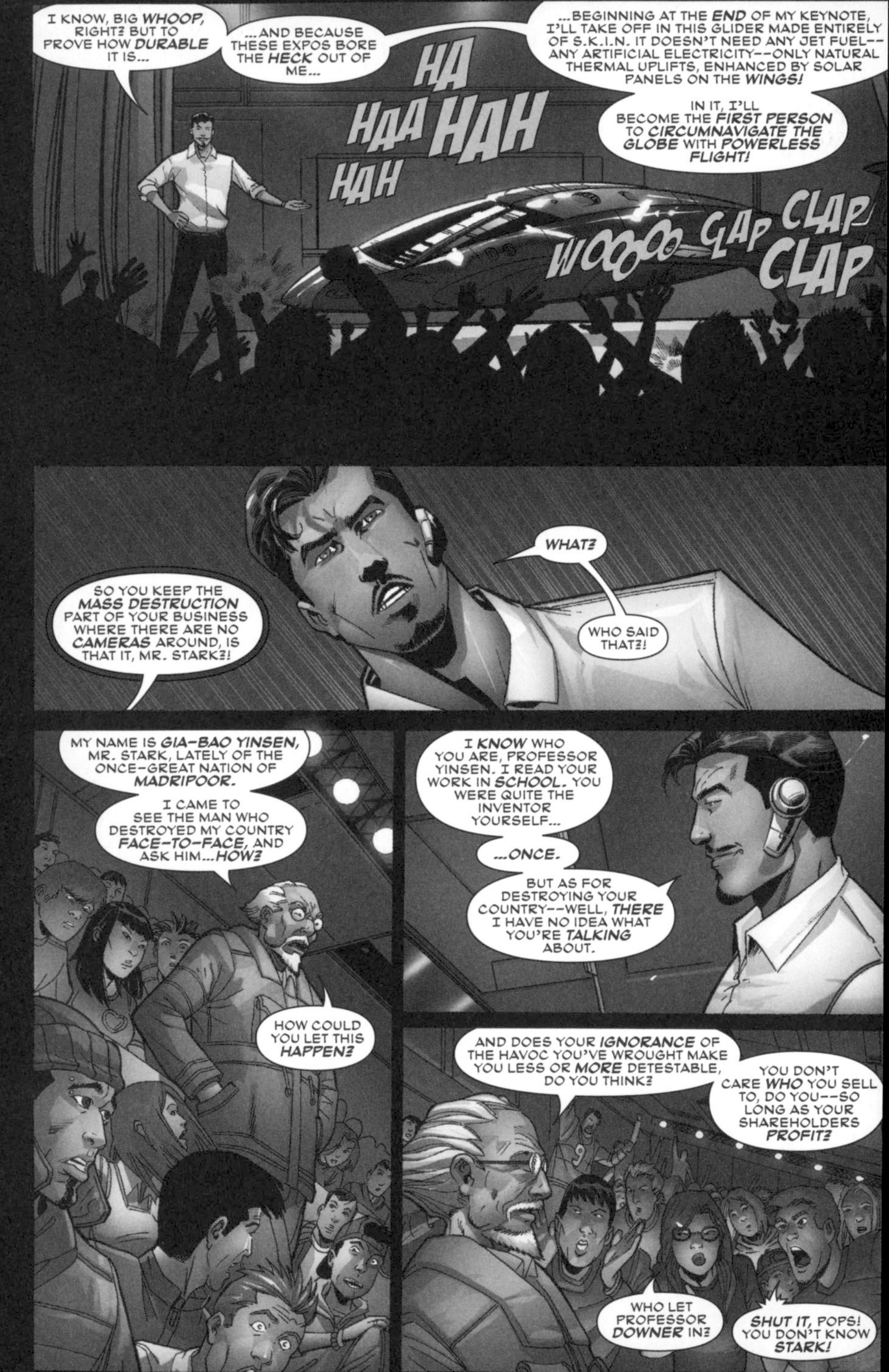
I KNOW, BIG WHOOP, RIGHT? BUT TO PROVE HOW DURABLE IT IS...
...AND BECAUSE THESE EXPOS BORE THE HECK OUT OF ME...
...BEGINNING AT THE END OF MY KEYNOTE, I'LL TAKE OFF IN THIS GLIDER MADE ENTIRELY OF S.K.I.N. IT DOESN'T NEED ANY JET FUEL--ANY ARTIFICIAL ELECTRICITY--ONLY NATURAL THERMAL UPLIFTS, ENHANCED BY SOLAR PANELS ON THE WINGS!
IN IT, I'LL BECOME THE FIRST PERSON TO CIRCUMNAVIGATE THE GLOBE WITH POWERLESS FLIGHT!
HA HAA HAH HAH
WOOOOO CLAP CLAP CLAP
WHAT?
SO YOU KEEP THE MASS DESTRUCTION PART OF YOUR BUSINESS WHERE THERE ARE NO CAMERAS AROUND, IS THAT IT, MR. STARK?!
WHO SAID THAT?!
MY NAME IS GIA-BAO YINSEN, MR. STARK, LATELY OF THE ONCE-GREAT NATION OF MADRIPOOR.
I CAME TO SEE THE MAN WHO DESTROYED MY COUNTRY FACE-TO-FACE, AND ASK HIM...HOW?
HOW COULD YOU LET THIS HAPPEN?
I KNOW WHO YOU ARE, PROFESSOR YINSEN. I READ YOUR WORK IN SCHOOL. YOU WERE QUITE THE INVENTOR YOURSELF...
...ONCE.
BUT AS FOR DESTROYING YOUR COUNTRY--WELL, THERE I HAVE NO IDEA WHAT YOU'RE TALKING ABOUT.
AND DOES YOUR IGNORANCE OF THE HAVOC YOU'VE WROUGHT MAKE YOU LESS OR MORE DETESTABLE, DO YOU THINK?
YOU DON'T CARE WHO YOU SELL TO, DO YOU--SO LONG AS YOUR SHAREHOLDERS PROFIT?
WHO LET PROFESSOR DOWNER IN?
SHUT IT, POPS! YOU DON'T KNOW STARK!

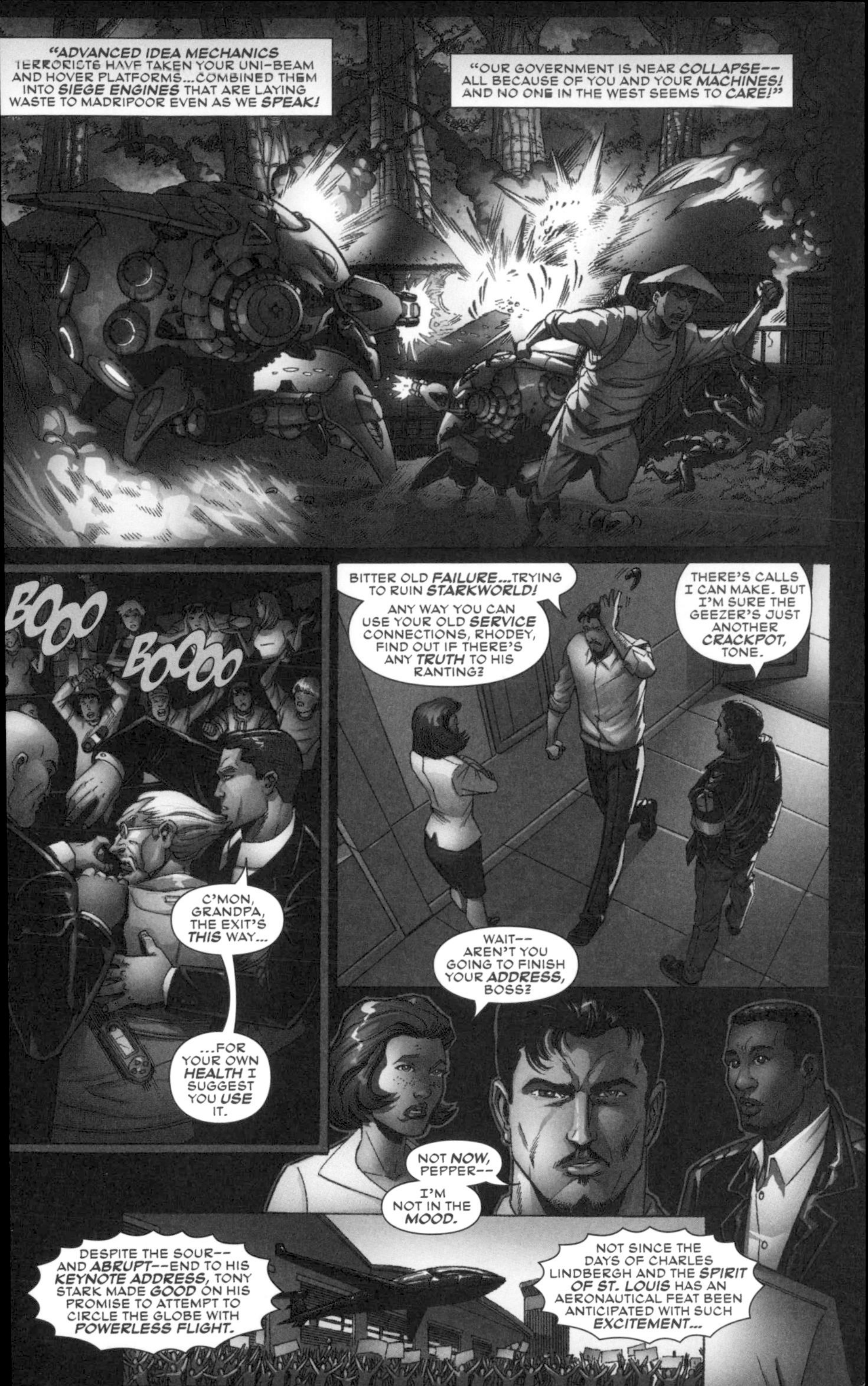
"ADVANCED IDEA MECHANICS TERRORISTS HAVE TAKEN YOUR UNI-BEAM AND HOVER PLATFORMS...COMBINED THEM INTO SIEGE ENGINES THAT ARE LAYING WASTE TO MADRIPOOR EVEN AS WE SPEAK!
"OUR GOVERNMENT IS NEAR COLLAPSE-- ALL BECAUSE OF YOU AND YOUR MACHINES! AND NO ONE IN THE WEST SEEMS TO CARE!"
BOOO
BOOOO
C'MON, GRANDPA, THE EXIT'S THIS WAY...
...FOR YOUR OWN HEALTH I SUGGEST YOU USE IT.
BITTER OLD FAILURE...TRYING TO RUIN STARKWORLD!
ANY WAY YOU CAN USE YOUR OLD SERVICE CONNECTIONS, RHODEY, FIND OUT IF THERE'S ANY TRUTH TO HIS RANTING?
THERE'S CALLS I CAN MAKE. BUT I'M SURE THE GEEZER'S JUST ANOTHER CRACKPOT, TONE.
WAIT-- AREN'T YOU GOING TO FINISH YOUR ADDRESS, BOSS?
NOT NOW, PEPPER--
I'M NOT IN THE MOOD.
DESPITE THE SOUR-- AND ABRUPT--END TO HIS KEYNOTE ADDRESS, TONY STARK MADE GOOD ON HIS PROMISE TO ATTEMPT TO CIRCLE THE GLOBE WITH POWERLESS FLIGHT.
NOT SINCE THE DAYS OF CHARLES LINDBERGH AND THE SPIRIT OF ST. LOUIS HAS AN AERONAUTICAL FEAT BEEN ANTICIPATED WITH SUCH EXCITEMENT...

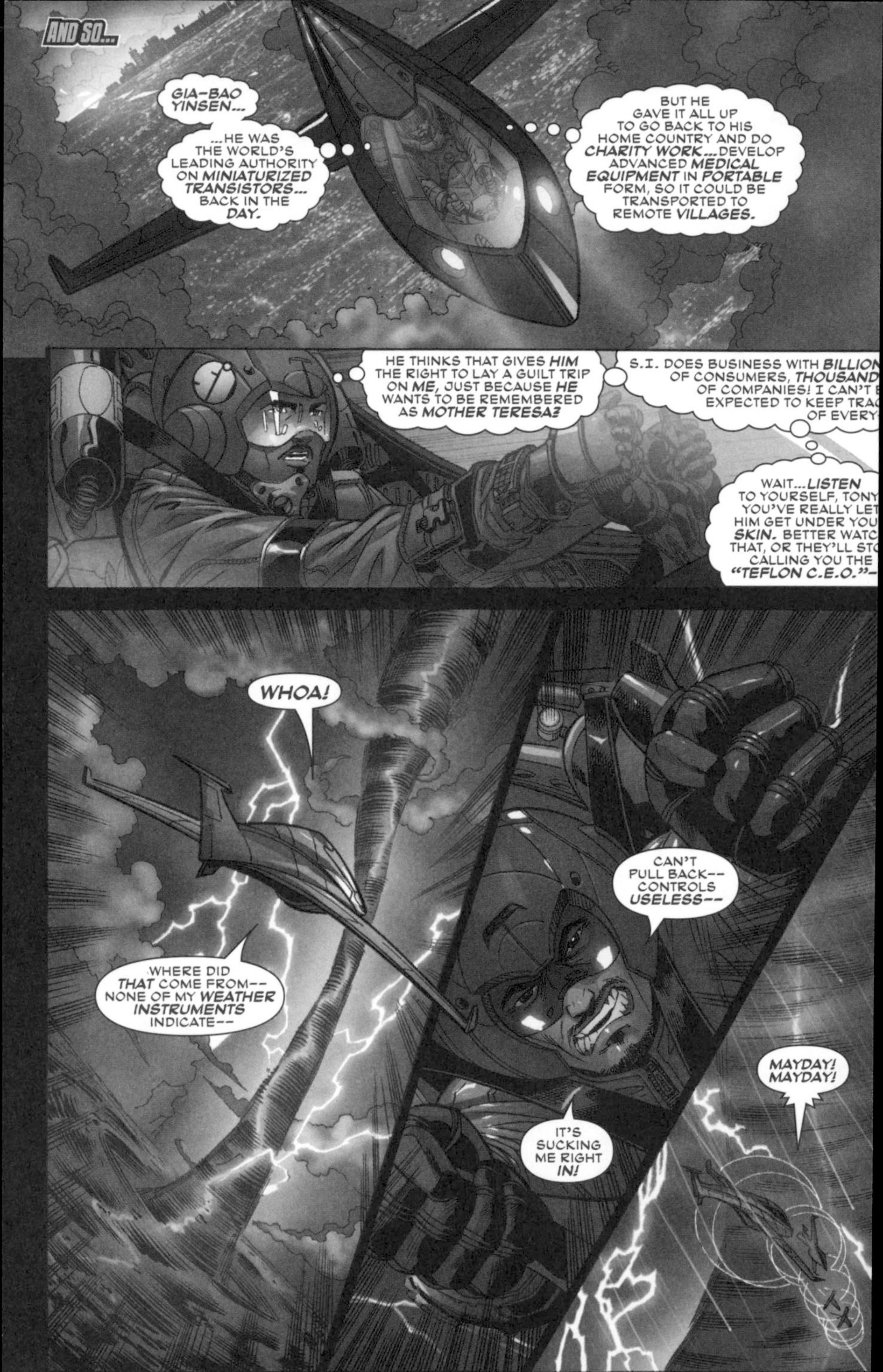
AND SO...
GIA-BAO YINSEN...
...HE WAS THE WORLD'S LEADING AUTHORITY ON MINIATURIZED TRANSISTORS... BACK IN THE DAY.
BUT HE GAVE IT ALL UP TO GO BACK TO HIS HOME COUNTRY AND DO CHARITY WORK...DEVELOP ADVANCED MEDICAL EQUIPMENT IN PORTABLE FORM, SO IT COULD BE TRANSPORTED TO REMOTE VILLAGES.
HE THINKS THAT GIVES HIM THE RIGHT TO LAY A GUILT TRIP ON ME, JUST BECAUSE HE WANTS TO BE REMEMBERED AS MOTHER TERESA?
WAIT...LISTEN TO YOURSELF, TONY
WHOA!
WHERE DID THAT COME FROM-- NONE OF MY WEATHER INSTRUMENTS INDICATE--
CAN'T PULL BACK-- CONTROLS USELESS--
IT'S SUCKING ME RIGHT IN!
MAYDAY! MAYDAY!

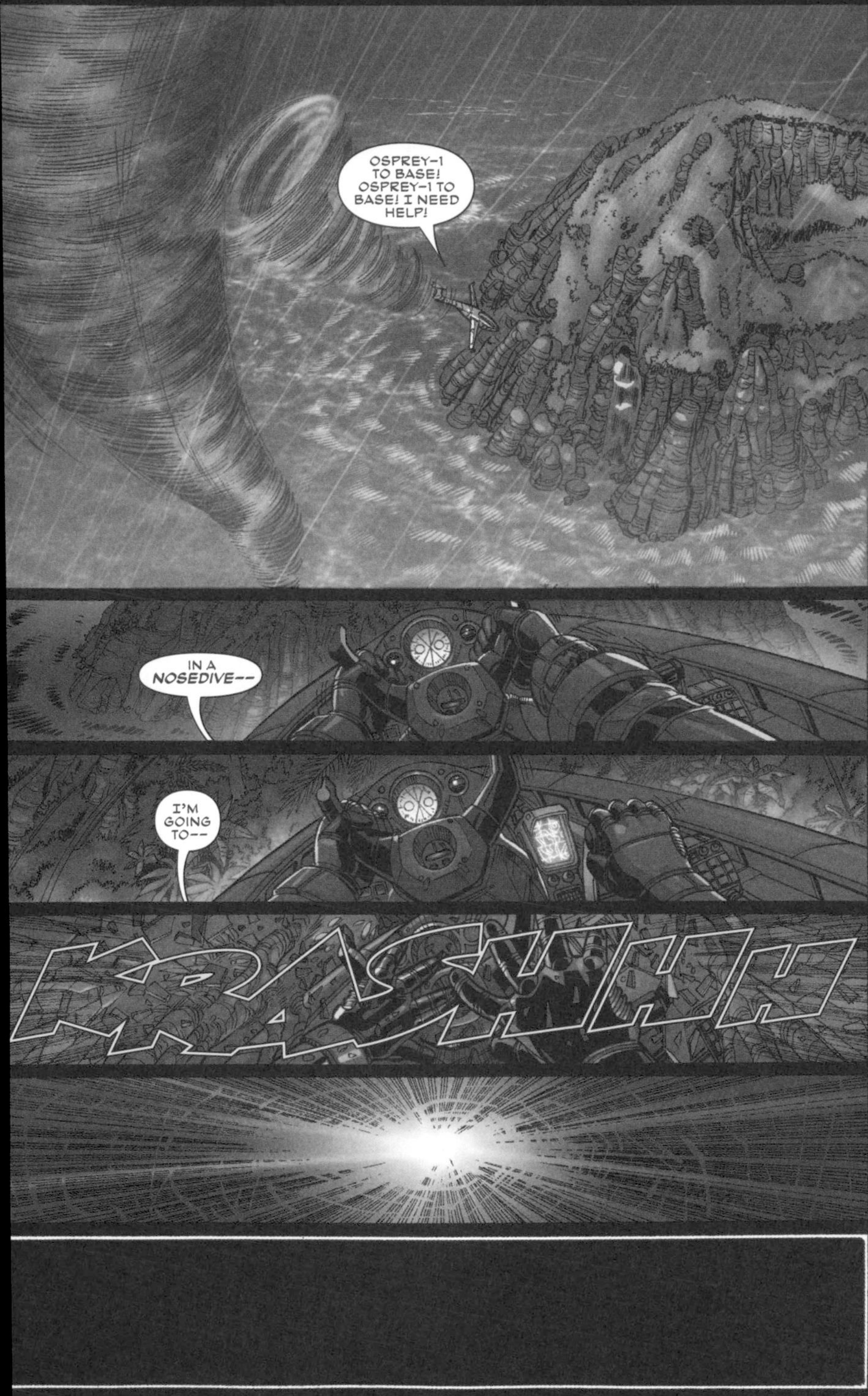
OSPREY-1 TO BASE! OSPREY-1 TO BASE! I NEED HELP!
IN A *NOSEDIVE*--
I'M GOING TO--
KRASHHH

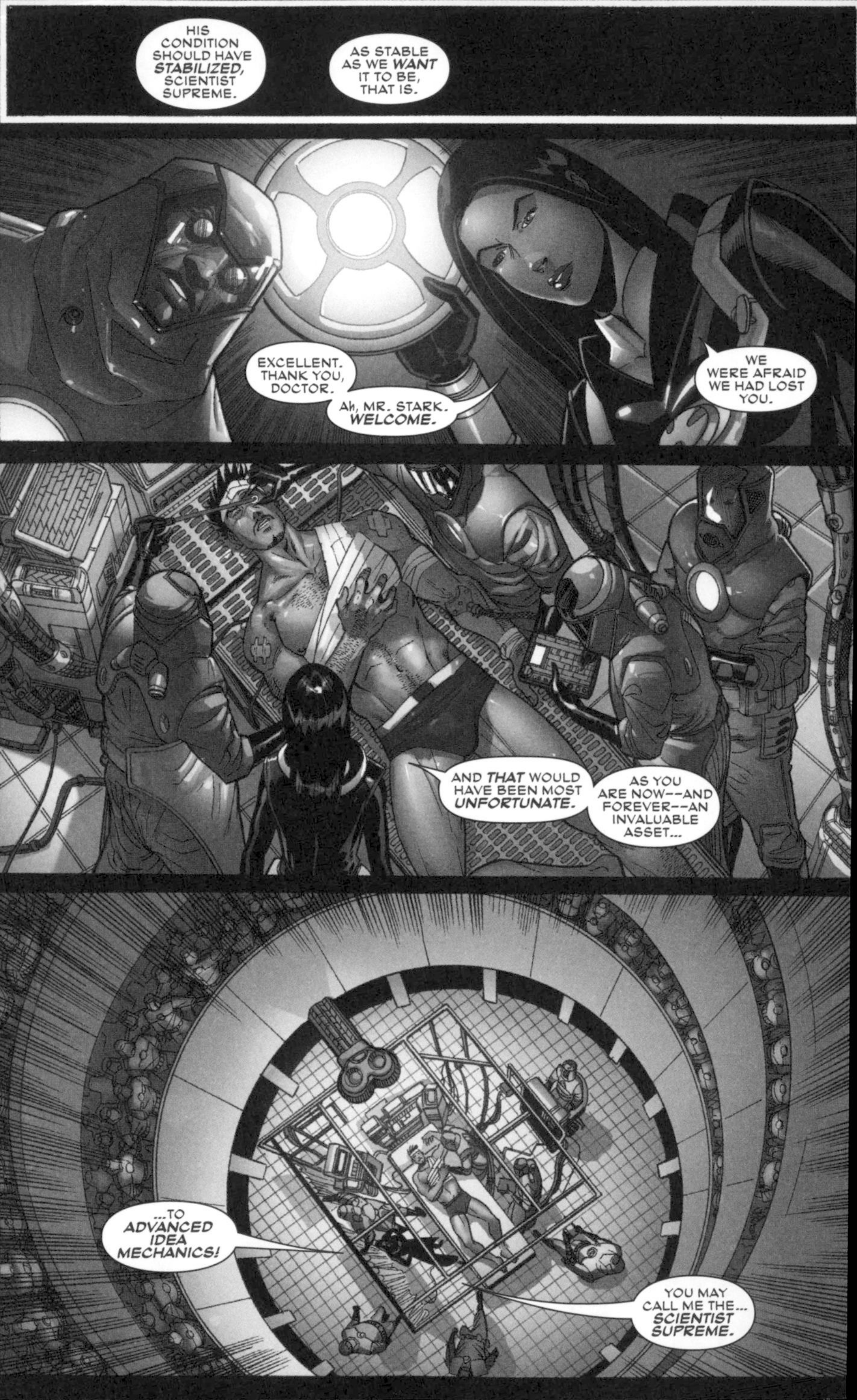
HIS CONDITION SHOULD HAVE STABILIZED, SCIENTIST SUPREME.
AS STABLE AS WE WANT IT TO BE, THAT IS.
EXCELLENT. THANK YOU, DOCTOR.
Ah, MR. STARK. WELCOME.
WE WERE AFRAID WE HAD LOST YOU.
AND THAT WOULD HAVE BEEN MOST UNFORTUNATE.
AS YOU ARE NOW--AND FOREVER--AN INVALUABLE ASSET...
...TO ADVANCED IDEA MECHANICS!
YOU MAY CALL ME THE... SCIENTIST SUPREME.

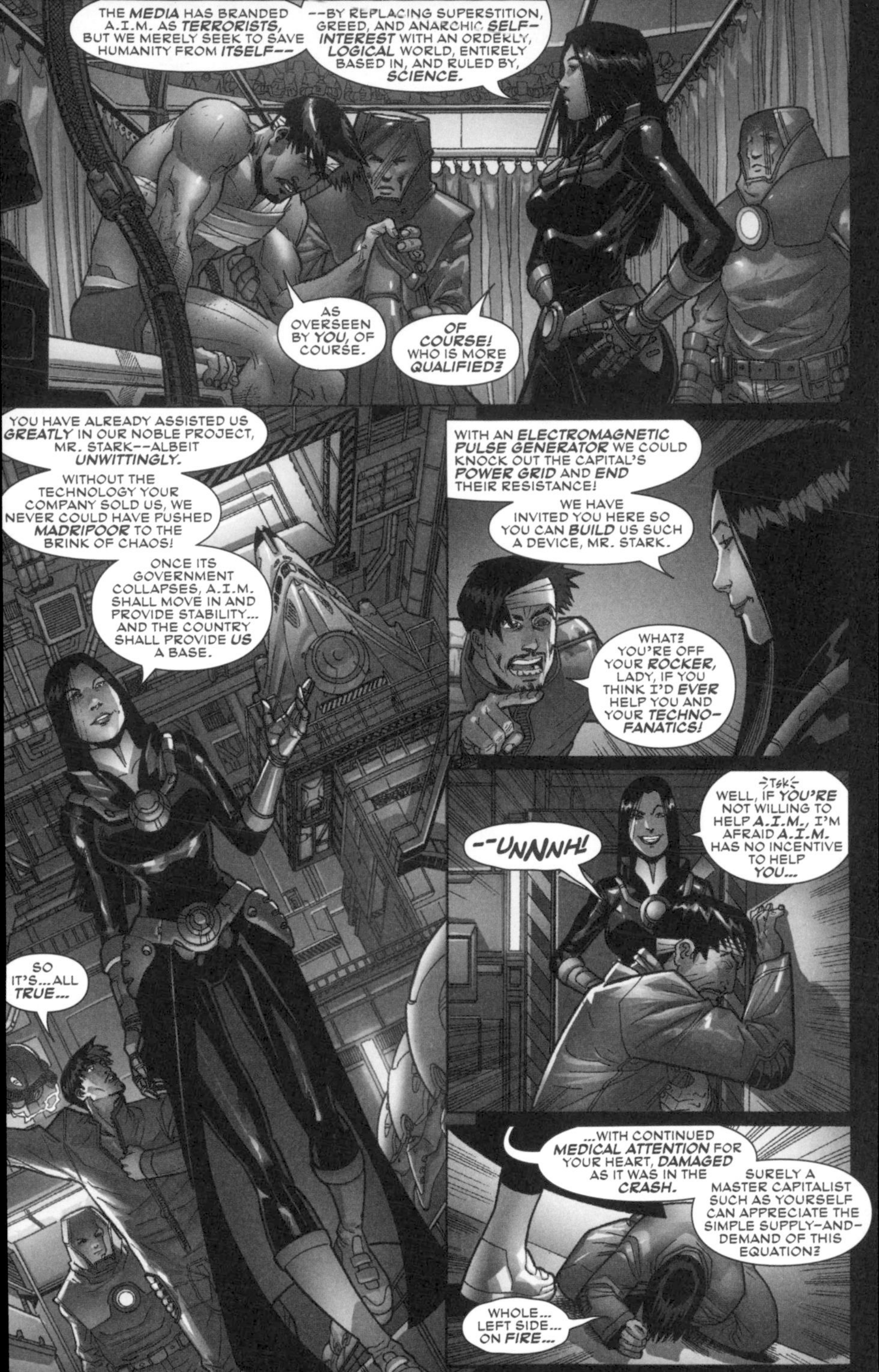
THE MEDIA HAS BRANDED A.I.M. AS TERRORISTS, BUT WE MERELY SEEK TO SAVE HUMANITY FROM ITSELF--
--BY REPLACING SUPERSTITION, GREED, AND ANARCHIC SELF-INTEREST WITH AN ORDERLY, LOGICAL WORLD, ENTIRELY BASED IN, AND RULED BY, SCIENCE.
AS OVERSEEN BY YOU, OF COURSE.
OF COURSE! WHO IS MORE QUALIFIED?
YOU HAVE ALREADY ASSISTED US GREATLY IN OUR NOBLE PROJECT, MR. STARK--ALBEIT UNWITTINGLY.
WITHOUT THE TECHNOLOGY YOUR COMPANY SOLD US, WE NEVER COULD HAVE PUSHED MADRIPOOR TO THE BRINK OF CHAOS!
ONCE ITS GOVERNMENT COLLAPSES, A.I.M. SHALL MOVE IN AND PROVIDE STABILITY... AND THE COUNTRY SHALL PROVIDE US A BASE.
SO IT'S...ALL TRUE...
WITH AN ELECTROMAGNETIC PULSE GENERATOR WE COULD KNOCK OUT THE CAPITAL'S POWER GRID AND END THEIR RESISTANCE!
WE HAVE INVITED YOU HERE SO YOU CAN BUILD US SUCH A DEVICE, MR. STARK.
WHAT? YOU'RE OFF YOUR ROCKER, LADY, IF YOU THINK I'D EVER HELP YOU AND YOUR TECHNO-FANATICS!
TSK
WELL, IF YOU'RE NOT WILLING TO HELP A.I.M., I'M AFRAID A.I.M. HAS NO INCENTIVE TO HELP YOU...
--UNNNH!
...WITH CONTINUED MEDICAL ATTENTION FOR YOUR HEART, DAMAGED AS IT WAS IN THE CRASH.
SURELY A MASTER CAPITALIST SUCH AS YOURSELF CAN APPRECIATE THE SIMPLE SUPPLY-AND-DEMAND OF THIS EQUATION?
WHOLE... LEFT SIDE... ON FIRE...

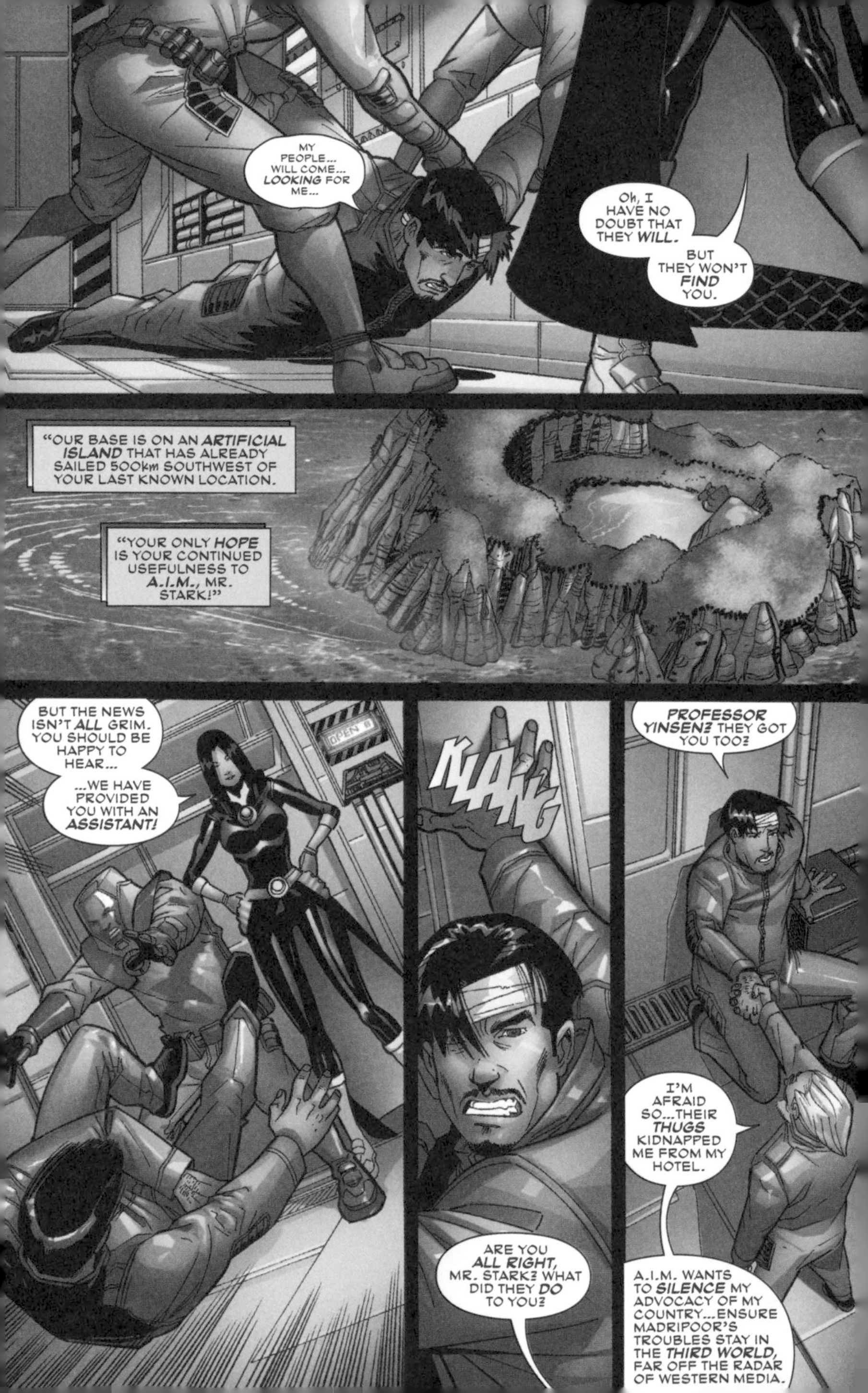
MY PEOPLE... WILL COME... LOOKING FOR ME...
Oh, I HAVE NO DOUBT THAT THEY WILL.
BUT THEY WON'T FIND YOU.
"OUR BASE IS ON AN ARTIFICIAL ISLAND THAT HAS ALREADY SAILED 500km SOUTHWEST OF YOUR LAST KNOWN LOCATION.
"YOUR ONLY HOPE IS YOUR CONTINUED USEFULNESS TO A.I.M., MR. STARK!"
BUT THE NEWS ISN'T ALL GRIM. YOU SHOULD BE HAPPY TO HEAR...
...WE HAVE PROVIDED YOU WITH AN ASSISTANT!
OPEN
KLANG
ARE YOU ALL RIGHT, MR. STARK? WHAT DID THEY DO TO YOU?
PROFESSOR YINSEN? THEY GOT YOU TOO?
I'M AFRAID SO...THEIR THUGS KIDNAPPED ME FROM MY HOTEL.
A.I.M. WANTS TO SILENCE MY ADVOCACY OF MY COUNTRY...ENSURE MADRIPOOR'S TROUBLES STAY IN THE THIRD WORLD, FAR OFF THE RADAR OF WESTERN MEDIA.

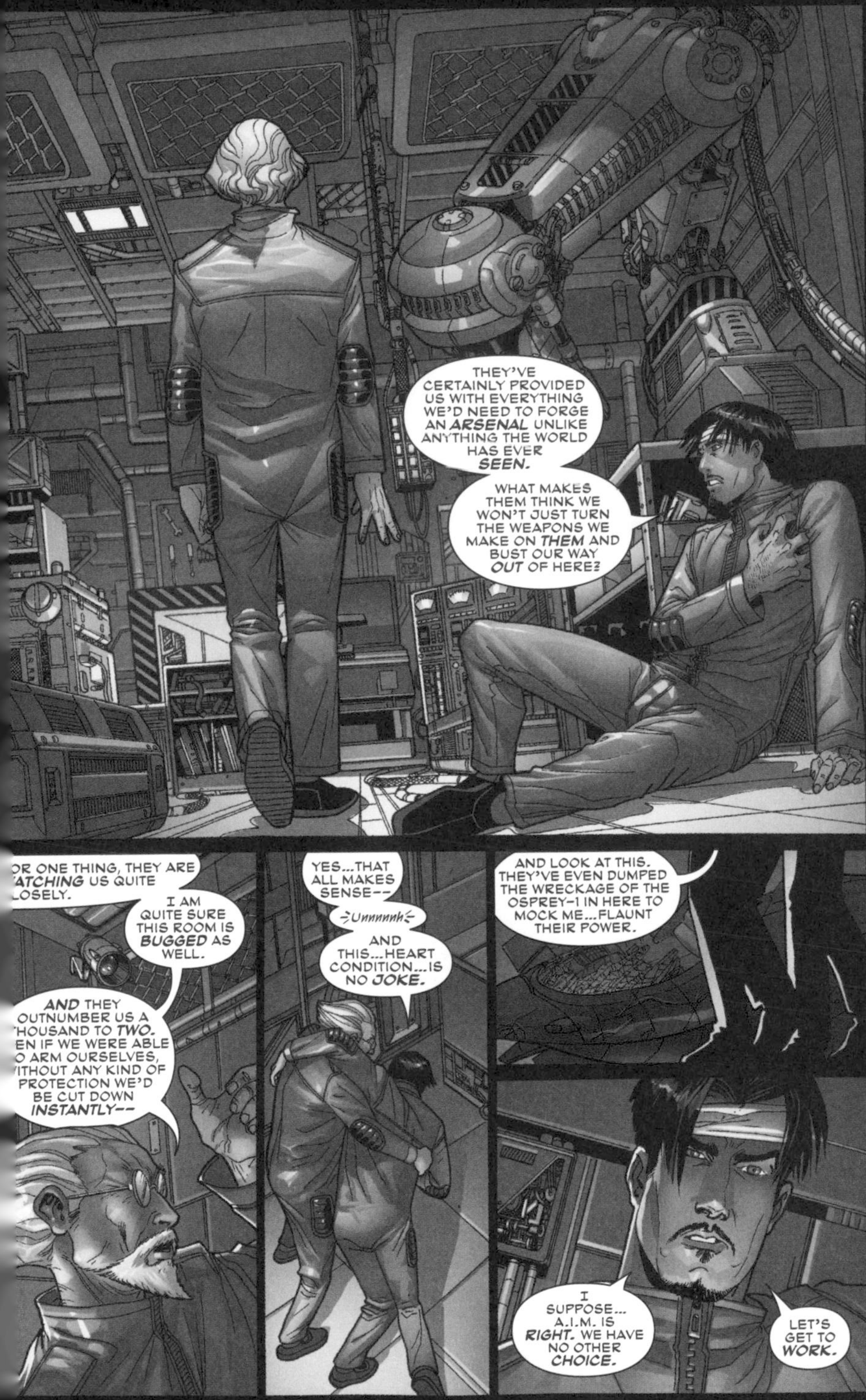
THEY'VE CERTAINLY PROVIDED US WITH EVERYTHING WE'D NEED TO FORGE AN ARSENAL UNLIKE ANYTHING THE WORLD HAS EVER SEEN.
WHAT MAKES THEM THINK WE WON'T JUST TURN THE WEAPONS WE MAKE ON THEM AND BUST OUR WAY OUT OF HERE?
OR ONE THING, THEY ARE ATCHING US QUITE LOSELY.
I AM QUITE SURE THIS ROOM IS BUGGED AS WELL.
AND THEY OUTNUMBER US A THOUSAND TO TWO. EN IF WE WERE ABLE O ARM OURSELVES, WITHOUT ANY KIND OF PROTECTION WE'D BE CUT DOWN INSTANTLY--
YES...THAT ALL MAKES SENSE--
Unnnnnh
AND THIS...HEART CONDITION...IS NO JOKE.
AND LOOK AT THIS. THEY'VE EVEN DUMPED THE WRECKAGE OF THE OSPREY-1 IN HERE TO MOCK ME...FLAUNT THEIR POWER.
I SUPPOSE... A.I.M. IS RIGHT. WE HAVE NO OTHER CHOICE.
LET'S GET TO WORK.

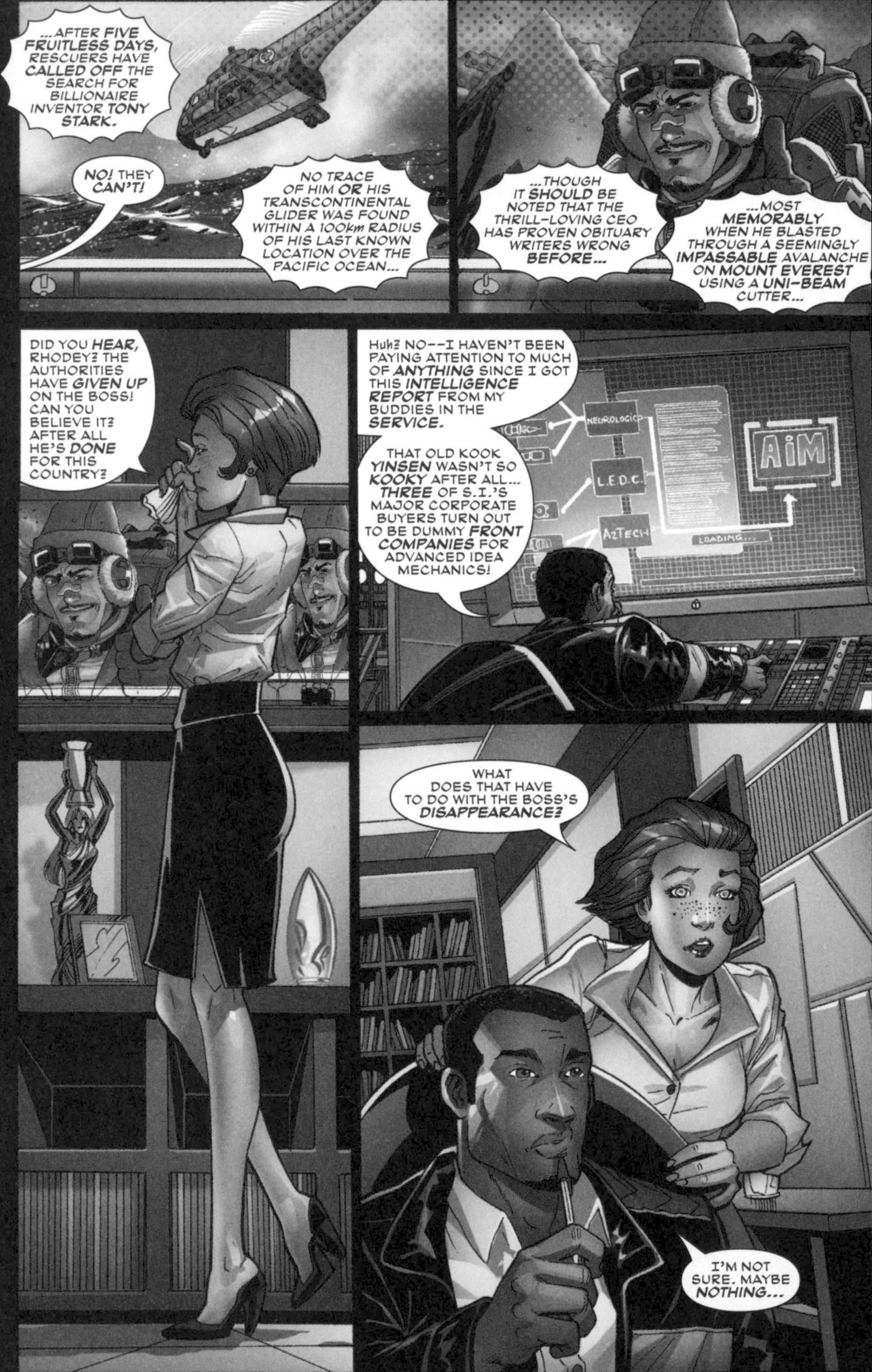
...AFTER FIVE FRUITLESS DAYS, RESCUERS HAVE CALLED OFF THE SEARCH FOR BILLIONAIRE INVENTOR TONY STARK.
NO! THEY CAN'T!
NO TRACE OF HIM OR HIS TRANSCONTINENTAL GLIDER WAS FOUND WITHIN A 100km RADIUS OF HIS LAST KNOWN LOCATION OVER THE PACIFIC OCEAN...
...THOUGH IT SHOULD BE NOTED THAT THE THRILL-LOVING CEO HAS PROVEN OBITUARY WRITERS WRONG BEFORE...
...MOST MEMORABLY WHEN HE BLASTED THROUGH A SEEMINGLY IMPASSABLE AVALANCHE ON MOUNT EVEREST USING A UNI-BEAM CUTTER...
DID YOU HEAR, RHODEY? THE AUTHORITIES HAVE GIVEN UP ON THE BOSS! CAN YOU BELIEVE IT? AFTER ALL HE'S DONE FOR THIS COUNTRY?
HUH? NO--I HAVEN'T BEEN PAYING ATTENTION TO MUCH OF ANYTHING SINCE I GOT THIS INTELLIGENCE REPORT FROM MY BUDDIES IN THE SERVICE.
THAT OLD KOOK YINSEN WASN'T SO KOOKY AFTER ALL... THREE OF S.I.'S MAJOR CORPORATE BUYERS TURN OUT TO BE DUMMY FRONT COMPANIES FOR ADVANCED IDEA MECHANICS!
NEUROLOGIC
L.E.D.C.
AZTECH
AIM
LOADING...
WHAT DOES THAT HAVE TO DO WITH THE BOSS'S DISAPPEARANCE?
I'M NOT SURE. MAYBE NOTHING...

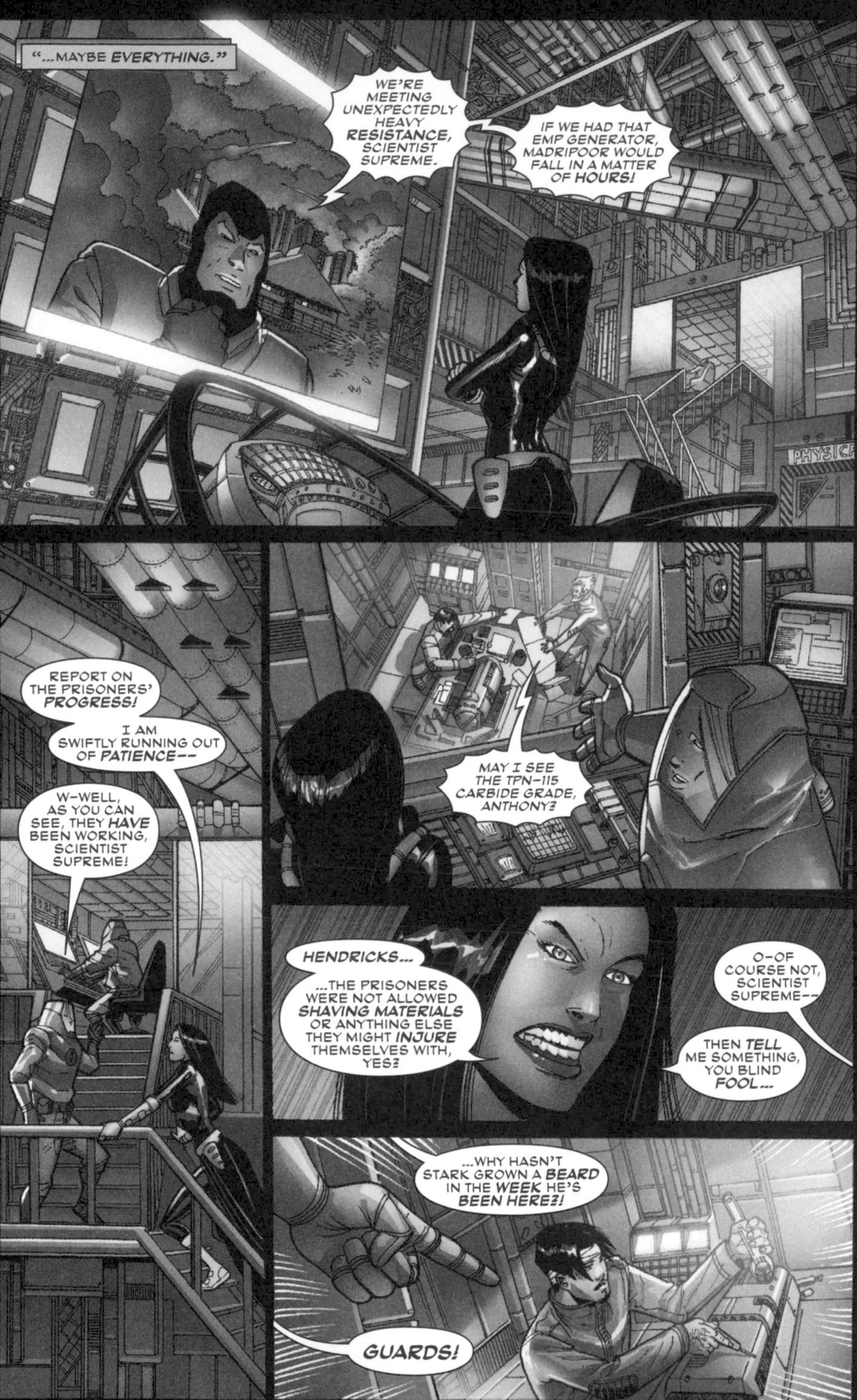
"...MAYBE EVERYTHING."
WE'RE MEETING UNEXPECTEDLY HEAVY RESISTANCE, SCIENTIST SUPREME.
IF WE HAD THAT EMP GENERATOR, MADRIPOOR WOULD FALL IN A MATTER OF HOURS!
PHYSIC
REPORT ON THE PRISONERS' PROGRESS!
I AM SWIFTLY RUNNING OUT OF PATIENCE--
W-WELL, AS YOU CAN SEE, THEY HAVE BEEN WORKING, SCIENTIST SUPREME!
MAY I SEE THE TPN-115 CARBIDE GRADE, ANTHONY?
HENDRICKS...
...THE PRISONERS WERE NOT ALLOWED SHAVING MATERIALS OR ANYTHING ELSE THEY MIGHT INJURE THEMSELVES WITH, YES?
O-OF COURSE NOT, SCIENTIST SUPREME--
THEN TELL ME SOMETHING, YOU BLIND FOOL...
...WHY HASN'T STARK GROWN A BEARD IN THE WEEK HE'S BEEN HERE?!
GUARDS!

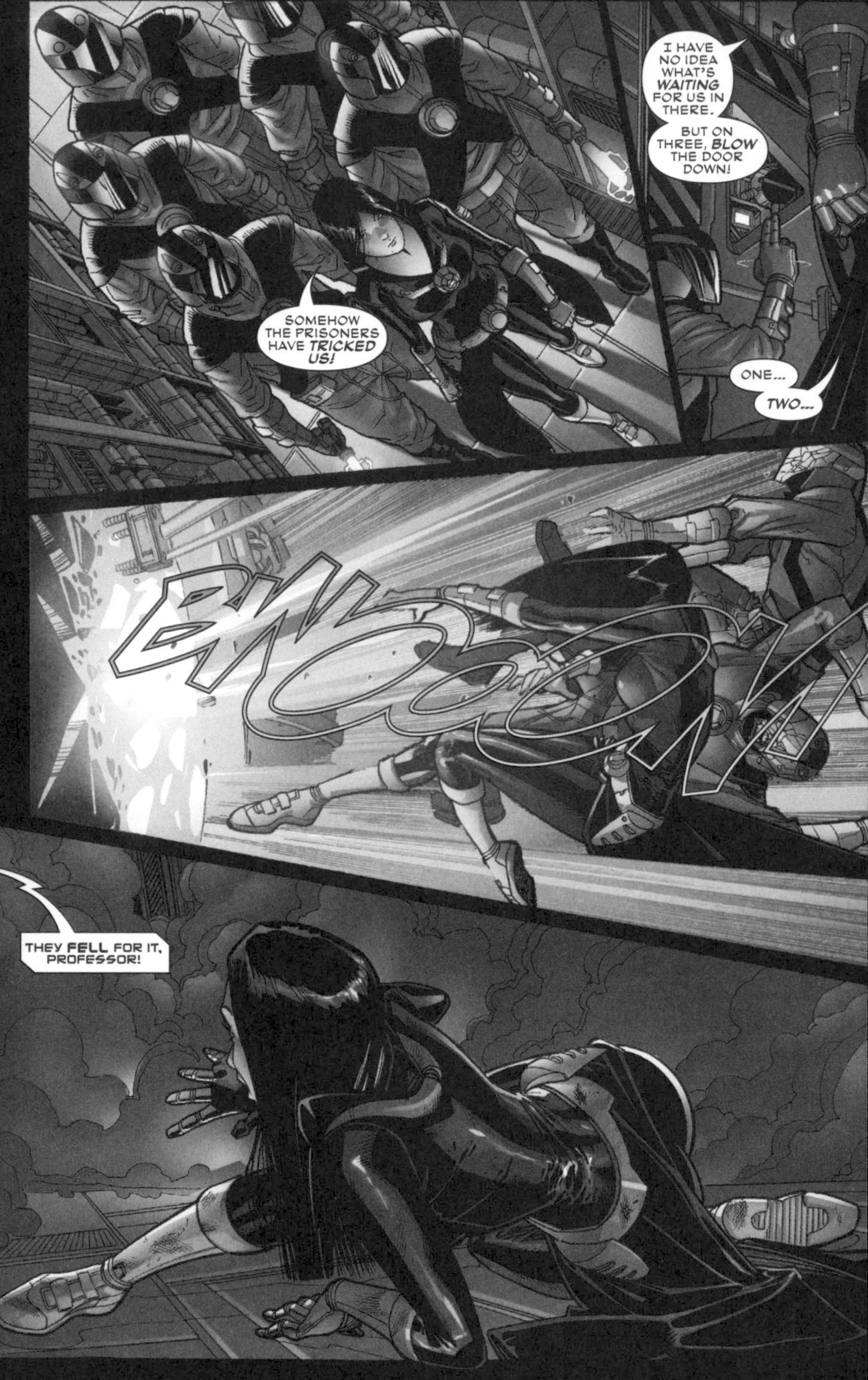
SOMEHOW THE PRISONERS HAVE *TRICKED* US!
I HAVE NO IDEA WHAT'S *WAITING* FOR US IN THERE.
BUT ON THREE, *BLOW* THE DOOR DOWN!
ONE...
TWO...
BWOOOM
THEY **FELL** FOR IT, PROFESSOR!

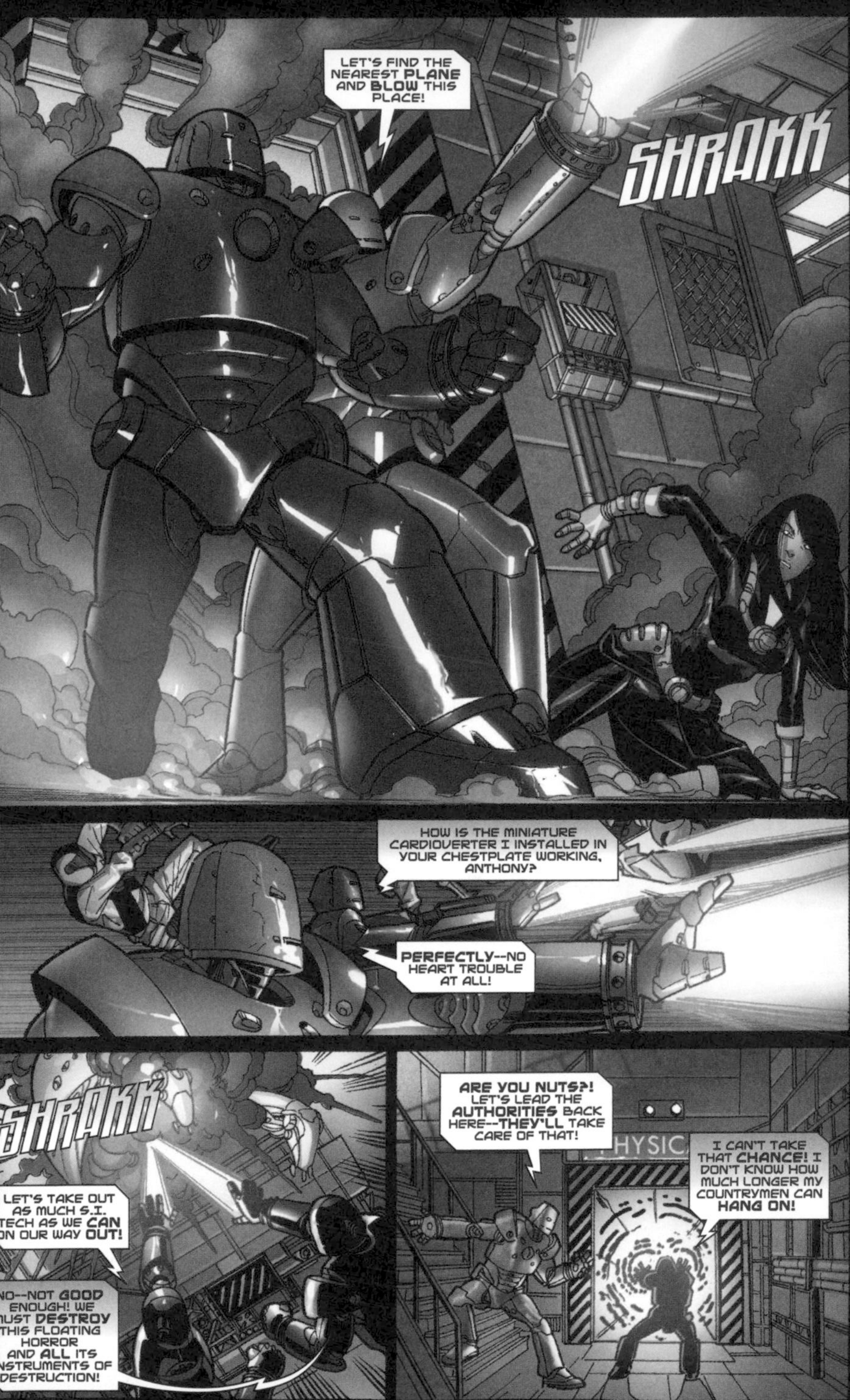

LET'S FIND THE NEAREST PLANE AND BLOW THIS PLACE!
SHRAKK
HOW IS THE MINIATURE CARDIOVERTER I INSTALLED IN YOUR CHESTPLATE WORKING, ANTHONY?
PERFECTLY--NO HEART TROUBLE AT ALL!
SHRAKK
LET'S TAKE OUT AS MUCH S.I. TECH AS WE CAN ON OUR WAY OUT!
NO--NOT GOOD ENOUGH! WE MUST DESTROY THIS FLOATING HORROR AND ALL ITS INSTRUMENTS OF DESTRUCTION!
ARE YOU NUTS?! LET'S LEAD THE AUTHORITIES BACK HERE--THEY'LL TAKE CARE OF THAT!
I CAN'T TAKE THAT CHANCE! I DON'T KNOW HOW MUCH LONGER MY COUNTRYMEN CAN HANG ON!

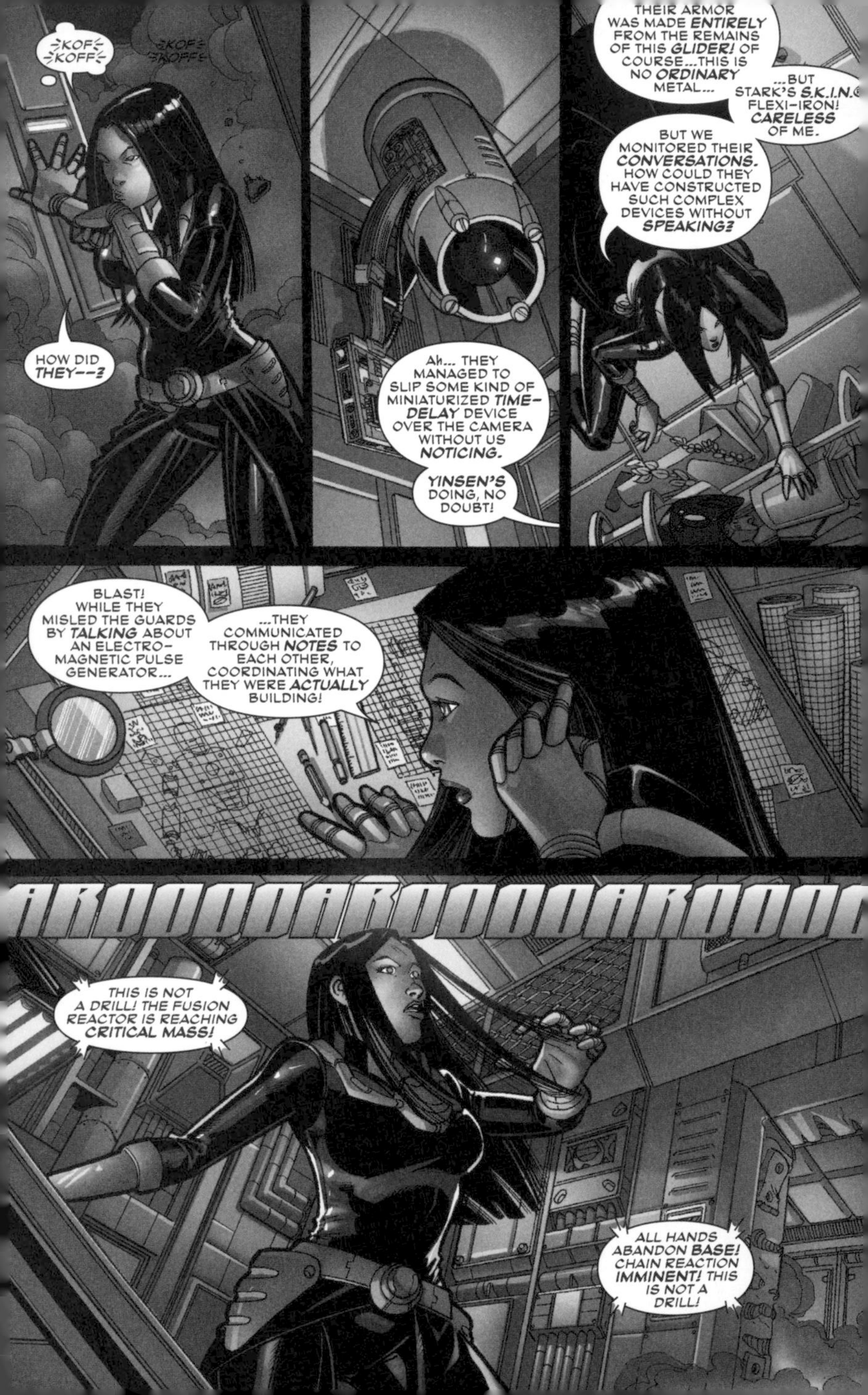

KOF KOFF
KOF KOFF
HOW DID THEY--?
Ah... THEY MANAGED TO SLIP SOME KIND OF MINIATURIZED TIME-DELAY DEVICE OVER THE CAMERA WITHOUT US NOTICING.
YINSEN'S DOING, NO DOUBT!
THEIR ARMOR WAS MADE ENTIRELY FROM THE REMAINS OF THIS GLIDER! OF COURSE...THIS IS NO ORDINARY METAL...
...BUT STARK'S S.K.I.N.© FLEXI-IRON! CARELESS OF ME.
BUT WE MONITORED THEIR CONVERSATIONS. HOW COULD THEY HAVE CONSTRUCTED SUCH COMPLEX DEVICES WITHOUT SPEAKING?
BLAST! WHILE THEY MISLED THE GUARDS BY TALKING ABOUT AN ELECTRO-MAGNETIC PULSE GENERATOR...
...THEY COMMUNICATED THROUGH NOTES TO EACH OTHER, COORDINATING WHAT THEY WERE ACTUALLY BUILDING!
AROOOOAROOOOAROOOO
THIS IS NOT A DRILL! THE FUSION REACTOR IS REACHING CRITICAL MASS!
ALL HANDS ABANDON BASE! CHAIN REACTION IMMINENT! THIS IS NOT A DRILL!

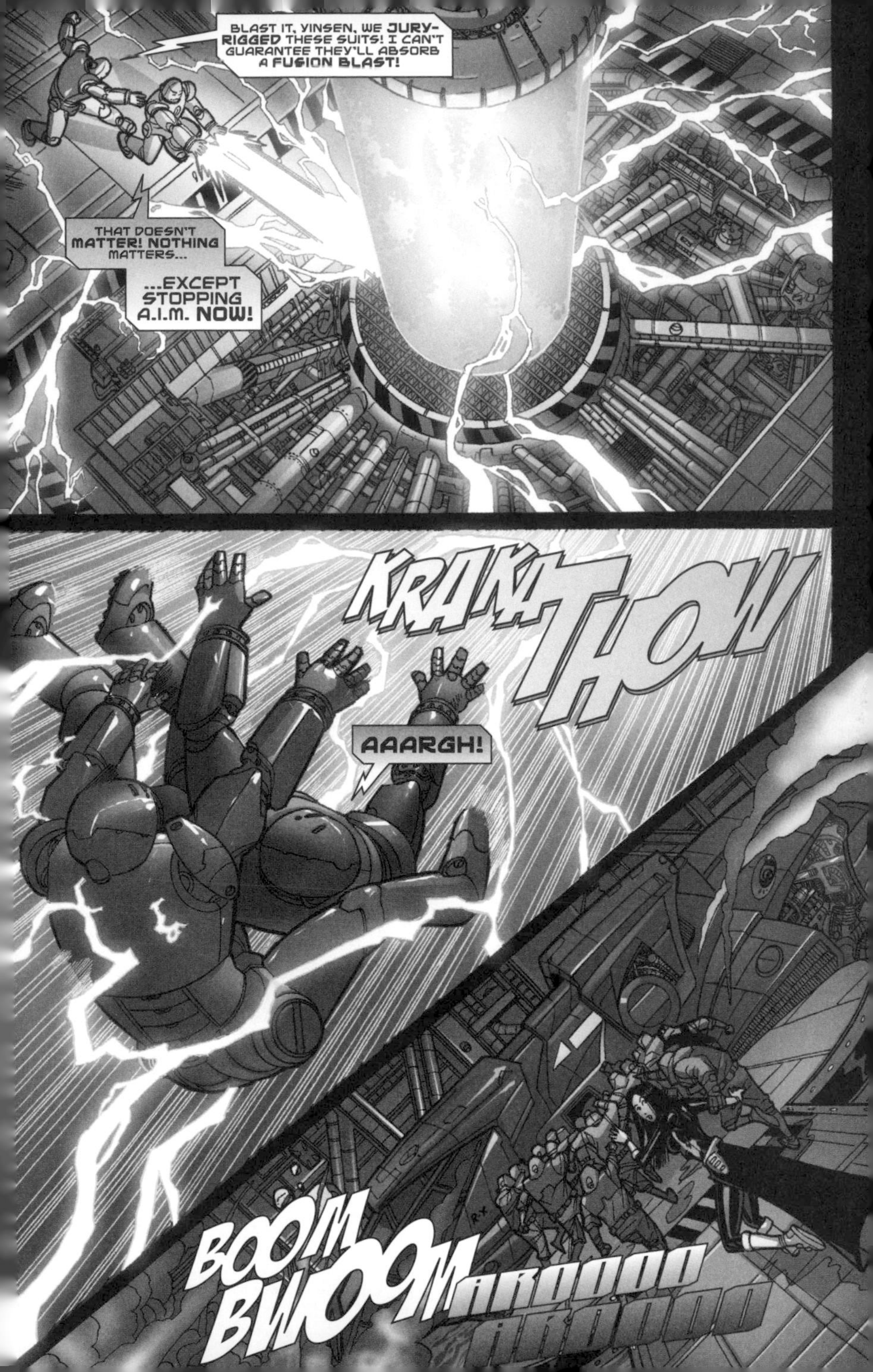
BLAST IT, YINSEN, WE JURY-RIGGED THESE SUITS! I CAN'T GUARANTEE THEY'LL ABSORB A FUSION BLAST!
THAT DOESN'T MATTER! NOTHING MATTERS...
...EXCEPT STOPPING A.I.M. NOW!
KRAKATHOW
AAARGH!
BOOM
BWOOM
AROOOO
AROOOO

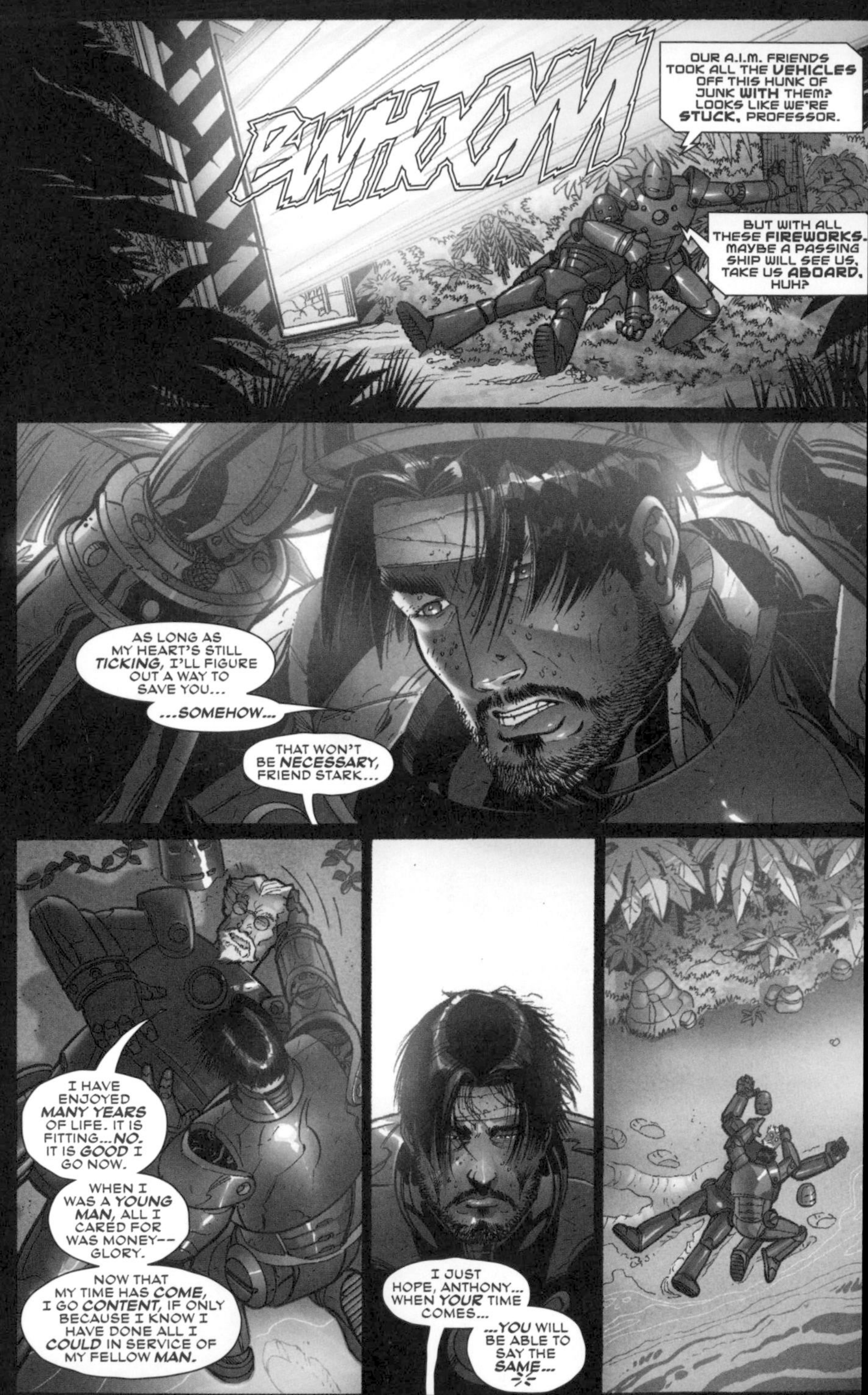

BWHOOM
OUR A.I.M. FRIENDS TOOK ALL THE VEHICLES OFF THIS HUNK OF JUNK WITH THEM? LOOKS LIKE WE'RE STUCK, PROFESSOR.
BUT WITH ALL THESE FIREWORKS, MAYBE A PASSING SHIP WILL SEE US, TAKE US ABOARD, HUH?
AS LONG AS MY HEART'S STILL TICKING, I'LL FIGURE OUT A WAY TO SAVE YOU...
...SOMEHOW...
THAT WON'T BE NECESSARY, FRIEND STARK...
I HAVE ENJOYED MANY YEARS OF LIFE. IT IS FITTING... NO. IT IS GOOD I GO NOW.
WHEN I WAS A YOUNG MAN, ALL I CARED FOR WAS MONEY--GLORY.
NOW THAT MY TIME HAS COME, I GO CONTENT, IF ONLY BECAUSE I KNOW I HAVE DONE ALL I COULD IN SERVICE OF MY FELLOW MAN.
I JUST HOPE, ANTHONY... WHEN YOUR TIME COMES...
...YOU WILL BE ABLE TO SAY THE SAME...

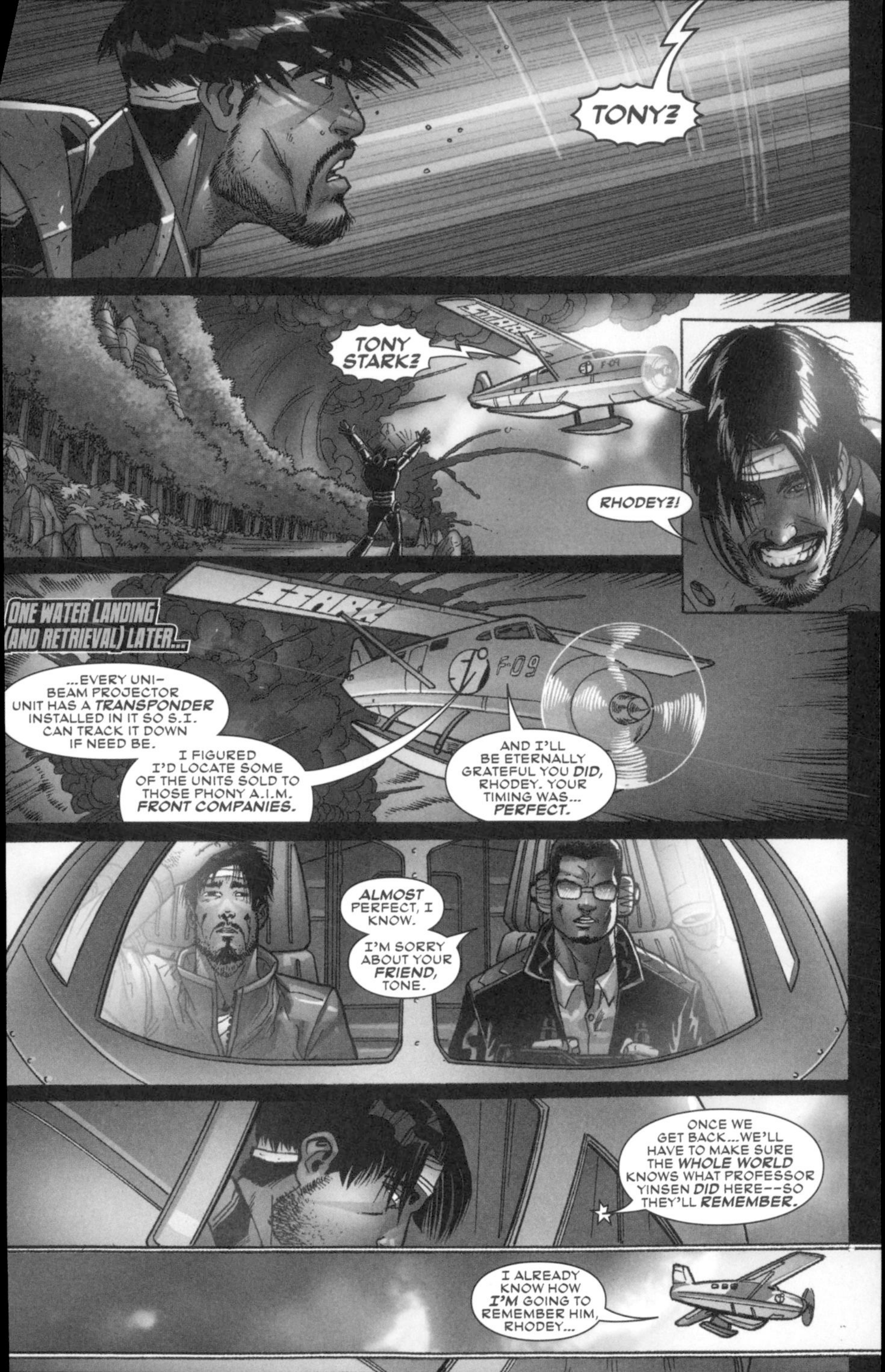
TONY?
TONY STARK?
RHODEY?!
ONE WATER LANDING (AND RETRIEVAL) LATER...
...EVERY UNI-BEAM PROJECTOR UNIT HAS A TRANSPONDER INSTALLED IN IT SO S.I. CAN TRACK IT DOWN IF NEED BE.
I FIGURED I'D LOCATE SOME OF THE UNITS SOLD TO THOSE PHONY A.I.M. FRONT COMPANIES.
AND I'LL BE ETERNALLY GRATEFUL YOU DID, RHODEY. YOUR TIMING WAS... PERFECT.
ALMOST PERFECT, I KNOW.
I'M SORRY ABOUT YOUR FRIEND, TONE.
ONCE WE GET BACK...WE'LL HAVE TO MAKE SURE THE WHOLE WORLD KNOWS WHAT PROFESSOR YINSEN DID HERE--SO THEY'LL REMEMBER.
I ALREADY KNOW HOW I'M GOING TO REMEMBER HIM, RHODEY...

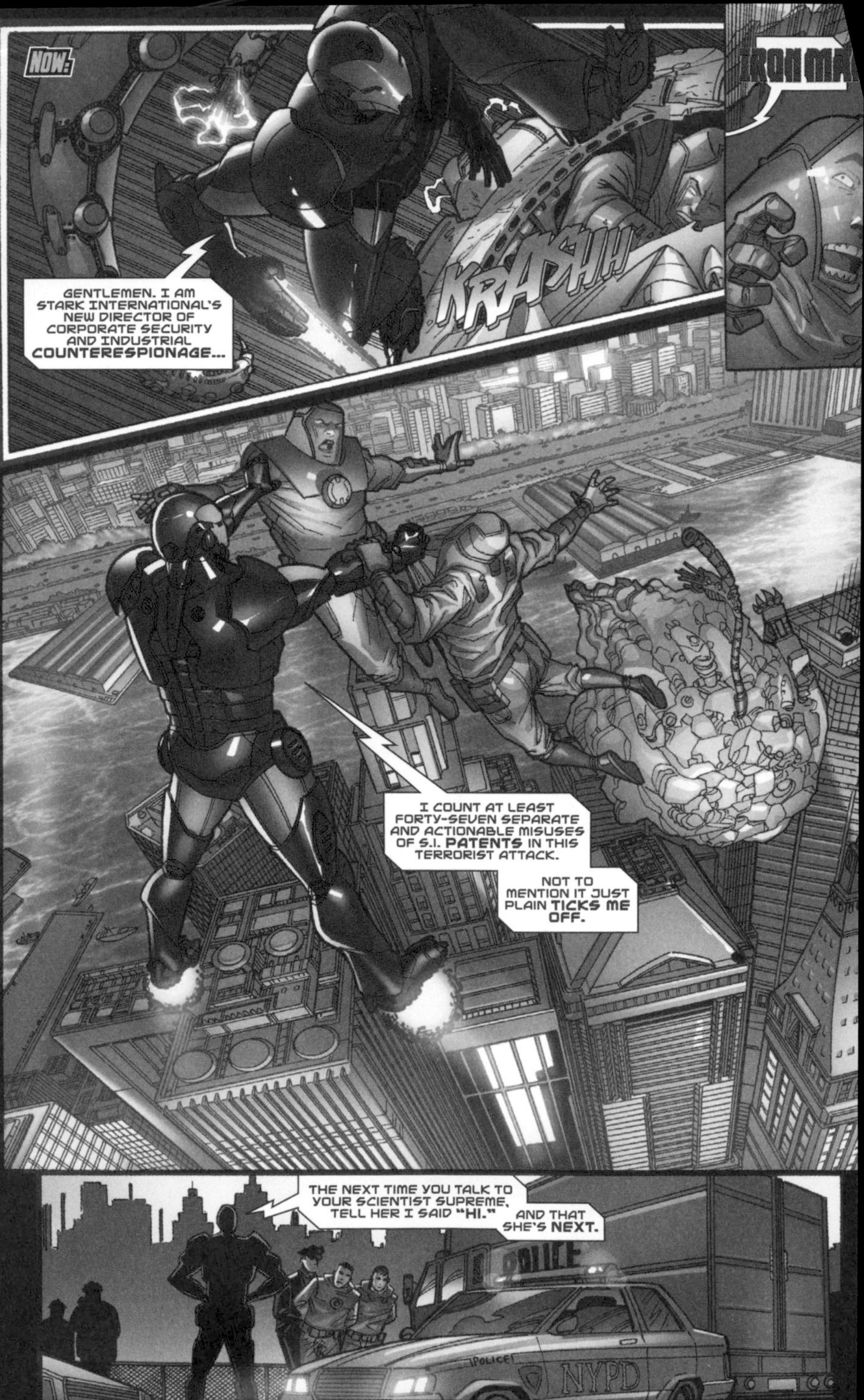
NOW:
IRON MA
GENTLEMEN. I AM STARK INTERNATIONAL'S NEW DIRECTOR OF CORPORATE SECURITY AND INDUSTRIAL COUNTERESPIONAGE...
KRASHH
I COUNT AT LEAST FORTY-SEVEN SEPARATE AND ACTIONABLE MISUSES OF S.I. PATENTS IN THIS TERRORIST ATTACK.
NOT TO MENTION IT JUST PLAIN TICKS ME OFF.
THE NEXT TIME YOU TALK TO YOUR SCIENTIST SUPREME, TELL HER I SAID "HI."
AND THAT SHE'S NEXT.
POLICE
POLICE
NYPD

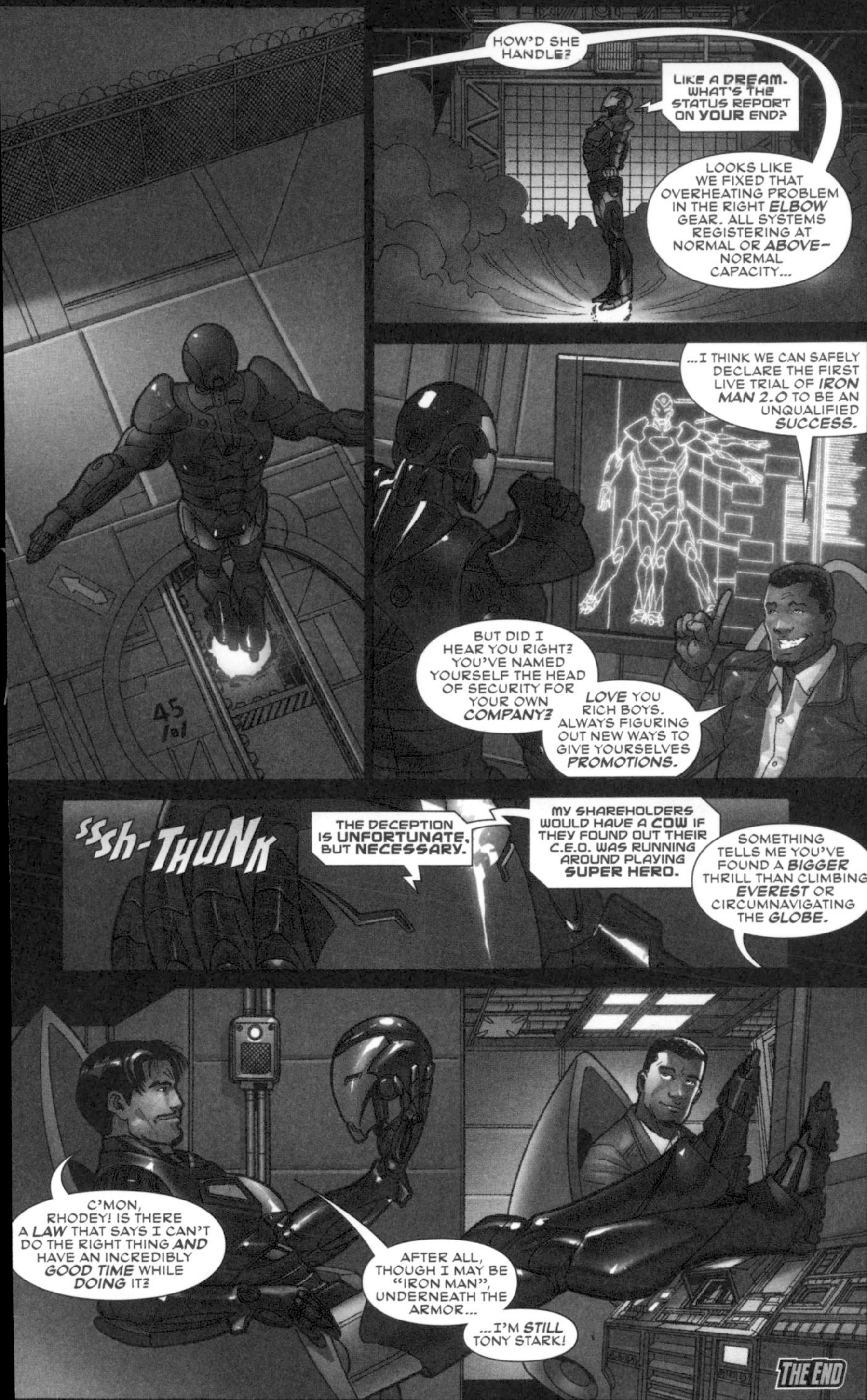
HOW'D SHE HANDLE?
LIKE A DREAM. WHAT'S THE STATUS REPORT ON YOUR END?
LOOKS LIKE WE FIXED THAT OVERHEATING PROBLEM IN THE RIGHT ELBOW GEAR. ALL SYSTEMS REGISTERING AT NORMAL OR ABOVE-NORMAL CAPACITY...
...I THINK WE CAN SAFELY DECLARE THE FIRST LIVE TRIAL OF IRON MAN 2.0 TO BE AN UNQUALIFIED SUCCESS.
BUT DID I HEAR YOU RIGHT? YOU'VE NAMED YOURSELF THE HEAD OF SECURITY FOR YOUR OWN COMPANY?
LOVE YOU RICH BOYS. ALWAYS FIGURING OUT NEW WAYS TO GIVE YOURSELVES PROMOTIONS.
45
SSSH-THUNK
THE DECEPTION IS UNFORTUNATE, BUT NECESSARY.
MY SHAREHOLDERS WOULD HAVE A COW IF THEY FOUND OUT THEIR C.E.O. WAS RUNNING AROUND PLAYING SUPER HERO.
SOMETHING TELLS ME YOU'VE FOUND A BIGGER THRILL THAN CLIMBING EVEREST OR CIRCUMNAVIGATING THE GLOBE.
C'MON, RHODEY! IS THERE A LAW THAT SAYS I CAN'T DO THE RIGHT THING AND HAVE AN INCREDIBLY GOOD TIME WHILE DOING IT?
AFTER ALL, THOUGH I MAY BE "IRON MAN", UNDERNEATH THE ARMOR...
...I'M STILL TONY STARK!
THE END

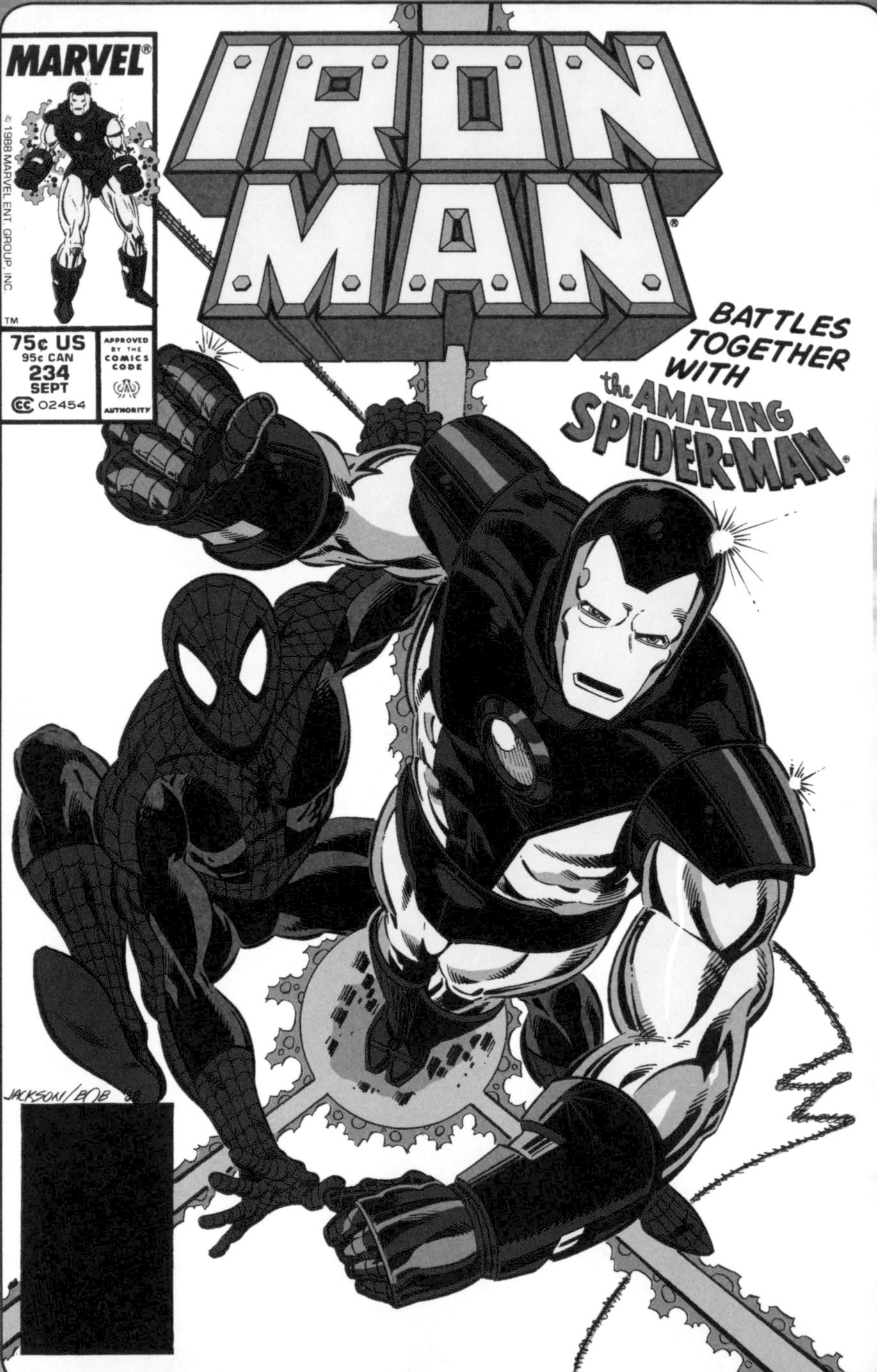
MARVEL®
© 1988 MARVEL ENT. GROUP, INC.
TM
75¢ US
95¢ CAN
234
SEPT
02454
APPROVED BY THE COMICS CODE AUTHORITY
IRON MAN®
BATTLES TOGETHER WITH
the AMAZING SPIDER-MAN®
JACKSON/BOB

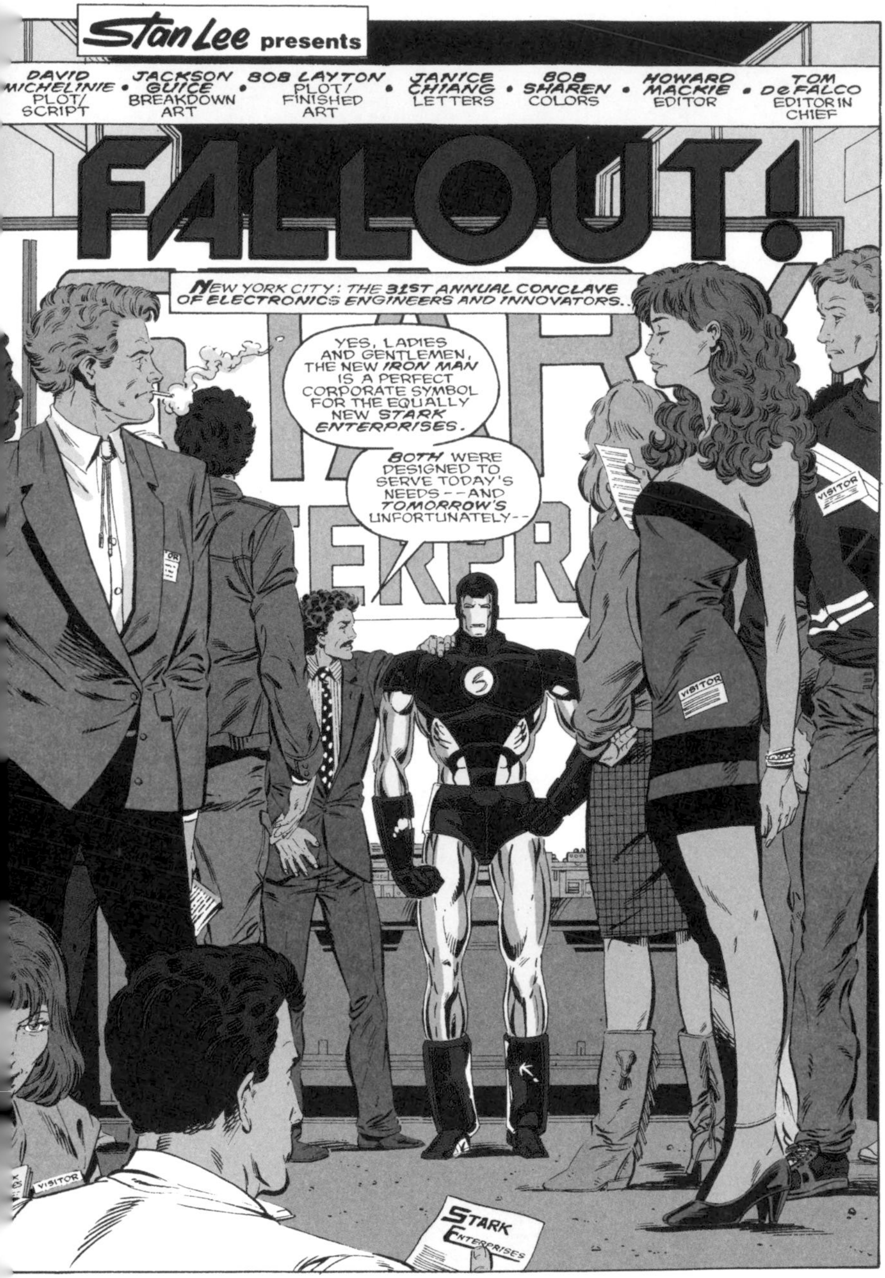
Stan Lee presents
DAVID MICHELINIE • PLOT/SCRIPT
JACKSON GUICE • BREAKDOWN ART
BOB LAYTON • PLOT/FINISHED ART
JANICE CHIANG • LETTERS
BOB SHAREN • COLORS
HOWARD MACKIE • EDITOR
TOM DeFALCO • EDITOR IN CHIEF
FALLOUT!
NEW YORK CITY: THE 31ST ANNUAL CONCLAVE OF ELECTRONICS ENGINEERS AND INNOVATORS...
YES, LADIES AND GENTLEMEN, THE NEW IRON MAN IS A PERFECT CORPORATE SYMBOL FOR THE EQUALLY NEW STARK ENTERPRISES.
BOTH WERE DESIGNED TO SERVE TODAY'S NEEDS--AND TOMORROW'S UNFORTUNATELY--
VISITOR
VISITOR
VISITOR
STARK ENTERPRISES

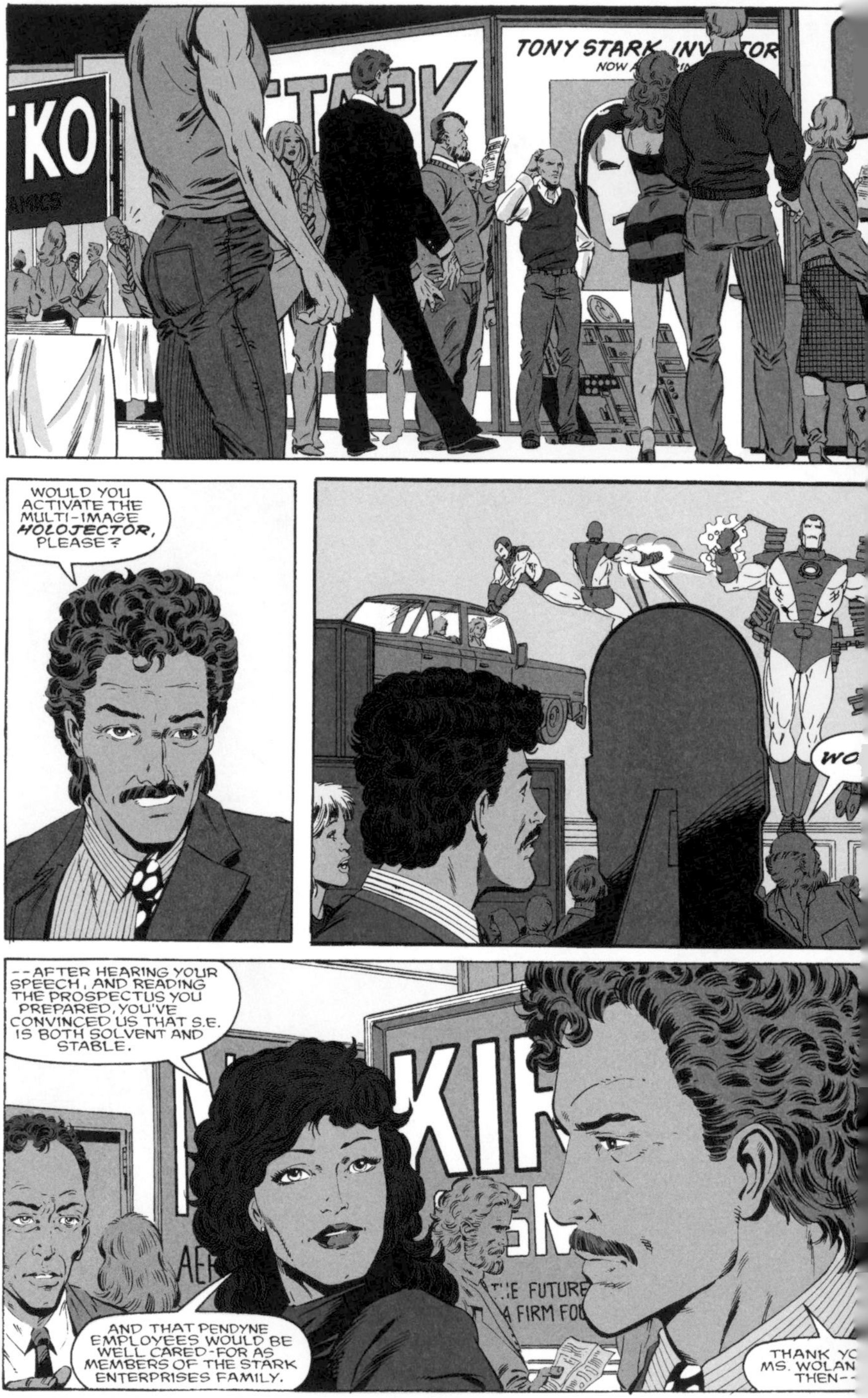
TONY STARK
WOULD YOU ACTIVATE THE MULTI-IMAGE *HOLOJECTOR*, PLEASE?
WO
--AFTER HEARING YOUR SPEECH, AND READING THE PROSPECTUS YOU PREPARED, YOU'VE CONVINCED US THAT S.E. IS BOTH SOLVENT AND STABLE.
AND THAT PENDYNE EMPLOYEES WOULD BE WELL CARED-FOR AS MEMBERS OF THE STARK ENTERPRISES FAMILY.
THANK YO MS. WOLAN THEN--

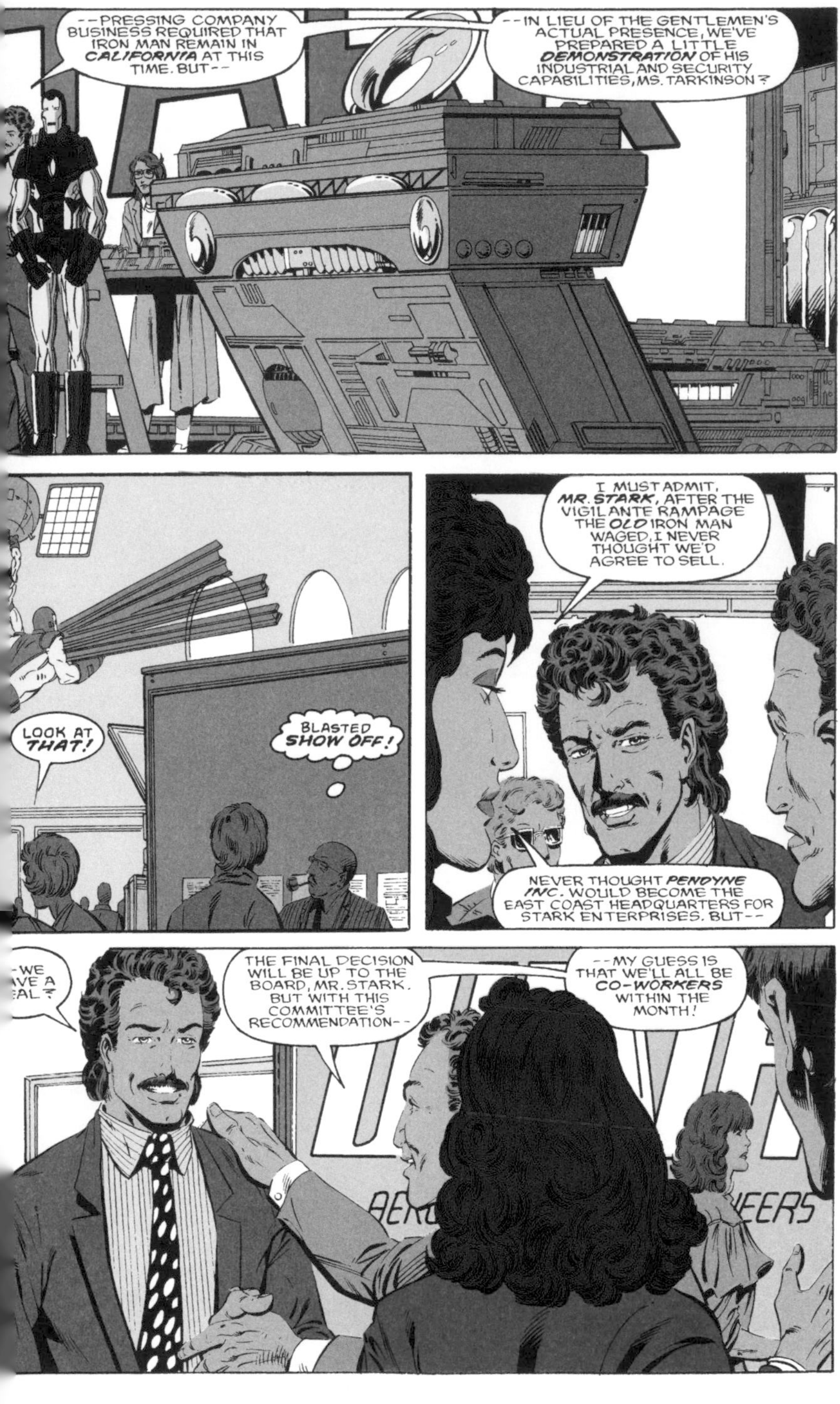
--PRESSING COMPANY BUSINESS REQUIRED THAT IRON MAN REMAIN IN CALIFORNIA AT THIS TIME. BUT--
--IN LIEU OF THE GENTLEMEN'S ACTUAL PRESENCE, WE'VE PREPARED A LITTLE DEMONSTRATION OF HIS INDUSTRIAL AND SECURITY CAPABILITIES, MS. TARKINSON?
LOOK AT THAT!
BLASTED SHOW OFF!
I MUST ADMIT, MR. STARK, AFTER THE VIGILANTE RAMPAGE THE OLD IRON MAN WAGED, I NEVER THOUGHT WE'D AGREE TO SELL.
NEVER THOUGHT PENDYNE INC. WOULD BECOME THE EAST COAST HEADQUARTERS FOR STARK ENTERPRISES. BUT--
-WE AVE A EAL?
THE FINAL DECISION WILL BE UP TO THE BOARD, MR. STARK. BUT WITH THIS COMMITTEE'S RECOMMENDATION--
--MY GUESS IS THAT WE'LL ALL BE CO-WORKERS WITHIN THE MONTH!

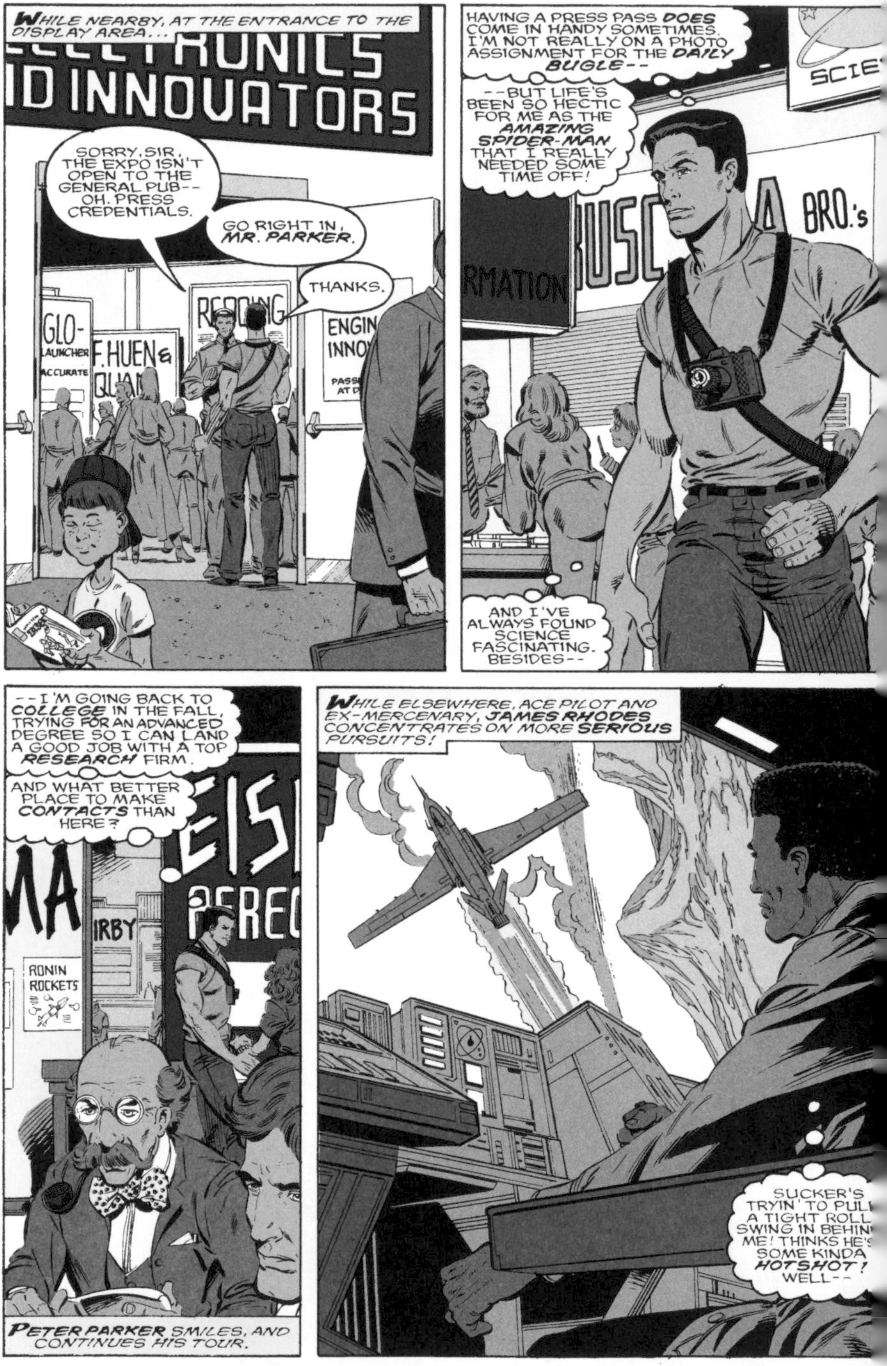
WHILE NEARBY, AT THE ENTRANCE TO THE DISPLAY AREA...
ELECTRONICS
ID INNOVATORS
SORRY, SIR, THE EXPO ISN'T OPEN TO THE GENERAL PUB-- OH. PRESS CREDENTIALS.
GO RIGHT IN, MR. PARKER.
THANKS.
HAVING A PRESS PASS DOES COME IN HANDY SOMETIMES. I'M NOT REALLY ON A PHOTO ASSIGNMENT FOR THE DAILY BUGLE--
--BUT LIFE'S BEEN SO HECTIC FOR ME AS THE AMAZING SPIDER-MAN THAT I REALLY NEEDED SOME TIME OFF!
AND I'VE ALWAYS FOUND SCIENCE FASCINATING. BESIDES--
--I'M GOING BACK TO COLLEGE IN THE FALL, TRYING FOR AN ADVANCED DEGREE SO I CAN LAND A GOOD JOB WITH A TOP RESEARCH FIRM.
AND WHAT BETTER PLACE TO MAKE CONTACTS THAN HERE?
RONIN ROCKETS
PETER PARKER SMILES, AND CONTINUES HIS TOUR.
WHILE ELSEWHERE, ACE PILOT AND EX-MERCENARY, JAMES RHODES CONCENTRATES ON MORE SERIOUS PURSUITS!
SUCKER'S TRYIN' TO PULL A TIGHT ROLL SWING IN BEHIND ME! THINKS HE'S SOME KINDA HOTSHOT! WELL--

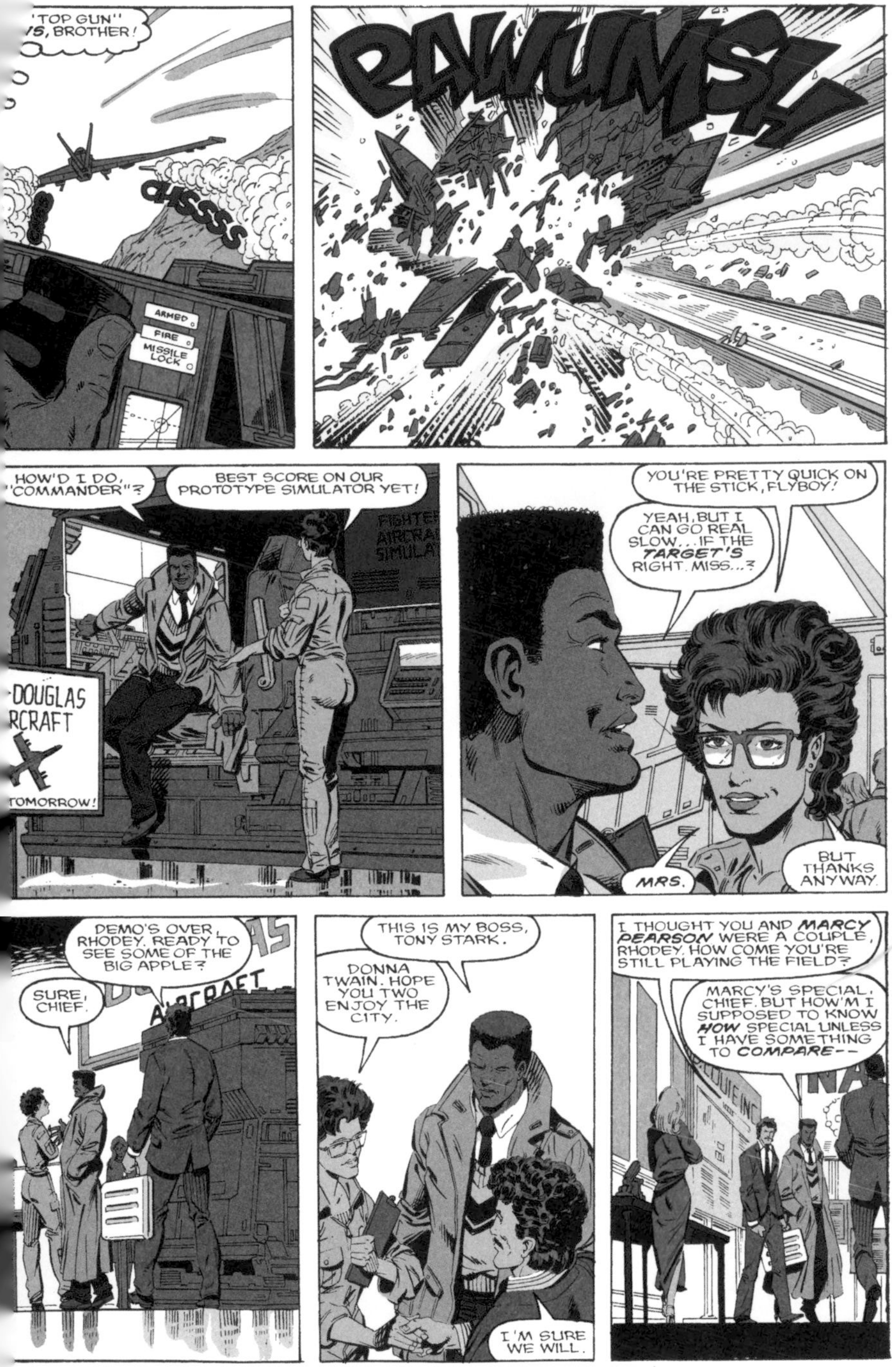
'TOP GUN''
IS, BROTHER!
CHSSS
CHSSSSS
ARMED
FIRE
MISSILE LOCK
RAWUMSH!
HOW'D I DO, "COMMANDER"?
BEST SCORE ON OUR PROTOTYPE SIMULATOR YET!
-DOUGLAS
RCRAFT
TOMORROW!
YOU'RE PRETTY QUICK ON THE STICK, FLYBOY!
YEAH, BUT I CAN GO REAL SLOW... IF THE TARGET'S RIGHT. MISS...?
MRS.
BUT THANKS ANYWAY.
DEMO'S OVER, RHODEY. READY TO SEE SOME OF THE BIG APPLE?
SURE, CHIEF.
AIRCRAFT
THIS IS MY BOSS, TONY STARK.
DONNA TWAIN. HOPE YOU TWO ENJOY THE CITY.
I'M SURE WE WILL.
I THOUGHT YOU AND MARCY PEARSON WERE A COUPLE, RHODEY. HOW COME YOU'RE STILL PLAYING THE FIELD?
MARCY'S SPECIAL, CHIEF. BUT HOW'M I SUPPOSED TO KNOW HOW SPECIAL UNLESS I HAVE SOMETHING TO COMPARE--

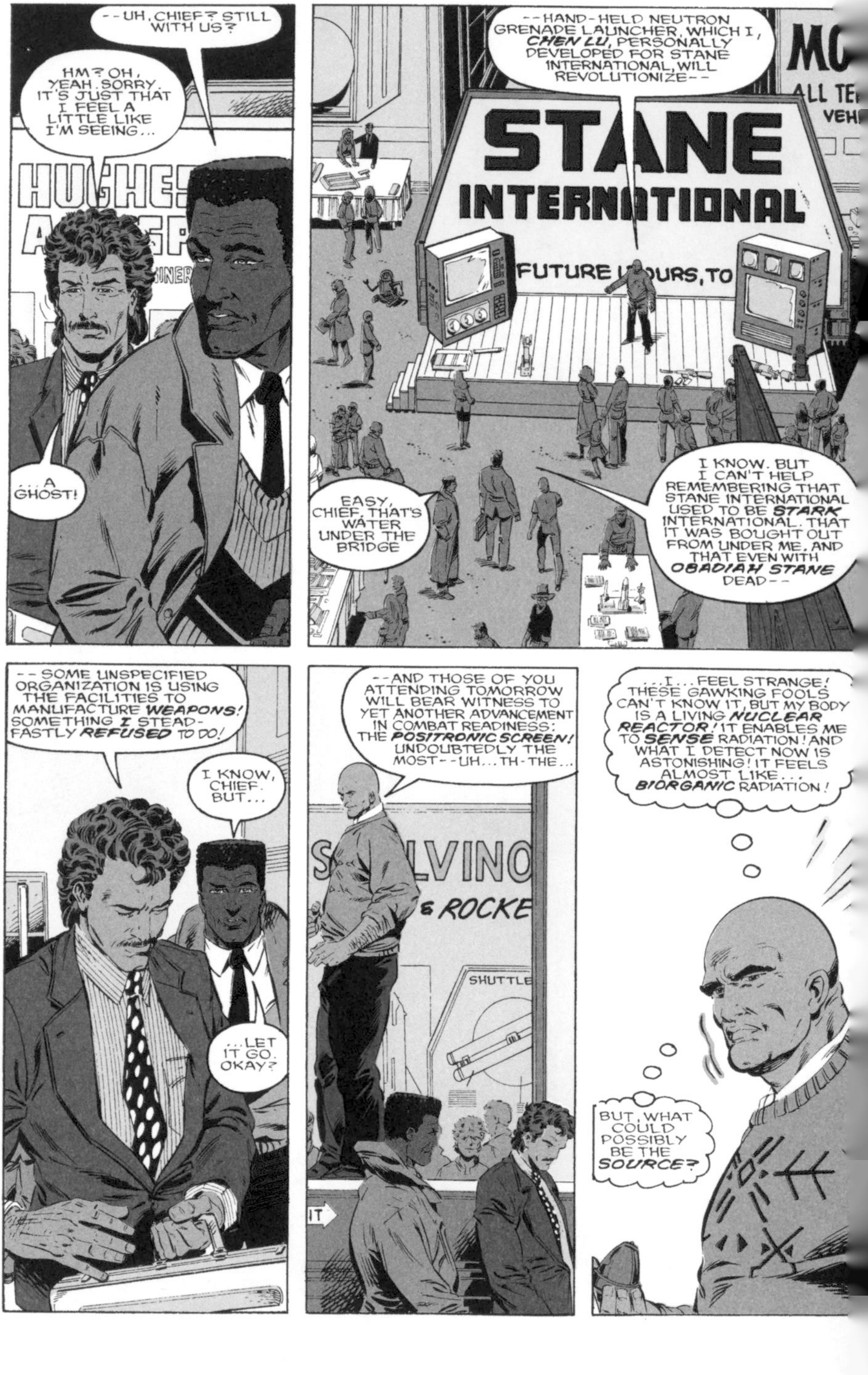
--UH, CHIEF? STILL WITH US?
HM? OH, YEAH. SORRY. IT'S JUST THAT I FEEL A LITTLE LIKE I'M SEEING...
...A GHOST!
--HAND-HELD NEUTRON GRENADE LAUNCHER, WHICH I, CHEN LU, PERSONALLY DEVELOPED FOR STANE INTERNATIONAL, WILL REVOLUTIONIZE--
STANE INTERNATIONAL
EASY, CHIEF. THAT'S WATER UNDER THE BRIDGE
I KNOW. BUT I CAN'T HELP REMEMBERING THAT STANE INTERNATIONAL USED TO BE STARK INTERNATIONAL. THAT IT WAS BOUGHT OUT FROM UNDER ME. AND THAT EVEN WITH OBADIAH STANE DEAD--
--SOME UNSPECIFIED ORGANIZATION IS USING THE FACILITIES TO MANUFACTURE WEAPONS! SOMETHING I STEADFASTLY REFUSED TO DO!
I KNOW, CHIEF. BUT...
...LET IT GO. OKAY?
--AND THOSE OF YOU ATTENDING TOMORROW WILL BEAR WITNESS TO YET ANOTHER ADVANCEMENT IN COMBAT READINESS: THE POSITRONIC SCREEN! UNDOUBTEDLY THE MOST--UH...TH-THE...
SHUTTLE
...I...FEEL STRANGE! THESE GAWKING FOOLS CAN'T KNOW IT, BUT MY BODY IS A LIVING NUCLEAR REACTOR! IT ENABLES ME TO SENSE RADIATION! AND WHAT I DETECT NOW IS ASTONISHING! IT FEELS ALMOST LIKE... BIORGANIC RADIATION!
BUT, WHAT COULD POSSIBLY BE THE SOURCE?

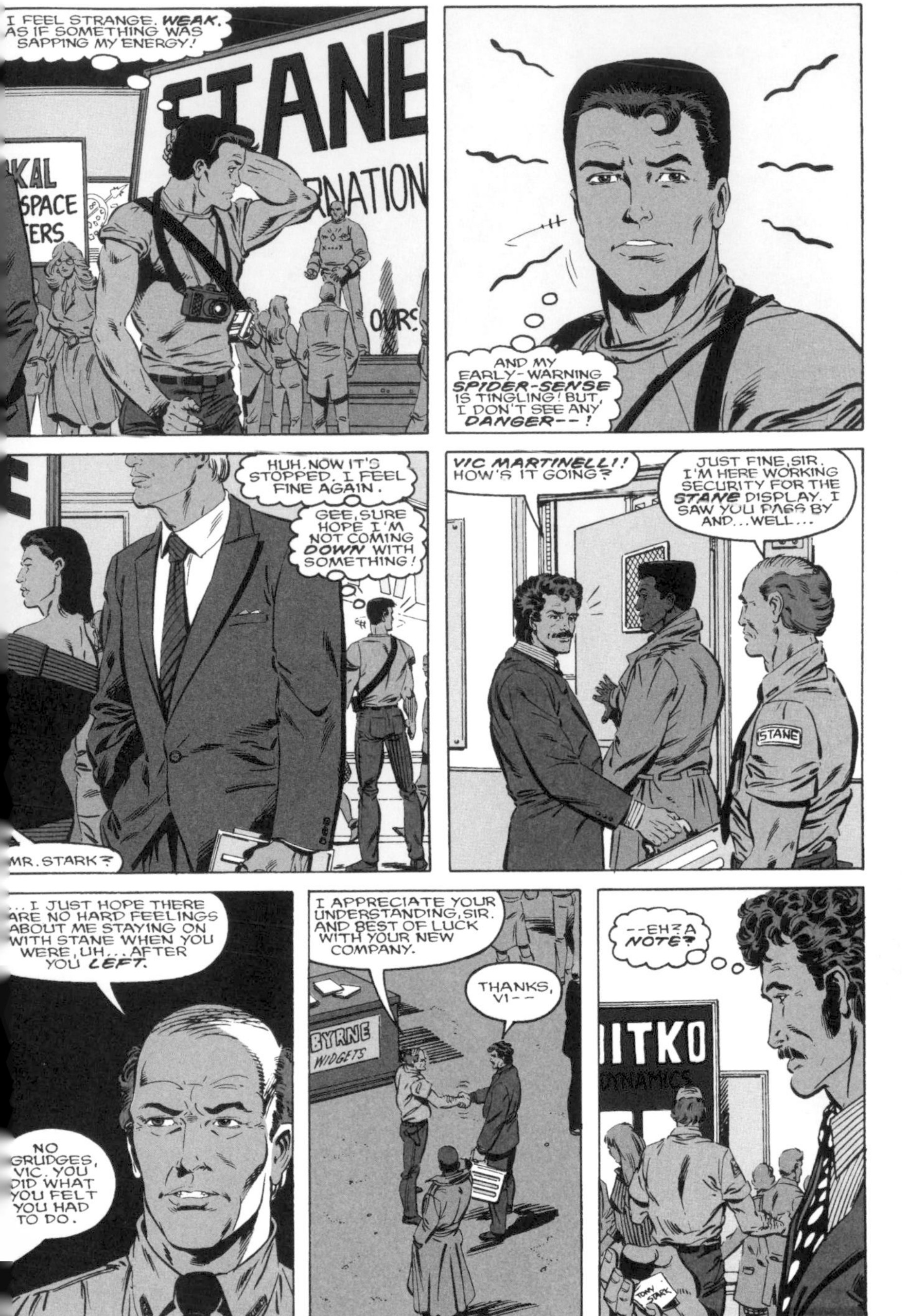

I FEEL STRANGE. WEAK. AS IF SOMETHING WAS SAPPING MY ENERGY!
STANE
AND MY EARLY-WARNING SPIDER-SENSE IS TINGLING! BUT, I DON'T SEE ANY DANGER--!
HUH. NOW IT'S STOPPED. I FEEL FINE AGAIN.
GEE, SURE HOPE I'M NOT COMING DOWN WITH SOMETHING!
MR. STARK?
VIC MARTINELLI!! HOW'S IT GOING?
JUST FINE, SIR. I'M HERE WORKING SECURITY FOR THE STANE DISPLAY. I SAW YOU PASS BY AND...WELL...
STANE
...I JUST HOPE THERE ARE NO HARD FEELINGS ABOUT ME STAYING ON WITH STANE WHEN YOU WERE, UH...AFTER YOU LEFT.
NO GRUDGES, VIC. YOU DID WHAT YOU FELT YOU HAD TO DO.
I APPRECIATE YOUR UNDERSTANDING, SIR. AND BEST OF LUCK WITH YOUR NEW COMPANY.
THANKS, VI--
BYRNE WIDGETS
--EH? A NOTE?
ITKO
TONY STARK

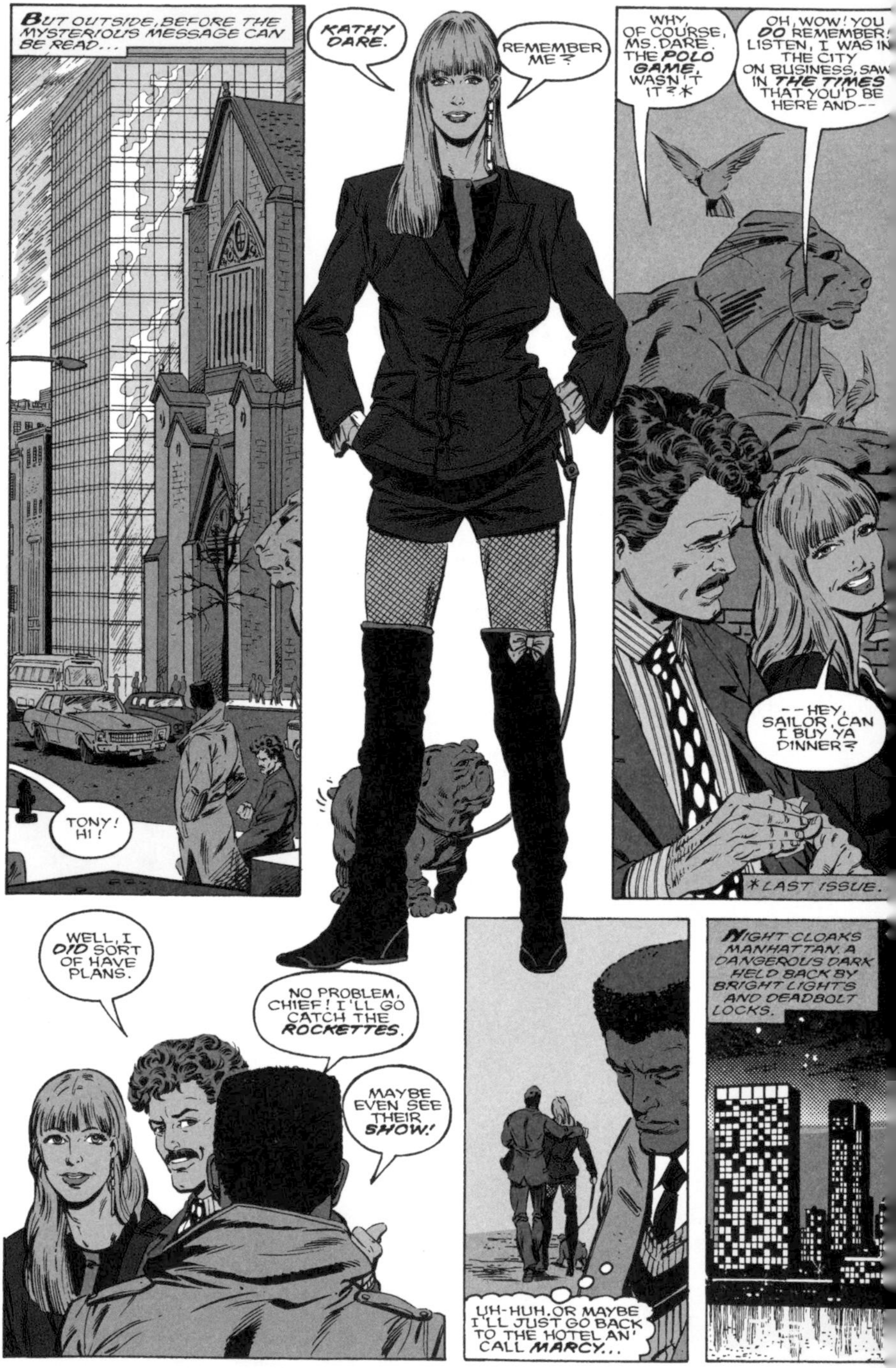
BUT OUTSIDE, BEFORE THE MYSTERIOUS MESSAGE CAN BE READ...
TONY! HI!
KATHY DARE.
REMEMBER ME?
WHY, OF COURSE, MS. DARE. THE POLO GAME, WASN'T IT?*
OH, WOW! YOU DO REMEMBER! LISTEN, I WAS IN THE CITY ON BUSINESS, SAW IN THE TIMES THAT YOU'D BE HERE AND--
--HEY, SAILOR, CAN I BUY YA DINNER?
*LAST ISSUE.
WELL, I DID SORT OF HAVE PLANS.
NO PROBLEM, CHIEF! I'LL GO CATCH THE ROCKETTES.
MAYBE EVEN SEE THEIR SHOW!
UH-HUH. OR MAYBE I'LL JUST GO BACK TO THE HOTEL AN' CALL MARCY...
NIGHT CLOAKS MANHATTAN. A DANGEROUS DARK HELD BACK BY BRIGHT LIGHTS AND DEADBOLT LOCKS.

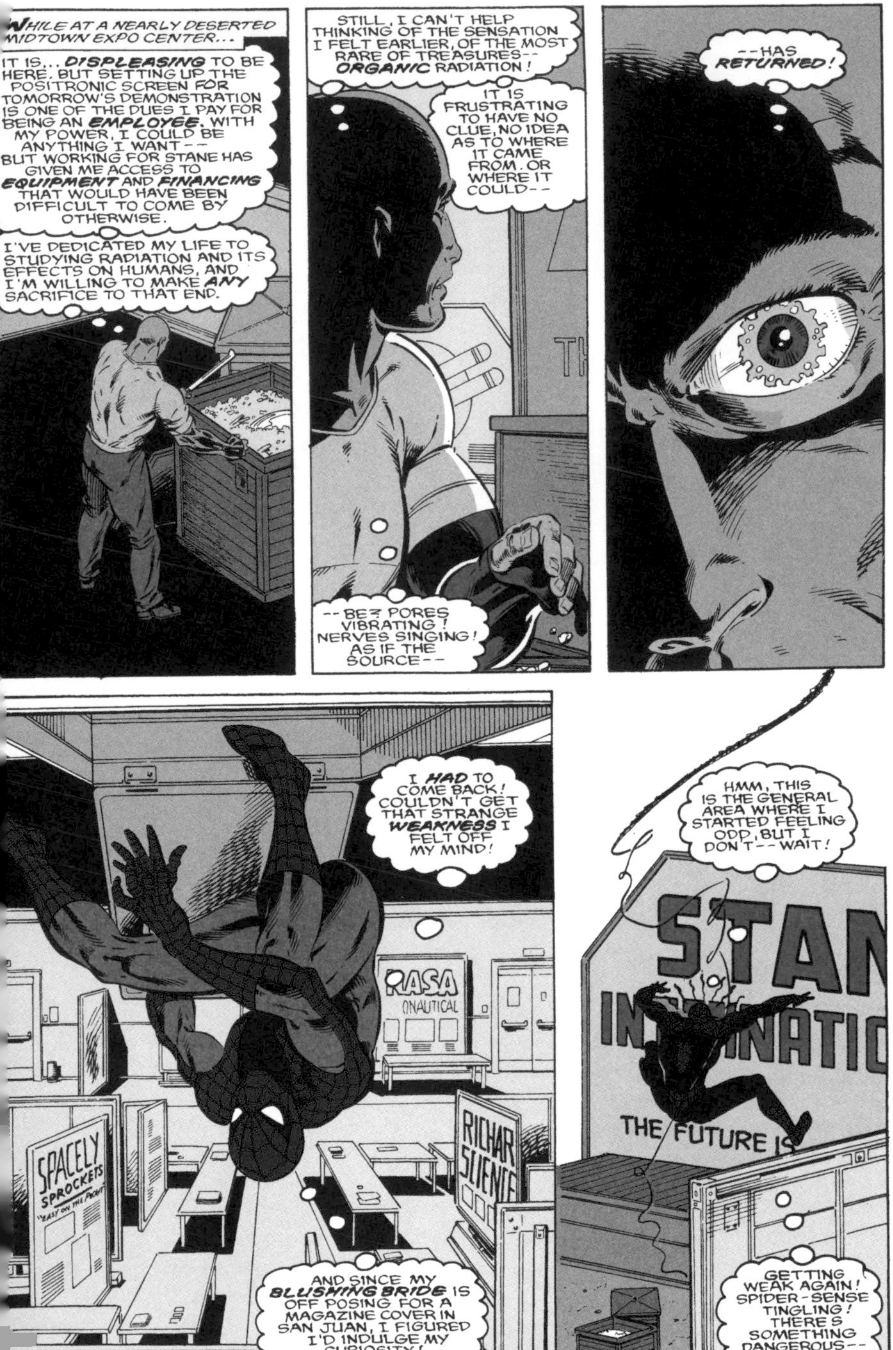
WHILE AT A NEARLY DESERTED MIDTOWN EXPO CENTER...
IT IS... DISPLEASING TO BE HERE. BUT SETTING UP THE POSITRONIC SCREEN FOR TOMORROW'S DEMONSTRATION IS ONE OF THE DUES I PAY FOR BEING AN EMPLOYEE. WITH MY POWER, I COULD BE ANYTHING I WANT-- BUT WORKING FOR STANE HAS GIVEN ME ACCESS TO EQUIPMENT AND FINANCING THAT WOULD HAVE BEEN DIFFICULT TO COME BY OTHERWISE.
I'VE DEDICATED MY LIFE TO STUDYING RADIATION AND ITS EFFECTS ON HUMANS, AND I'M WILLING TO MAKE ANY SACRIFICE TO THAT END.
STILL, I CAN'T HELP THINKING OF THE SENSATION I FELT EARLIER, OF THE MOST RARE OF TREASURES-- ORGANIC RADIATION!
IT IS FRUSTRATING TO HAVE NO CLUE, NO IDEA AS TO WHERE IT CAME FROM. OR WHERE IT COULD--
--BE? PORES VIBRATING! NERVES SINGING! AS IF THE SOURCE--
--HAS RETURNED!
I HAD TO COME BACK! COULDN'T GET THAT STRANGE WEAKNESS I FELT OFF MY MIND!
AND SINCE MY BLUSHING BRIDE IS OFF POSING FOR A MAGAZINE COVER IN SAN JUAN, I FIGURED I'D INDULGE MY CURIOSITY!
SPACELY SPROCKETS
"EASY ON THE POINT"
RASA
ONAUTICAL
RICHAR SCIENCE
HMM, THIS IS THE GENERAL AREA WHERE I STARTED FEELING ODD, BUT I DON'T-- WAIT!
STAN
INTERNATIO
THE FUTURE IS
GETTING WEAK AGAIN! SPIDER-SENSE TINGLING! THERE'S SOMETHING DANGEROUS--

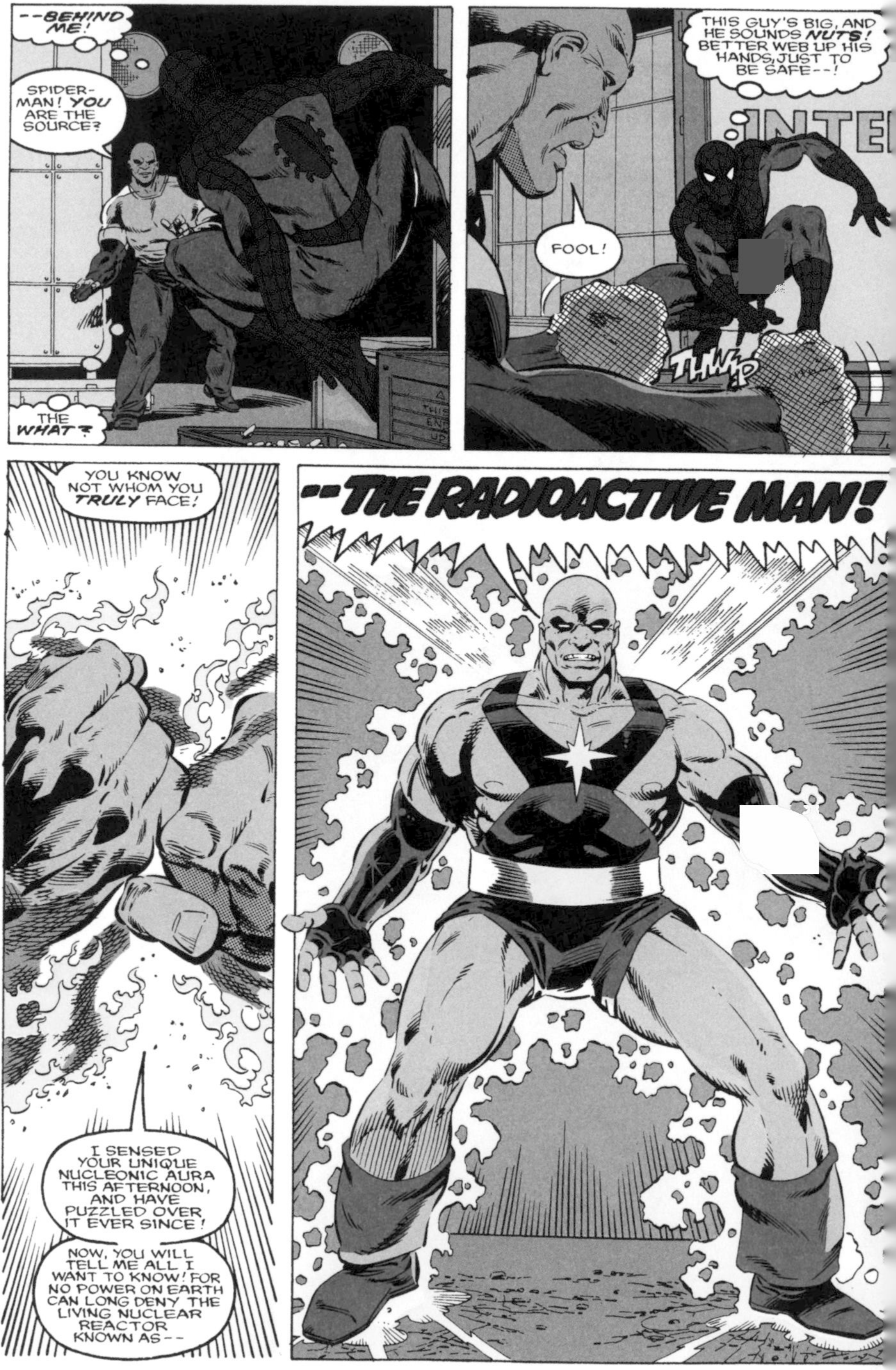
--BEHIND ME!
SPIDER-MAN! YOU ARE THE SOURCE?
THE WHAT?
THIS GUY'S BIG, AND HE SOUNDS NUTS! BETTER WEB UP HIS HANDS, JUST TO BE SAFE--!
FOOL!
THWAP
YOU KNOW NOT WHOM YOU TRULY FACE!
I SENSED YOUR UNIQUE NUCLEONIC AURA THIS AFTERNOON, AND HAVE PUZZLED OVER IT EVER SINCE!
NOW, YOU WILL TELL ME ALL I WANT TO KNOW! FOR NO POWER ON EARTH CAN LONG DENY THE LIVING NUCLEAR REACTOR KNOWN AS--
--THE RADIOACTIVE MAN!

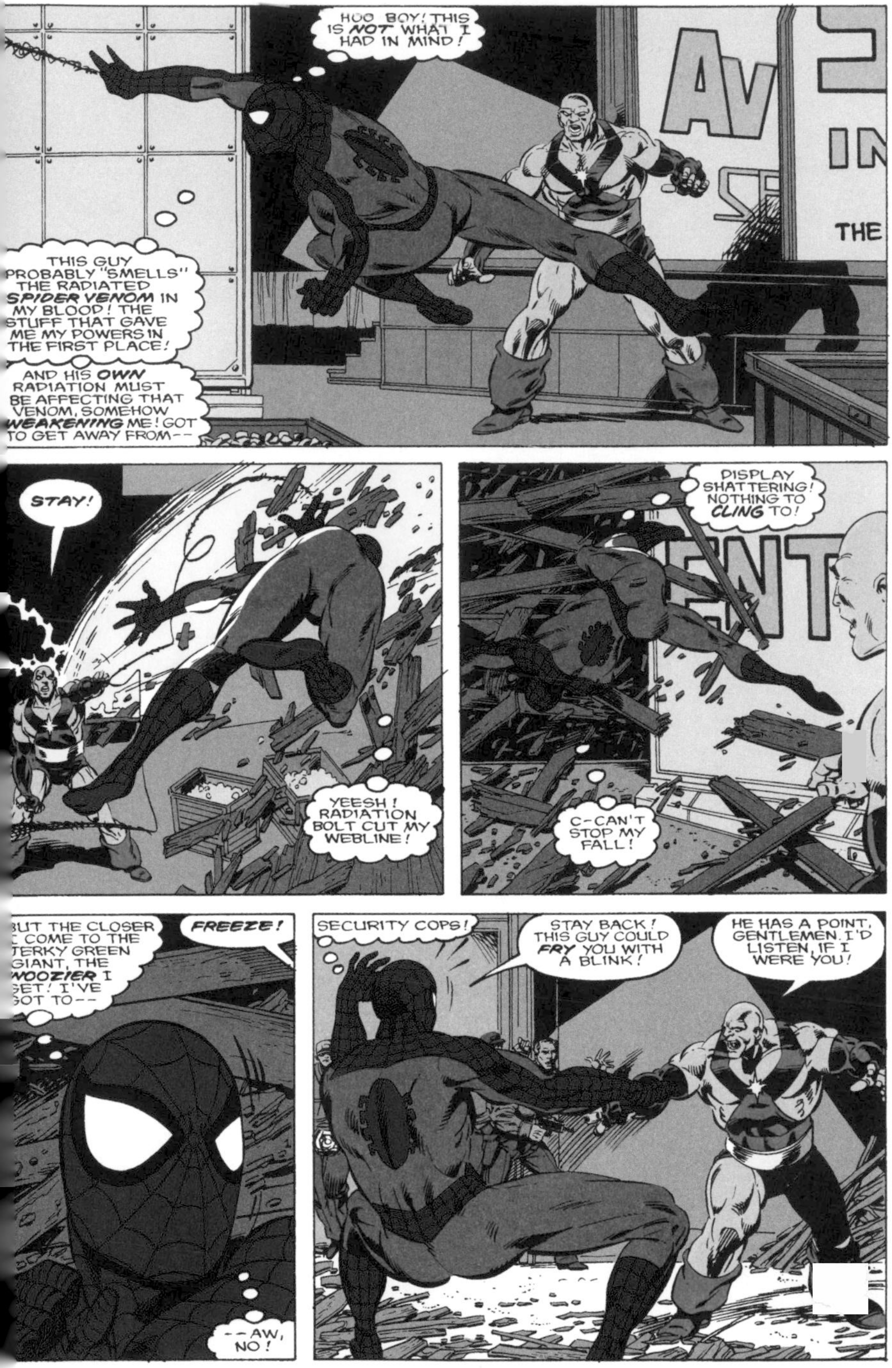
HOO BOY! THIS IS NOT WHAT I HAD IN MIND!
THIS GUY PROBABLY "SMELLS" THE RADIATED SPIDER VENOM IN MY BLOOD! THE STUFF THAT GAVE ME MY POWERS IN THE FIRST PLACE!
AND HIS OWN RADIATION MUST BE AFFECTING THAT VENOM, SOMEHOW WEAKENING ME! GOT TO GET AWAY FROM--
STAY!
YEESH! RADIATION BOLT CUT MY WEBLINE!
DISPLAY SHATTERING! NOTHING TO CLING TO!
C-CAN'T STOP MY FALL!
FREEZE!
--AW, NO!
SECURITY COPS!
STAY BACK! THIS GUY COULD FRY YOU WITH A BLINK!
HE HAS A POINT, GENTLEMEN. I'D LISTEN, IF I WERE YOU!

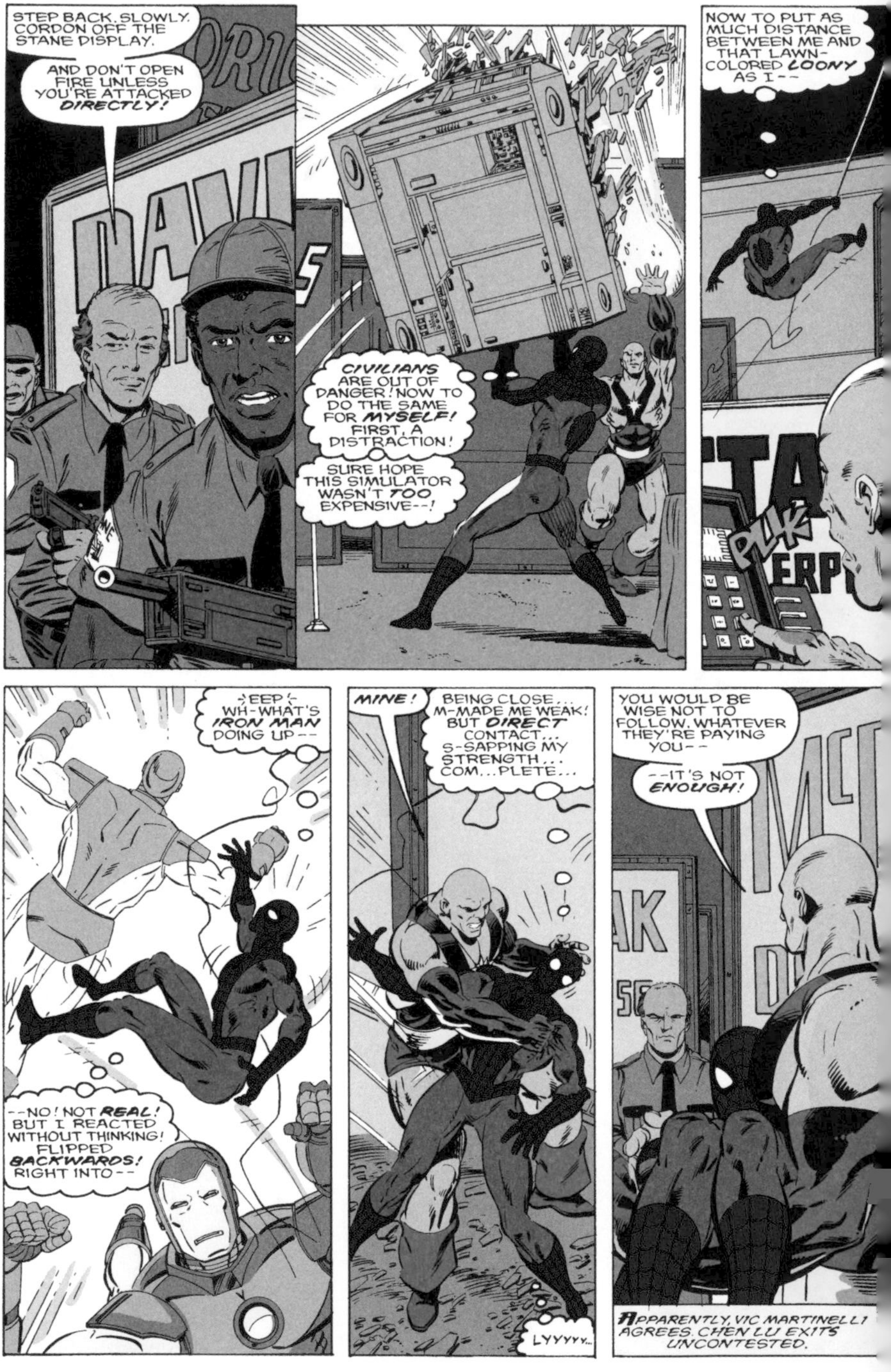
STEP BACK. SLOWLY. CORDON OFF THE STANE DISPLAY.
AND DON'T OPEN FIRE UNLESS YOU'RE ATTACKED DIRECTLY!
CIVILIANS ARE OUT OF DANGER! NOW TO DO THE SAME FOR MYSELF! FIRST, A DISTRACTION!
SURE HOPE THIS SIMULATOR WASN'T TOO EXPENSIVE--!
NOW TO PUT AS MUCH DISTANCE BETWEEN ME AND THAT LAWN-COLORED LOONY AS I--
PLIK
-EEP- WH-WHAT'S IRON MAN DOING UP--
--NO! NOT REAL! BUT I REACTED WITHOUT THINKING! FLIPPED BACKWARDS! RIGHT INTO--
MINE!
BEING CLOSE... M-MADE ME WEAK! BUT DIRECT CONTACT... S-SAPPING MY STRENGTH... COM...PLETE...
LYYYYY...
YOU WOULD BE WISE NOT TO FOLLOW. WHATEVER THEY'RE PAYING YOU--
--IT'S NOT ENOUGH!
APPARENTLY, VIC MARTINELLI AGREES. CHEN LU EXITS UNCONTESTED.

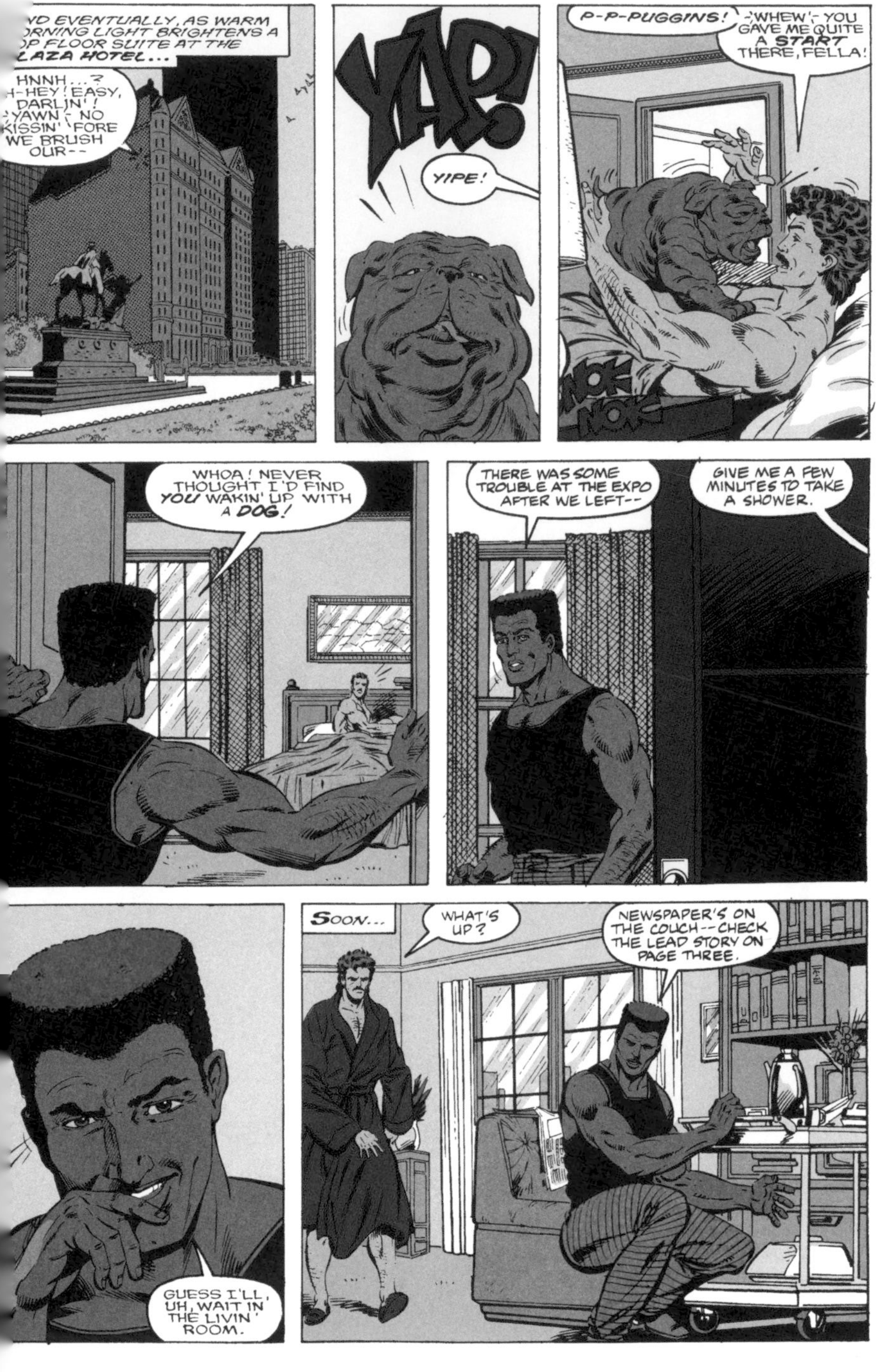

ND EVENTUALLY, AS WARM ORNING LIGHT BRIGHTENS A OP FLOOR SUITE AT THE LAZA HOTEL...
HNNH...? H-HEY! EASY, DARLIN'! -YAWN- NO KISSIN' 'FORE WE BRUSH OUR--
YAP!
YIPE!
P-P-PUGGINS!
-WHEW- YOU GAVE ME QUITE A START THERE, FELLA!
NOK NOK
WHOA! NEVER THOUGHT I'D FIND YOU WAKIN' UP WITH A DOG!
THERE WAS SOME TROUBLE AT THE EXPO AFTER WE LEFT--
GIVE ME A FEW MINUTES TO TAKE A SHOWER.
GUESS I'LL, UH, WAIT IN THE LIVIN' ROOM.
SOON...
WHAT'S UP?
NEWSPAPER'S ON THE COUCH--CHECK THE LEAD STORY ON PAGE THREE.

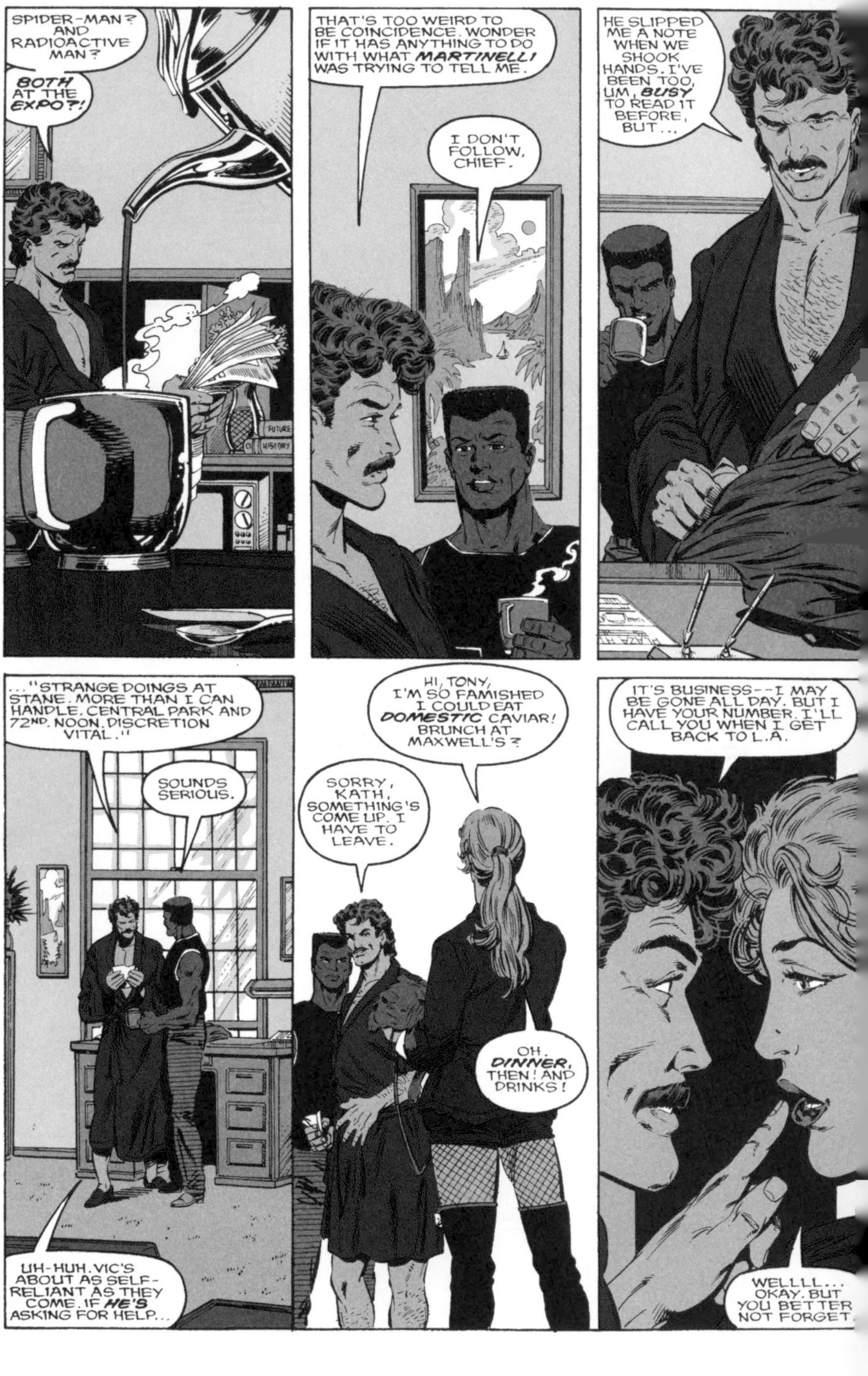
SPIDER-MAN? AND RADIOACTIVE MAN?
BOTH AT THE EXPO?!
THAT'S TOO WEIRD TO BE COINCIDENCE. WONDER IF IT HAS ANYTHING TO DO WITH WHAT MARTINELLI WAS TRYING TO TELL ME.
I DON'T FOLLOW, CHIEF.
HE SLIPPED ME A NOTE WHEN WE SHOOK HANDS. I'VE BEEN TOO, UM, BUSY TO READ IT BEFORE, BUT...
FUTURE
HISTORY
..."STRANGE DOINGS AT STANE. MORE THAN I CAN HANDLE. CENTRAL PARK AND 72ND. NOON. DISCRETION VITAL."
SOUNDS SERIOUS.
UH-HUH. VIC'S ABOUT AS SELF-RELIANT AS THEY COME. IF HE'S ASKING FOR HELP...
HI, TONY, I'M SO FAMISHED I COULD EAT DOMESTIC CAVIAR! BRUNCH AT MAXWELL'S?
SORRY, KATH, SOMETHING'S COME UP. I HAVE TO LEAVE.
OH. DINNER, THEN! AND DRINKS!
IT'S BUSINESS--I MAY BE GONE ALL DAY. BUT I HAVE YOUR NUMBER. I'LL CALL YOU WHEN I GET BACK TO L.A.
WELLLL... OKAY. BUT YOU BETTER NOT FORGET.

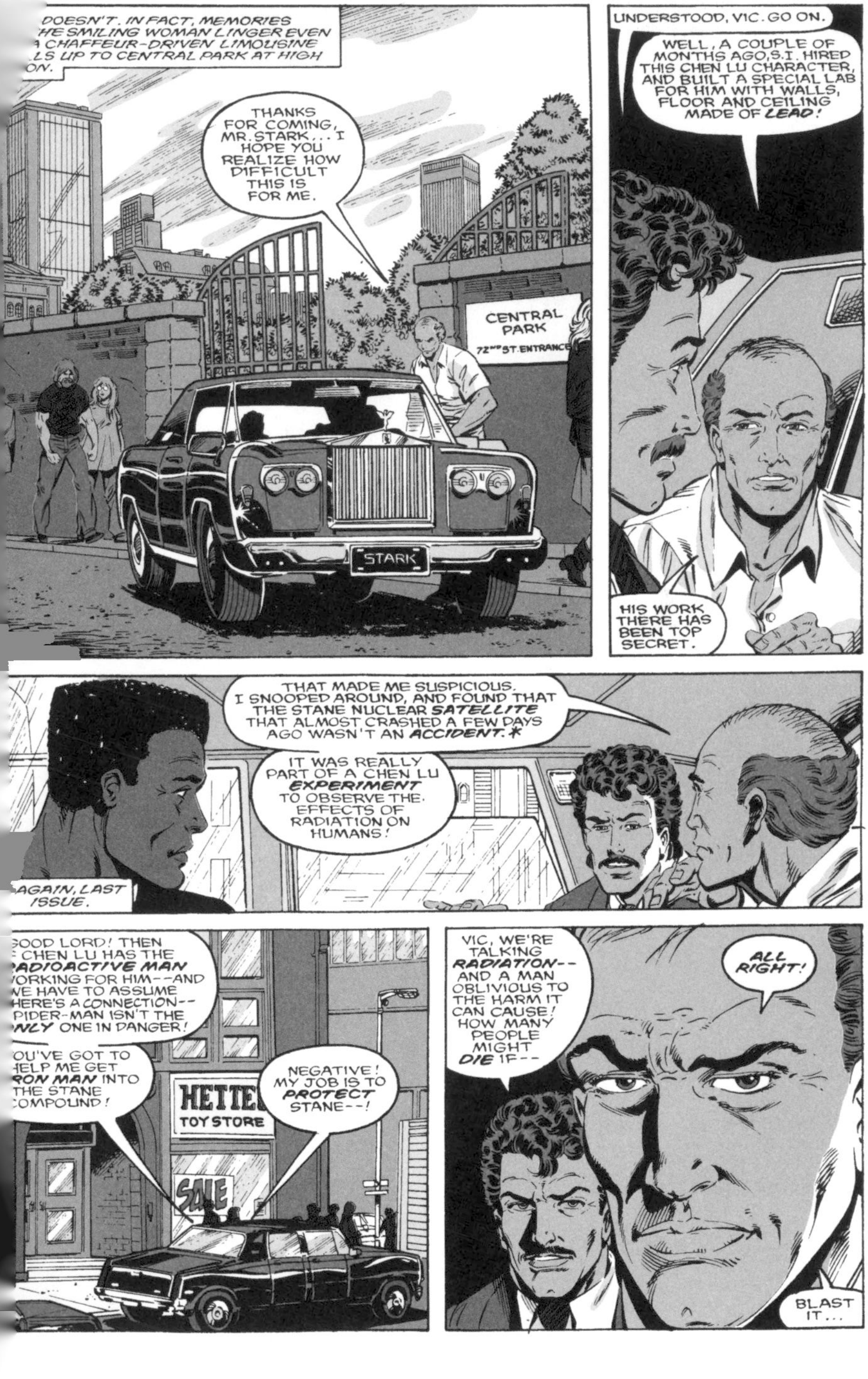

DOESN'T. IN FACT, MEMORIES
HE SMILING WOMAN LINGER EVEN
A CHAFFEUR-DRIVEN LIMOUSINE
LS UP TO CENTRAL PARK AT HIGH
ON.
THANKS FOR COMING, MR. STARK... I HOPE YOU REALIZE HOW DIFFICULT THIS IS FOR ME.
CENTRAL PARK
72ND ST. ENTRANCE
STARK
UNDERSTOOD, VIC. GO ON.
WELL, A COUPLE OF MONTHS AGO, S.I. HIRED THIS CHEN LU CHARACTER, AND BUILT A SPECIAL LAB FOR HIM WITH WALLS, FLOOR AND CEILING MADE OF LEAD!
HIS WORK THERE HAS BEEN TOP SECRET.
THAT MADE ME SUSPICIOUS. I SNOOPED AROUND, AND FOUND THAT THE STANE NUCLEAR SATELLITE THAT ALMOST CRASHED A FEW DAYS AGO WASN'T AN ACCIDENT.*
IT WAS REALLY PART OF A CHEN LU EXPERIMENT TO OBSERVE THE EFFECTS OF RADIATION ON HUMANS!
AGAIN, LAST ISSUE.
GOOD LORD! THEN F CHEN LU HAS THE RADIOACTIVE MAN WORKING FOR HIM--AND WE HAVE TO ASSUME HERE'S A CONNECTION--PIDER-MAN ISN'T THE NLY ONE IN DANGER!
OU'VE GOT TO HELP ME GET RON MAN INTO THE STANE COMPOUND!
NEGATIVE! MY JOB IS TO PROTECT STANE--!
HETTE
TOY STORE
SALE
VIC, WE'RE TALKING RADIATION--AND A MAN OBLIVIOUS TO THE HARM IT CAN CAUSE! HOW MANY PEOPLE MIGHT DIE IF--
ALL RIGHT!
BLAST IT...

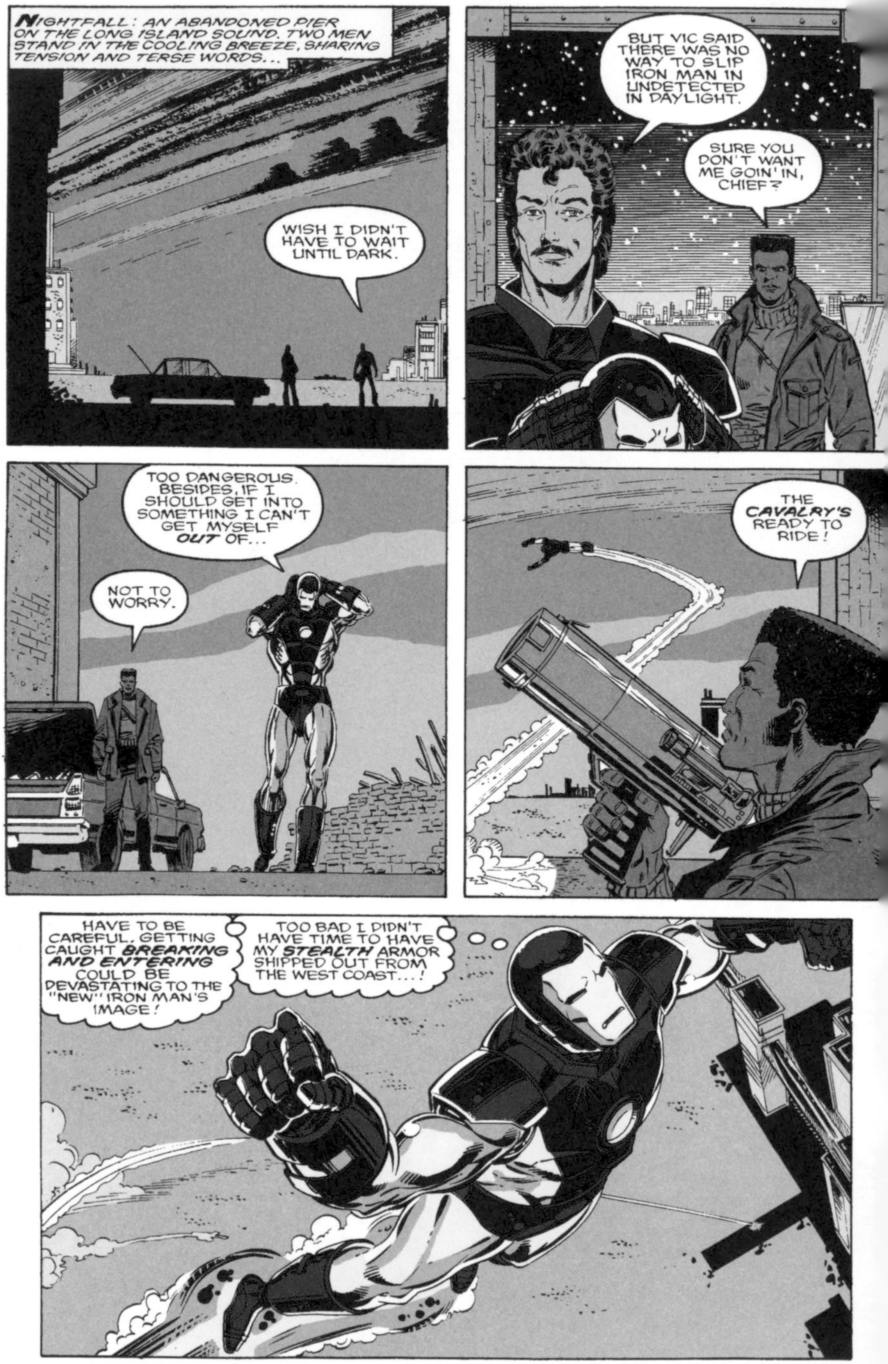

NIGHTFALL: AN ABANDONED PIER ON THE LONG ISLAND SOUND. TWO MEN STAND IN THE COOLING BREEZE, SHARING TENSION AND TERSE WORDS...
WISH I DIDN'T HAVE TO WAIT UNTIL DARK.
BUT VIC SAID THERE WAS NO WAY TO SLIP IRON MAN IN UNDETECTED IN DAYLIGHT.
SURE YOU DON'T WANT ME GOIN' IN, CHIEF?
TOO DANGEROUS. BESIDES, IF I SHOULD GET INTO SOMETHING I CAN'T GET MYSELF OUT OF...
NOT TO WORRY.
THE CAVALRY'S READY TO RIDE!
HAVE TO BE CAREFUL. GETTING CAUGHT BREAKING AND ENTERING COULD BE DEVASTATING TO THE "NEW" IRON MAN'S IMAGE!
TOO BAD I DIDN'T HAVE TIME TO HAVE MY STEALTH ARMOR SHIPPED OUT FROM THE WEST COAST...!

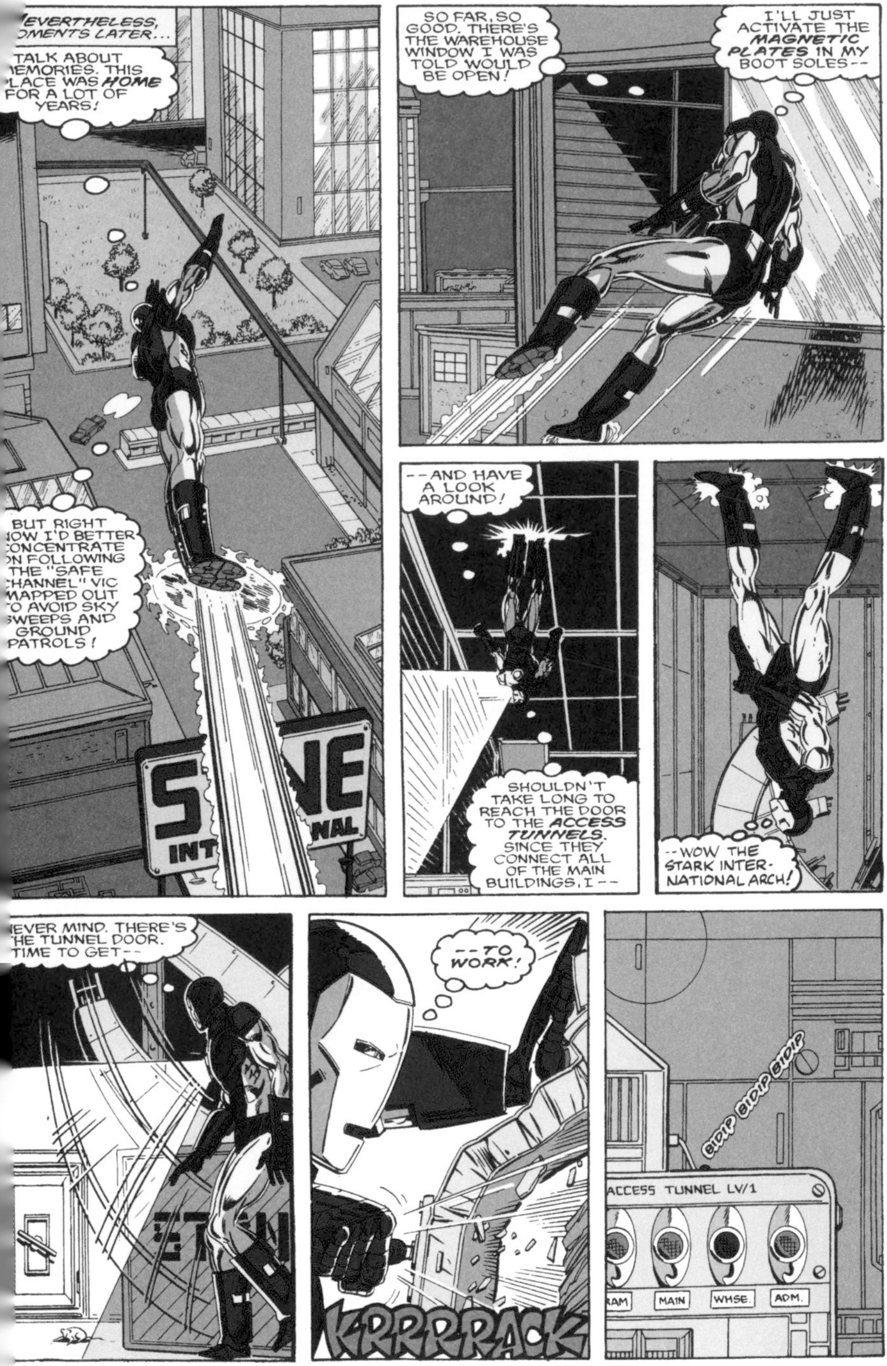
NEVERTHELESS, MOMENTS LATER...
TALK ABOUT MEMORIES. THIS PLACE WAS HOME FOR A LOT OF YEARS!
BUT RIGHT NOW I'D BETTER CONCENTRATE ON FOLLOWING THE "SAFE CHANNEL" VIC MAPPED OUT TO AVOID SKY SWEEPS AND GROUND PATROLS!
SO FAR, SO GOOD. THERE'S THE WAREHOUSE WINDOW I WAS TOLD WOULD BE OPEN!
I'LL JUST ACTIVATE THE MAGNETIC PLATES IN MY BOOT SOLES--
--AND HAVE A LOOK AROUND!
SHOULDN'T TAKE LONG TO REACH THE DOOR TO THE ACCESS TUNNELS. SINCE THEY CONNECT ALL OF THE MAIN BUILDINGS, I--
--WOW THE STARK INTER-NATIONAL ARCH!
NEVER MIND. THERE'S THE TUNNEL DOOR. TIME TO GET--
--TO WORK!
KRRRRACK
BIDIP BIDIP BIDIP
ACCESS TUNNEL LV/1
RAM
MAIN
WHSE.
ADM.

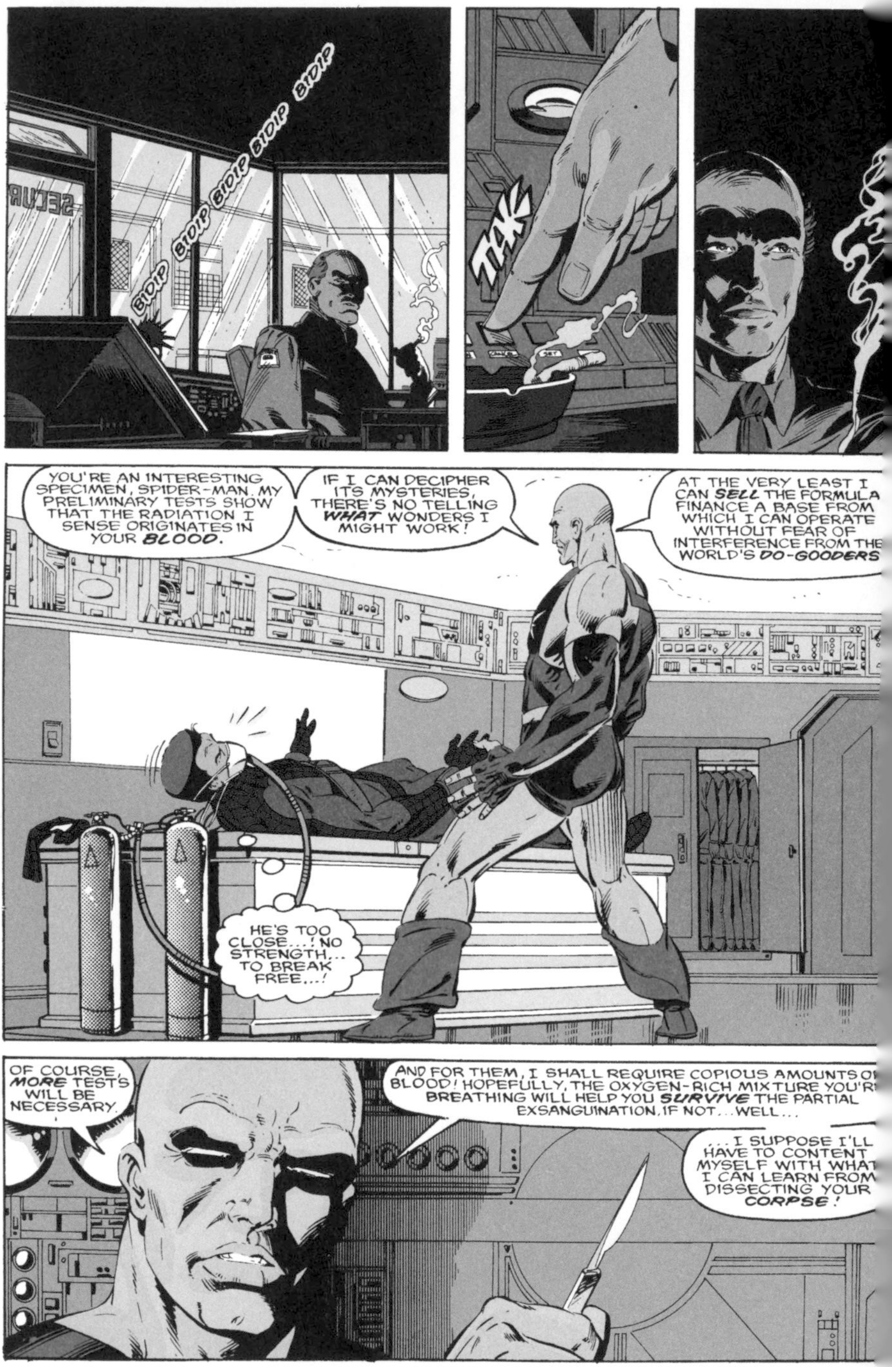

BIDIP BIDIP BIDIP BIDIP BIDIP
TAK
YOU'RE AN INTERESTING SPECIMEN, SPIDER-MAN. MY PRELIMINARY TESTS SHOW THAT THE RADIATION I SENSE ORIGINATES IN YOUR BLOOD.
IF I CAN DECIPHER ITS MYSTERIES, THERE'S NO TELLING WHAT WONDERS I MIGHT WORK!
AT THE VERY LEAST I CAN SELL THE FORMULA FINANCE A BASE FROM WHICH I CAN OPERATE WITHOUT FEAR OF INTERFERENCE FROM THE WORLD'S DO-GOODERS
HE'S TOO CLOSE...! NO STRENGTH... TO BREAK FREE...!
OF COURSE, MORE TESTS WILL BE NECESSARY.
AND FOR THEM, I SHALL REQUIRE COPIOUS AMOUNTS OF BLOOD! HOPEFULLY, THE OXYGEN-RICH MIXTURE YOU'RE BREATHING WILL HELP YOU SURVIVE THE PARTIAL EXSANGUINATION, IF NOT... WELL...
...I SUPPOSE I'LL HAVE TO CONTENT MYSELF WITH WHAT I CAN LEARN FROM DISSECTING YOUR CORPSE!

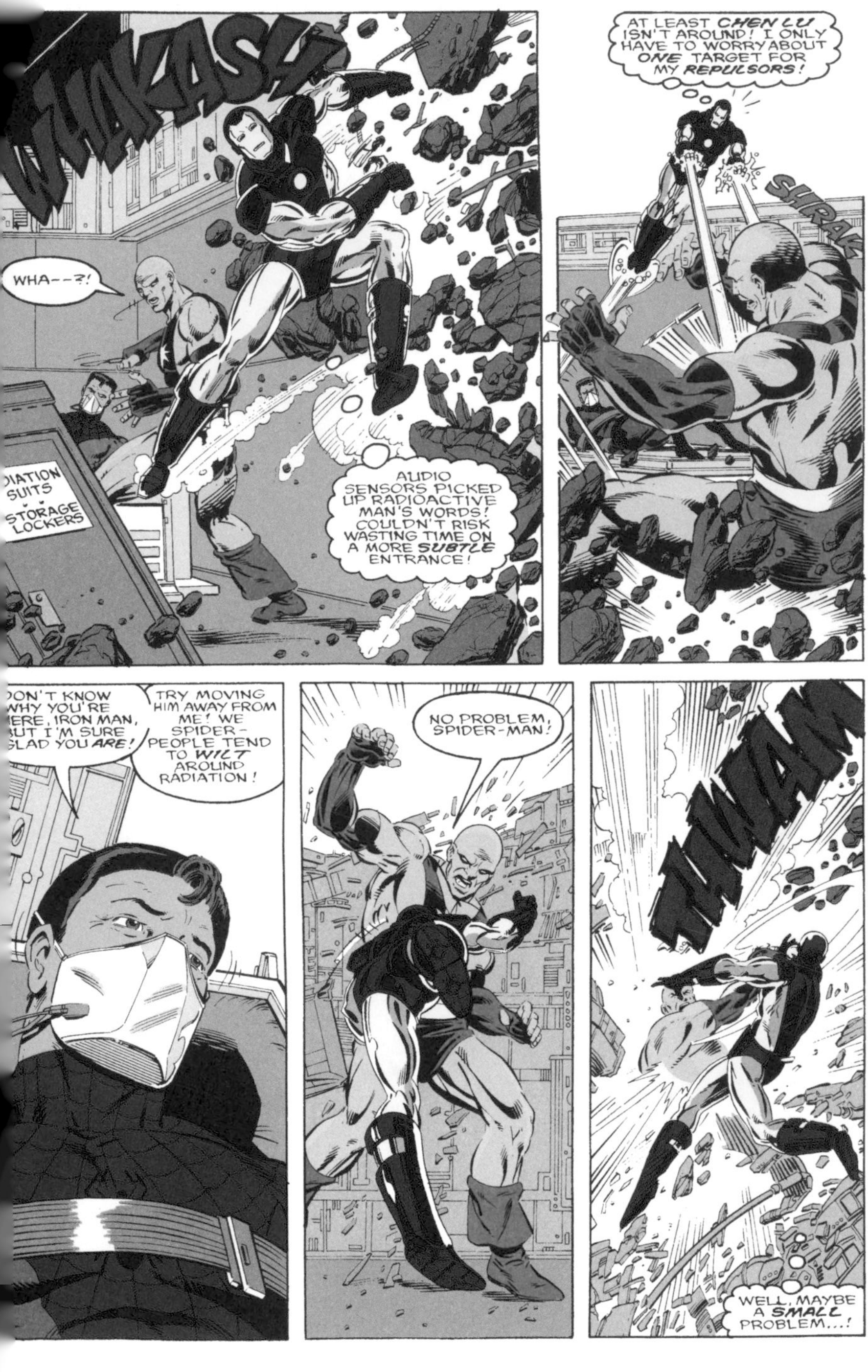
WHAKASH
WHA--?!
AUDIO SENSORS PICKED UP RADIOACTIVE MAN'S WORDS! COULDN'T RISK WASTING TIME ON A MORE SUBTLE ENTRANCE!
DIATION SUITS • STORAGE LOCKERS
AT LEAST CHEN LU ISN'T AROUND! I ONLY HAVE TO WORRY ABOUT ONE TARGET FOR MY REPULSORS!
SHRAK
DON'T KNOW WHY YOU'RE HERE, IRON MAN, BUT I'M SURE GLAD YOU ARE!
TRY MOVING HIM AWAY FROM ME! WE SPIDER-PEOPLE TEND TO WILT AROUND RADIATION!
NO PROBLEM, SPIDER-MAN!
THWAM
WELL, MAYBE A SMALL PROBLEM...!

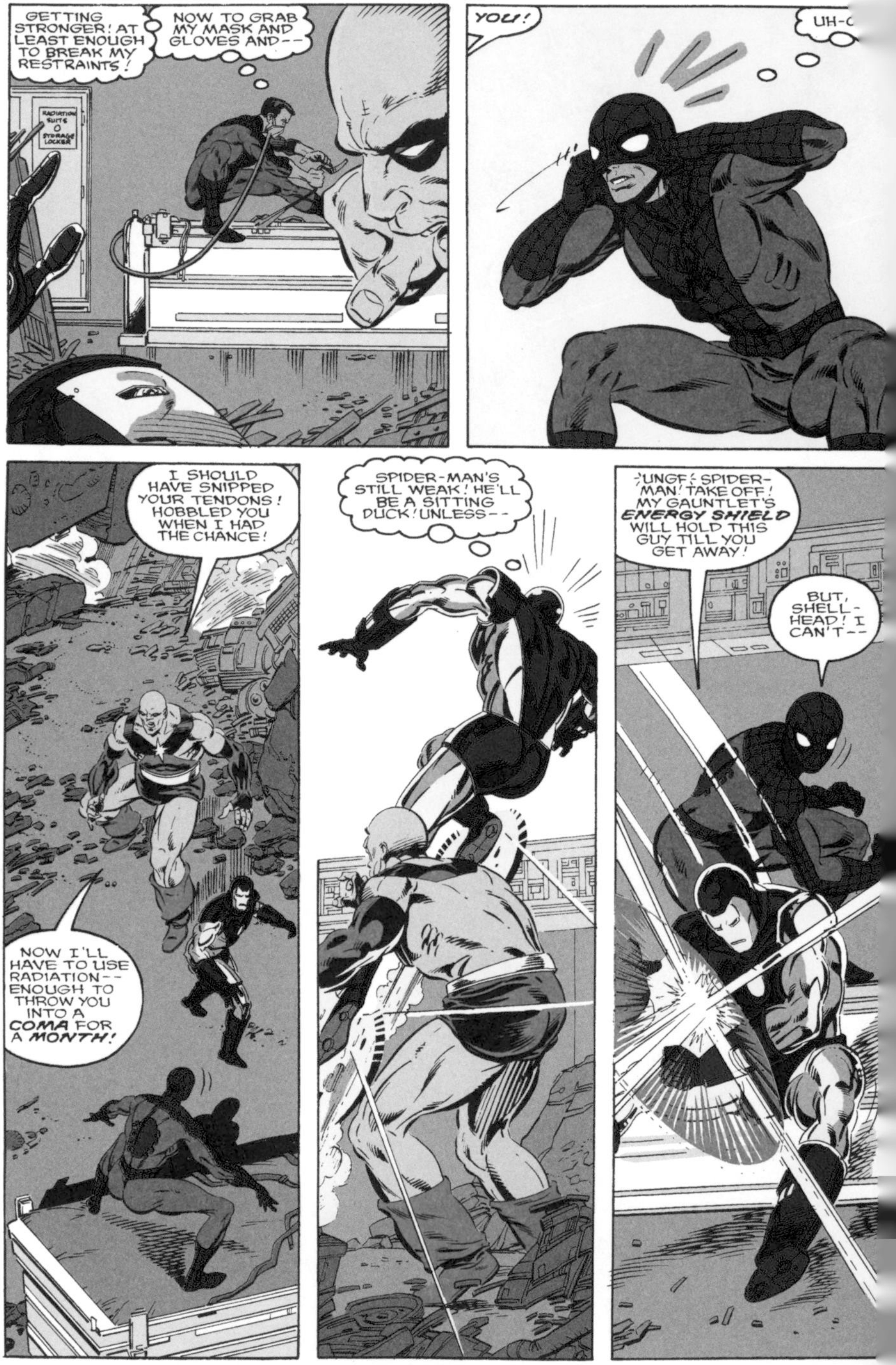
GETTING STRONGER! AT LEAST ENOUGH TO BREAK MY RESTRAINTS!
NOW TO GRAB MY MASK AND GLOVES AND--
RADIATION SUITS STORAGE LOCKER
YOU!
UH-O
I SHOULD HAVE SNIPPED YOUR TENDONS! HOBBLED YOU WHEN I HAD THE CHANCE!
NOW I'LL HAVE TO USE RADIATION--ENOUGH TO THROW YOU INTO A COMA FOR A MONTH!
SPIDER-MAN'S STILL WEAK! HE'LL BE A SITTING DUCK! UNLESS--
UNGF! SPIDER-MAN! TAKE OFF! MY GAUNTLET'S ENERGY SHIELD WILL HOLD THIS GUY TILL YOU GET AWAY!
BUT, SHELL-HEAD! I CAN'T--

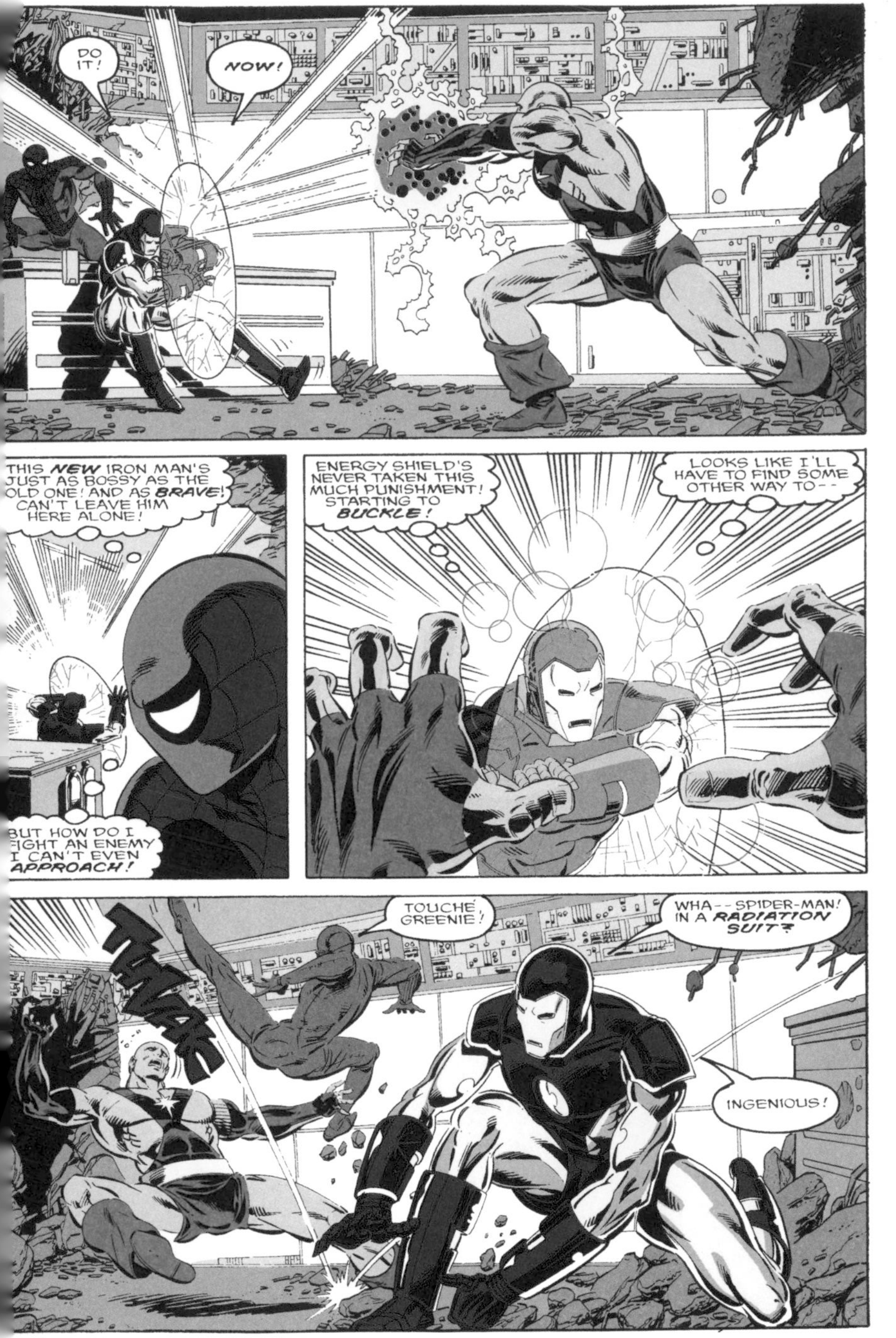
DO IT!
NOW!
THIS NEW IRON MAN'S JUST AS BOSSY AS THE OLD ONE! AND AS BRAVE! CAN'T LEAVE HIM HERE ALONE!
BUT HOW DO I FIGHT AN ENEMY I CAN'T EVEN APPROACH!
ENERGY SHIELD'S NEVER TAKEN THIS MUCH PUNISHMENT! STARTING TO BUCKLE!
LOOKS LIKE I'LL HAVE TO FIND SOME OTHER WAY TO--
THWAK
TOUCHE, GREENIE!
WHA-- SPIDER-MAN! IN A RADIATION SUIT?
INGENIOUS!

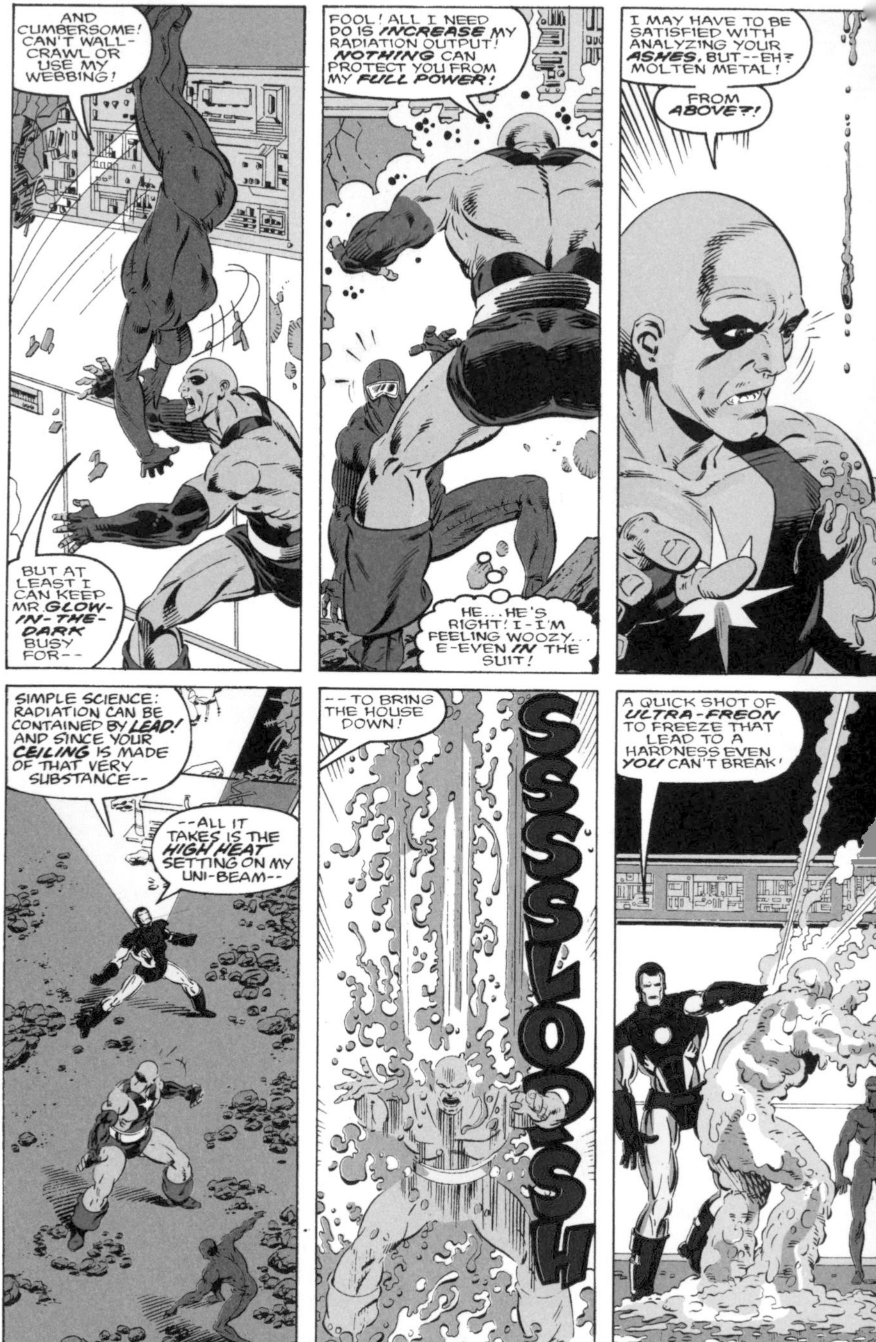
AND CUMBERSOME! CAN'T WALL-CRAWL OR USE MY WEBBING!
BUT AT LEAST I CAN KEEP MR GLOW-IN-THE-DARK BUSY FOR--
FOOL! ALL I NEED DO IS INCREASE MY RADIATION OUTPUT! NOTHING CAN PROTECT YOU FROM MY FULL POWER!
HE... HE'S RIGHT! I-I'M FEELING WOOZY... E-EVEN IN THE SUIT!
I MAY HAVE TO BE SATISFIED WITH ANALYZING YOUR ASHES. BUT--EH? MOLTEN METAL!
FROM ABOVE?!
SIMPLE SCIENCE: RADIATION CAN BE CONTAINED BY LEAD! AND SINCE YOUR CEILING IS MADE OF THAT VERY SUBSTANCE--
--ALL IT TAKES IS THE HIGH HEAT SETTING ON MY UNI-BEAM--
--TO BRING THE HOUSE DOWN!
SSSSLOOOSH
A QUICK SHOT OF ULTRA-FREON TO FREEZE THAT LEAD TO A HARDNESS EVEN YOU CAN'T BREAK!

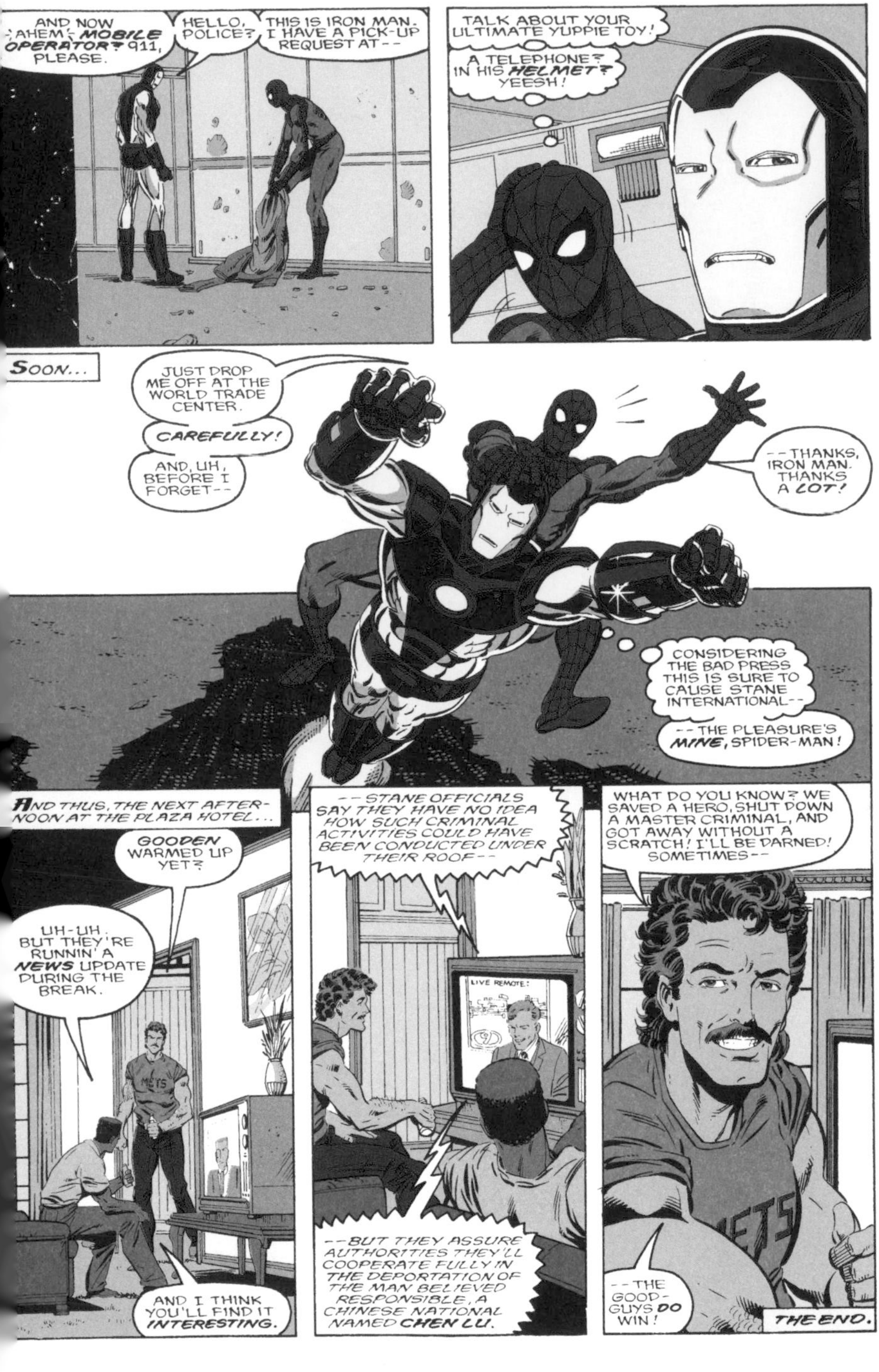
AND NOW -AHEM- MOBILE OPERATOR? 911, PLEASE.
HELLO, POLICE?
THIS IS IRON MAN. I HAVE A PICK-UP REQUEST AT--
TALK ABOUT YOUR ULTIMATE YUPPIE TOY!
A TELEPHONE? IN HIS HELMET? YEESH!
SOON...
JUST DROP ME OFF AT THE WORLD TRADE CENTER.
CAREFULLY!
AND, UH, BEFORE I FORGET--
--THANKS, IRON MAN. THANKS A LOT!
CONSIDERING THE BAD PRESS THIS IS SURE TO CAUSE STANE INTERNATIONAL--
--THE PLEASURE'S MINE, SPIDER-MAN!
AND THUS, THE NEXT AFTERNOON AT THE PLAZA HOTEL...
GOODEN WARMED UP YET?
UH-UH. BUT THEY'RE RUNNIN' A NEWS UPDATE DURING THE BREAK.
AND I THINK YOU'LL FIND IT INTERESTING.
--STANE OFFICIALS SAY THEY HAVE NO IDEA HOW SUCH CRIMINAL ACTIVITIES COULD HAVE BEEN CONDUCTED UNDER THEIR ROOF--
LIVE REMOTE:
--BUT THEY ASSURE AUTHORITIES THEY'LL COOPERATE FULLY IN THE DEPORTATION OF THE MAN BELIEVED RESPONSIBLE, A CHINESE NATIONAL NAMED CHEN LU.
WHAT DO YOU KNOW? WE SAVED A HERO, SHUT DOWN A MASTER CRIMINAL, AND GOT AWAY WITHOUT A SCRATCH! I'LL BE DARNED! SOMETIMES--
--THE GOOD-GUYS DO WIN!
THE END.

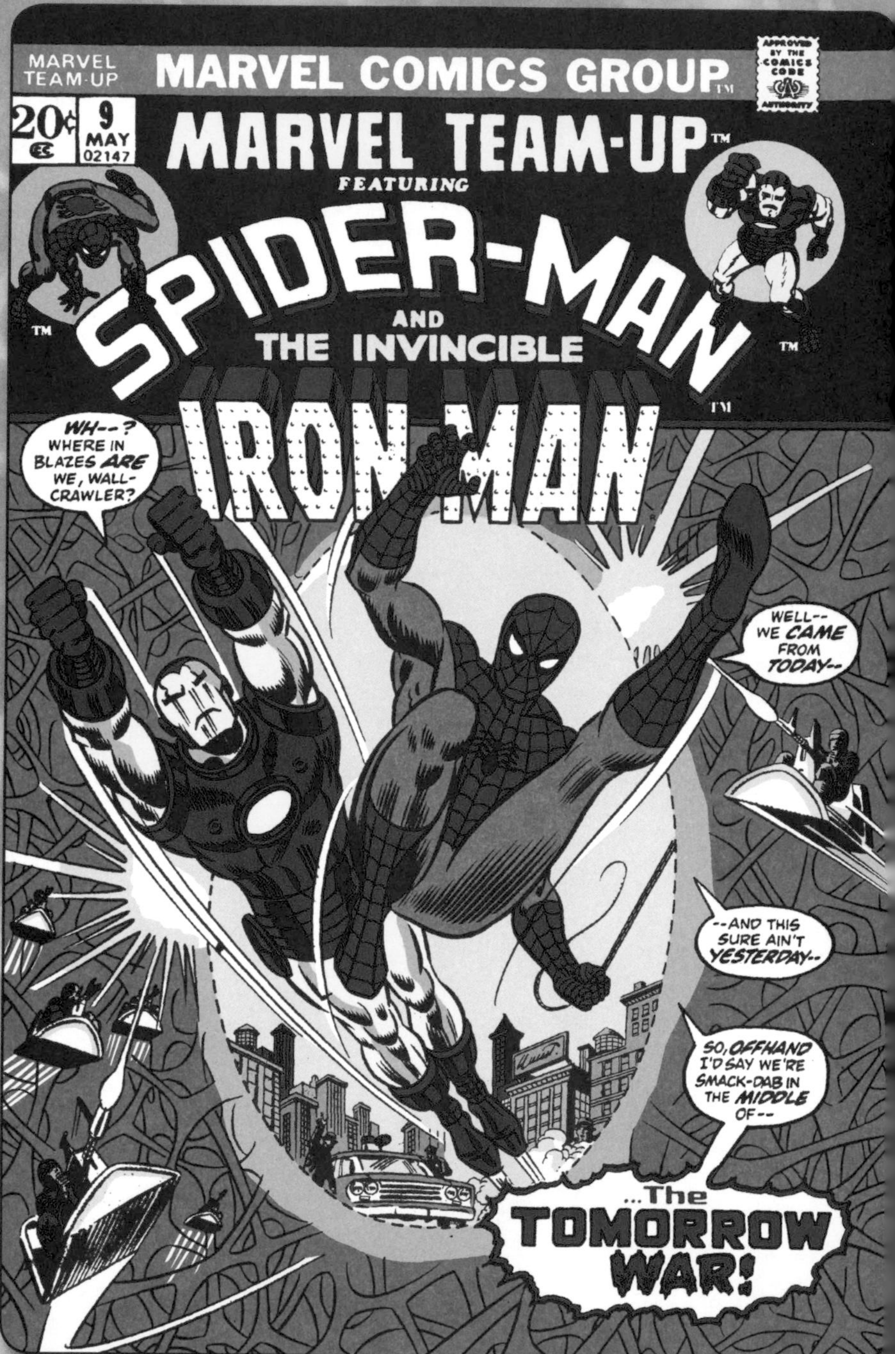
MARVEL TEAM-UP
MARVEL COMICS GROUP
APPROVED BY THE COMICS CODE AUTHORITY
20¢
9 MAY 02147
MARVEL TEAM-UP
FEATURING
SPIDER-MAN
AND THE INVINCIBLE
IRON MAN
WH--? WHERE IN BLAZES ARE WE, WALL-CRAWLER?
WELL-- WE CAME FROM TODAY--
--AND THIS SURE AIN'T YESTERDAY--
SO, OFFHAND I'D SAY WE'RE SMACK-DAB IN THE MIDDLE OF--
...The TOMORROW WAR!

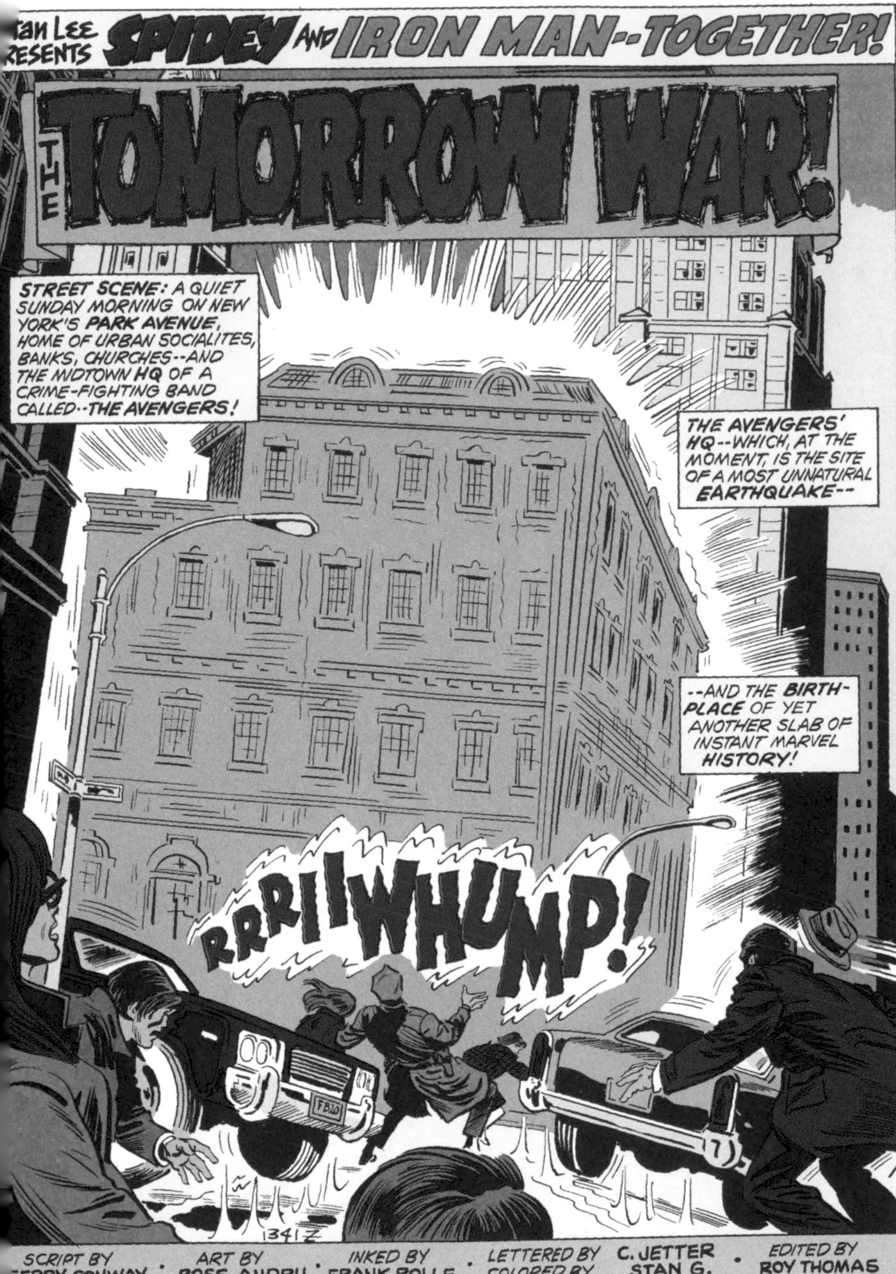

Stan Lee Presents SPIDEY AND IRON MAN--TOGETHER!
THE TOMORROW WAR!
STREET SCENE: A QUIET SUNDAY MORNING ON NEW YORK'S PARK AVENUE, HOME OF URBAN SOCIALITES, BANKS, CHURCHES--AND THE MIDTOWN HQ OF A CRIME-FIGHTING BAND CALLED--THE AVENGERS!
THE AVENGERS' HQ--WHICH, AT THE MOMENT, IS THE SITE OF A MOST UNNATURAL EARTHQUAKE--
--AND THE BIRTH-PLACE OF YET ANOTHER SLAB OF INSTANT MARVEL HISTORY!
RRRIIWHUMP!
SCRIPT BY GERRY CONWAY • ART BY ROSS ANDRU • INKED BY FRANK BOLLE • LETTERED BY C. JETTER COLORED BY STAN G. • EDITED BY ROY THOMAS

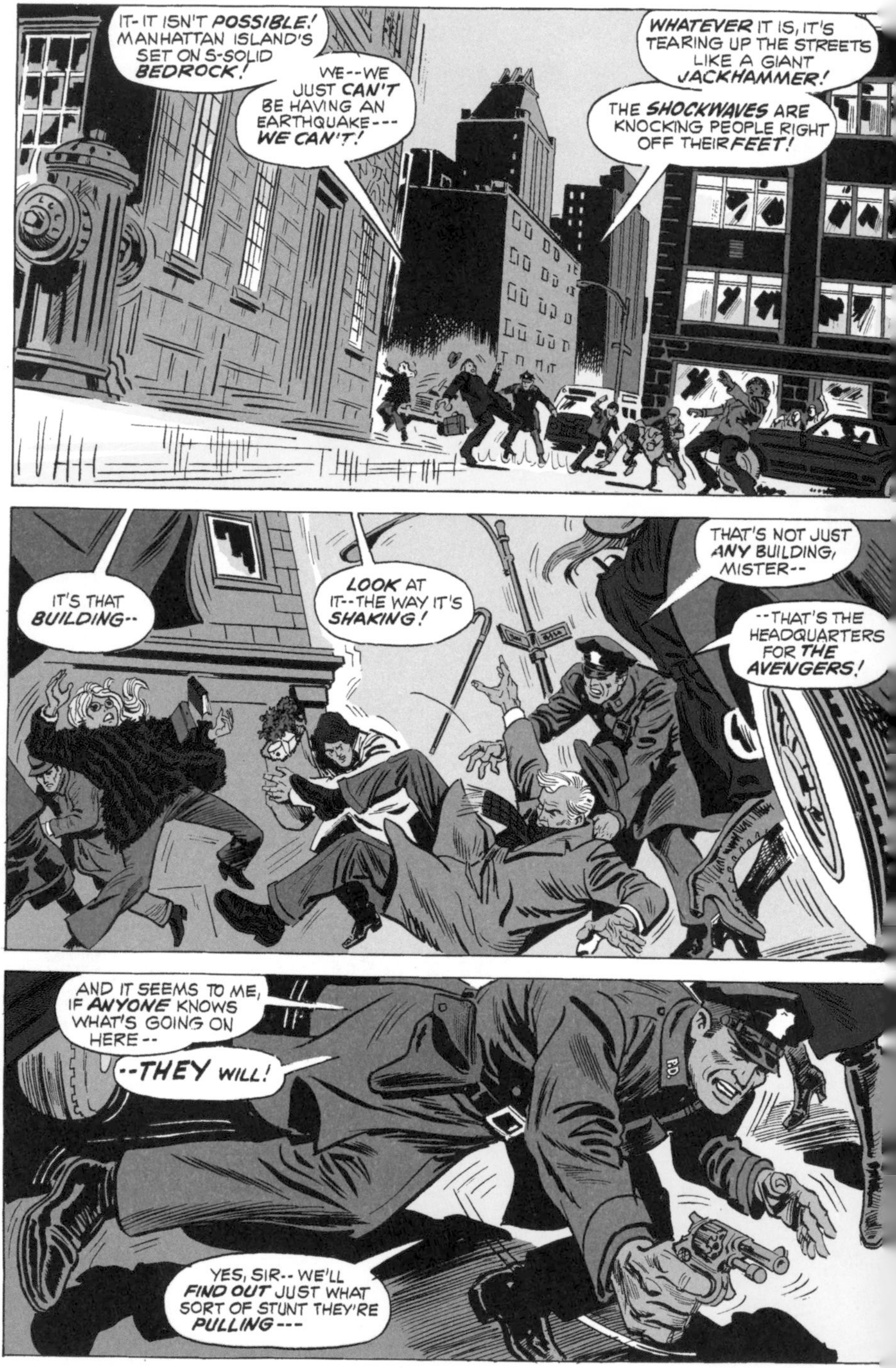
IT-IT ISN'T POSSIBLE! MANHATTAN ISLAND'S SET ON S-SOLID BEDROCK!
WE--WE JUST CAN'T BE HAVING AN EARTHQUAKE--- WE CAN'T!
WHATEVER IT IS, IT'S TEARING UP THE STREETS LIKE A GIANT JACKHAMMER!
THE SHOCKWAVES ARE KNOCKING PEOPLE RIGHT OFF THEIR FEET!
IT'S THAT BUILDING--
LOOK AT IT--THE WAY IT'S SHAKING!
THAT'S NOT JUST ANY BUILDING, MISTER--
--THAT'S THE HEADQUARTERS FOR THE AVENGERS!
AND IT SEEMS TO ME, IF ANYONE KNOWS WHAT'S GOING ON HERE--
--THEY WILL!
YES, SIR--WE'LL FIND OUT JUST WHAT SORT OF STUNT THEY'RE PULLING---

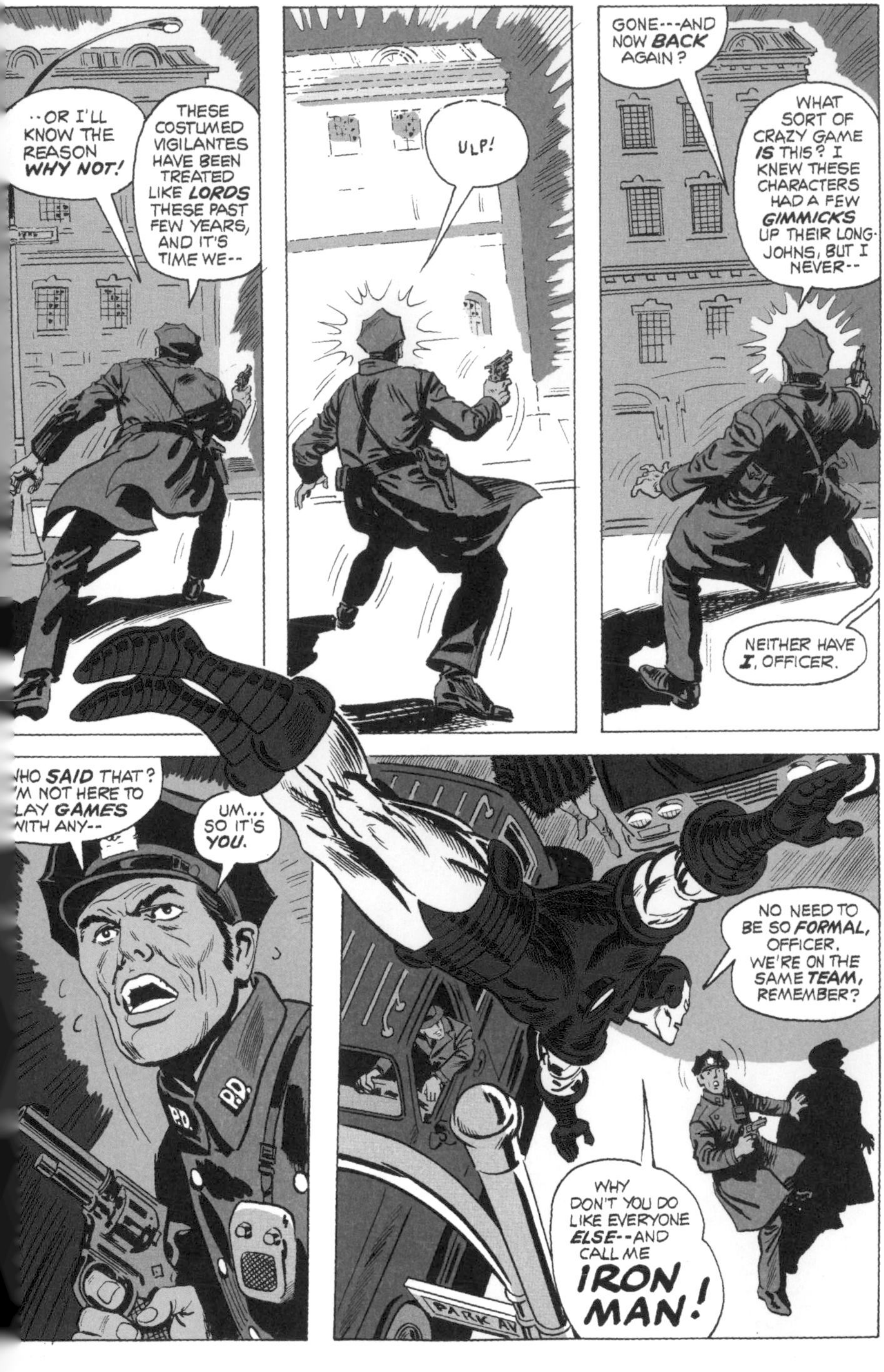
--OR I'LL KNOW THE REASON WHY NOT!
THESE COSTUMED VIGILANTES HAVE BEEN TREATED LIKE LORDS THESE PAST FEW YEARS, AND IT'S TIME WE--
ULP!
GONE---AND NOW BACK AGAIN?
WHAT SORT OF CRAZY GAME IS THIS? I KNEW THESE CHARACTERS HAD A FEW GIMMICKS UP THEIR LONG-JOHNS, BUT I NEVER--
NEITHER HAVE I, OFFICER.
WHO SAID THAT? I'M NOT HERE TO PLAY GAMES WITH ANY--
UM... SO IT'S YOU.
NO NEED TO BE SO FORMAL, OFFICER. WE'RE ON THE SAME TEAM, REMEMBER?
WHY DON'T YOU DO LIKE EVERYONE ELSE--AND CALL ME IRON MAN!
P.D.
PARK AV

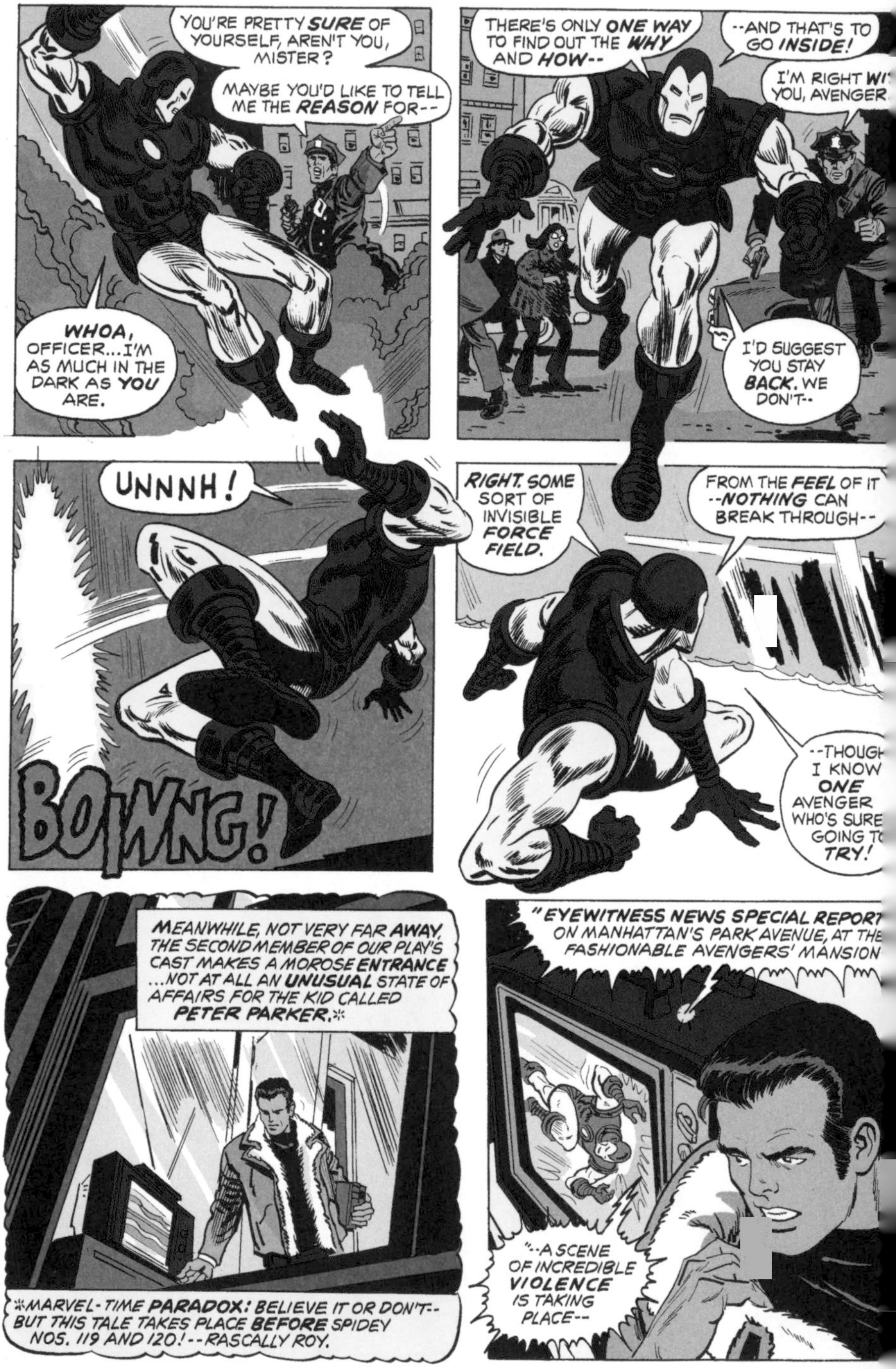
YOU'RE PRETTY SURE OF YOURSELF, AREN'T YOU, MISTER?
MAYBE YOU'D LIKE TO TELL ME THE REASON FOR--
WHOA, OFFICER...I'M AS MUCH IN THE DARK AS YOU ARE.
THERE'S ONLY ONE WAY TO FIND OUT THE WHY AND HOW--
--AND THAT'S TO GO INSIDE!
I'M RIGHT WI YOU, AVENGER
I'D SUGGEST YOU STAY BACK. WE DON'T--
UNNNH!
BOIWNG!
RIGHT. SOME SORT OF INVISIBLE FORCE FIELD.
FROM THE FEEL OF IT --NOTHING CAN BREAK THROUGH--
--THOUG I KNOW ONE AVENGER WHO'S SURE GOING T TRY!
MEANWHILE, NOT VERY FAR AWAY, THE SECOND MEMBER OF OUR PLAY'S CAST MAKES A MOROSE ENTRANCE ...NOT AT ALL AN UNUSUAL STATE OF AFFAIRS FOR THE KID CALLED PETER PARKER.*
*MARVEL-TIME PARADOX: BELIEVE IT OR DON'T--BUT THIS TALE TAKES PLACE BEFORE SPIDEY NOS. 119 AND 120!--RASCALLY ROY.
"EYEWITNESS NEWS SPECIAL REPORT ON MANHATTAN'S PARK AVENUE, AT THE FASHIONABLE AVENGERS' MANSION
"--A SCENE OF INCREDIBLE VIOLENCE IS TAKING PLACE--

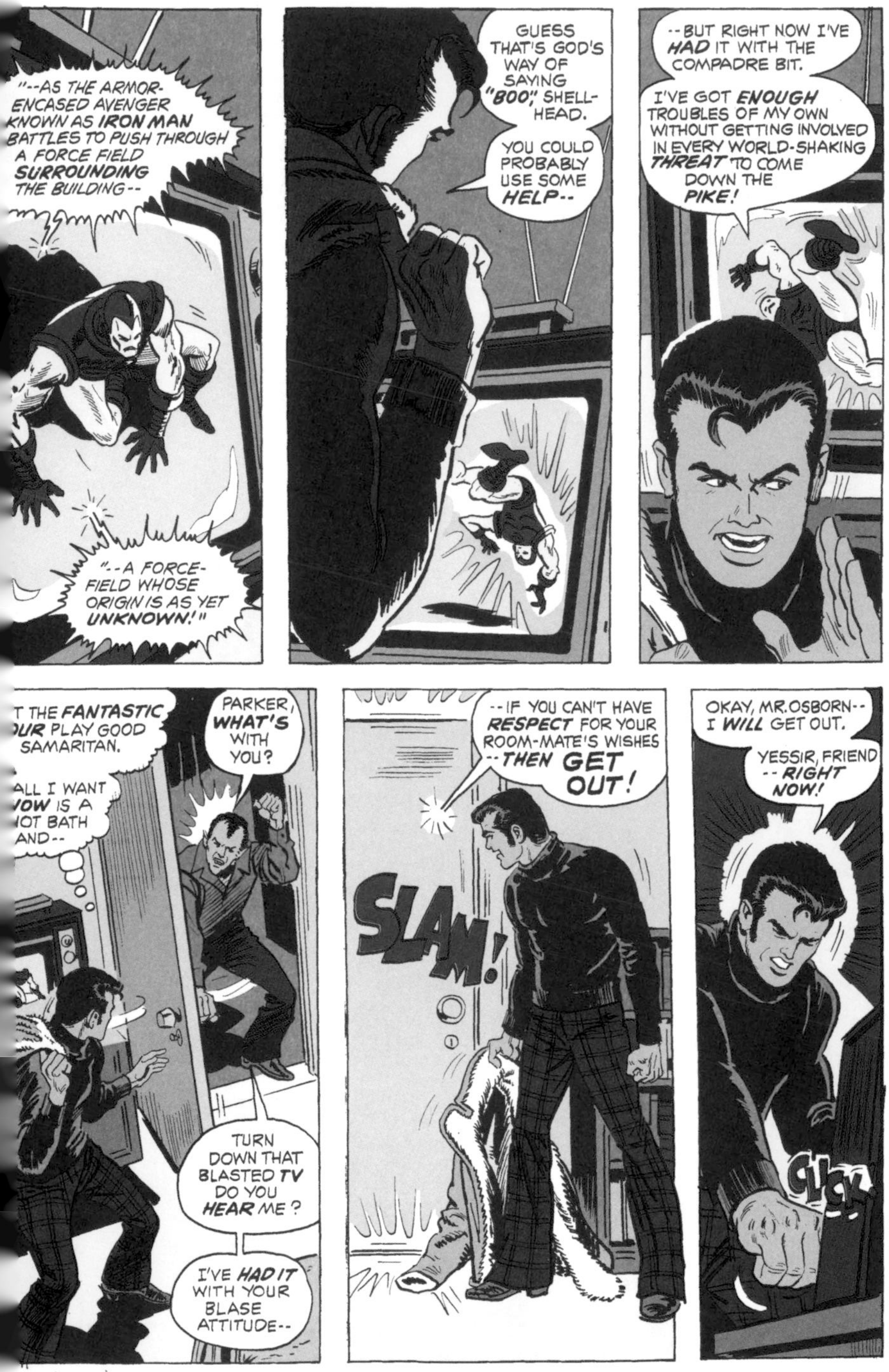
"--AS THE ARMOR-ENCASED AVENGER KNOWN AS IRON MAN BATTLES TO PUSH THROUGH A FORCE FIELD SURROUNDING THE BUILDING--
"--A FORCE-FIELD WHOSE ORIGIN IS AS YET UNKNOWN!"
GUESS THAT'S GOD'S WAY OF SAYING "BOO," SHELL-HEAD.
YOU COULD PROBABLY USE SOME HELP--
--BUT RIGHT NOW I'VE HAD IT WITH THE COMPADRE BIT.
I'VE GOT ENOUGH TROUBLES OF MY OWN WITHOUT GETTING INVOLVED IN EVERY WORLD-SHAKING THREAT TO COME DOWN THE PIKE!
T THE FANTASTIC OUR PLAY GOOD SAMARITAN.
ALL I WANT OW IS A OT BATH AND--
PARKER, WHAT'S WITH YOU?
TURN DOWN THAT BLASTED TV DO YOU HEAR ME?
I'VE HAD IT WITH YOUR BLASE ATTITUDE--
--IF YOU CAN'T HAVE RESPECT FOR YOUR ROOM-MATE'S WISHES --THEN GET OUT!
SLAM!
OKAY, MR. OSBORN-- I WILL GET OUT.
YESSIR, FRIEND --RIGHT NOW!
CLICK

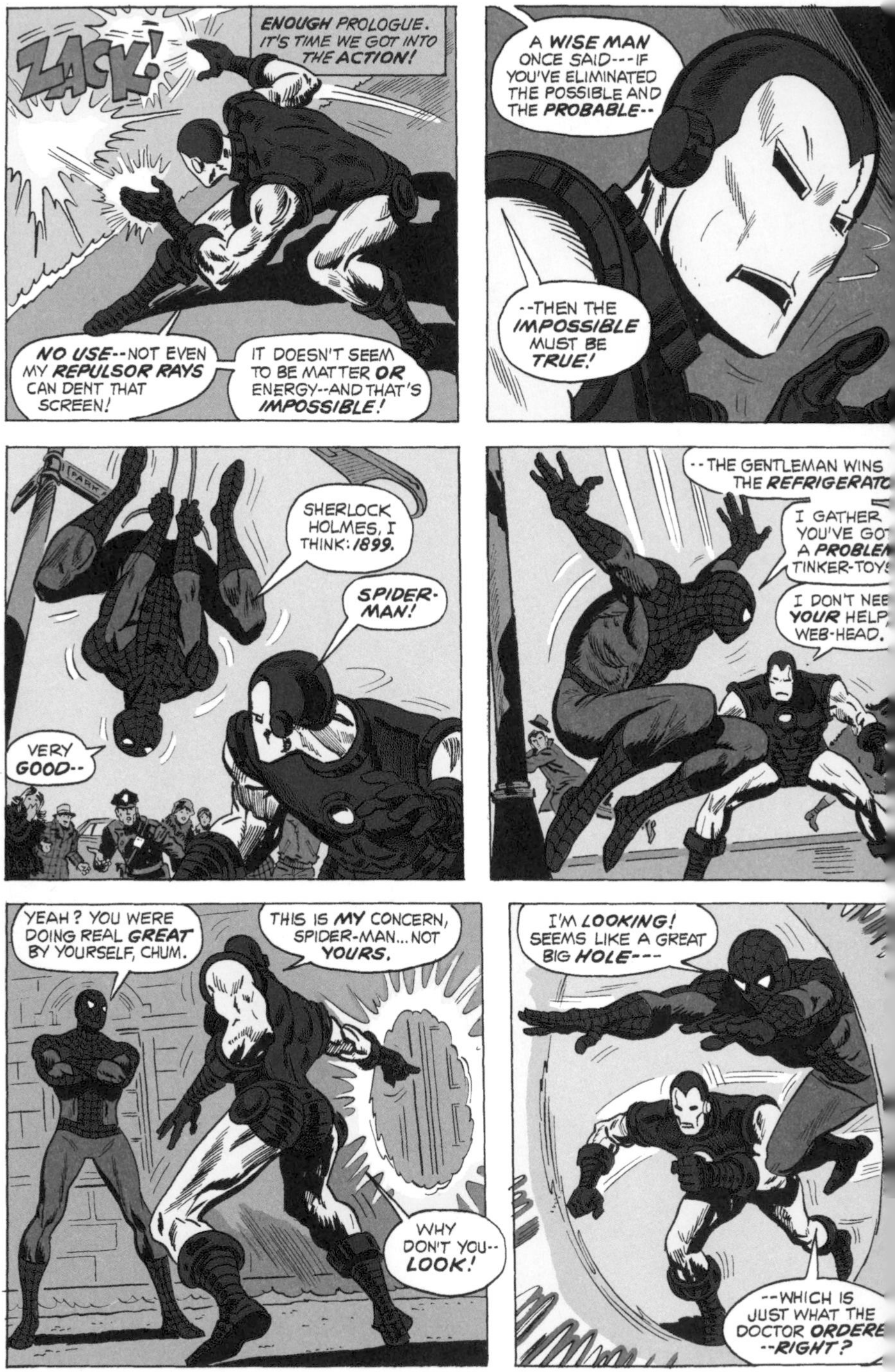

ZACK!
ENOUGH PROLOGUE. IT'S TIME WE GOT INTO THE ACTION!
NO USE--NOT EVEN MY REPULSOR RAYS CAN DENT THAT SCREEN!
IT DOESN'T SEEM TO BE MATTER OR ENERGY--AND THAT'S IMPOSSIBLE!
A WISE MAN ONCE SAID---IF YOU'VE ELIMINATED THE POSSIBLE AND THE PROBABLE--
--THEN THE IMPOSSIBLE MUST BE TRUE!
PARK
SHERLOCK HOLMES, I THINK: 1899.
SPIDER-MAN!
VERY GOOD--
--THE GENTLEMAN WINS THE REFRIGERATO
I GATHER YOU'VE GOT A PROBLEM TINKER-TOYS
I DON'T NEE YOUR HELP WEB-HEAD.
YEAH? YOU WERE DOING REAL GREAT BY YOURSELF, CHUM.
THIS IS MY CONCERN, SPIDER-MAN... NOT YOURS.
WHY DON'T YOU--LOOK!
I'M LOOKING! SEEMS LIKE A GREAT BIG HOLE---
--WHICH IS JUST WHAT THE DOCTOR ORDERE --RIGHT?

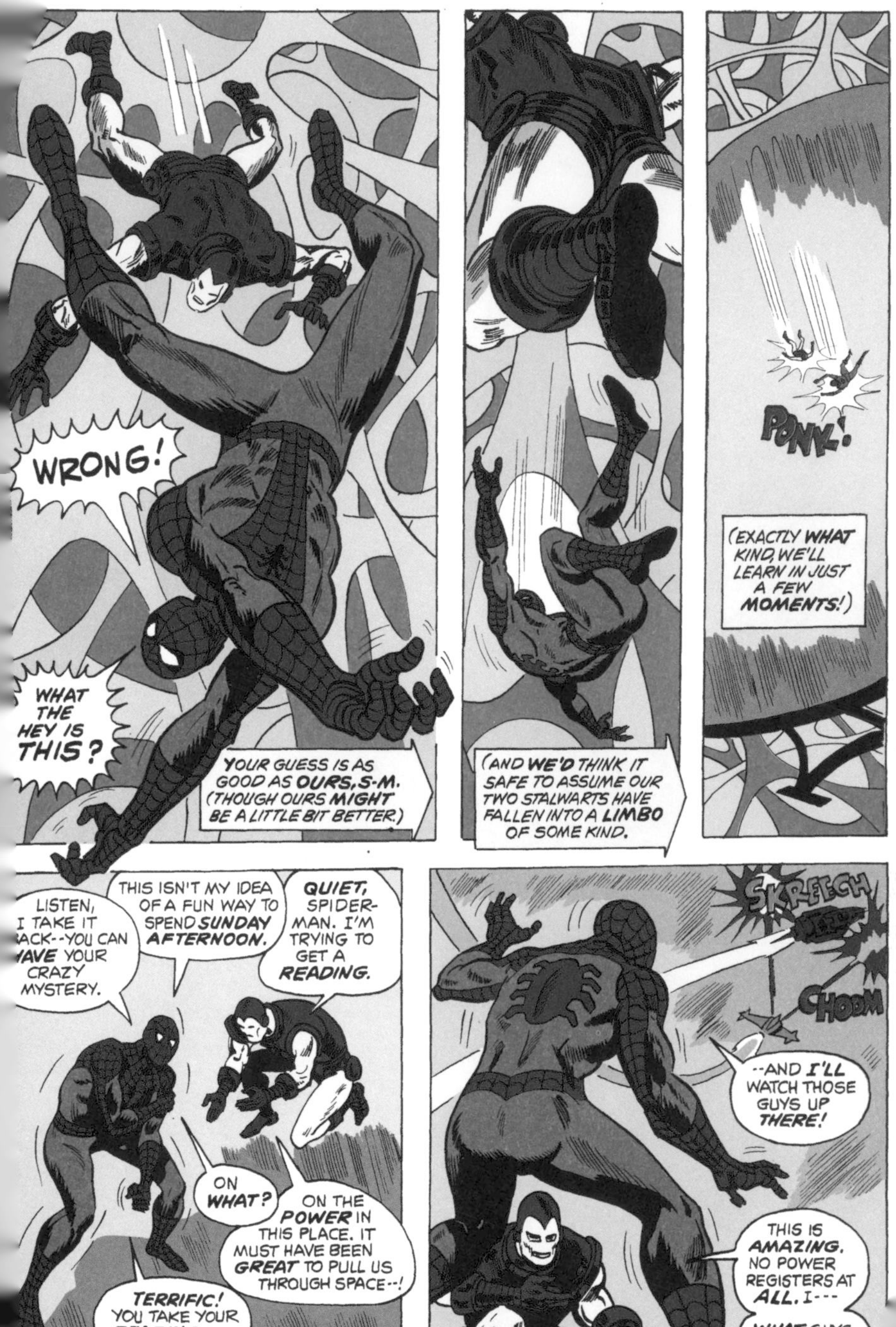
WRONG!
WHAT THE HEY IS THIS?
YOUR GUESS IS AS GOOD AS OURS, S-M. (THOUGH OURS MIGHT BE A LITTLE BIT BETTER.)
(AND WE'D THINK IT SAFE TO ASSUME OUR TWO STALWARTS HAVE FALLEN INTO A LIMBO OF SOME KIND.
PONK!
(EXACTLY WHAT KIND, WE'LL LEARN IN JUST A FEW MOMENTS!)
LISTEN, I TAKE IT BACK--YOU CAN HAVE YOUR CRAZY MYSTERY.
THIS ISN'T MY IDEA OF A FUN WAY TO SPEND SUNDAY AFTERNOON.
QUIET, SPIDER-MAN. I'M TRYING TO GET A READING.
ON WHAT?
ON THE POWER IN THIS PLACE. IT MUST HAVE BEEN GREAT TO PULL US THROUGH SPACE--!
TERRIFIC! YOU TAKE YOUR READINGS--
SKREECH
CHOOM
--AND I'LL WATCH THOSE GUYS UP THERE!
THIS IS AMAZING. NO POWER REGISTERS AT ALL. I---
WHAT GUYS--WHERE?

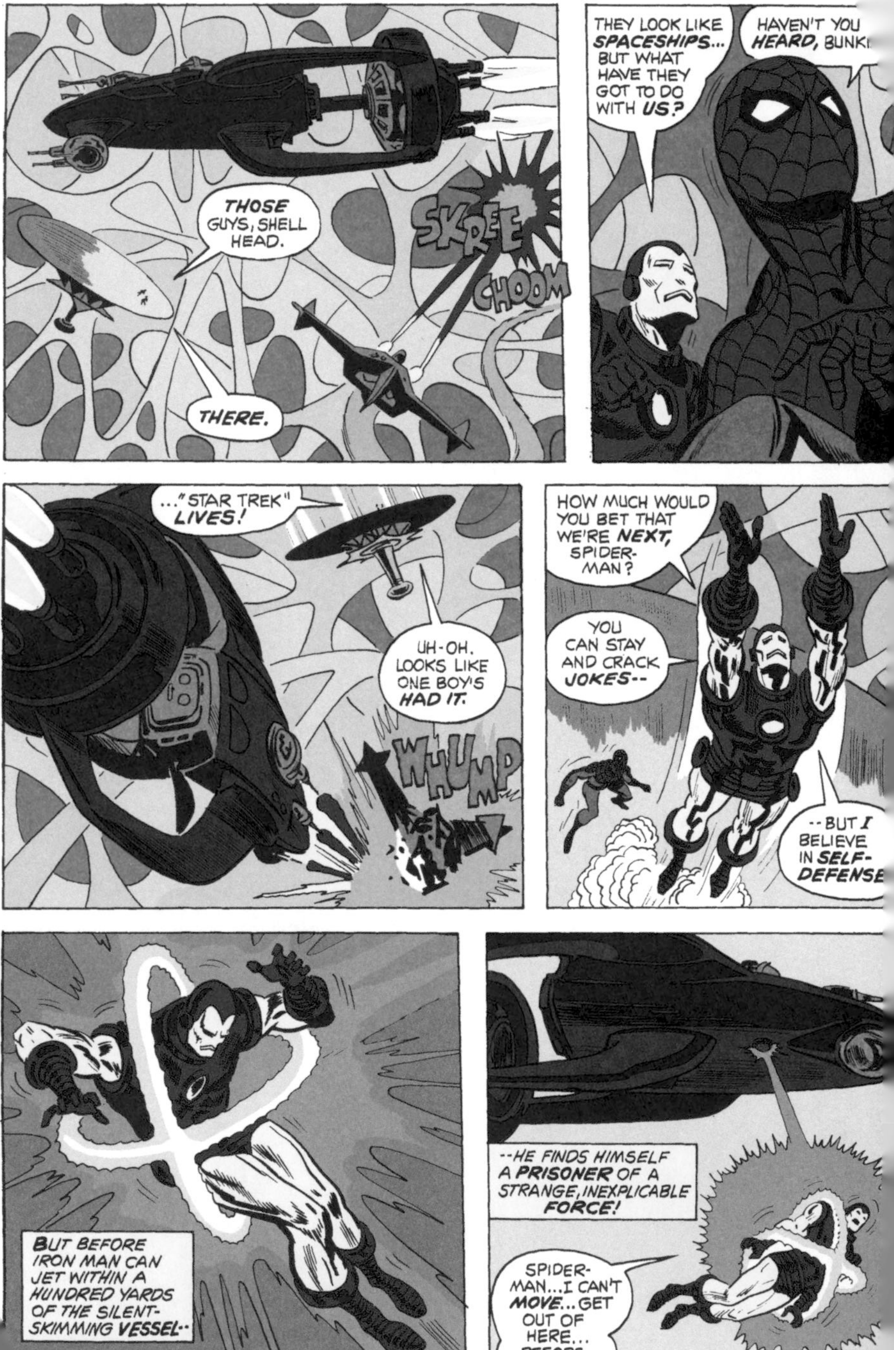

THOSE GUYS, SHELL HEAD.
SKREE
CHOOM
THERE.
THEY LOOK LIKE SPACESHIPS... BUT WHAT HAVE THEY GOT TO DO WITH US?
HAVEN'T YOU HEARD, BUNKI
..."STAR TREK" LIVES!
UH-OH. LOOKS LIKE ONE BOY'S HAD IT.
WHUMP
HOW MUCH WOULD YOU BET THAT WE'RE NEXT, SPIDER-MAN?
YOU CAN STAY AND CRACK JOKES--
--BUT I BELIEVE IN SELF-DEFENSE
BUT BEFORE IRON MAN CAN JET WITHIN A HUNDRED YARDS OF THE SILENT-SKIMMING VESSEL--
--HE FINDS HIMSELF A PRISONER OF A STRANGE, INEXPLICABLE FORCE!
SPIDER-MAN...I CAN'T MOVE...GET OUT OF HERE... BEFORE...

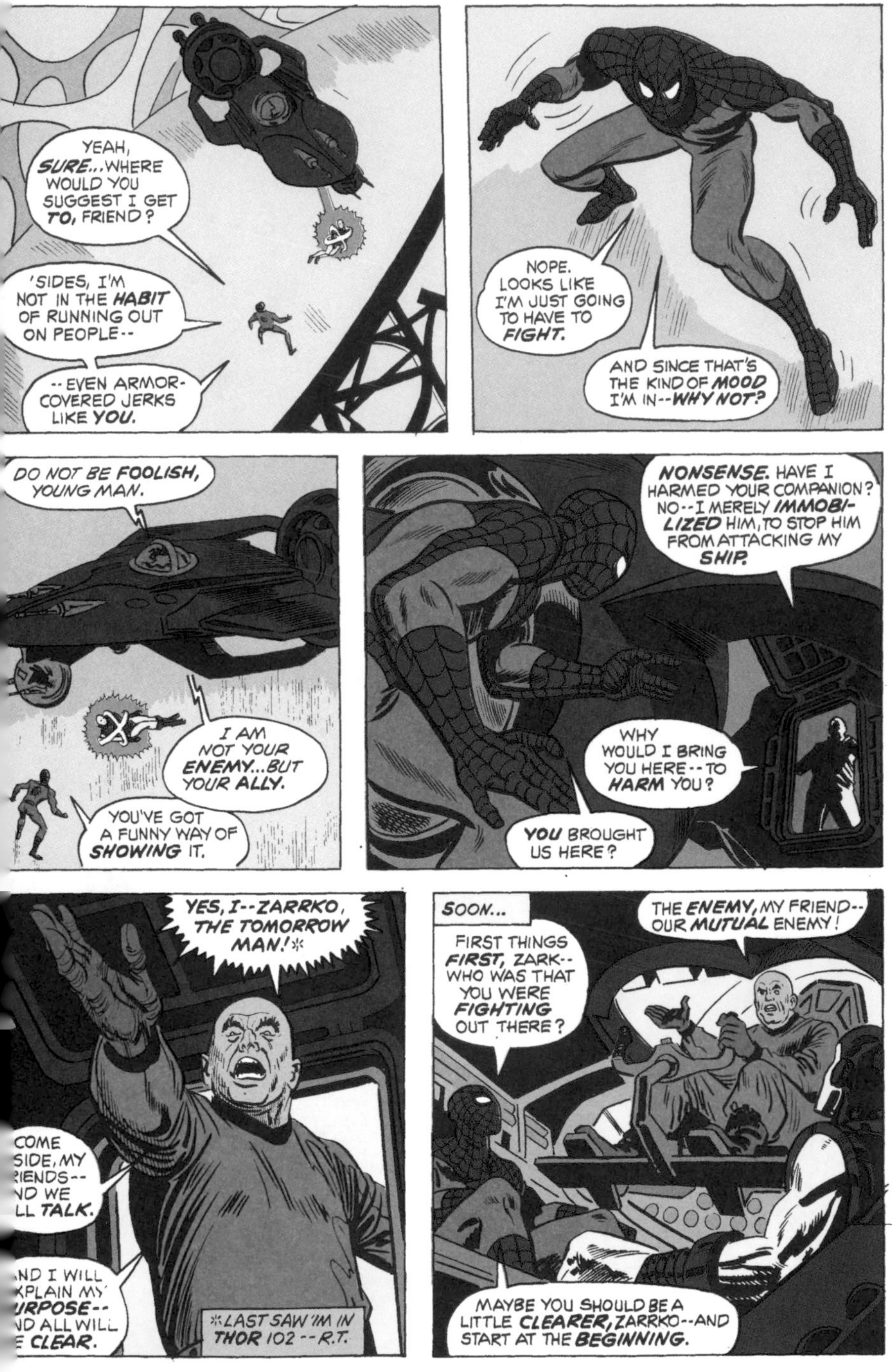

YEAH, SURE... WHERE WOULD YOU SUGGEST I GET TO, FRIEND?
'SIDES, I'M NOT IN THE HABIT OF RUNNING OUT ON PEOPLE--
--EVEN ARMOR-COVERED JERKS LIKE YOU.
NOPE. LOOKS LIKE I'M JUST GOING TO HAVE TO FIGHT.
AND SINCE THAT'S THE KIND OF MOOD I'M IN--WHY NOT?
DO NOT BE FOOLISH, YOUNG MAN.
I AM NOT YOUR ENEMY...BUT YOUR ALLY.
YOU'VE GOT A FUNNY WAY OF SHOWING IT.
NONSENSE. HAVE I HARMED YOUR COMPANION? NO--I MERELY IMMOBILIZED HIM, TO STOP HIM FROM ATTACKING MY SHIP.
YOU BROUGHT US HERE?
WHY WOULD I BRING YOU HERE--TO HARM YOU?
YES, I--ZARRKO, THE TOMORROW MAN!*
COME SIDE, MY RIENDS-- ND WE LL TALK.
ND I WILL XPLAIN MY URPOSE-- ND ALL WILL CLEAR.
*LAST SAW 'IM IN THOR 102 --R.T.
SOON...
FIRST THINGS FIRST, ZARK-- WHO WAS THAT YOU WERE FIGHTING OUT THERE?
THE ENEMY, MY FRIEND-- OUR MUTUAL ENEMY!
MAYBE YOU SHOULD BE A LITTLE CLEARER, ZARRKO--AND START AT THE BEGINNING.

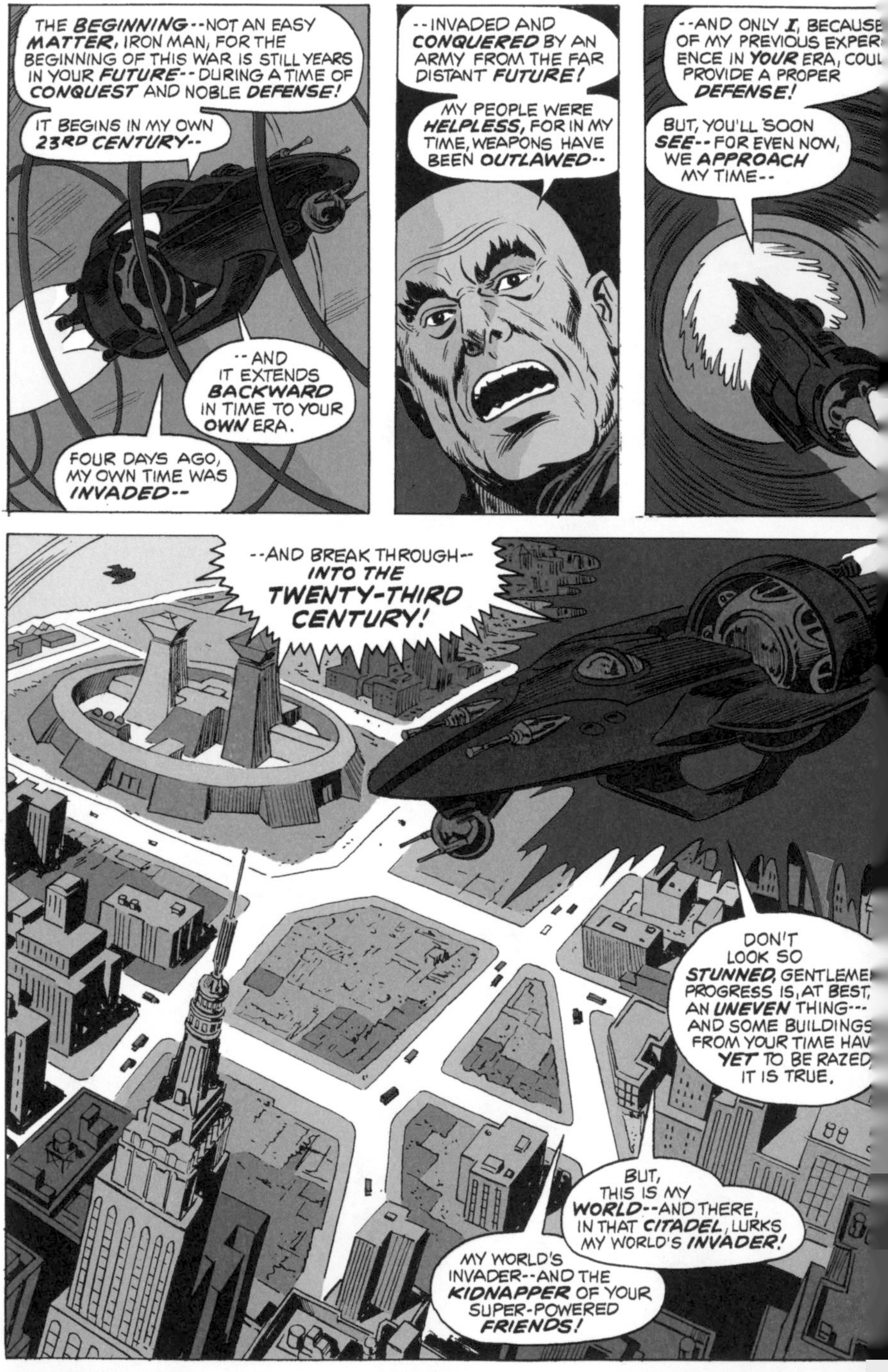
THE BEGINNING--NOT AN EASY MATTER, IRON MAN, FOR THE BEGINNING OF THIS WAR IS STILL YEARS IN YOUR FUTURE--DURING A TIME OF CONQUEST AND NOBLE DEFENSE!
IT BEGINS IN MY OWN 23RD CENTURY--
--AND IT EXTENDS BACKWARD IN TIME TO YOUR OWN ERA.
FOUR DAYS AGO, MY OWN TIME WAS INVADED--
--INVADED AND CONQUERED BY AN ARMY FROM THE FAR DISTANT FUTURE!
MY PEOPLE WERE HELPLESS, FOR IN MY TIME, WEAPONS HAVE BEEN OUTLAWED--
--AND ONLY I, BECAUSE OF MY PREVIOUS EXPER ENCE IN YOUR ERA, COUL PROVIDE A PROPER DEFENSE!
BUT, YOU'LL SOON SEE--FOR EVEN NOW, WE APPROACH MY TIME--
--AND BREAK THROUGH--INTO THE TWENTY-THIRD CENTURY!
DON'T LOOK SO STUNNED, GENTLEME PROGRESS IS, AT BEST, AN UNEVEN THING---AND SOME BUILDINGS FROM YOUR TIME HAV YET TO BE RAZED, IT IS TRUE.
BUT, THIS IS MY WORLD--AND THERE, IN THAT CITADEL, LURKS MY WORLD'S INVADER!
MY WORLD'S INVADER--AND THE KIDNAPPER OF YOUR SUPER-POWERED FRIENDS!

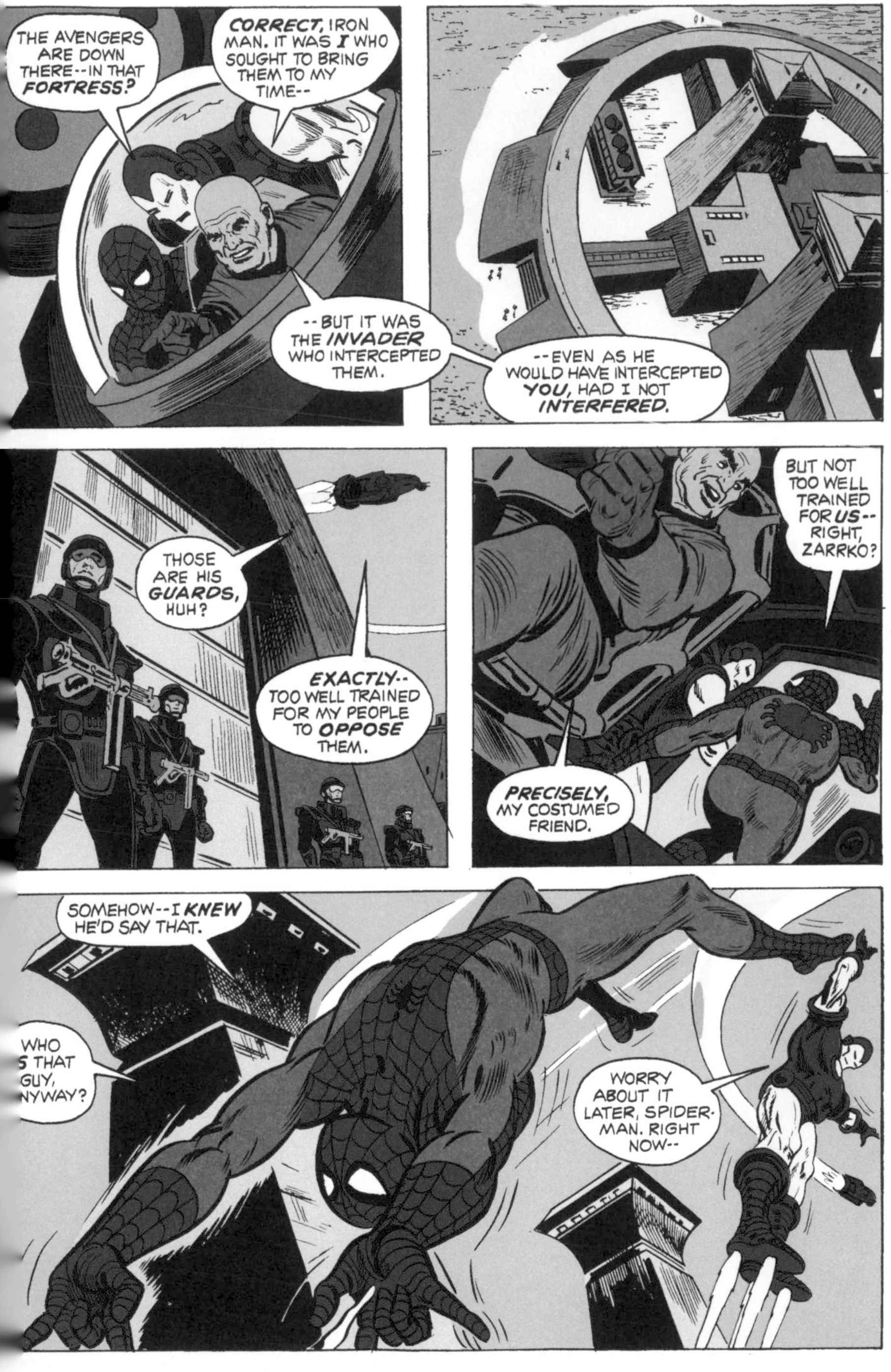

THE AVENGERS ARE DOWN THERE--IN THAT FORTRESS?
CORRECT, IRON MAN. IT WAS I WHO SOUGHT TO BRING THEM TO MY TIME--
--BUT IT WAS THE INVADER WHO INTERCEPTED THEM.
--EVEN AS HE WOULD HAVE INTERCEPTED YOU, HAD I NOT INTERFERED.
THOSE ARE HIS GUARDS, HUH?
EXACTLY-- TOO WELL TRAINED FOR MY PEOPLE TO OPPOSE THEM.
BUT NOT TOO WELL TRAINED FOR US-- RIGHT, ZARRKO?
PRECISELY, MY COSTUMED FRIEND.
SOMEHOW--I KNEW HE'D SAY THAT.
WHO S THAT GUY, NYWAY?
WORRY ABOUT IT LATER, SPIDER-MAN. RIGHT NOW--

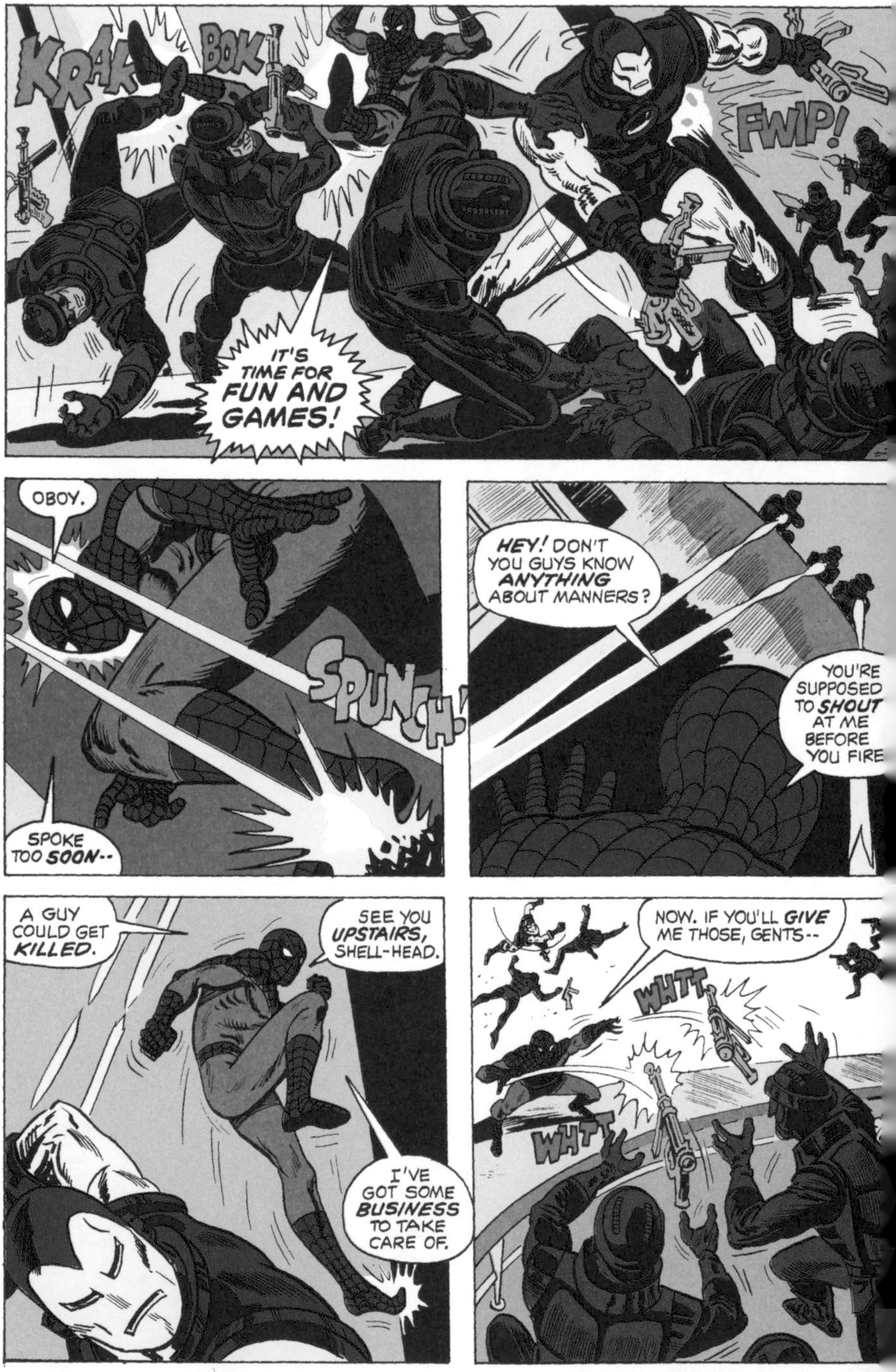
KRAK
BOK
FWIP!
IT'S TIME FOR FUN AND GAMES!
OBOY.
SPUNCH!
SPOKE TOO SOON--
HEY! DON'T YOU GUYS KNOW ANYTHING ABOUT MANNERS?
YOU'RE SUPPOSED TO SHOUT AT ME BEFORE YOU FIRE
A GUY COULD GET KILLED.
SEE YOU UPSTAIRS, SHELL-HEAD.
I'VE GOT SOME BUSINESS TO TAKE CARE OF.
NOW. IF YOU'LL GIVE ME THOSE, GENTS--
WHTT
WHTT

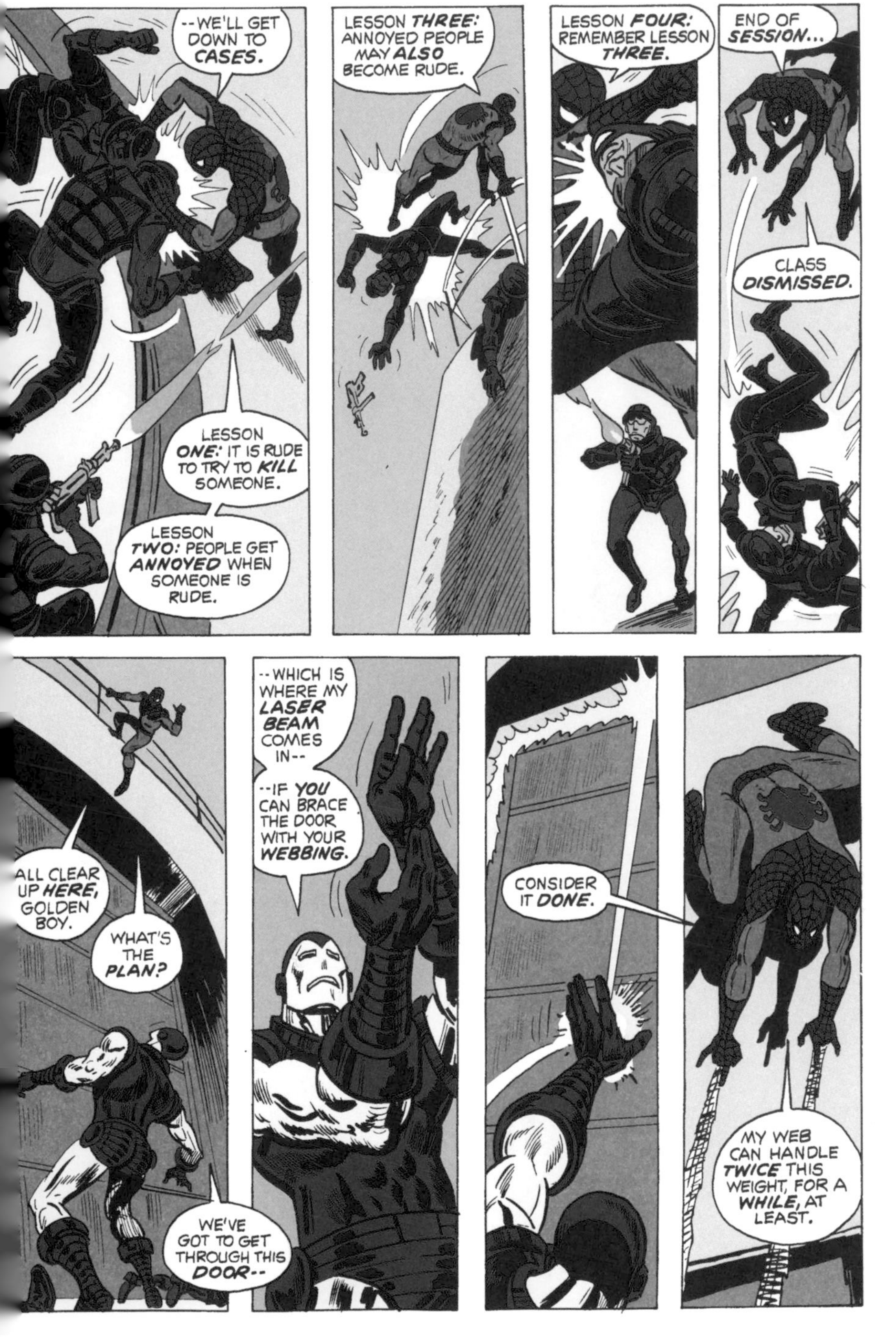
--WE'LL GET DOWN TO CASES.
LESSON ONE: IT IS RUDE TO TRY TO KILL SOMEONE.
LESSON TWO: PEOPLE GET ANNOYED WHEN SOMEONE IS RUDE.
LESSON THREE: ANNOYED PEOPLE MAY ALSO BECOME RUDE.
LESSON FOUR: REMEMBER LESSON THREE.
END OF SESSION...
CLASS DISMISSED.
ALL CLEAR UP HERE, GOLDEN BOY.
WHAT'S THE PLAN?
WE'VE GOT TO GET THROUGH THIS DOOR--
--WHICH IS WHERE MY LASER BEAM COMES IN--
--IF YOU CAN BRACE THE DOOR WITH YOUR WEBBING.
CONSIDER IT DONE.
MY WEB CAN HANDLE TWICE THIS WEIGHT, FOR A WHILE, AT LEAST.

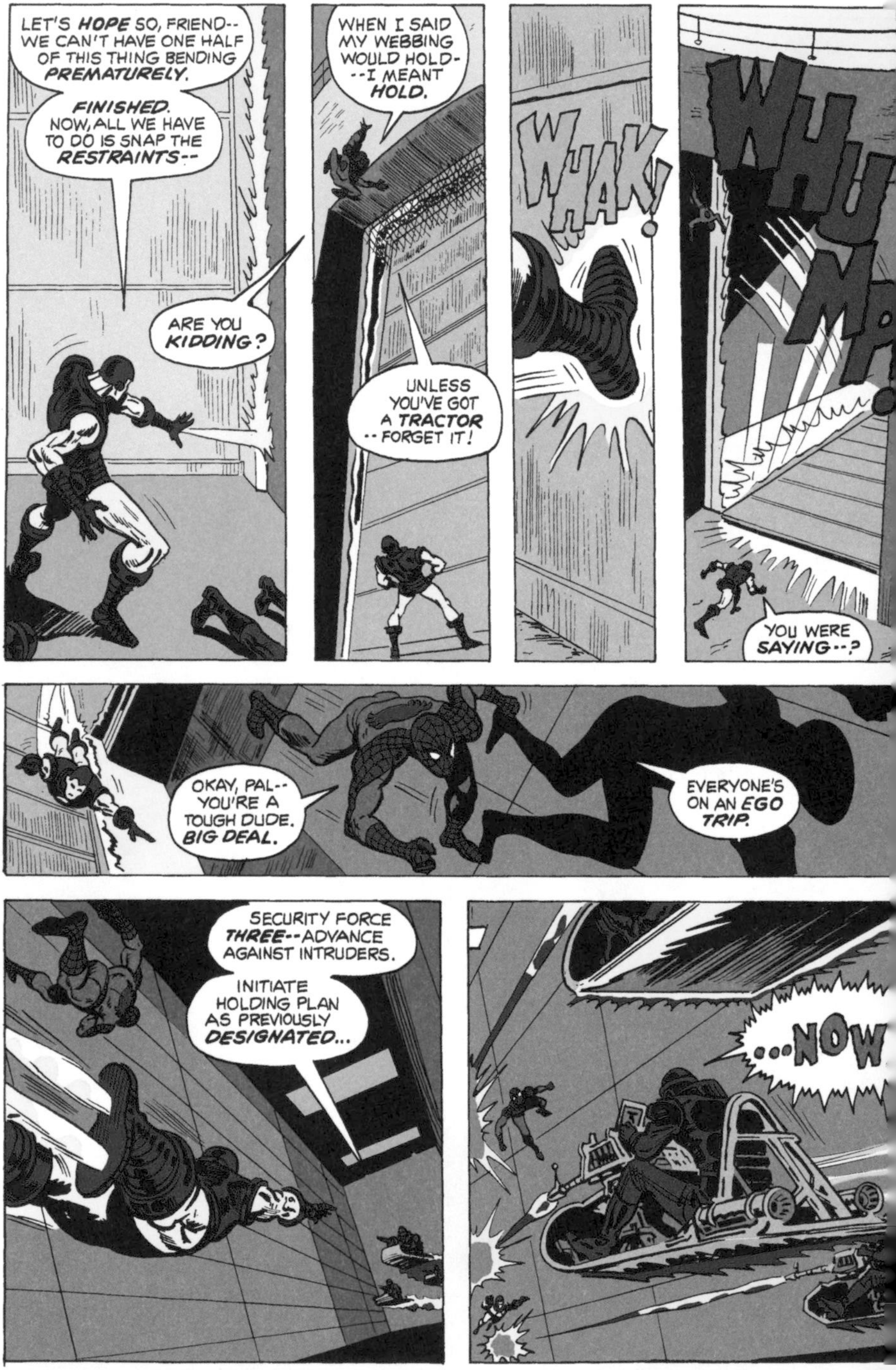
LET'S HOPE SO, FRIEND-- WE CAN'T HAVE ONE HALF OF THIS THING BENDING PREMATURELY.
FINISHED. NOW, ALL WE HAVE TO DO IS SNAP THE RESTRAINTS--
ARE YOU KIDDING?
WHEN I SAID MY WEBBING WOULD HOLD- --I MEANT HOLD.
UNLESS YOU'VE GOT A TRACTOR --FORGET IT!
WHAK!
WHUMP!
YOU WERE SAYING--?
OKAY, PAL-- YOU'RE A TOUGH DUDE. BIG DEAL.
EVERYONE'S ON AN EGO TRIP.
SECURITY FORCE THREE--ADVANCE AGAINST INTRUDERS.
INITIATE HOLDING PLAN AS PREVIOUSLY DESIGNATED...
...NOW

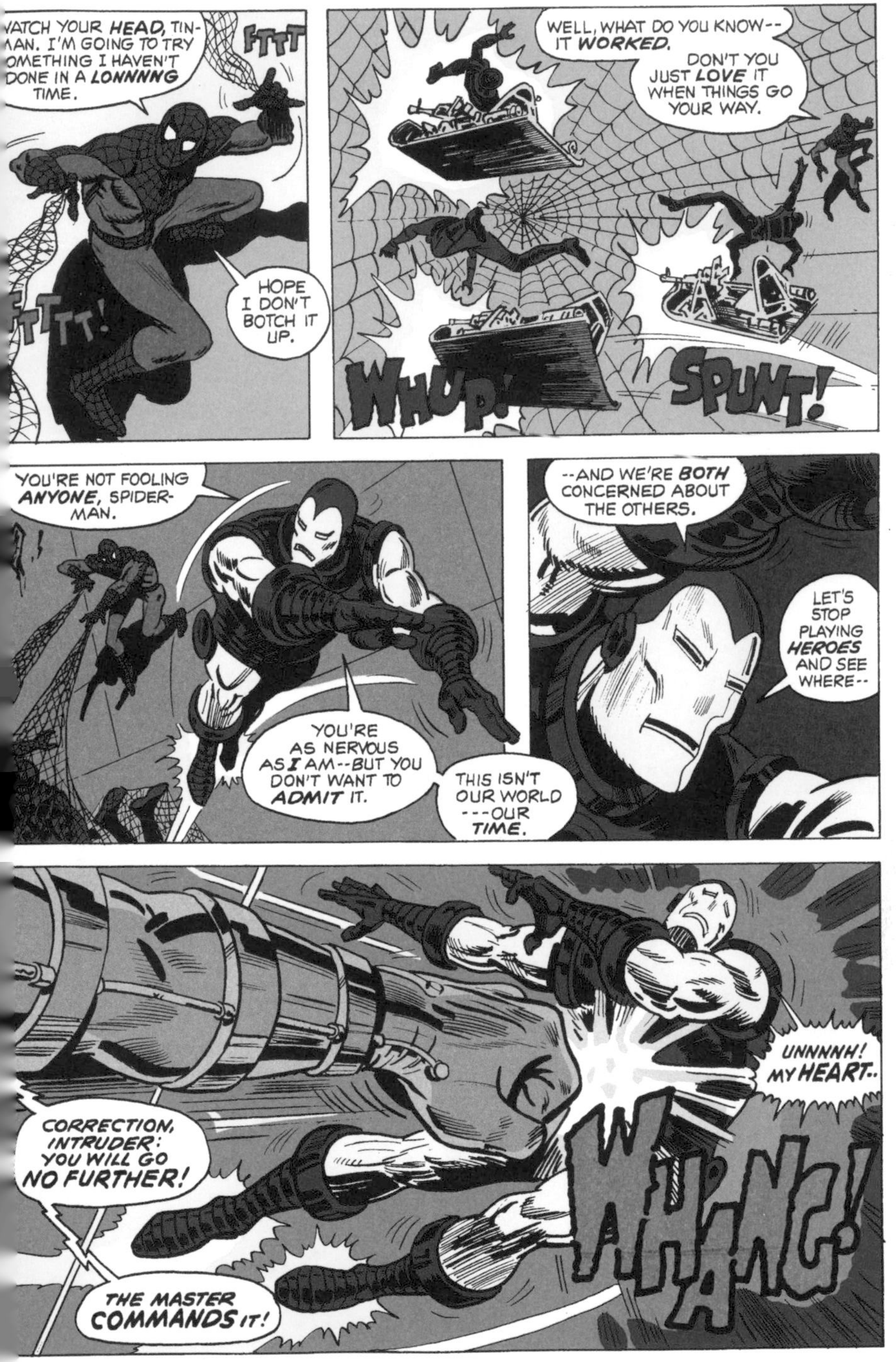
WATCH YOUR HEAD, TIN-MAN. I'M GOING TO TRY SOMETHING I HAVEN'T DONE IN A LONNNNG TIME.
FTTT
FTTTTT!
HOPE I DON'T BOTCH IT UP.
WELL, WHAT DO YOU KNOW-- IT WORKED.
DON'T YOU JUST LOVE IT WHEN THINGS GO YOUR WAY.
WHUP!
SPUNT!
YOU'RE NOT FOOLING ANYONE, SPIDER-MAN.
YOU'RE AS NERVOUS AS I AM--BUT YOU DON'T WANT TO ADMIT IT.
THIS ISN'T OUR WORLD ---OUR TIME.
--AND WE'RE BOTH CONCERNED ABOUT THE OTHERS.
LET'S STOP PLAYING HEROES AND SEE WHERE--
UNNNNH! MY HEART..
CORRECTION, INTRUDER: YOU WILL GO NO FURTHER!
THE MASTER COMMANDS IT!
WHANG!

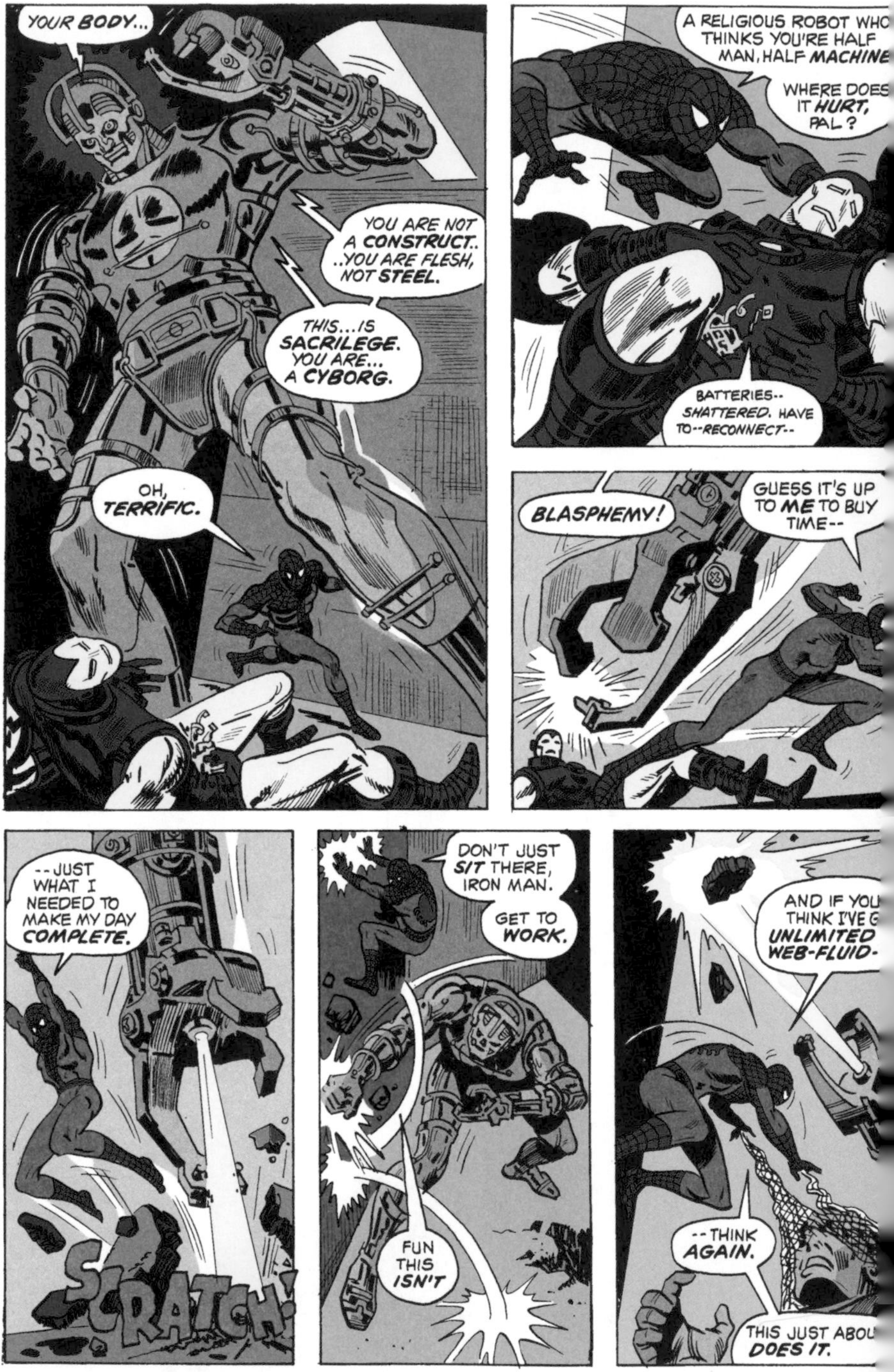
YOUR BODY...
YOU ARE NOT A CONSTRUCT.. ..YOU ARE FLESH, NOT STEEL.
THIS...IS SACRILEGE. YOU ARE... A CYBORG.
OH, TERRIFIC.
A RELIGIOUS ROBOT WHO THINKS YOU'RE HALF MAN, HALF MACHINE
WHERE DOES IT HURT, PAL?
BATTERIES-- SHATTERED. HAVE TO--RECONNECT--
BLASPHEMY!
GUESS IT'S UP TO ME TO BUY TIME--
--JUST WHAT I NEEDED TO MAKE MY DAY COMPLETE.
SCRATCH
DON'T JUST SIT THERE, IRON MAN.
GET TO WORK.
FUN THIS ISN'T
AND IF YOU THINK I'VE G UNLIMITED WEB-FLUID-
--THINK AGAIN.
THIS JUST ABOU DOES IT.

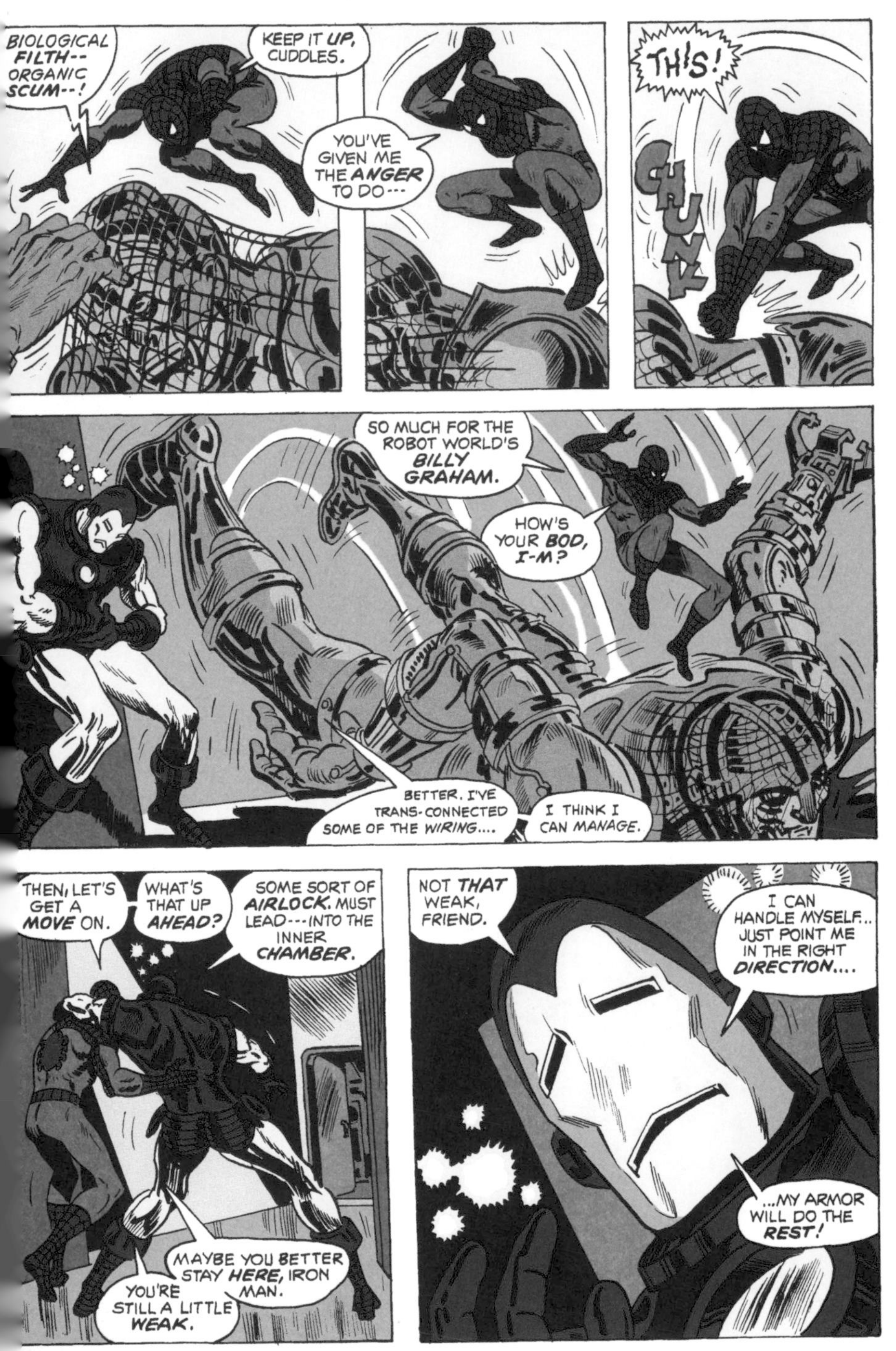
BIOLOGICAL FILTH-- ORGANIC SCUM--!
KEEP IT UP, CUDDLES.
YOU'VE GIVEN ME THE ANGER TO DO---
THIS!
CHUNK
SO MUCH FOR THE ROBOT WORLD'S BILLY GRAHAM.
HOW'S YOUR BOD, I-M?
BETTER. I'VE TRANS-CONNECTED SOME OF THE WIRING....
I THINK I CAN MANAGE.
THEN, LET'S GET A MOVE ON.
WHAT'S THAT UP AHEAD?
SOME SORT OF AIRLOCK. MUST LEAD---INTO THE INNER CHAMBER.
MAYBE YOU BETTER STAY HERE, IRON MAN.
YOU'RE STILL A LITTLE WEAK.
NOT THAT WEAK, FRIEND.
I CAN HANDLE MYSELF... JUST POINT ME IN THE RIGHT DIRECTION....
...MY ARMOR WILL DO THE REST!

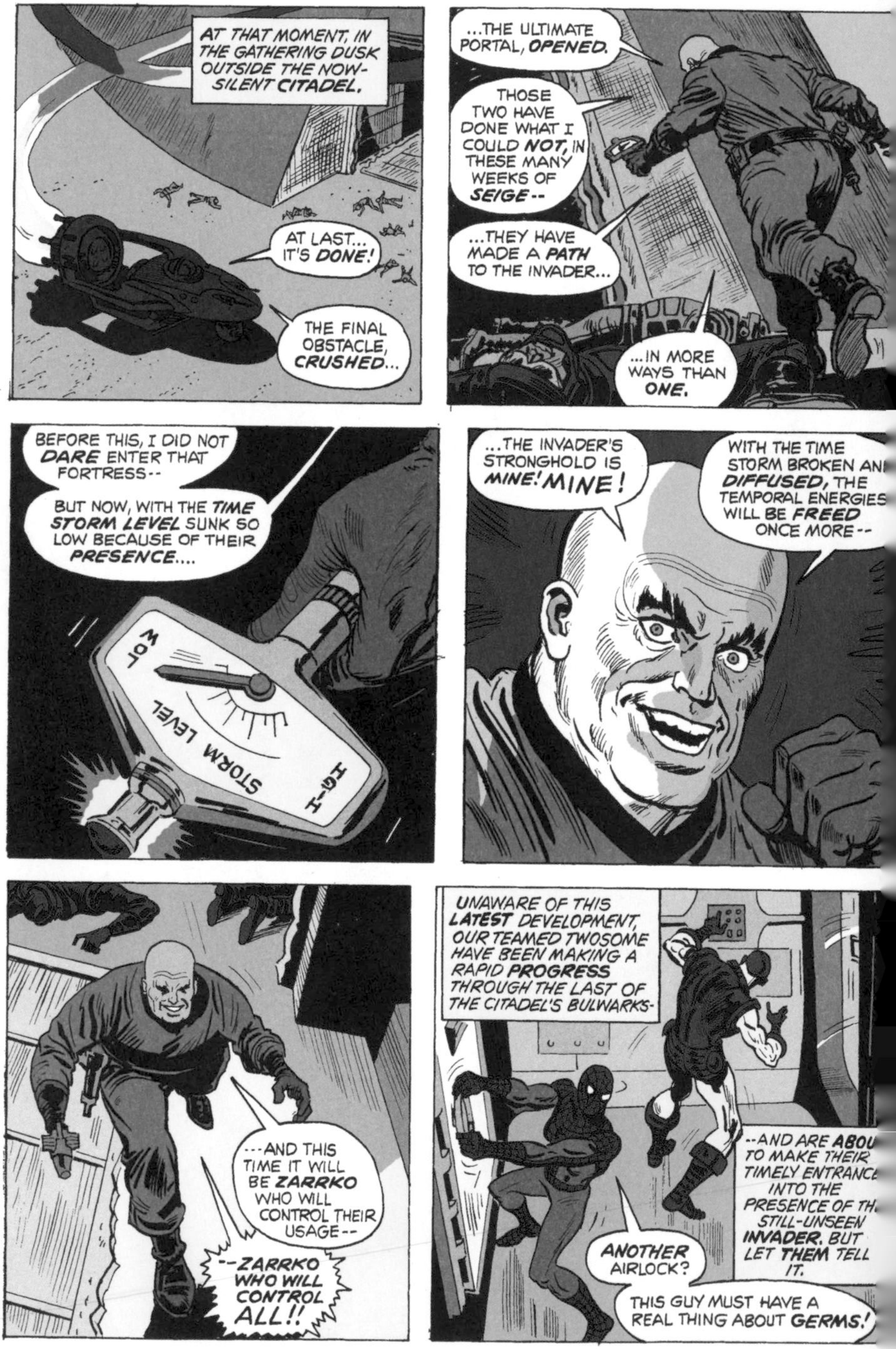

AT THAT MOMENT, IN THE GATHERING DUSK OUTSIDE THE NOW-SILENT CITADEL.
AT LAST... IT'S DONE!
THE FINAL OBSTACLE, CRUSHED...
...THE ULTIMATE PORTAL, OPENED.
THOSE TWO HAVE DONE WHAT I COULD NOT, IN THESE MANY WEEKS OF SEIGE--
...THEY HAVE MADE A PATH TO THE INVADER...
...IN MORE WAYS THAN ONE.
BEFORE THIS, I DID NOT DARE ENTER THAT FORTRESS--
BUT NOW, WITH THE TIME STORM LEVEL SUNK SO LOW BECAUSE OF THEIR PRESENCE....
LOW
STORM LEVEL
HIGH
...THE INVADER'S STRONGHOLD IS MINE! MINE!
WITH THE TIME STORM BROKEN AN DIFFUSED, THE TEMPORAL ENERGIES WILL BE FREED ONCE MORE--
---AND THIS TIME IT WILL BE ZARRKO WHO WILL CONTROL THEIR USAGE--
--ZARRKO WHO WILL CONTROL ALL!!
UNAWARE OF THIS LATEST DEVELOPMENT, OUR TEAMED TWOSOME HAVE BEEN MAKING A RAPID PROGRESS THROUGH THE LAST OF THE CITADEL'S BULWARKS-
--AND ARE ABOU TO MAKE THEIR TIMELY ENTRANCE INTO THE PRESENCE OF TH STILL-UNSEEN INVADER. BUT LET THEM TELL IT.
ANOTHER AIRLOCK?
THIS GUY MUST HAVE A REAL THING ABOUT GERMS!

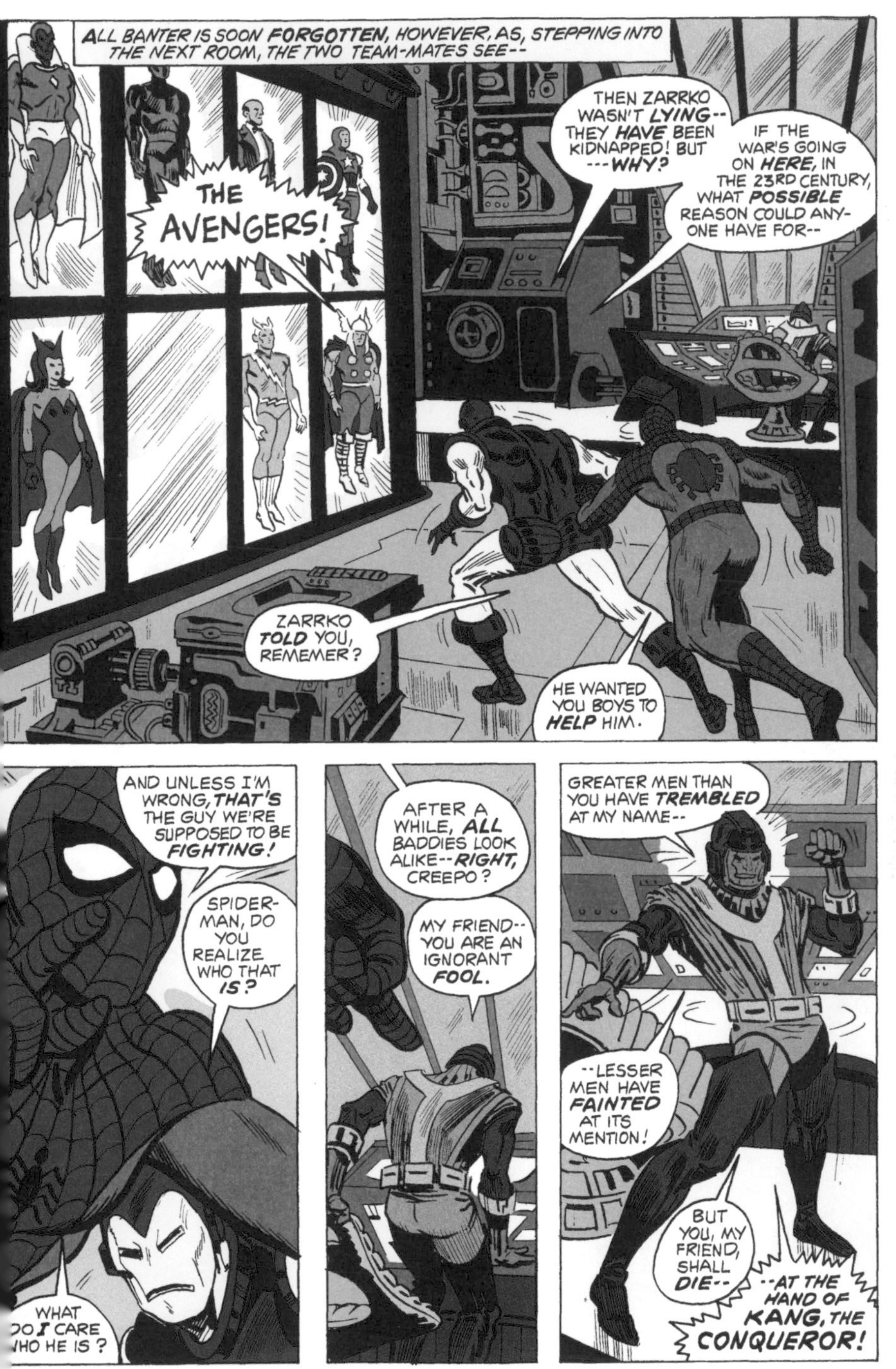
ALL BANTER IS SOON FORGOTTEN, HOWEVER, AS, STEPPING INTO THE NEXT ROOM, THE TWO TEAM-MATES SEE--
THE AVENGERS!
THEN ZARRKO WASN'T LYING--THEY HAVE BEEN KIDNAPPED! BUT ---WHY?
IF THE WAR'S GOING ON HERE, IN THE 23RD CENTURY, WHAT POSSIBLE REASON COULD ANYONE HAVE FOR--
ZARRKO TOLD YOU, REMEMER?
HE WANTED YOU BOYS TO HELP HIM.
AND UNLESS I'M WRONG, THAT'S THE GUY WE'RE SUPPOSED TO BE FIGHTING!
SPIDER-MAN, DO YOU REALIZE WHO THAT IS?
WHAT DO I CARE WHO HE IS?
AFTER A WHILE, ALL BADDIES LOOK ALIKE--RIGHT, CREEPO?
MY FRIEND--YOU ARE AN IGNORANT FOOL.
GREATER MEN THAN YOU HAVE TREMBLED AT MY NAME--
--LESSER MEN HAVE FAINTED AT ITS MENTION!
BUT YOU, MY FRIEND, SHALL DIE--
--AT THE HAND OF KANG, THE CONQUEROR!

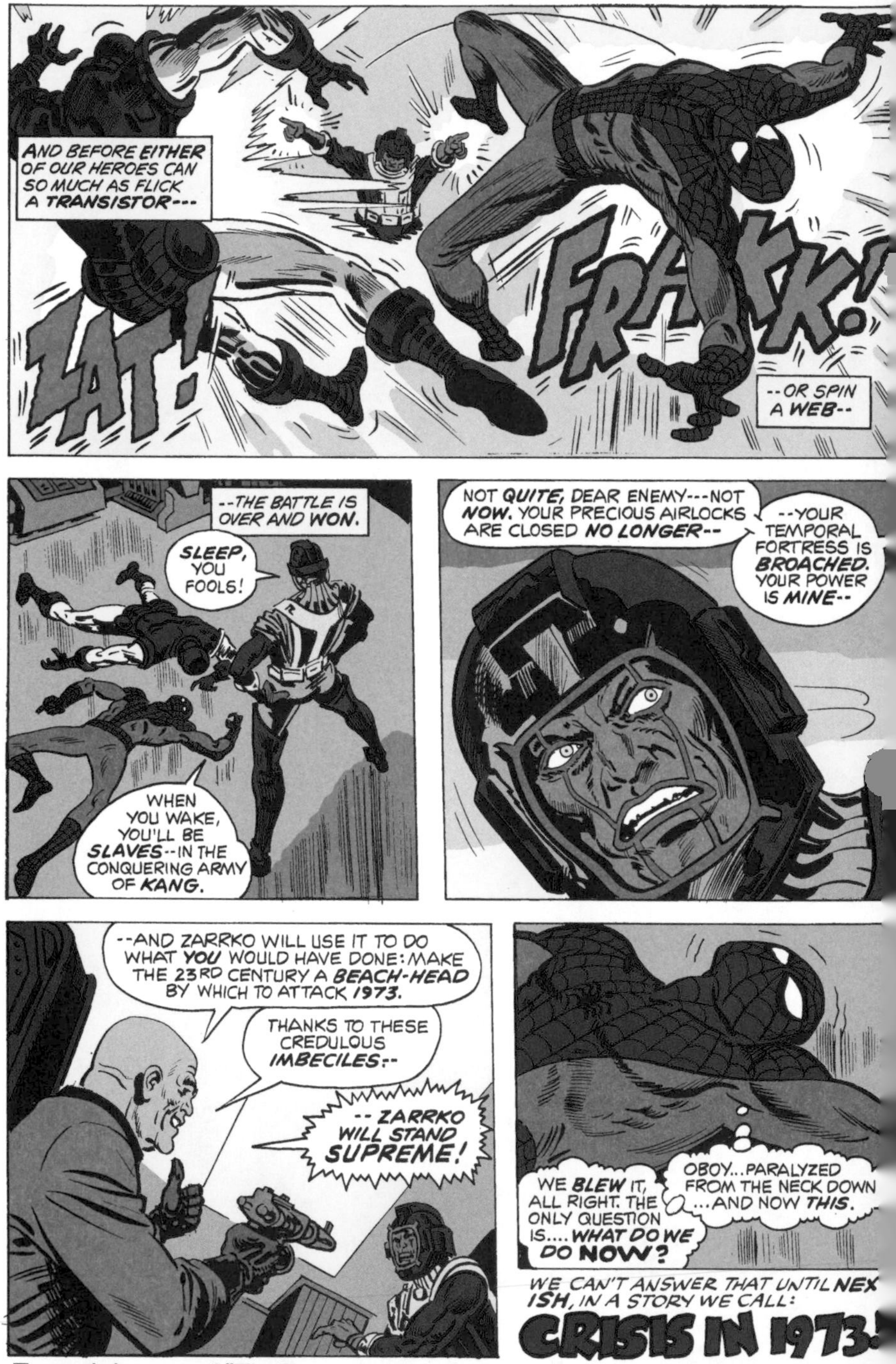
AND BEFORE EITHER OF OUR HEROES CAN SO MUCH AS FLICK A TRANSISTOR---
ZAT!
FRAKK!
--OR SPIN A WEB--
--THE BATTLE IS OVER AND WON.
SLEEP, YOU FOOLS!
WHEN YOU WAKE, YOU'LL BE SLAVES--IN THE CONQUERING ARMY OF KANG.
NOT QUITE, DEAR ENEMY---NOT NOW. YOUR PRECIOUS AIRLOCKS ARE CLOSED NO LONGER--
--YOUR TEMPORAL FORTRESS IS BROACHED. YOUR POWER IS MINE--
--AND ZARRKO WILL USE IT TO DO WHAT YOU WOULD HAVE DONE: MAKE THE 23RD CENTURY A BEACH-HEAD BY WHICH TO ATTACK 1973.
THANKS TO THESE CREDULOUS IMBECILES:-
-- ZARRKO WILL STAND SUPREME!
WE BLEW IT, ALL RIGHT. THE ONLY QUESTION IS.... WHAT DO WE DO NOW?
OBOY...PARALYZED FROM THE NECK DOWN ...AND NOW THIS.
WE CAN'T ANSWER THAT UNTIL NEX
ISH, IN A STORY WE CALL:
CRISIS IN 1973

To read the rest of "The Tomorrow War," check out *Essential Marvel Team-Up Vol.*